NORDIC LIGHTNING

AN INTERNATIONAL LEGACIES ROMANCE

CAMILLA STEVENS

Copyright © 2019 by Camilla Stevens

All rights reserved.

No part of this book may be reproduced in any form or by any electronic or mechanical means, including information storage and retrieval systems, without written permission from the author, except for the use of brief quotations in a book review.

Author: Camilla Stevens

Thank you Å and B, for helping make this book as authentic as possible...and for that one summer.

ABOUT THE AUTHOR

Camilla Stevens is a New York resident. At night you can find her typing away, often with a glass of wine, getting all the steamy, suspenseful or humorous, Happily Ever After stories out of her head and down on the page.

SIGN UP FOR HER NEWSLETTER:
http://eepurl.com/cbc3BD

AMAZON AUTHOR PAGE:
amazon.com/author/camillastevens

Want to Join the ARC Team? Sign up Here:

http://eepurl.com/cvJzfP

Next page for more!
www.camillastevens.com
author@camillastevens.com

ALSO BY CAMILLA STEVENS

WRIGHT BROTHERS SERIES
Mr. Wright & Mr. Wrong
Mr. & Mrs. Wright
So Wrong

STAND ALONE
One Night
Sweet Seduction

EX-CLUB ROMANCE SERIES
Archer: Ex-Bachelor

TEXAS HEAT ROMANCE SERIES
Home Run
High Stakes
Hard Sell

INTERNATIONAL LEGACIES ROMANCE
The Italian Heir
The French Thief

DESCRIPTION

Hockey is my game.
She's my goal.

ERIK SØRENSON
Fast. Hot. Electrifying.
With a grin that could melt ice.
My life was going just fine here in Brooklyn where I've lived all my life.
Then, the player they call the Nordic Lightning came skating into it.
What I know about hockey I could fit on the tip of my little finger.
I know even less about Erik Sørenson.
But I'm a fast learner.
Almost as fast as he is in those skates.
I've learned he's a Swedish import...or is it Norwegian?
I've learned he does things on the ice that make my head spin.
I've learned he's the playmaker, the one that helps his teammates score—both on and off the ice.

Which is why I'm more shocked than anyone when he's the one asking me out…in the most public way possible.
But our worlds are as different as night and day.
So what happens when the player who is constantly on the move meets up with the woman who is happily rooted in place?

From Brooklyn to Scandinavia, this is another BWWM Stand Alone in the International Legacies Romance series.
WARNING: *Due to adult content, 18+ Only*

Other Titles in the *International Legacies Romance* Series:
The Italian Heir
The French Thief
The Nordic Lightning
Her Icelandic Protector (Coming November)
The Russian Defender (Coming Soon)
The Luxembourg Betrayal (Coming Soon)
The Aussie Try (Coming Soon)
The Armenian Saint (Coming Soon)
The Spanish Pirate (Coming Soon)

CONTENTS

Author's Note   xiii

Prologue   1

PART I
Chapter 1   9
Chapter 2   18
Chapter 3   22
Chapter 4   32
Chapter 5   42
Chapter 6   48
Chapter 7   53
Chapter 8   62
Chapter 9   70
Chapter 10   79
Chapter 11   89
Chapter 12   98
Chapter 13   105
Chapter 14   119
Chapter 15   128
Chapter 16   133
Chapter 17   142
Chapter 18   151
Chapter 19   160
Chapter 20   167
Chapter 21   173
Chapter 22   179
Chapter 23   183
Chapter 24   191
Chapter 25   196
Chapter 26   203
Chapter 27   206

Chapter 28	213
Chapter 29	218
Chapter 30	224
Chapter 31	231
Chapter 32	239
Chapter 33	244
Chapter 34	250
Chapter 35	262
Chapter 36	271
PART II	
Chapter 37	279
Chapter 38	286
Chapter 39	292
Chapter 40	297
Chapter 41	302
Chapter 42	309
Chapter 43	318
Chapter 44	329
Chapter 45	337
Chapter 46	345
Chapter 47	353
Chapter 48	359
Chapter 49	361
Chapter 50	364
Epilogue	368
The Monte Carlo Shark PREIVEW	371
Next Up in the International Legacies Romance	375

AUTHOR'S NOTE

This book, as with all of the ***International Legacies Romance*** books that will follow, is a romance, not just between the two characters but also between me and the places I've personally been and loved. An ode of sorts to countries/cities I've visited.

Thus, I'd just like to offer the following caveats and explanations:

Language and Writing Style

Since most of these books take place in countries around the world, in order to have some semblance of authenticity, I had to have some way to include the local language (in this case Norwegian and Swedish) without a) writing it in Norwegian/Swedish and translating for the reader (ugh!) or b) including "he/she/they said in Norwegian/Swedish" after every bit of dialogue.

As such, I've distinguished anything that isn't said in English by putting it in italics. I realize that some readers may find this annoying, and I apologize, but I'd rather have you

AUTHOR'S NOTE

annoyed than confused, or worse, assuming everyone speaks English with one another.

That said...welcome to Norway and a wee bit of Sweden (and New York)! I hope you enjoy it as much as I personally did and one day have the chance to visit yourself.

Norway/Sweden

My descriptions of all locations are taken from personal experience and interviewing (or interrogating) others, as well as individual research. As with most of the International Legacies Romance, bits and pieces of this are biographical, which means there will be things in here that differ from your experiences in these locales. Trust me, it happened! That said, although I've done my best to obtain the most up-to-date information, do your research before deciding you'd like to visit. I don't take artistic liberties with things that can easily be figured out via a simple Google search or asking others—only when it comes to romance. :)

PROLOGUE

ÖRNSKÖLDSVIK, SWEDEN

TWELVE YEARS AGO

The puck drops.

I don't even think. I just go. That's what I do best: go. I can guide this puck around any player or other obstacle quicker than lightning.

I'm already in the attacking zone with Simon Gustafsson in my periphery. His grin of anticipation is the only cue I need. I shift my arm, preparing to pass to him.

Before I can, I feel my body thwarted forward. Instead of falling, I quickly find my feet and swivel around to confront the culprit.

Liam, my half-brother.

Once again, I don't think I just go. Or rather, my fist does.

He's just as quick to fight back. It doesn't take long before we're both on the ice, a tangle of punches and shouts. The distant sound of a whistle is ignored and only the act of the other players pulling us apart stops the fight. The coach slides in, looking back and forth at both of us.

"What the hell was that?" he yells. "Almost every practice, it's something with you two. Both of you need to figure out how to get along or you're out for good. For today, go home and cool off."

"You always have to ruin it, don't you? Everything was just fine until you came to live here."

I ignore Liam, used to this same crap that I've been subject to since we were both twelve. That's when my mother died and I was forced to move here from Norway. After almost four years, nothing has changed.

I don't know why my father insisted I come to Sweden to live with them. I would have loved to stay in Oslo, moving in with my grandpa or going to live with my aunt, uncle, and cousins.

Liam and I are walking back home—*his* home, and I know the misery that will be waiting for me there after what happened today.

"Hockey is my game. Mine. I've been playing since I could walk. You only started because you have to copy everything I do, but good luck making it to the professional league like I will one day. Do you think I don't know why you spend all that time practicing after hours? It still won't make you better than me."

I laugh and turn on him.

"I am *better than you*. Not that I give a shit about hockey or you. The only reason I play is because it's the only thing to do in this shitty town, and hopefully, it will one day get me out of here."

Örnsköldsvik, or Ö-vik as everyone calls it, is nothing like Oslo, where I grew up, but I actually like the city. Hockey is the most popular sport here, and I like it more than I thought I would as well. Hell if I'll let Liam know that. "*Your mother can't stand me. Dad barely tolerates me. I only practice so often to avoid all of you.*"

It's just the opening he needs. A small, taunting smile curls his mouth. "*So all this is just because Dad chose my mom, not yours?*"

Before I can respond, we're interrupted.

"*Hey, Erik. How did it go at hockey practice?*"

We both turn to find Sigrid and her friends approaching. Her eyes rake down my long body in a way that tells me she doesn't give a damn about how hockey practice was. The girls with her all giggle in a way I have no interest in entertaining right now.

But the jealous look on Liam's face *is* something of interest to me. His eyes are focused on her like flies on a drop of honey.

I hitch one side of my mouth up into that grin I've learned girls like.

"*I got sent home early for fighting.*" Yet another thing I've learned girls like.

The way Sigrid bites her bottom lip, as well as the gleam that comes to her eye tells me my intuition was right. "*So that means you can finally do something other than hockey tonight?*"

The anger radiating from my half-brother next to me only fuels my petty vengeance. I think of all the subtle snubs from his mother, the indifference of our father, the animosity he's met me with since day one.

I nod my head in his direction. "*I could, but his mom probably won't let me.*"

The brief look of irritation and resentment she casts his way sends a mild wave of regret through me. Any hope Liam had of Sigrid ever liking him is now gone.

I think of what happened today on the ice and every ounce of guilt disappears.

"Well, I should get home and face my punishment." Never mind that Liam will probably be in just as much trouble as I am. Despite his other failings, our dad doesn't play favorites when it comes to grounding us.

After giving Liam one more harsh look, Sigrid lingers, eyes still glued to me before one of her friends eventually drags her away with another round of giggles.

"Maybe next time," she calls out.

"Unless I get in trouble again." I add another killer smirk that has them giggling even more excitedly.

A part of me knows I shouldn't have rubbed it in. Another part of me knows that tonight his mother is going to be less subtle than usual to remind me I'm not wanted here. I might as well enjoy this moment.

"She's just a stupid slut anyway," Liam mutters, shoulder checking me as he continues walking. "Like your mother."

I feel the rage start to burn inside me. It's a sore point, and he knows it. The fact that our dad chose to marry Freja instead of my mother always seemed to be a stain on her reputation. Never mind that Liam and I are both the unfortunate evidence of *his* days of being young and reckless with the opposite sex.

Neither my mother nor my grandfather ever gave me the details of what happened between my father and her before I was born. But facts don't matter when it comes to the taunting of one's peers...specifically that of my half-brother.

"Take it back," I growl.

He knows better than to give in so easily. He just digs the claws in deeper.

"It's not my fault that Dad had no interest in settling down with Norwegian trash."

I rush at him, all the force of my bodyweight barreling into him so hard I hear the breath escape his lungs. He's only an inch shorter than me but heavy with the sort of brawn that may one day turn to fat or brute muscle. Right now, it's almost enough to withstand yet another one of our physical brawls. It's a powerful impact but nothing he wouldn't be able to withstand and bounce back from with only his dignity bruised.

This time is different.

The small brick wall surrounding the yard we're next to catches him at the backs of his legs before he can find his footing. Rather than fall back onto his ass, he lifts one leg to try and step over it, no doubt to save some of that dignity. His leg twists and somehow catches on the wall, forcing the other to get caught up and land at an odd, but vicious angle.

The sound of his bone cracking is sickening. The sight of the jagged edge protruding from the fabric of his pants is even more nauseating.

Both of us stare at the compound fracture in shock before our brains can even register what happened.

It hits us at the same time, and we lock eyes with one another before his pain receptors can deliver the message.

Liam's dream of playing professional hockey has just come to a screeching halt.

PART I

WINTER & SPRING

CHAPTER ONE

MAYA

"How do you feel about hockey?"
"Hmm?" I hum around the pencil trapped between my teeth. I continue checking the last few citations of the legal memo for Whitney Howard, one of the attorneys for whom I paralegal.

"What was that?" I finally say, giving Liza Santorini my full attention when I'm done.

"Hockey. How do you feel about it?"

"I...don't?" I reply warily.

"You don't," she echoes, her face probably matching the same look of confusion on mine.

"I don't have feelings about hockey."

She rolls her eyes and waves that comment away.

"Here's the thing, Fuckface bailed on hockey with Joey tonight—yet again."

Fuckface. Frank "Fuckface" Santorini, the man who took off with "some skank," leaving Liza to do most of the heavy lifting when it comes to their son, Joey.

"Frank plays hockey?" I ask, picturing the infamous ex-husband who, based on the handful of times I saw him with his slicked-back hair and fake tan, had more of a squash at an overpriced fitness club vibe than hockey.

Not that I know anything about hockey.

"Right, and I'm Venus Williams." Liza coughs out a sarcastic laugh. With a coifed head of blonde hair and a reed-thin body, she looks nothing like the famous tennis player. "The only time that man ever lifts a stick is to put his in some sleazy skank who—"

"What's this about hockey?" I interrupt.

"The Blades are playing tonight at the Barclays Center. Frank got tickets for Joey and him but, surprise, surprise, had a last-minute thing he couldn't get out of. Probably in the form of trashy and easy, hopefully, disease-ridden to boot."

"Wait...you want *me* to take Joey instead?"

"I'd go myself, but I got this deposition thing with Spencer. You know how he likes to use us to practice. I'd try to get out of it if it was Meyer, who's a sweetheart, but you know—*Spencer*." She rolls her eyes, and her jaw tightens.

"And you thought I would be the best stand-in?" I reply with a laugh.

"Come on. It'll be no different than watching him for me after work like you used to. He loves you, Maya."

When Liza first started here, she was a perfect mess. She'd literally never had a paying job before, and I occasionally offered to pick her son up from school and watch him for a while if she was working overtime or just needed a break.

"Any love he has for me will go down the drain when he realizes I'm clueless about the sport."

"He'll teach you. That boy lives and breathes hockey, which makes what Fuckface did even shittier."

Before I can even finish transforming my face into one of

reluctance as a precursor to verbally backing out, she tries to butter me up.

"I'll give you forty bucks for food. You'll both need to eat anyway."

"Forty dollars? Liza, you don't have to—"

"Don't worry; I'll put it on Fuckface's tab—reminding him what he's missing out on."

"It's too much."

"It's the Barclays Center. Trust me, you'll need it," she says in a dry tone. "Get yourself a beer. You're seriously saving my life here, Maya. Think of Joey."

That plea and her puppy-dog eyes are stronger than my willpower or my desire to settle in after work with Wednesday-night popcorn and Netflix.

"I guess I'm going to my first hockey game," I sigh as the last bit of my resistance goes out the window.

As usual, she's over the top with the theatrics. "Oh Maya, you are a lifesaver," she gushes, practically melting over me with thanks and hugs. "It'll be fun. Trust me, you won't regret it."

"Right," I reply with a tight smile.

"He's not coming?" Joey asks when he sees me standing at the front of his school to pick him up instead of his father. Having myself been a child of divorce, and all the baggage that comes with it, I can empathize with that feeling of disappointment. The look on his face almost breaks my heart.

"I know. You wanted your dad."

At eight years old, he's mature enough to consider my feelings and quickly recover with an unconvincing smile.

"No, it's fine," he mutters.

"If it makes you feel better, your mom insisted I ply you with junk food."

The smile hitches up just a little but still doesn't reach his eyes.

"Hey," I say, bringing my arm around him and bumping my hip against his side. His shoulders barely reach the waist of my long trench coat, especially in these heels. "I can be fun too. It's Wednesday, the week is almost half over. Let's have a good time tonight. What do you say?"

I bump my hip against him again, and that at least gets a laugh as I walk him through the chilly January air toward the subway to get to Barclays Center.

"...and when the Islanders permanently moved to the Coliseum, he spent like fifty-million dollars redoing the Barclays Center so it was more suited for hockey, but the Nets could also play basketball here too," Joey says.

"Really?" I reply, trying to sound interested as Joey tells me the entire history of the Brooklyn Blades. The last time I was here was for a John Legend concert several years ago, and I swear the overall layout looks the same. Whoever this Magnus Reinhardt, owner of the Blades is, he seems to have more money than sense.

"It's not obvious, but you can tell," Joey assures me.

"I'll take your word for it."

It's over an hour later. We're settled into our seats with our food. Liza wasn't joking about the cost. I felt guilty about using the money she gave me on a beer—which cost fourteen dollars!—so I used my own for that. Not that there was much money left after a burger, fries, and peanut M&M's for Joey, and just a burger for me.

I wasn't able to go home and change out of my work clothes with enough time left to pick Joey up. Beneath the coat I've removed, I'm still in my blouse, pencil skirt, thick tights, and work heels, all of which definitely make me stand out from the crowd of Blades black and light blue jerseys, sweatshirts, and hats.

There's also the fact that, after a thorough search to make sure, I'm probably one of only twenty black people in the arena, or at least the part of it I can see clearly enough. I vaguely remember all the fanfare about Brooklyn finally getting its own hockey team when the Blades were first announced. No more de facto rooting for the Islanders just because they happened to play here occasionally. Not that it mattered much in my neck of Brooklyn where ball (as in basketball) is still life. There were hints that the Blades would make hockey fans a more "diverse" group, but if this crowd is any indication, that isn't the case at all.

"So are you going to finally let me see what's on that sign you have?" I ask, pointing down at the piece of folded cardboard Joey carried all the way here. I didn't want to embarrass him on the train by asking about it, but now my curiosity has the better of me.

"It's a sign for Erik Sørenson," he says in a proud voice, putting aside his food to reach down and grab it.

"Really?" I say in an excited tone if only to match his obvious enthusiasm for the player. I have no idea who he is. "Let me see."

As I take another bite of my burger, Joey unfolds the cardboard to show me.

"'**Hey Erik! #28 is Great!**'" I read. "It rhymes. That's sure to get his attention. I assume Erik is number twenty-eight?"

Joey nods, finally showing off that smile I'm used to. "Erik Sørenson. He's my favorite player."

"Why is that?"

"He's just really fast on the ice. Like *really* fast. They once had a contest with a bunch of players from different teams and he clocked in as the fastest. I think he used to be into speed skating. He handles the puck really well too, but he doesn't *hog* it. He makes it easy for other players to score. Everyone calls him the Nordic Lightning, because he used to play for that team in Florida and he was so fast that it stuck even when he moved to the Blades. It's kind of a joke because they threatened to sue the blogger who started it for um...trademark in—in-something?"

"Infringement?" I hint.

"Yeah, I think that's it. Anyway, everyone was making fun of that so they gave it up. But really he should be called the Nordic Playmaker because he's so good at setting up plays for other players."

I nod along, pretending that I understand half of what he's said. It'll probably fall into place once I actually see the game played firsthand. Instead, I latch on to the one bit of information that's semi-interesting.

"So Nordic Lightning. Because he's from...Norway?"

"Yeah—I mean, no. He was born in Norway, but he played in the Swedish Hockey League before he was picked up by the NHL. Thankfully, we got him a few years ago."

"And now you're hoping to get a photo with him?"

Joey nods again. "Last time when Dad brought me, Robert LaPointe gave a kid who was holding a sign a puck during warm-up. I figured my chances were better to get a puck if I have a sign too."

"When does warm-up start?"

As if on cue, the lights in the stadium lower and loud music blasts through the air. My hamburger is stalled halfway to my mouth as I look around.

"This is it!"

"Now?"

"Yeah, I wanna get down there before all the free spots are taken," he says, jumping out of his seat.

"Wait, what?" I ask as his back disappears down the row. "Joey!"

I toss what's left of my burger into his box, grab my purse, and follow him. Or at least try to. His smaller child-sized body easily maneuvers between, around, and over the legs of the people sitting next to us.

"Sorry!" I say to a man who just suffered a good jab from my heeled shoe. I should have stopped at the Target across the street to buy a pair of flats or something. Usually, I don't bother switching shoes for work since the subway stop near my home is a five-minute walk away and the one near work is even closer. These shoes are more than comfortable enough for that simple commute.

"Not a problem," he says with a grin. I'm not sure if it's me or my ass in this skirt he's talking to.

Joey is already down the stairs in our section, which has a pretty decent view of the rink from what I can tell. It's not the fifty-yard line—or whatever the hockey version is—but at least I can see both goals clearly.

"Joey, wait!" I yell, carefully traversing the stairs in my heels. They may be well suited for dashing around at work and getting to and from the subway, but on this steep stairway, they might as well be six-inch stilettos.

The lights come back on and I'm close enough to see Joey find a decent spot for himself by the glass. I stop to smile at him jumping up and down, slapping his sign against the glass as the players circle the rink with their sticks.

I think about Liza stuck at work. Even if Joey doesn't get a puck, she should at least get a memento from tonight.

With my iPhone rescued from my purse, I pull up the camera app and point it at Joey's back as he tries to get Erik's attention.

Snap!

"Joey!" I shout as the players continue to guide random pucks across the rink beyond him. He turns to give me a quick, distracted look. I return a broad smile as a hint for him to do the same. When he does, I snap the photo before he's facing the ice again.

Having caught two decent shots, I take a moment to look at the result. The first is great, just a kid and his sign as the players go by—like something out of a Norman Rockwell painting. The second would have been practically perfect…if I hadn't screwed it up.

Joey is caught halfway through shooting me an impatient smile…just as a player with "28" emblazoned on his jersey speeds by with a thumbs up and a set of white teeth glowing in a grin. That's nothing compared to the pair of eyes that might as well be breaking free from the screen and searing my own retinas. Even through the shield of his helmet and the clear partition circling the rink, I can see them bright as day. He was staring right at me while I took the photo.

Joey's going to kill me if he sees that he just missed his favorite player in order to turn and give me a smile.

I search the ice for #28 again, camera ready to snap a shot, but all I see is a blur of black and arctic blue. I'm still so focused on trying to read jersey numbers that I at first miss the player who comes to a stop right in front of Joey. When my eyes finally focus on what's before me, I'm too stunned to react. Mr. 28 was something when he was staring up at me from the screen of my phone. The live version is…

Whoa.

For some dumb reason, "My Love is Like...Wo" by Mýa—which I used to play behind my parents back nonstop when I was much younger (mostly for all the obvious similarities in our name, but also, awesome song)—pops into my head. I don't see much of the man behind that helmet, mask, hockey uniform, and the number 28, but what I do take in is like...*Whoa.*

His eyes are glued to mine and almost perfectly match the light blue details of his uniform. There's something brief but intense and electrifying in them, like a flash of lightning striking me right at my core. And just like lightning, it lasts for only a few seconds before his gaze softens to stare down at Joey in front of him. He reaches down to pick up a puck and toss it over the glass. Joey is practically having a conniption over that, dropping the sign to catch it. I'm still recovering when I see the player mouthing something to me and pointing down at Joey, who might as well be a jackrabbit for how happily he's jumping up and down, puck in one hand and the recovered sign in the other.

I realize Mr. 28 wants me to take a photo. Now, even Joey is turned around with an exasperated expression. And here I am playing love (sex?) songs in my head from my silly schoolgirl days.

"Smile!" I say to both of them through a tight smile of my own.

Joey's smile couldn't be any bigger.

Mr. 28 is sporting one that seems anything but family-friendly. Or maybe that's just my wishful thinking.

I take the photo.

The wink and grin I get from Mr. 28—what the hell did Joey say his name was, Erik something?—as he skates away makes the slight chill of the arena completely disappear.

Whoa.

CHAPTER TWO

ERIK

"*Nydelig,*" I whisper in Norwegian under my breath with the grin still plastered on my face.

Gorgeous.

Maybe it was the clothes: heels, a skirt that hugs those very noticeable curves, a blouse that leaves enough to the imagination to make her even more tempting. Far different from the puck bunnies in Blades baby tees or jerseys over leggings or microscopic mini skirts

At first, I thought she was working for someone in the head office, babysitting some VIP's son whose parents can't be bothered to be here with him personally. Either way, I'm a sucker for any kid who goes to the trouble of creating a handmade sign for me, so I stopped for the shot. That deer in the headlights look she gave me definitely didn't spell corporate. No Blades representative on babysitting duty would be that damn starstruck.

Or that damn...*nydelig.*

"Nice one," Corey Swanson says with a shit-eating grin as

he skates past me. As a notorious manwhore, he spends half the time during warm-up scouting the crowd for "prospects."

Something about him putting this woman in that category has me racing to catch up with him. I easily surpass him as I spy a puck to slap into the net.

"Showoff!" he shouts with a laugh.

Looping back around to where the boy was, I see both him and the woman who took the photo walking back up the stairs to their seat. Her arm is around him as he continues to jump up and down with excitement. I get a kick out of watching the boy. The woman gives me a different kind of kick.

I make one more turn around, and this time, I catch Preston McDouglas from the L.A. Kings, our rival team tonight. The glare he shoots my way gets my adrenaline going. For some reason, he's still sore about me beating him in that idiotic speed contest to see who the fastest skater in hockey is. Even though I had an obvious advantage from my years of speed skating as a kid in Norway, tonight I welcome the challenging look on his face.

I feel a fierce game coming on—my favorite kind.

The horn sounds to clear the ice, and I follow my teammates to the bench. From this moment on, my mind is strictly on the game. All thoughts of McDouglas, the woman and the boy, or that lingering guilt that always hits me at the start of each game, the one that tells me I shouldn't be here—it all disappears under the lights and the rink before me.

Face-off.

The puck drops and, as usual, I'm quicker than my opponent. The nickname some blogger labeled me with and managed to make stick, Nordic Lightning, briefly flashes through my head as I snap the puck back to Swanson on my left. He's ready for it and the game is on.

While the Kings' right-winger and defense go after him in the attacking zone, I swerve around and past them, waiting for an opening for him to pass it back to me. I see McDouglas already gearing up to body check me as soon as I get possession of the puck.

I'll have to be fast.

Swanson passes to me, and I work the puck toward the goal. I sense McDouglas before I see him and even I'm impressed with how I manage to control the puck while swiveling my body around as he barrels past me, head down like a charging bull. He misses me by barely an inch. The collective yell of the home crowd is enough to piss him off even more, stirring those flames of old resentment.

With too many players blocking my way, I pass down to Peter Shaw in the neutral zone.

Shaw works along the right side until he gets a hip check right into the boards and loses control of the puck.

The Kings player who takes control of it heads down toward the Blades goal, and I fly across the ice to recover it.

As soon as I'm close enough to make a try for the puck, he passes to another player.

I skate back to help protect the goal while Grigory Mikhailov, our powerhouse of a defensive player tries to rescue the puck.

Instead, the Kings' player passes to a teammate, Kowalski.

...or tries to.

I swing my stick and hit the puck to Swanson before it can reach him. That earns me a scowl from Kowalski.

I ignore it and head down the ice to assist Swanson. He's our best scorer, but his weakness is getting to the net.

Sure enough, the puck is stolen by a Kings player who gets it down the ice by passing between players.

Mikhailov body checks the one with the puck in possession, forcing that unfortunate player to encounter a six-foot-six wall of pure muscle. Grigory is one of the tallest players in the entire league, probably the strongest as well.

I don't stop to watch the carnage as I go after the puck, crashing into an opponent as a struggle for the prize ensues. Sticks clack against one another until I manage to claim it and speed my way back to the goal.

Before I get even one meter, I feel my legs buckle as something rams into the backs of my knees. The outraged roar of the crowd matches that in my head as I fall back, my helmet bouncing off the ice. I quickly recover, rising back up to the sound of the ref's whistle as I spin to face my attacker.

It's #58 McDouglas, still scowling at me. Now seeing red, I drop my stick and lunge.

From there it's chaos.

CHAPTER THREE

THE GAME

"*Yes!*" I scream as I catch the first punch. I shoot up from my seat, mostly because the row in front of me is already out of theirs.

I'm not quite sure what happened—he's so damn fast, all I saw was him falling to the ice—but the angry roar of the crowd tells me the other player did something worth getting punched for.

"What did he do?" I ask Joey.

"Slew foot. McDouglas kicked him from behind to trip him up."

The two players go at it below us, #58 bunching up Erik's jersey in his hand while punching him with the other.

"The refs are just letting them fight!"

"Yeah, that's part of the fun," Joey shouts with enthusiastic delight as he stands on his seat to get a better look. I let him plant his hand on my shoulder to keep himself steady.

"So they aren't going to stop it?"

"Eventually, especially if it becomes a bench clearer. That's when all the players pile on."

Yet another thing I'm learning about the sport. During the long introduction to the game, Joey gave me a quick lesson on the basics: the play of the game, the rules, who's who, and more.

But this is something different.

And I kind of like it.

Erik lands a good punch on #58, which has my heart accelerating more than ever. He manages to break free of the hold the other player has on him. That doesn't stop one of Erik's teammates, who looks like a mix between a giant redwood and Mount Everest in a hockey uniform, from coming in and taking over where Erik left off. He is met with a good right hook, which might as well have hit a brick wall for what little impact it had. Erik steps back in, pushing his teammate away to land a good punch on the other player which has him on his ass.

The players from both teams are now joining in, either swinging fists or trying to pull players away. A sea of white, black, and silver (Kings) and black and light blue (Blades) pours out from the sides to fill the ice which only encourages the crowd of fans, who are now working themselves into a frenzy. Any earlier righteous outrage is now replaced by fanatical glee.

By the time the referees have settled the teams, my heart is still pounding. Erik and his giant of a teammate #47 are sent to a separate seating area behind the glass—penalty box, or "sin bin" as Joey explained it—and the Kings player who attacked Erik heads to a similar area on the other side.

And the game has only just begun!

"You should have let me finish him," Grigory growls beside me in the penalty box.

"Finishing him is exactly what I was trying to avoid," I say

23

with a laugh as I watch the game play out before us, impatient to return and join it. "Though I appreciate the thought."

The fierce Russian sitting next to me is not only two inches taller than I am but a good sixty pounds heavier, all of it muscle. He's also got a permanent chip on his shoulder the size of his home country. I'm probably the closest thing he has to a friend on the team—mostly due to us being the only two foreigners if you discount the Canadians, who really shouldn't count—and even I'm not sure what his internal anger stems from. He's closed-mouthed about most of it, but from what little I've picked up, it's either a woman or his family back home in Russia, maybe both.

Typical.

"I would not have killed him," he assures me.

"I'm not so sure about that," I say, shaking my head. I rest a hand on his mountain of a shoulder. "Let's just focus on getting back in the game."

"I am ready," he says with an expression on his face that makes me think perhaps this time out is a good thing.

Considering my own lingering anger, it's probably a good thing for me as well. The NHL isn't as lax as it used to be about throwing punches. Too many of these fighting penalties and I'll soon start facing a game suspension.

"What do you think of the pics?" I ask, showing Joey the photos of him and #28 that I snapped. I make sure to avoid showing him the unfortunate one of Erik flying by while Joey's head was turned to face me.

The "ice crew" is, yet again, clearing the rink of ice shavings in between plays right now, so we have a moment to ourselves.

"They're so awesome, Maya!" he says with a toothy grin. "A puck *and* a photo? I can't wait to show everyone at school!"

"Let's send them to your mom, show her how much fun you're having."

"Okay," he says with a smile and a shrug. Apparently, mom is a less impressive target for showing off. I won't ask about dear old dad. That one hits just a little too close to home, and neither of us deserves to have our night ruined by that jerk.

I text Liza:

Having a blast!

I attach the photos I took, lingering a bit on the second good one I took with Erik staring right at the camera.

"Let's get one of us in our seats with your sign," I suggest after quickly sending those two pics.

"M'kay."

I wrap one arm around him, and he plasters an obligatory, huge smile on his face. I laugh at it as I snap the selfie, then pull the phone down to add it to the two I just sent.

Liza replies immediately:

Looks like fun! Ur a lifesaver!

Another face-off.

I'm still pumped up from the earlier fight. I can't tell whether McDouglas being off the ice the rest of the game for his dirty play is a good thing or a bad thing.

The puck drops, and he disappears from my thoughts as I take control of it again. Instead of passing, I circle my way around my opponent and make a break for the attack zone. I'm not selfish or lucky enough to try for the goal, so I scope Shaw situated near the net and pass.

He's ready for it. I'm shocked, as is probably everyone else on the ice and in the arena when he makes a perfect slap shot into the net.

The whole play lasted less than a minute.

"*Holy shit!*" I exclaim, then quickly turn to Joey. "Don't tell your mom I said that."

He laughs as he joins the crowd around us out of their seats to cheer. "It's okay; she curses all the time."

Considering her nickname for his father, even though she assures me she's never used it around Joey, I believe it.

"Does it usually happen that fast? A goal?"

"No way. I mean, Sørenson is great at assists, but that was amazing."

I watch Erik fly into his teammate and lift him up from the ice in an embrace. I'm too busy wondering what that would feel like to care about what's on the scoreboard, which now reads in favor of the Blades.

I've most likely used up my good luck in this game, but it's worth it. There is still one period left after this one, which leaves plenty of time to lose our lead.

And the Kings are now even more amped up. I can practically smell the testosterone filling the air.

When the puck drops, my opponent takes control and swipes by me with a barely noticeable shoulder check. I swivel around to watch him go. Swanson and another Blades player, Terry Keats are already on his tail, so I hang back just in case control of the puck changes suddenly.

Mikhailov is the one to body check the player, sending him

crashing into the boards behind the net as the puck goes flying, completely up for grabs.

I brace myself, and when Shaw takes control, I come in closer, ready to help out if needed. It passes a few times between five of the Blades players as we get closer to the Kings' goal.

A player manages to swipe the puck from Shaw and speed down to our goal. I fly across the ice to catch up to him, but I'm not fast enough to stop the pass to another player who chucks it right past Hughes, our goalie, to score a point for the Kings.

"*No!*" Yet again, I'm out of my seat, this time in protest.

The angry energy of the crowd spurs me on. I am officially one of them now.

The teams are tied, which has just made the game that much more tension-filled. I have a feeling I'm going to be spending plenty of time on my feet like the other fans.

Who knew hockey was this fun?

It's the third period, and we're still tied with the Kings. The energy of the crowd has been infectious, but with only five minutes to go, it's getting damn near rebellious at this point.

I'm back on the ice after being relieved for a bit, well-rested and ready to end this game in our favor. Facing me, Kopitar from the Kings can see it in my eyes. We both grin just before the puck drops.

I win the face-off.

I round him and, in the presence of two Kings players headed toward me I pass to Ben Kavaler who's open.

I swiftly skate toward the attacking zone now that I'm no longer a focus, ready to accept the puck if Kavaler gets into a tight squeeze. He manages for about five seconds before being slammed into the boards by an opponent.

The puck flies away, and there's a mad scramble on both sides for control of it.

I'm fast, but too far away to claim it before a Kings player seizes it and heads down toward our goal. My instinct is to follow, but I already see two of my own teammates flying after him, not to mention Mikhailov going into defense mode like a massive bull ready to charge.

Lucky for the Kings player, Kavaler is the one to meet him first, slipping his stick in to swipe the puck away. He passes to Swanson, who manages to get as far as the neutral zone before realizing he's got a wall of Kings players headed his way.

I'm on the edge of the neutral zone, closest to the goal, so he passes to me.

With only one rival close enough to catch up to me, it's an easy play. Even he can't outrun my speed. There are two Kings defense ready to prevent the goal, and I surprise them by swinging around, forcing at least one of them to follow me around the net.

The other one is smart enough to hang back, but he can't prevent me using my last bit of good luck in the game to slap the puck toward a small opening I see as I pass back around in front of the goal.

The puck slices right past the goalie's stick...then underneath his knee before he can bring it down to block the shot.

I've scored.

"*Yes!*"

This time I beat the crowd around me as I jump to my feet. The sound of them joining me is deafening, and for good reason. I don't need Joey to explain what just happened. I know a kickass goal when I see it.

I had briefly wondered what the hell Erik was doing when he swung right past the goal instead of trying to make a shot. But it obviously paid off.

My eyes flash up to the timer and see there's less than a minute left in play. I'd be amazed if something happened to shift the lead in that amount of time.

"A fuckin' Gordie Howe Hat Trick," the man in front of me shouts with a laugh. "Leave it to Sørenson."

"What's that?" I ask Joey.

He laughs before answering. "When a player scores, assists, and gets into a fight in a single game."

I nod, kind of understanding why it might be a big deal. Obviously, it's impressive that he scored, something that seems to happen rarely in hockey. Joey already told me he's good with assists. Fighting seems like it came pretty naturally to him.

I wonder how often he gets into fights on the ice.

There are two distinctly opposite reactions from an opposing team when they are behind this close to the final countdown: defeatism or determination.

The Kings have gone with the latter.

Perfect.

I love a good last-minute scrap, especially with the adrenaline and thrill of victory still running through my veins.

This time, what happens after face-off is less of a play than a tussle on the ice. Everyone is more vicious. Players are slammed into the boards too often to even skate for any length of time.

I'm not one to give them any leeway just because they have no chance at winning—the puck is still in the neutral zone with less than thirty seconds of play. I slam into Brett Davies who has the puck.

Without thinking, and no doubt fueled by frustrated rage, he swings his stick out and I trip over it. I fall to the ice just as the buzzer sounds to end the game.

The, now useless puck is forgotten in the face of that incident, and I'm the first to jump up and attack him, joined by a few of my teammates who are also filled with the rush of complete victory and certainly not willing to let this pass.

The Blades have won, but it's lost in the roar of battle as both teams duke it out on the ice.

I stare at the rink below, my heart racing.

I saw the other player trip Erik, and I was filled with the same rage that seems to be completely taking over the players below me. Even the crowd around me is caught up in it, shouting their outrage down toward the scuffle.

It lasts less than a minute, dying down as soon as the refs have cleared the ice.

The blood pumping through my veins tempers down, and I'm not sure if the high it's left me with is thrilling or worrying.

Erik is a fighter, that much is obvious.

A base part of me savors it, no doubt tapping into some prehistoric urge for safety and protection.

The rational part of me is less impressed. Growing up where I did, I've seen too many acts of bravado and boys trying to prove themselves lead to nothing but trouble.

At any rate, the man is impressive on the ice. That much I can't deny.

We're still breathless as the game is called for the Blades.

"Way to end on a high note, Sørenson," LaPointe, our team captain says, shaking his head. I see the hint of a smirk on his face, despite the critique of how I closed out the game.

I shrug and grin back. Davies deserved it. Anyone who saw what he did can say that much.

Yes, I probably should have held back, what with the win we had, but...something inside of me couldn't let it go. I'm certainly not the worst player in the league when it comes to fighting, especially since they began cracking down on it, but my lightning-quick reaction to foul play is probably also what gave me my nickname of Nordic Lightning.

My eyes roll up to the stands. The attendees who don't give a damn about the post-game ceremonies are already leaving their seats.

Now that the game is over, my mind shifts back to the woman who took that photo. Is she sticking around? Maybe she'll stay long enough to join the particularly rabid fans and puck bunnies who try to meet the players as we head to the locker rooms, or even much later when we head out.

All I know is, I've got to see her again.

CHAPTER FOUR

MAYA

"So, why can't they just get someone really big like a sumo wrestler to sit there to block the net?"

Joey laughs and slaps his hand against his forehead. "Everyone always asks that."

We're walking out of the arena now that the escaping crowd has thinned. I'm feeling heady and still a little high from the thrill of the game. The tension and excitement, not to mention the impressive skill I saw on the ice have officially bumped hockey up a few places from nonexistent as far as my interest in watching various sports goes.

Hell, I might even splurge on a Blades sweatshirt.

"So what's wrong with my idea?" I ask as we ride down the escalator.

"First, you'd have to teach them to ice skate."

"That's the beauty of it. They wouldn't have to do much more than get to the net and sit there."

He laughs again. "Plus, there are regulation sizes for the uniforms and pads. Then, even with a really big goalie, there'd be holes that any good player could get a puck through. It takes a lot of skill to stop one, and they'd have to be able to move fast. Finally, it really hurts getting hit by a puck, even with pads. Also...it's boring to play that way."

"Hmm, I guess I need to start doing my research."

"You definitely do."

"So did you have a good time with boring old Maya?"

"You weren't boring," he says with a sheepish smile. "You got me a picture with Erik Sørenson. Dad never even did that. He doesn't even come down to the ice with me."

That casts a sobering cloud over the moment and I throw my arm over his shoulders. "Hey, I've got a little more money left from your mom. You want a hot chocolate or something to take with you?"

Liza's money is long gone, but Joey should end the evening on a happier note than memories of his dad falling down on the job.

"Nah," he says. "Mom will be waiting outside to go home. I've still got some M&Ms left."

"Alright. You all buttoned up nice and warm?"

"Yes," he says, rolling his eyes.

I laugh and lead him out the doors to the frigid January air.

Liza is standing on the left side of the subway entrance nearby shivering her ass off even in the fur coat she has on. It's probably real, leftover from her days as a Long Island housewife. Her face lights up when she sees us.

"Mom!" Joey shouts and speeds up to run to her. She pulls him in for a hug until he wriggles free to tell her about the game.

"I got a puck! And Erik took a picture with me! And we won!"

"I saw," she says in that enthusiastic way moms do when they want to feign as much interest in something as their kid. "I guess Maya is a good luck charm!" she adds, giving me a conspiratorial wink.

"Did you see the photos? Can you send them to Dad?"

I hope I'm the only one who notices the slight grimace that comes to her face at that. "I have a better idea. Why don't I post them to Instagram?"

Joey seems less enthusiastic about that suggestion, obviously not being an Instagram junkie like his mother.

"That way everyone, including your dad, can see them. Maybe the news will catch it or something. I'll bet even Erik Sørenson will see it," she says. "Especially if I tag him?"

"Cool!" he says, his face brightening back up at that suggestion.

"Should we tag our photographer?" she offers, trying to loop me into the enthusiasm.

"Oh, I don't Instagram, but post away," I say with a smile and a wave of the hand.

I'm certainly not going to be the one to tell her about my long-neglected Instagram account, which most certainly doesn't use my real name. I can't even remember the last time I posted to it. I think it was when my friends and I went to The Bahamas right after we graduated from college almost four years ago. The thought of what other pictures are tied to that account, not to mention the ridiculous username I picked, make me cringe. The only reason I've kept it is because I'm still nostalgic about some of the memories captured, even those silly embarrassing ones. That is most definitely the old Maya Jackson.

"Alright, I'll do it first thing when we get home. Right now I'm freezing my ass off."

Liza reaches out to pull me into a surprisingly strong hug, considering her size. "Mmm, thanks again, Maya."

"Not a problem. It was actually fun. I think I have a new favorite sport."

"Well, I'm sure this won't be the last time that Fu—Joey's dad decides to—"

"Anytime," I interrupt with a gracious smile before sliding my eyes down to her son. "And thank *you* for teaching me all about hockey."

"Go ahead and thank her, Joey."

"Thanks, Maya," he says, bringing his arms around my waist.

"Again, anytime. It was an exciting game," I say, as I squeeze him back. I think about how exciting one man, in particular, was—on the ice at least. Despite the cold, my body temperature rises at least ten degrees.

"Don't tell me they kept you this late at work," Katie, my roommate says with a frown as soon as I step into our Prospect Lefferts apartment.

She's painting her toenails and as usual, wearing one of the ridiculous t-shirts from the cheese shop she works at "in-between acting jobs." It's called Wedge Appeal, and all the workers wear these shirts that I personally find a little bit much. Tonight, Katie's reads: Parmesan Lovers Like It Hard and Strong.

With impossibly long, pale legs, auburn hair that I don't think I've ever seen out of a messy bun, wide green eyes, and the sort of fresh-faced air of optimism that can only come from wealthy parents to fall back on, she looks like she belongs somewhere further northwest in Brooklyn, maybe even lower Manhattan. I suspect living here in the as-yet-to-be-*completely*-gentrified part of New York gives her the sort of cachet she's deliberately seeking by living in this city. There's also the idea that, based on what I've seen of her dating preferences, she's probably just in search of something decidedly not pale, auburn-haired, or green-eyed.

"No, I was actually at my first hockey game."

She stops painting her nails to give me a confused look. "Why?"

"I can't go to a hockey game?" I say, feeling a little indignant.

She smirks and drags her eyes up and down my body. "Did you like it?"

"What are you getting at?" I ask, noting the suggestive tone of her question. I wonder if she can read the lingering excitement flowing through my veins.

"I'll take that as a yes," she says with a laugh.

"What's *that* supposed to mean?"

"Come off it, Maya," she says, laughing even louder. "Thanks to my brothers, I sat through enough games up in Boston to know it's basically like foreplay."

"Katie, eww," I groan, wrinkling my nose.

"Oh, stop! Like you weren't turned on by the aggression, even if you don't date white guys, which is all hockey pretty much still is."

"What makes you think I don't date white guys?" I ask in surprise.

"I've never seen you with one."

"I'm...open to dating white guys," I protest.

"Have you though?"

"You've known me for less than two years. You have no idea what my past dating life has been like," I say, somewhat defensively.

"That doesn't answer my question," Katie teases with a

smirk. She squints her eyes with speculation. "Do you even find them attractive?"

Instantly, my mind races to that wink from those blue eyes seen through a face mask. I didn't get a good look at Erik Sørenson on the screen during the Blades roll-call, but that did nothing to diminish his appeal. I got zero reception on the subway so I couldn't look him up on my phone during my ride home. Now, I'm wondering if the man underneath all that hockey gear is as hot as my intuition seems to think he is.

"Oh, my God!" Katie yelps as she leaps off the couch to drag me back down next to her. "I knew it! Is this crush of yours one of those boring Ralph Lauren or Brooks Brothers types, or something more...edgy? Please tell me he's not some basic hipster. I'd have to move out."

"*He's* not anything," I say standing back up and dropping my purse on the used coffee table to shrug out of my heavy coat. "Because there is no he. I went to a hockey game. It was fun. End of discussion."

"I don't know why you're so shy about it. It's the twenty-first century, Maya. No one cares," she says as I hang my coat on the stand by the door and grab my purse again.

"Good to know," I say, mostly as a way to escape the interrogation. The last person I want to talk this out with is Katie, who'd probably have some sort of ecstatic seizure from multicultural overload. She's cool, and certainly one of the least problematic roommates I've ever had, but way too much of a busybody with absolutely no filter.

"Oh hey, I almost forgot. There's pepper brie in the fridge if you want some," she calls out as I'm headed to my room.

Then again, there's the free cheese I always get from her job.

"Thanks," I shout before closing the door.

Back in my room, I dump my purse, kick off my shoes, and

fall back onto my bed with my phone to pull up Instagram. I start with Liza's account, where I see she's already posted the three shots I sent her from the game. She's tagged each of them with every hashtag under the sun, including #eriksørenson and @eriksørenson.

I waste no time clicking over to his account, which is a nice mix of professional and personal photos. After scrolling through a few photos of him on the ice playing hockey, still hidden underneath all that gear, I'm pleasantly surprised by some of the other pics where I finally get a full picture of him, sans hockey gear.

Very nice.

Christmas was only about two weeks ago, and there's one shot of him that stands out. It's a selfie that he's taken, so it definitely fits into the "personal" set of photos. Erik's blonde hair is slightly rustled, giving him a boyish look. I see glimpses of what looks like a modern loft behind him, complete with a Christmas tree. He's wearing a sweater with a pattern that looks distinctly Scandinavian, adding to the holiday feel of the photo. There's that grin on his face that I'm beginning to think only comes in the form of "devilish." He's holding up a heart-shaped gingerbread cookie, which makes the whole photo seem precious in a way. But still damn sexy as hell. The caption underneath reads:

God Jul! Couldn't find any ribbe, lutefisk, or pinnekjøtt for a proper Julaften here in New York, so I have to settle for pepperkake sent to me by my aunt in Oslo. Takk, Vilde!

I have no idea what half of what he wrote is but I'm suddenly wondering what Christmas is like in Norway. Here in New York, it's definitely commercialized, but I still love it more than any other holiday.

I scroll further, seeking out more photos like that one. Instead, my attention is arrested by some shots taken from *Ideal Gentleman* magazine that get my heart racing, and I have to stop to take a closer look:

Happy to be selected as one of Ideal Gentlemen's "Northern Lights," a spotlight on Scandinavians in American sports.

One of the two in his Instagram feed has Erik in a well-tailored suit, lounging on the bench in the "sin bin," arms crossed under the back of his head with that devilish smile on his face as he stares up at the camera. It's an above shot of him lengthwise, and my eyes crawl across his long body. Just how tall is he?

The other—and definitely my favorite—is of him in another sharp suit, taken outside. He's looking straight ahead with a fierce gaze while the windswept snow is practically a blizzard surrounding him. His hands are in his pockets, causing his strong shoulder muscles to flex underneath the jacket. The sharp edges of his jaw and that hard stare into the camera with those Nordic-blue eyes cut right through the harsh elements around him.

Tough in the face of anything. At least that's what I'm getting from it.

And I like it.

I bite back a smile of pleasure and keep scrolling, hoping for more.

I see several of him surrounded by a group of boys. The captions underneath these indicate that he's an active participant in the Big Brother organization. So there's a soft gooey center under that hard exterior after all.

Along the way, there are many photos of him on various beaches with locations tagged in all parts of the world, from Australia to California.

Scrolling further back, I stop on some of Erik, apparently back in Norway during warmer months with an older man, their arms wrapped around each other's shoulders.

The man has the same blue eyes as Erik, but with a gleam of joy in them and laugh lines that are on full display. He's probably in his sixties, with a full beard that would make him look like a jolly Santa Claus if he wasn't so obviously fit. Here, Erik's smile still has that hint of mischief, but there is absolute pleasure that overshadows it.

My happiest moments are spent with this man. Gratulerer med dagen, Morfar!

I quickly use Google translate to figure out what the last sentence is: *Happy birthday, Grandpa!* I return to the photo, with an even bigger smile on my face. I can definitely see the love between these two.

I scroll a bit more, suddenly realizing that there are no photos of him with his parents, or even mentioning them. Why is that?

I switch back to Google to do another proper search of Erik. It's all well and good to have cutesy photos nicely curated for Instagram, but what is the unfiltered public view of him?

For the most part, the image search pulls up shots of him playing hockey, or being interviewed after a game. There are some more with him as a Big Brother.

I'm a tiny bit relieved to see that there aren't a *ton* of him with other women, at least not beyond the female fans holding up signs that range from the desperate to the completely inappropriate. There are more than a few of one woman in particular, who I'm pretty sure I've seen in a few Victoria's Secret ads —Tessa something.

It would seem that the Nordic Lightning has a particular favorite flavor and it's decidedly leggy, busty...and strictly vanilla.

Then again, who am I to judge? My tastes have definitely leaned toward some flavor of chocolate my entire life. In fact, my dating pool has hardly expanded too far outside of Brooklyn. Working in downtown Manhattan has broadened that circle somewhat. But now that I think about it, the furthest away from me anyone I've ever dated has lived was way up in Harlem—the very reason it didn't work out. He might as well have lived in...

Norway.

I scroll through the photos of Erik. I certainly wouldn't kick him out of bed in the morning. But the idea of dating a white man...who's a professional hockey player...from *Norway* (Sweden?) is...a completely foreign concept to me. I imagine myself in his home country, which I know even less about than I do hockey.

"Good grief, Maya," I laugh to myself. "We think pretty highly of ourself, don't we?"

After all, it was just a wink. He probably does the same thing to one lucky lady every game.

Erik Sørenson is a nice thought but completely unrealistic. I'm sure that he's already forgotten about me—*if* I even lasted long enough in his memory bank to survive the game.

CHAPTER FIVE

ERIK

It's definitely her.
    I'm lying back on my bed, looking at a photo of the woman and the boy from tonight that I finally managed to find after a bit of searching on Instagram. Joey and Maya, enjoying the game, or so the caption reads. That's all I've got, at least as far as she goes.
    The glimpse I had of her face, even through my mask, the clear partition bordering the rink, and the distance separating us told me she'd look amazing up close, and I was right.
    Maya's large eyes are dark brown but still manage to sparkle, framed by thick lashes like those of a character in a cartoon fairytale. Impossibly deep dimples dot both full cheeks as she beams for the camera. Her mouth is spread into almost a caricature of those huge American smiles that always throw off foreigners who aren't used to such bold displays of cheerfulness, especially us Scandinavians. I love it.
    The Instagram account it's posted to is certainly not hers, at least not based on the profile photo, which is that of an older blonde woman holding a martini. I searched the rest of the

hundred or so photos on that feed and found plenty more of Joey but no more of Maya. She hasn't even been tagged in this one, making it all the more frustrating, especially since the woman who posted it made sure to use every tag in existence. I had to go through each # and @ attached to this picture in search of my own version of Cinderella.

At least the prince in that fairytale had a shoe to help him along.

All I have is this photo.

I stare at it a moment longer, my eyes etching that slightly heart-shaped face to memory before closing out the app.

Technically, I shouldn't even have been looking. It's a violation of that silly game LaPointe set up. The player with the most tags on Instagram or Twitter after a game gets a hundred dollars. The unspoken rule is that he then has to buy a round for the team the next time we hit up a bar, which always ends up costing far more than the prize money.

In order to give fans time to post their photos and tweets, we have to wait until the next day before looking. Never mind that everyone violates the no-peeking rule—LaPointe being the biggest offender.

Before I can put it away, the phone buzzes in my hand and a smile comes to my face when I see who it is. I click to accept the FaceTime and feel my smile get bigger when I see my grandfather's face fill the screen.

"*Morfar.*"

"*Erik!*" he replies in a cheerful tone. "*Congratulations on your win tonight.*"

"Thanks."

"*How many fights was it this time?*" he asks in a deceptively idle tone as he sips his mug of something warm and steaming.

"My coach has already spanked me. Don't you start too."

He laughs and shakes his head, but drops it all the same.

"*Okay, okay. I sometimes forget you aren't that boy who came to stay during the summers.*"

That gets me thinking about my usual upcoming trip back home this summer. "*How is everyone?*"

"*Oh, not much to report. Vilde likes to check up on me these days. I don't know why. I still hike every morning and I'm perfectly healthy.*"

I smile, feeling reassured by that fact. My *morfar* is probably more fit than men half his age. With any luck, and for my own selfish reasons, I hope he lives a long, healthy life.

"*Whenever she comes, she stays longer than necessary and talks, talks, talks. Plus, I always have to hide my beer, or she'll give me a lecture. As if I'm not the man who helped raise her. Sometimes I think she forgets that.*"

I grin to myself, knowing exactly from whom she inherited that talking trait. Morfar has a way of getting even me to talk more than I usually do, which isn't much.

"*Alf is…Alf,*" he says, referring to Vilde's husband, who is as quiet as she is talkative. "*Emma will only talk about that silly bus nonsense. She keeps trying to sell me socks.*"

I laugh at that. The bus is part of a Norwegian tradition called *Russefeiring*, for students who will be graduating. They buy buses and decorate them just prior to final exams, and for about a month they go wild with parties and concerts. I gave money to sponsor my cousin's bus, but often students do things like sell products to raise the money.

"*You know Bård is at university. That's another thing Vilde keeps going on and on about. He won't come home to visit often enough. The only obvious conclusion is that there is a girl in the picture.*"

We both laugh at this.

"*Speaking of which, how is your love life these days? Still avoiding relationships?*"

I feel my body go tense and the remembrance of my last actual relationship. Tessa Ogden, a bona fide Victoria's Secret model...and eventual nightmare. My agent, Doug Lidwell, was the one to introduce us. In the beginning, it was fine. She was gorgeous, presented a good "image" and "brand" according to him, and she was wild in bed—a little too wild perhaps, even for me. That could explain how fiercely she erupted when things began to cool off, at least on my end.

It didn't take me long to realize that she was catering to my likes and dislikes, never offering a contrary opinion or conflicting thought. When she started learning Norwegian, I thought it a nice gesture at first, until she began discussing our future life together in my home country, simply because I expressed a passing desire to move back to Norway after my hockey career in America was over.

As overly accommodating as she was during our relationship, she became nothing but a burden afterward: stalking me in person, creating fake profiles to bash me on social media, even going so far as to interfere with the next two women I only casually dated, turning their lives to hell until they broke up with me. Fortunately, most of it was kept away from the media, thanks to the same man who initially set us up. Mostly, I think Doug felt bad about his blunder, so he worked at putting an eventual stop to it all. I haven't had a serious relationship since.

"*You shouldn't let one bad relationship ruin your views on the opposite sex, Erik,*" he says, reading my mind. "*At some point, you'll want to settle down, won't you?*"

"*There* was *a pretty face in the crowd tonight,*" I say, mostly in a teasing manner, despite the rush that hits me just thinking about that face.

"*Oh?*" he responds, his brows raised. "*Just a face, or do you plan on finding out more about her?*"

"Right now, all I have is a name and a photo. That's not much to go on. In fact, she may already be taken."

That thought sends a vicious spark of envy through me so violent it might as well be the lightning that gave me my nickname.

"Do you want to get to know her?"

"Yes," I say with such intensity that I surprise both of us.

Morfar smiles knowingly. "Well then what do you plan on doing about it?"

I laugh. "I guess I could send out a public notice asking, do you know who this woman is?"

"Why not?" he replies without laughing.

I wrinkle my brow. "That's...ridiculous."

He gives me a keen look before speaking. "You're too young to have gotten to know your grandmother, unfortunately. She died when you were just a baby. But she was a spectacular woman; I knew that the first moment I met her. I also knew I was going to be with her no matter what, even if that meant shouting from the rooftops. Some women are worth it, Erik. Often, you just know."

I recall how Maya was my first thought when the game ended, how I knew I had to see her again.

"But what does this old man know?" he says with a laugh, though that speculative look hasn't left his eyes.

"More than you let on," I say with a wry grin.

"Yes, yes," he says, waving a hand in the air. "Well, it's late there, and early here, so I'll let you get your rest. I know you have another game tomorrow. Congratulations on your win...and hopefully on getting the girl," he adds with a wink.

"Goodnight, Morfar," I say with a chuckle, before closing out.

I'm instantly met with a single message glowing from the

screen that stirs almost as much emotion in me as Maya's face did:

Grattis till vinsten. -Pappa
Congratulations on winning. -Dad

It's from my father. He's recently been sending them after every game this season.

Since the first message, I've always just sent a simple "Takk," (Thanks) in response—in Norwegian. What else is there to say to the man I don't speak to other than to wish each other Happy Birthday or Merry Christmas?

I should be grateful that he's in touch at all. After I officially joined the Swedish Hockey League, I cut all contact with my "family" in Örnsköldsvik. Freja probably wrote me off just as easily; no love lost there. My relationship with Liam was... complicated, certainly not the kind that would lend toward keeping in touch. Dad tried at first, but when I hardly ever responded (for good reason, at least in my mind) he gradually stopped trying to reach out to me.

Now, I look at the long feed of the same messages sent back and forth over the past month or so, and I wonder yet again, what it's about. Rather than waste time thinking over it, I continue the thread by giving my usual one-word response:

Takk

I quickly close out the messaging app and open Instagram one last time mostly to end the night on a more pleasant note. I seek out the picture of Maya and Joey.

Is she worth shouting from the rooftops for?

I stare at the photo once more, then the comment box below the photo and the answer comes to me. Definitely worth it.

I begin to type.

CHAPTER SIX

ERIK

The next morning, I'm first on the team bus as usual. As the rest of the players trickle in, I'm surprised to see not even a hint of a reaction from what I did last night. Mostly, it's just the usual nods of acknowledgment or a "what's up?"

I'm too jaded by the antics of this team to even remotely think I've gotten off the hook that easily.

Grigory takes his usual seat next to me, and I'm not surprised to see a lack of reaction from him. His social media is painstakingly handled by a personal rep hired by his agent so that he has at least *some* online presence. I don't know if the man has ever even opened the Instagram app, let alone personally posted to it. Which means he definitely hasn't been searching out the hashtags of his teammates.

When the bus starts up and begins moving, I relax only slightly.

"Okay, okay," LaPointe announces, standing up once we finally get going. I brace myself. "We all know what time it is. Time to find out who's buying rounds tonight after the game."

The bus gets louder from players either excited at the prospect of being noticed online by fans, or, more likely, the free drink that will come after the game tonight. I sit back, not quite as stoic as my seatmate but tempering my enthusiasm all the same.

"I'm just going to go ahead and cut to the chase by pointing out a cheater in our midst," LaPointe says, staring straight at me with a shit-eating grin. He pulls up his phone, which is already opened to the Instagram account I spent far too much time staring at last night.

"'Maya and Joey enjoying the game.'" He reads. It's followed by a round of taunting coos from my teammates. "And what do we have here? Our very own Erik Sørenson went ahead and posted a message."

That's when it really starts.

Corporate America's love affair with getting a head start on every holiday means that only two weeks after New Year's Day shelves are already packed with those boxes of small Valentine's Day cards children pass around at school.

They are also good ammunition for teasing teammates, as I find out when a barrage of them are thrown my way. I hold up my arms to shield myself. Grigory grunts with displeasure next to me as a few of them manage to smack him as well.

"Okay, okay," LaPointe says with laughter still in his voice as he holds up a hand to stop the attack. "I think we all deserve to know what endearing words of love our heartstruck center had for his Valentine."

Obviously, word spread long before we boarded the bus since I see most of my teammates pulling out their phones to read along.

LaPoint loudly clears his throat as though he's about to make some important proclamation. "I should point out how diplomatic it was of you, Sørenson, to start by cozying up to the kid. Anyway, here goes: 'Hey, Jocy, it's always "great" to meet a fan in person.' Complete with great in quotes, I might add. Right number twenty-eight?" He winks at me.

That one gets a "hyuk hyuk" from somewhere, followed by a round of laughs. Joey's sign is in the photo, telling the world "28 is Great!"

I sit back and take my hazing with a perfectly neutral expression. I fully expected something like this once I posted the message last night and now it's time to face the fire.

"'Hope you enjoyed the game and the puck. The next game you want to attend is on me, complete with a signed Jersey,'" LaPointe reads. "Now, if that doesn't get you laid, I don't know what will."

I feel the first signs of irritation start to hit me. The last thing I want is Maya being thrown around by my teammates like a cheap shot. Before I can protest LaPointe moves on.

"Here's the part where he really sells it. 'I'd love to meet your friend Maya in person as well, preferably on a date. If you could put me in touch with her, then I could properly ask her out.'"

He lowers his phone to look my way. "Have to say, it was a nice touch there at the end. Very gentlemanly."

That gets another round of jeers and laughter.

"Apparently, class is in short supply on this team," I say with a smirk. I'd only make it worse for myself if I didn't respond.

The chorus of *oohs* fills the bus, and I settle back in my seat, arms crossed as I pretend to fall asleep.

"Okay, so we all know that any post we respond to personally doesn't count in the tally, even if it's in the spirit of true love. As such!" he continues with a dramatic pause. I open one eye to see him with one finger raised in the air. "I'm going to change the rules just for today and make this a bittersweet experience for you. If this Maya of yours replies by the time we make it to the bar tonight, then all your drinks are on me personally, and I will pay you the hundred bucks out of my own meager funds. However, if she doesn't, the round of drinks is on you—minus the hundred bucks. That's what you get for breaking the rules."

A round of applause fills the bus at that idea.

"On that note, we all know the other team rule. The Viking has officially claimed his woman, which means?"

"Hands off," the rest of the bus shouts in unison.

"Hands off," LaPointe repeats before shooting me a smirk. "She's all yours, Sørenson. For her sake, I hope your nickname the Nordic Lightning is only applicable on the ice."

I lift one middle finger in response, which earns me a smirk amid the round of laughs that follows his joke.

LaPointe finally takes a seat, and everyone is back to minding their own business or getting some sleep in. Grigory, who as usual has stayed out of the fuss, turns to me.

"If you like a woman, you must let her know. You did right thing. In my country, only bold ones get what they want. Women? Money? Hockey? No difference. You made statement to them." He nods toward the rest of our teammates. "You claimed your woman."

"That's awfully progressive of you," I say with a laugh. "All the same, glad to have your approval."

"No approval needed. You know what you want. You go for it. End of story."

"Well, the story's not quite over yet. She actually has to respond first."

"If she is right one, she will respond," he says in such a growled voice I turn to him, wondering from where this sudden intensity came.

But he has a point. I've done what I can. Now I just have to wait and find out if Maya is the right one.

CHAPTER SEVEN

MAYA

"Oh my God, Maya!" I nearly drop the coffee I'm carrying from the break room as Liza practically runs me over on my way to my desk.

"What is it?" I ask, slightly alarmed as I carefully set the cup down.

"I can't believe you don't Instagram," she says, as though doing so is the key to life.

"No," I say slowly, hoping she doesn't start probing me on whether I've used it before or not. "What's this about?"

"It just happened last night. I only found out this morning."

"What just happened last night?"

"This," she says, proudly holding her phone so close to my face I have to back up to see what's displayed.

"The photo from last night," I comment, wrinkling my brow to discover what's worth such an alarming start to the workday.

"*Look!*" She urges.

The only thing I note is an unusually large number of

"likes." I'm not even on Instagram regularly and I know that over seven-hundred likes is a lot. Like...*really* a lot.

"That's a lot of likes," I say in a decidedly unenthusiastic voice.

"Not the likes!" she says, pulling the phone away, to tap something. "Here, look at the top comment!"

The first thing I notice is the username: @eriksørenson.

Oh shit.

Then I read the message:

Hey Joey, it's always "great" to meet a fan in person. Hope you enjoyed the game and the puck. Next game you want to attend is on me, complete with a signed Jersey! I'd love to meet your friend Maya in person as well, preferably on a date. If you could put me in touch with her, then I could properly ask her out.

Both my heart and stomach do summersaults—for entirely different reasons. Without thinking, I snatch the phone from her hand to reread it. I can see Liza's huge grin in my periphery.

"First of all, Joey couldn't be more in love with you. That'll show Fuckface to miss a game with him. But seriously...Erik Sørenson?"

"You didn't tag me or anything did you?" I ask, snapping my eyes back up to her.

"No? I thought you didn't have an account."

"Never mind," I say, quickly dismissing that thought. "Why would he ask me out?"

Liza straightens up in surprise. "Maya, you're an absolute doll. Why *wouldn't* he ask you out? With those eyes of yours and that mouth, which I personally know at least a few women who have paid *mucho dinero* just to replicate."

"What I mean is…I'm not even into hockey," I say. I think of the rush I got from watching last night's game. "Not the way Joey is."

"Maya, he's not asking you to coach the team. He's asking you out!"

"Yeah but…" My mind races with how *crazy* this is.

I bring my eyes back down to the phone still in my hand. My thumb scrolls through the several hundred messages underneath Erik's ranging from, "**I'm free for a date!**" to the prototypical self-pimping of "**Follow me!**" to those that are just a little too off-color for my tastes.

"So, do you want me to DM him your number?"

"What? No!" I say, my eyes snapping back up to Liza.

"Why not?" she asks with genuine surprise. "He's one of the hottest players on the team."

"That's not the point. He's just…too…" Good looking? Famous? Out of my league?

"Wait a sec, is this because," she leans in close, putting one hand up next to her mouth, and I know exactly what she's about to say before she whispers "he's white?"

"*No*," I say firmly.

She's lucky I know her like that. With anyone else, such a question would be a major HR faux pas.

But really, why does everyone keep asking about race?

Once again, I'm hit with the reminder that I've never dated a white man…not really. There was that one study date in college, which was more studying in my mind and, as it turned out, more of a date in his. It ended poorly when I squeaked a surprised "no!" as he leaned in for a kiss afterward. I did feel bad for him. There really is no way to recover what's left of a man's ego after sending it through the shredder that way.

Since then, I've mostly stuck to various shades of brown, which I'm definitely most comfortable with. It's just a natural offshoot of my inclination to stick with the familiar. Not that I'm opposed to dating white men or anything.

"Oh," she says, pulling back. "Well then, what's the problem? You DM him your number, go out for a fantastic night and..." She smiles and shrugs.

"And nothing," I insist.

I want to plead with her to delete the photo, but then I think of how ecstatic Joey probably was at his half of the message.

Smart move, Sørenson.

Surely this will blow over soon enough. Despite all the likes and comments, it isn't as though it's gone viral or anything. I don't know anything about the man, but if he's this bold, I can't be the first woman he's hit up on Instagram. Tomorrow some celebrity couple will break up, or some politician will say something stupid or some funny video will capture the hearts of America, and the mysterious Maya will be yesterday's news.

"Listen, I've got to get to work. Don't DM him anything about me!"

She heaves an aggrieved sigh. "Okay, but Joey is gonna be so disappointed. He was really excited at the thought of you two dating."

"Joey got his reward." At least he's happy about his.

Once she's gone, I pull out my phone to open Instagram. The app is buried somewhere on the fourth screen of my phone, and it takes me a moment to find it.

I don't really have an online presence. I'd like to say it's because I don't consider my life that interesting, but I know the real reason why: my dad. Anything I can do to keep off social media, mostly to avoid him.

Now, I feel an even more urgent need to remain anonymous on the Internet. I press the Home button for my own account. As I assumed, my most recent photos are from that trip to The Bahamas with my friends.

Not too terrible, I think, looking at myself and my friends in bikinis with drinks in our hands.

I continue to scroll, watching my days of youthful carelessness unravel before me. I started the account when I was working at a sports bar in Midtown, the kind where females (and only females) work their asses off for tips—some might say literally. It wasn't a strip club or even something quite as in-your-face as Hooters, but the tank tops and shorts were...clingy. And the tips proved it.

Still, I can't help but smile, even as I cringe when I see myself being silly with some of the other girls who worked there. It's the usual hot mess of duck faces, sticking tongues out, exaggerated poses you see splattered all over social media.

I land on the one that lead to my username. It's me bent over, showing my ass—in *almost* every sense of the word—as one of my coworkers slightly lifts the back of my tank top to show off the butterfly tattoo tramp stamp.

As though the list of regrets couldn't get any longer.

@Barbackbutterfly.

At the time it seemed like a "genius" username. Now it just seems tawdry. A part of me itches to delete the whole damn account, especially now.

But as I scroll through the photos, I realize why I've held onto them. These are fond memories in part because they are so ridiculous. Me and my girls. Me and my past antics. Even some of Mom and me, and old boyfriends, and places and events I've been to. This is a part of who I am—was.

That doesn't mean the entire world has to be a party to it. I head to the account settings and switch it to private. My profile picture is just a blue butterfly and always has been, so I'm not worried about being identified that way.

If my job at a law firm has taught me anything, it's that no one can completely stay anonymous online. It won't take long before someone figures out who "Maya" is and links this account. Suddenly, I'm filled with righteous indignation. So what if I had fun in my youth? So what if people decide to judge me based on that? So what if this Erik Sørenson decides the woman he met at the Barclays Center isn't worth his time after all? Should this even matter?

I hear a cough above me and react without thinking.

"No!" I exclaim, before becoming thoroughly horrified at who I've just addressed.

It's Sloane Alexander who, along with Whitney Howard, is one of the only two black female senior associates working here. Both of them are only a few years older than me. While Whitney is far more laid back and even fun at times, Sloane is strictly business, almost to an intimidating degree. She always fills me with this sense of awe at her intelligence and...just everything about her, from the way she walks to the way she talks. All the more so because she does it without ever making me feel like I'm beneath her, nor does she treat me like a brainless serf the way some attorneys do.

Mostly, I admire her because she absolutely holds her own at *Douglas & Foster*. She's ten times smarter than everyone and manages to take zero shit from them, all while still maintaining a complete image of grace and dignity. Which makes her finding me like this so much worse.

"Excuse me?" she responds, not in a curt or hostile manner, more *very mildly* amused than anything. She does make sure to direct a pointed look at my phone, which is still glaringly displaying Instagram.

Douglas & Foster bans any form of social media on work computers for liability reasons. They obviously have no control over what people do on their personal phones, but they definitely still frown on using them for said purposes while on the job.

"I'm sorry," I rush to say, flipping the phone over on my desk. "I was just—how can I help you?"

"I've just come back from the M&A attorneys meeting, this Gaultier Financial business is a mess—which is obviously good for us," she says, with a mildly disgusted sigh, "but it's both time-sensitive and costly, so whatever you have on your plate for me, just get as much done today and tomorrow as you can because starting Monday it's all Gaultier."

"Got it."

"And...be a little more discreet when it comes to social media. Next time it may not be me who catches you," she warns before walking off.

I let out a long, slow breath as she leaves. Then drop my head into the palms of my hands.

I haven't even so much as messaged Erik Sørenson and already he's wreaking havoc on my life.

"How in the world did I miss it this morning?" Katie exclaims.

Thankfully, I'm usually gone before she even gets out of bed in the morning. I would never have made it out of the apartment on time If she'd learned about this before I left.

"I knew there was something in your face last night."

"Hold up just a second," I say, pausing as I take off my coat. "Just because this guy has decided to blast my name on Instagram, doesn't mean I'm—"

"Oh, stop," she laughs. "It's okay to admit he's hot, and you're flattered."

"How would you feel, being publicized like this?"

Stupid question.

59

Katie stares at me as though I've asked how she'd feel winning the lottery.

"Never mind, don't answer that."

"You're already a hashtag on Twitter."

"*What?*" On Twitter I'm a definite lurker, enjoying tweets from comedians and random funny accounts I follow, getting the latest news, and having a laugh at whatever Black Twitter has to say about anything. On that site, I don't even have a profile picture, let alone a real "presence."

"Seriously." She pulls out her phone and starts typing, then shows me. I take the phone and scroll through the tweets with my very own official hashtag used in each. #WhosMaya

Am I the only one out here tryna figure out #WhosMaya so I can assume her identity and get me some @EricSørenson?

#WhosMaya if you don't jump on this, the rest of the collective female population will. (This one has attached that striking photo of Erik in the snow from *Ideal Gentleman* magazine).

#WhosMaya obviously ain't down with the swirl. Good on her! #staystrong! #blacklove!

#WhosMaya I don't blame her for staying silent. Who wants to be under that kind of public microscope? Look how they did Meghan with Prince Harry, and she was already famous. Let Maya be.

#WhosMaya is basic as hell. #sorrynotsorry #Erikcandobetter

#WhosMaya is HOT af. #jealous

"I would kill for that kind of publicity!" Katie says, practically swooning.

"No offense, Katie, but I'm not trying to sell cheese."

"But *I* am, at the very least you could give a shoutout. They'd probably make me assistant manager or something."

I pause to consider her shirt today: Pepper Jack Lovers Like a Good Bite.

Good grief.

CHAPTER EIGHT

ERIK

Philly can be particularly brutal when it comes to sports. It doesn't help that our own Ben Kavaler was traded from the Flyers just last year.

Already, the sea of black and orange feels like a tsunami, waiting to overtake us on the ice, if their team doesn't first.

I love it.

I work best under pressure. Taking the fight to another team's home turf sparks something in me that can't wait to absolutely conquer them. Maybe there's a bit of a Viking streak in me after all. I grin as my name is called and I take the ice to a chorus of booing.

Usually, nothing can ruin this feeling for me.

Until tonight.

It's a good thing my phone is still in my locker since I'm pretty sure, even here on the ice I'd be checking it to see if Maya has responded yet. It isn't because of the bet made back on the bus. I'd buy the entire bar drinks if it meant some kind of communication from her, hell, even an acknowledgment. I wouldn't go so far as to say that a "thanks but no thanks" would be acceptable, but at least then I could put her firmly out of my head.

Eventually.

As the saying goes, the silence is deafening.

I force my mind on the game before me, knowing that once the action gets going everything else, including Maya, will fade away.

Taking up position in the center, I brace myself, gripping my stick just tightly enough.

The ref is in place.

The noise of the crowd dies down only a little, ready to let loose again once the puck is dropped.

Hayes stares at me with the same intensity I feel radiating from my own gaze, right before we focus on the spot before us.

The puck is dropped.

Game on.

"Those are all on me," I tell the waitress serving our section.

She gives me a smile with a direct gaze that hints at something more, but quickly shifts it back into professional mode, perhaps because of the lack of reciprocal interest in mine.

We're in a bar here in Philly, making sure it's one that doesn't cater to sports. This place has more of a dance club vibe than I'd prefer, making it harder to talk over the music. None of the other players seem to mind since it means the dresses are shorter and tighter.

"There he goes again," Swanson says, shaking his head with wonder. "She could be all yours, Erik. Something to ease the pain of tonight's game."

"The game wasn't too bad, even if we did lose," LaPointe

says. "What Sørenson needs is some tail to take his mind off Who's Maya."

I give him a hard look. "Watch it LaPointe."

"He bought us drinks, so we need to give the guy a break," Brian Trager, one of the older players, says. He claps me on the back. "Speaking of which, thanks for the beer, Erik."

I lift my glass in a silent salute.

From there, it's our usual drifting apart for the night. All the married or otherwise taken players wander off to a less vibrant section of the bar, leaving the rest of us "open for business."

Some more than others.

"I wonder what time she gets off?" Shaw says, staring longingly after our waitress.

"She's on the job," I say. "Let's not make it harder for her."

I point the mouth of my bottle toward a group of women who have been eyeing us since the moment we walked in. "Let's go say hello."

Peter Shaw is one of the youngest players, just barely old enough to be allowed to drink. He was plucked out of some small town in Minnesota when he was only nineteen and his lack of experience with the opposite sex shows even after two years.

"Remember, confidence is key."

"Yeah," he says, nodding his head and already starting to sweat.

"Try that move I showed you."

"Yeah," he repeats, nodding his head.

"And stop nodding your head."

"Yeah." He chuckles nervously but stops.

"Hello ladies," he says, using the worst introduction ever.

I inwardly sigh.

They give him a doubtful, but not a completely closed-off look.

"Can I buy you a drink?"

"We're good," one says, though not unkindly as she holds up her completely full glass of beer.

My eyes wander the table, noting that all four of them have only just begun drinking. Definitely not lubricated enough to be forgiving toward what is likely to be a disastrous attempt at flirting, at least based on the nervous laughter escaping my teammate's lips.

"How'd you like to make a bet?" he begins, sounding slightly more confident again. "If I win, you let me buy you all the next round. If I lose, you're rid of me."

I'm hopeful once again, especially when all four of them look at each other than shrug and smile.

"Okay," says the same one that spoke before. She seems the most open toward him.

Shaw smiles at her. "I bet I could turn your drink over without spilling a drop."

Now, I'm inwardly groaning. He's doing it all wrong.

"What?" she asks with a wary laugh.

Shaw stares at her for a second, then down at the drink. "Oh, shit—I mean, sorry about that!—what I meant to say was..."

I see that deer in the headlights look and decide a little interception is necessary.

"Forgive my buddy here," I say, throwing my arm around his shoulders. "He's just pissed off at me because I lost him the game tonight. What you have here is the best damn left-winger on the Brooklyn Blades."

That lights those eyes right up. Obviously they have no particular favoritism for the home team, which is a good sign.

"You play professional hockey?" the first one asks, eyes boring right into him.

"Yeah," Shaw replies, falling into his element again.

"You too?" It's the one closest to me.

"Yes, but not nearly as good as this one," I say nodding my head toward him.

Not even a flicker his way.

"You have an interesting hint of an accent. Where is it from?" Eyes gleaming, tongue sliding across lips, body leaning forward with interest.

I have to tread carefully. Pissing off one member of this quartet will earn Shaw an instant Do Not Disturb sign from the rest of them.

"A mix of Norwegian and Swedish," I say, backing up slightly.

She just leans in further, somehow intrigued at this Scandinavian concoction.

"Say something in Norwegian...or Swedish."

Suddenly all eyes are ignoring Shaw in favor of me.

"*Jeg er ikke interessert.*"

"What's it mean?" She asks eagerly.

I give her my most gracious smile. "It's shorthand for, I would love to spend more time with you, but I don't think my girlfriend would appreciate it."

Technically, it's the more curt: *I'm not interested.*

"She's a lucky girl," the one closest to me says with a conceding smile.

"I wish she'd tell me that," I say with a smirk. *There's* some wishful thinking on my part.

"At any rate, I should return to my buddies. I leave you in good hands here with Peter," I say, slapping his back. "Maybe you can show them that trick again," I hint.

He smirks and turns back to them. "Okay, I've got it now. I

bet I could turn that drink upside down without spilling it..."

I smile as I walk away, hoping he succeeds tonight. The girls seemed nice and were certainly attractive.

It isn't unusual for me to put my teammates first, especially when it comes to women. After Tessa, I've been even more generous when it comes to bowing out from female attention. Until now.

The one woman I want might as well not exist. Maybe that's what makes me want her so much. I've seen the hashtag all over Twitter, and a part of me hoped that would do the trick of getting someone to at least give me a last name to work with.

So far, no such luck.

Who the hell are you, Maya?

I pull out my phone, just in case. That, of course, gets the taunting going back at our table.

"No luck yet, lover boy?" one of them teases.

"O Juliet, Juliet, wherefore art thou, Juliet?" Swanson croons, doing his best impression of a lovesick teenage boy.

"You do know she's asking 'why,' not 'where' Romeo is in that play, right?" I say, putting the phone back into my pocket.

He gives me a look of confusion, but it quickly disappears under a grin. "Well, they don't love me for my brains."

I feel my phone vibrate in my back pocket indicating a text-message and I pull it out, feeling slightly hopeful.

By now, I shouldn't be surprised at getting an after-game message from my father, even if it's still early in Sweden:

Synd. Hoppas det går bättre nästa gång. -Pappa

A pity. Hope you do better next time. -Dad

As usual, I stare at the message as though the letters are ancient runes I have to decipher instead of the simple message that stares back at me. What is he trying to say with this? What is he trying to say with any of it?

I could just reach out to him and ask instead of suffering

through this passive-aggressive texting of ours. My mind races back to the day I was headed to the United States to play for the NHL after a few years in Stockholm with Djurgårdens of the Swedish Hockey League. I thought my father would have at least come down to see me off, but it never happened.

I haven't heard from him, nor Freja or Liam since then, at least until this text messaging started.

I close out the messaging app only to have the phone ring just as I'm about to put it away. When I see who it is and, more importantly, what's coming, I walk away to a more private spot.

"Erik." The grim tone hints at the tongue lashing I'm about to get from my agent Doug.

"Doug."

"Before you hang up on me, I think this whole Instagram thing is great!" I can hear the fake enthusiasm in his voice, and I just imagine that tight smile on his face. "I wanted to wait until you finished your game before I got in touch."

"And I appreciate that," I say, taking a sip of my beer.

"Thankfully, nothing too serious has happened in the meantime."

"Like finding out who she is?"

"Like the poor girl being discovered and splashed across social media against her wishes."

I sigh and take another sip.

"Don't get me wrong; the message you wrote was...tactful."

"Hmmm," I say, noncommittally.

"We just need to manage this if it goes any further. At the very least find out more about her first."

"Manage it?" I repeat.

"Yes, in this era you can't be too careful, especially when you decide to go off the rails and make it so public."

"What exactly did I do wrong here?"

"Nothing...yet. Of course, the whole hashtag WhosMaya

Twitter expansion on this thing hasn't helped, but thankfully that's starting to die down. Listen, I'm sure you're tired after the game, why don't I take you out to dinner tomorrow, and we can discuss this."

"I'm not discussing my private life with you for the sake of having it managed."

"Not managed, just...a bit of relationship advice."

"Haven't you been divorced three times?"

"All the more reason to listen to me."

I laugh.

"I've also got some nibbles from prospective sponsors I want to run by you. Meet me after practice tomorrow. I'll come to you. We'll do dinner. I'll order the good wine."

"Nice carrot and stick there."

"I'll take that as a yes."

CHAPTER NINE

MAYA

How the hell are you a hashtag on Twitter and I didn't know?? And what's up with this Instagram business?

Demi tells me some hockey player asked you out? On Instagram? Are you even still using that account?

Girl....Spill It! ALL!

I had worked myself up so much overnight, I expected to find TMZ hanging outside my front door ready to accost me with questions as soon as I left my apartment building this morning.

Obviously, that didn't happen.

That doesn't stop my friends Demetria, Zia, and Gabrielle from blowing up my phone once it finally spread enough to create a blip on their radar.

All of them are met with a firm: **Tonight!**

As though they couldn't be bothered to wait for our usual Friday night get together. For the rest of the day, I put my phone on silent so I can actually get some work done.

"What I want to know is, how the hell you ended up at a hockey game in the first place?"

Work is done for the week, and I'm with my girls at our usual spot in the last booth of the bar. We've all changed into more casual clothing before arriving, just to get started on the weekend.

Demetria is hands down the most successful of us, having graduated valedictorian of our high school. She now works at an investment firm near the *Douglas & Foster* offices downtown. In fact, more than half the time she barely even leaves work early enough to make it here most Fridays.

Gabrielle is an executive assistant to some producer at ABC studios and is getting married this year.

Zia does a little bit of everything, mostly revolving around the term "holistic."

This is the place where I got my first gig as a barback (hence the Instagram username) before moving on to the more lucrative pastures of that sports bar in Manhattan. Ralph, the same bartender I worked with back then is still here and gives us all a beer on the house when we come every Friday.

I love this because it's that one point in the week where I can turn off and be real.

"Exactly," Gabrielle says, agreeing with Demetria. "Especially since your only response to our *multiple* texts is, 'tonight.' Now it's tonight, so spill, girl. I wanna know all about this hockey player of yours and how he knows about you in the first place?"

"Joey's dad bought him tickets to the game but, surprise, surprise, he dropped out last minute, so I took him instead."

There's the briefest moment of silence after that. They all know about the hot-button topic that is my own father.

I quickly move on.

"Anyway, he had this sign—you saw it on Instagram—and managed to get Erik Sørenson's attention and...the rest is history."

"So the *sign* is what got his attention?" Gabrielle asks with a teasing smirk.

"Yes," I say in a needling voice, though I can't help the smile that comes to my face. "I just...happened to be nearby."

"So what was the game like?" Zia, next to me asks with a frown. "I've heard it can get pretty violent."

My face lights up. I know my friend is a bit on the touchy-feely, frou-frou side—which is why I love her—but my excitement about the game is still too fresh in my veins.

"It was the shit! The players crash right into each other. And I'm sorry, but the fights are the best part. The referees just let them go at it, at least until it gets too crazy."

"See? That's how you know it's a white sport," Demetria chimes in. "The second they get a Tiger Woods playin' for them, what do you want to bet all that fighting suddenly becomes a foul, or whatever they call it in hockey?"

"Oh, here we go," Zia groans, throwing her head back.

"Seriously, Demetria. Every time, it's gotta be race with you," Gabrielle says, rolling her eyes.

"Where's the lie though?" she retorts swiveling her head around to look each of us in the eye. "Remember what they did with football? Just because a brotha wants to dance to celebrate his goal, next thing you know—banned."

"First of all, the NFL relaxed that rule, so there goes that argument," I say, snatching my fingers her way. "And whatever, I enjoyed the hell out of the game, fights included."

"And just how many *sistahs* were sitting in the audience enjoying the hell out of it with you?" she asks.

I use the moment to sip my beer, which causes Gabrielle and Zia to laugh.

Demetria is relentless. "Mmm-hmm, I thought so. I'll bet you can count on one hand the number of black faces you saw."

Not quite *that* low.

"Just another sign of gentrification in Brooklyn."

None of us let that one fly.

"Girl, stop. Your ass lives in Williamsburg," I say.

"The Blades have been here in Brooklyn for years already," Zia points out.

"Oh come on, Demi. Now you're just reaching," Gabrielle says, elbowing her side.

"Reaching to the right conclusion," she says to Gabrielle, then turns to me. "As for Williamsburg, there's nothing wrong with living close to work. After living there, I'm an expert as to how it goes down. First, we get a hockey team, the next thing you know there's a...I don't know, an *avocado toast* food truck in Brownsville."

"And my ass would be the first one in line," I say with a laugh.

"Girl, me too," Gabrielle chimes in, lifting her glass so I can tap mine against it.

"I heard that," Zia says with a laugh as she joins us with her glass. "Have you ever even had avocado toast, Demi?"

"Okay fine but, getting back to the *main* point," she says, giving each of us another hard look. "It's all fine and good for him to rack up Instagram points, but what are Mommy and

Daddy gonna say when they finally guess who's coming to dinner?"

"He's Norwegian," I point out.

"I thought he was Swedish," Zia says.

"Aren't they uncircumcised over there?" Gabrielle asks, with a wrinkled nose.

"What am I, the expert on Scandinavian dick, all of a sudden?" I say, giving her an incredulous look.

"There's nothing wrong with leaving a penis intact the way Mother Nature intended," Zia says. "Foreskin can be fun to play with."

"Too, *too* much information, Zia," Gabrielle says, grimacing at her.

"Every day we stray further from God's light," Demetria says, closing her eyes and shaking her head, making me laugh.

"Girl, it's hard enough for us to work with what's left *after* circumcision. Foreskin is just another feature for men to obsess over like they do the rest of it," Gabrielle continues.

"You're engaged, what are you doing talking about another man's dick in the first place?" Demetria scolds.

"Yes, I am engaged, quite happily. I'm just pointing out something Maya should be...*aware* of."

"Thank you for the anatomy lesson, Mom, but maybe I should at least go out with the man first? *Not* that his penis is a topic that would *ever* come up for discussion, mind you."

"So you're going to go out with him?" Zia asks with a smile.

"I think we need another round of drinks," I say, finishing off the rest of mine.

Despite the cries of protest, I walk up to the bar and order four more beers.

"Okay, enough stalling!" Gabrielle urges when I come back.

"I haven't decided if I'm going to date him yet," I say.

"Because he's white?"

"It's not because he's white!" I insist for the umpteenth time now.

"I hope not, Maya," Gabrielle says. "Even I've dated a white guy before. It's the twenty-first century. And if I wasn't with Marcus, this Erik whatshisface could definitely get it. Did you see him in that suit from *Ideal Gentleman*? Girl, bring on the snow!"

"I've dated plenty of white men too," Zia says, laughing with her.

Demetria coughs out a laugh at that. "Girl, what haven't you dated? When the aliens come for us, you'll be the first one out there sayin' 'Where the green men at?'"

"Demi, stop," I say, feeling the usual tension begin to simmer between the two of them.

As much as they have each other's back, race—specifically color—has always been a tricky subject between my two friends, what with Zia being lighter than all of us. Her skin and natural hair are the color of light honey, and tiny specks of hazel dot her big brown eyes. She's always been the favorite among the boys we grew up with. Demetria is darker than all of us with flawless skin and striking features that I've always envied. If only she'd get rid of whatever hang-up she has when it comes to men. She's always been judicious when it comes to dating, mostly because of her strict parents, but since she started working at an investment firm, she's been especially caustic about the opposite sex.

"It's fine Maya. You know we cool," Zia says to me, then turns to Demetria. "I just want to know how it's going for *you* waiting on your black knight in shining armor? Because they sure as hell aren't waiting on you, especially up there on Wall Street. Broaden your horizons, Demi. Hell, when the aliens come, you might just find that green is your favorite flavor of swirl."

That gets a laugh out of us all, even Demetria.

"Maya, there's nothing wrong with stayin' true to the brothas and finding yourself a good black man," Demetria insists. "They're still out there."

"It's not a race thing! And what does that even mean, stayin' true? I'm not throwing black men under the bus just because I date one white guy, *which* I haven't even agreed to in the first place!"

There's silence for a moment before they speak up again.

"Then what is it, Maya?" Gabrielle asks, slightly exasperated. "You just wanna leave the man hanging?"

"Yeah, Maya, I thought the way he asked was sweet. Totally respectful," Zia adds.

"And public," I point out.

"Now, you're just trying to find reasons."

"Seriously, Maya," Demetria, of all people says. "Either tell the man no or give him your number."

Gabrielle laughs and lifts her glass. "Now, you know you have to do something if even Demi says so."

"Okay, fine!" I say after taking an extended sip during this session of peer pressure.

If I'm honest with myself, this is exactly the sort of urging I needed. Just the thought of seeing Erik in person has my insides sizzling, despite everything.

I pull out my phone and make sure to give each of them a direct look before opening up Instagram.

"What are you going to say?" Zia asks.

"I'm just going to give him my number. If he calls, he calls, if he doesn't..." The thought has my stomach suddenly dropping. "Then I guess I can finally move on with my life."

"As thirsty as that message was, he'll call," Demetria says.

"It wasn't thirsty, it was nice," Zia insists.

"Thirsty. Nice. The man wants you, so you're doing the right thing, Maya," Gabrielle says, ending the debate.

"Wait, how will he even know it's from you? He probably gets a hundred phone numbers from women a day, and we all saw how you changed your account to private as soon as all this dropped," asks Zia.

"Y'all just don't want to see me get away with anything do you?" I say with a smirk.

"I just want to see you with a man again," she replies, bumping me with her shoulder. "Or just have some fun."

I shake my head and stare at the screen. I'm sure as hell not switching my profile photo to a picture of my face. I think about how to distinguish myself, letting Erik know the message is from the Maya he's been seeking. Then, it finally comes to me.

With a smirk, I pull up his Instagram account, ignoring the distraction of his most recent photos, which would just have me salivating as I scroll through them yet again until I've lost all track of time.

After direct messaging a quick note and adding my number, I quickly close out, feeling the rush of adrenaline at what I've just done. "Done. Happy?"

Zia lifts her glass. "Cheers, to...Maya finally finding her inner goddess."

Gabrielle and Demetria both roll their eyes.

"Cheers to finally growing a pair," Demetria says, tapping her glass to Zia's

"Girl, cheers to hopefully getting laid, circumcised or not," Gabrielle says with a laugh.

I groan with the others as I tap my glass to theirs.

"Okay, so real talk now," Gabrielle says, leaning in toward me. "What's your mom gonna say when she finds out about all this?"

My mother is even more anti-social media than I am. She swore off Twitter, Facebook, Instagram, even MySpace back in the day, long before any of them were even a thing. I know it stems from avoiding all temptation to check in and see how my dad is doing—the man who can't get enough of showing off his new life—new *family*—on every platform.

I know for a fact that it's the same reason I've stayed offline. The day he sent a "friend" request to my barely updated Facebook account is the day I deleted it.

"Well, she obviously doesn't know, otherwise my phone would be lit up right now," I say with a wary smile. "But I guess I'll find out when I see her tomorrow."

CHAPTER TEN

THE CALL

"That spread in *Ideal Gentleman* magazine worked wonders, just like I told you it would. As far as sports go, you're Sweden's most famous export."

"I'm Norwegian," I remind Doug.

"Right, right," he says, nodding in that way that tells me it's just a segue into something he's not sure I'll want to discuss. "The thing is, I've had a call again from Sven Lindström. He's opening a new hotel in Malmö."

"And you know exactly how I feel about representing a Swedish brand."

"What's this opposition you have to Sweden? Isn't it the country that started it all for you?"

"In a manner of speaking," I say, wondering where the steak I ordered is. I pull out my phone and idly scroll through the DMs on Instagram, mostly as a distraction. "And I don't have an opposition to Sweden, per se, I just—"

I've been scrolling through the usual noise in my DM feed, which has been louder than usual lately, mostly with random phone numbers, email addresses, and @ tags to follow or get in touch with.

This one is different.

@barbackbutterfly:**Just because of the wink.**

It's followed by a phone number.

I sit up straight in my chair and click on the profile photo, which is nothing but a blue butterfly. The account is private, which is infuriating, mostly because I know it's Maya —*my* Maya.

And I want to see more.

I definitely remember the wink I gave her after she snapped the photo. At the time it was a spur of the moment afterthought, practically an involuntary reflex. But what came before it was definitely something special. The woman who looked like she was dressed to head off to work instead of a hockey game. That wasn't the only thing that made her stand out.

"It's her," I say...stupidly.

"Wait, what?" Doug's droning spiel about Sven and his hotel group comes to an abrupt stop. "She actually got back to you?"

"With a number," I say, standing up.

"Wait, where are you going? You're not calling her, are you? Erik...."

I ignore him as I make my way past the tables around us, pulling up the app to make the call.

Doug is behind me, saying something to our waiter about using his credit card to pay for everything and saving our table since we'll be right back.

I'm not so sure about that.

"I'm a grown woman. I don't need my mother's permission to date a man."

"Yeah, but she's so..." Demetria's face is strained as she mimics my mother's silent judgment regarding almost everything.

I get it, mostly because I was a first-hand witness to the disastrous ending to her marriage to my dad.

"She's not *that* bad when it comes to men. She's just—"

"Is that your phone?" Zia asks, looking down at my purse between us.

I stare down at it, only to hear the faint ring from the phone inside. "Probably a telemarketer."

"The hell it is!" Gabrielle exclaims. "Right on the heels of you sending him your number?"

It rings again, and I just stare at the bag holding it.

"Girl, if you don't answer that phone..." Gabrielle warns.

"Then, I will!" Zia says with a laugh, reaching for my bag.

It's a mad scramble as I try to reach it before she does something too...Zia. She's one of those weird believers in things like "fate" and "meant to be" and "kismet." What she needs to believe in is "weak ass" and "triflin'" and "no good" when it comes to the men she chooses.

I finally snatch it from her, only to have it stop ringing.

We all stare at the phone in my hands, wondering what to do next.

———

Hi, you've reached Maya Jackson. You know what to do after the beep!

It's her voicemail. I don't waste time by being disappointed. Frankly, the way her voice sounds in the message is enough to sate me until I meet the real thing.

"Maya—I'm pretty sure you're the right one—I just received your number. I'm going to try again just in case. But, as I said in my message, I'd love to meet you in person, and take you out on a date."

We all listen to the message.

"Just as I thought. Thirsty," Demetria says.

"Demi, stop," Zia says.

"This time, answer, Maya!" Gabrielle insists. "He knows it's you!"

"Or I'm taking the phone back," Zia warns.

We all jump in surprise as the phone rings again.

"Erik!" Doug hisses, his face practically the color of hot embers as I call again.

I grin at him.

"Wait, you can't just call some random number you got—"

I place a finger against his lips and give him a look of mocking condemnation. "Shhh, it's ringing."

He flails his arms and pulls away. It's almost enough to make me laugh. Which would be a shame, because this time the call is answered.

"Erik?" I say, pressing one finger to my other ear to drown out the noise of the bar.

"Maya." His voice sounds so self-assured and pleased, I feel a smile come to my face. There's a hint of an accent touching even that one word, which for some reason tickles me.

It isn't lost on my friends, who start making even more noise around me.

"Hold on; I'm in a bar. I have to go outside," I say, giving them all a hard, warning glare.

As if that would stop them.

"I can call you right back," he says. "I'm headed outside as well."

"Um," I say, trying to fumble my way into my heavy coat. "That would be a good idea."

I hang up and set the phone down to put my coat on.

"Don't even think about following me outside."

As if.

They just laugh, already putting their coats on.

"Oh, thank God," Doug says when I hang up. "Okay, there's a certain way to approach this, Erik."

"Is that so?" I say, in a patronizing tone.

"As I said, if you hadn't made this so public, I wouldn't be interfering. But this? This can be very lucrative if you—"

"I'm sorry, are you talking about monetizing my dating life?"

His eyes light up as though that was the best idea he'd heard this century. "Since you put it that way—"

"No."

"I'm just saying—"

"I'm calling. You stay here." I head outside in nothing but my jeans and a heavy sweater. Having grown up in some of the coldest places on Earth, I'm used to the chill. Besides, my insides are practically on fire now.

Doug follows me out, then quickly reverses course once the cold hits him, muttering something that sounds distinctly like "fuck this shit."

There's something to be said for having Norwegian genes. I call Maya again.

"Erik? Hi," I say as I answer in the freezing cold. Good grief, how could it be this frigid without so much as a snowflake yet?

"This better be short," Gabrielle whispers, shivering beside me, even in her heavy coat.

I have my hood up, the faux fur edge getting in the way of the phone I'm trying to hold up to my ear.

"Oh, just put it on speaker," Demetria mutters through chattering teeth. "You know we'll get it out of you eventually."

I frown at her.

"Hello Maya," he says, sounding as calm and collected as if he were lounging on a beach in Miami. He's probably used to the cold. I adjust my hood, which has slipped down and miss most of what he says next.

"So, I....nted to.....formally...ou out...like I...ised on....agram."

"What?" I say, sounding more exasperated than I wanted to. "Hold on. Do you mind if I put you on speakerphone? I should warn you, I couldn't get rid of my friends, so they are all here—despite my very specifically telling them *not* to follow me." I glare at all of them in the glow of the street light.

They just smile.

"Not a problem," he says, seemingly not bothered at all. He even laughs a little.

Point one in favor of confidence.

I pull the phone from my ear and jerk my hood back firmly

on my head before my ears freeze off. Then, I put him on speakerphone.

"I'm sorry, what were you saying before?"

"I said, I wanted to formally ask you out on a date, as I promised on Instagram. Perhaps someplace warm?" I say, finally starting to feel the bite of the frigid air.

I hear her laugh nervously on the other end. There are distinct female whispers, most of which I can't quite comprehend. It still amuses me.

I'm not intimidated by "friends." I certainly wouldn't have gotten this far with Maya if they were there to play interference. The fact that she seemed reluctant to have them as an audience makes me think that she doesn't need them as a crutch in situations like this, which is admirable.

"A date," she repeats, almost as though she's confirming what I've just said.

"Yes, a date," I repeat with a smile.

"A date," she repeats.

"Yes...a date," I say slower this time.

What's going on over there?

My mind feels like a carousel, mostly because of my so-called friends.

Zia is grabbing my free arm and practically jumping up and down with glee. "Say yes!" she whispers.

Gabrielle has a smile that threatens to split her lower face in two as she nods eagerly. *You got this, girl!,* she mouths.

Demetria just shakes her head and rolls her eyes. I'm not

sure if it's meant for me, Erik, or our two friends acting a fool next to us.

I put the phone on mute.

"Will you all *stop!*"

"I know you didn't just put that man on mute," Gabrielle admonishes.

"Thanks to *you!*"

"Just say yes and be done with it, Maya," Zia says. "So we can go inside."

"No one's stopping you!"

"If you think we're missing out on this, you're outta your damn mind," Gabrielle—oh, she of drama not to be missed—says.

"He already said it was okay that we're here," Zia adds.

"Which, if I'm honest, is a point in his favor," Demetria says. "Frankly, I'm just here to make sure none of you act a complete fool. But I'm about to freeze my ass off, so say yes, Maya so we can go back inside."

"If you three would just—"

"Wait, is he still on mute?" Zia asks.

I pull the phone away and stare at it, making sure she didn't hang up on me.

I'm still clueless as to what's going on on the other end. Any other man might start to feel uncomfortable, knowing full well that Maya's friends are all discussing him.

My confidence level is high enough to withstand it.

But the silence lingers.

I blink in surprise when it's shattered by her voice.

"Sorry, Erik! Yes!"

The cringes on each of their faces point out how terrible that was, and I wince.

"I mean, yes, I will go out with you."

Why do I feel like a damn teenager?

"Great," Erik says on the other end. "How about tonight? I mean…if you're not busy with your friends?"

Once again, there's silence, except this time there's just enough background noise to tell me I haven't been put on mute.

I stare wide-eyed at each of my friends, all of whom are now sending animated silent messages.

Zia: *Yes! Yes!*

Gabrielle: *No! No!*

Demetria: aggrieved sigh of *whatever*.

Gabrielle reaches out to touch mute again.

"Gabby!"

"You know the rule. Don't you dare take a man up on a request for a date the same night he asks."

"What are we, in the Victorian Era?" Zia snaps. "If you want to meet him, meet him. To-night! And get laid if you want to."

I wrinkle my nose at her.

"Girl," Demetria says, with a laugh of disbelief. "Do *something*. I'm pretty sure I have icicles growing out of my ass."

"Good grief, Demi," Gabrielle says, frowning at her. "Make sure I actually hit mute, Maya."

"Shut up!" I shout.
While they're still in shock, I un-mute my phone.

I'm still staring down at my phone when I hear the sound of it coming out of mute.
"Yes, Erik. I'd love to meet tonight."

CHAPTER ELEVEN

ERIK

Doug's only parting words when I told him where I was headed to meet Maya were, "Don't screw this up!" Unusually curt for someone who is typically a talker, but in his defense, the weather wasn't particularly conducive to extended conversation.

I've taken an Uber down from DUMBO, where I live, to the coffee bar Maya suggested.

Asking her out tonight instead of planning for a later date, which is definitely the usual custom here, was yet another instinctive move. I figured if going with my gut worked twice, it would work again. The wink, then the Instagram message both led me this far. What's one more bold move?

And there she is.

The place is nearer to where she already was, so it's no surprise she's arrived earlier than me. I grin as I stand there watching her through the window of the coffee shop.

She's sitting at one of the booths next to the floor-to-ceiling window, bouncing one leg up and down. The puffy coat necessary in weather like this is balled up next to her side underneath her purse. She's in a long sweater one side slipping down and leaving a peek of her tank top underneath. It ends half-way down the thighs of the skin-tight jeans she has on, all leading to brown, suede booties. The hair that was up in some kind of bun or twist when I first saw her at the game is now down, just past her shoulders and mostly covered by a knit cap over most of her head.

She's on her phone, no doubt texting the same friends who were privy to our conversation earlier, based on her facial expressions. I laugh as I see her roll her eyes and exhale an exaggerated sigh at something on her screen, then laugh and text something back to them.

She's cute.

Scratch that—*nydelig*.

I quickly head toward the front door and swing it open so hard that the bell above rings loud enough to draw the attention of the patrons who are still buying coffee this late at night. It's more than I would have normally expected. New York.

Of all the eyes focused on me, some with avid recognition, there is only one pair my own are interested in. They are large enough to put the average Disney princess' to shame, framed by dark lashes that stand at attention like tiny little guards keeping those eyes from popping right out of their sockets.

I know just the thing to put those lashes at ease.

When I make it to her table, I wink.

She stares at me like I'm an apparition, large eyes somehow impossibly wider.

I wink again, now in an exaggerated way, if only to show I am human after all.

This time she laughs.

"I feel bad. Is it not the rule here that the person asking for the date buys?" I say, nodding toward the coffee she has her hands wrapped around.

"I guess that means a rain check," she says, staring down at it. "You can buy next time. This one was more to keep me from making a trip to the ER to have my fingers amputated from standing in the cold during that phone call."

"Already a second date? Usually, I have to work much harder for it."

She smirks at me. "I somehow doubt that, but there's still plenty of opportunity to screw up this first one."

I grin back at her. "Well, believe it or not, but my hands need a little bit of warmth as well. So excuse me while I get a coffee."

I'm not above wondering how my hands could otherwise warm themselves. The way Maya watches as I shrug out of the thick peacoat and unwrap the scarf from my neck, makes me think her mind is also swimming with ideas. Underneath, I'm wearing a simple dark gray wool sweater and black jeans with black shoes.

As a six-foot-four natural blond, I'm used to getting lingering looks even without the professional hockey status. I ignore it as I order my coffee from the cashier with the dark-rimmed glasses, stretched out ear-lobes, and a thoroughly bored expression on his face. He's indifferent enough toward me that I actually find it amusingly refreshing.

"Just one large coffee."

While he turns around to fill the cup, the barista next to him with no specialized order to make leans on the bar with one hand and smiles at me. She has a neon-orange pixie-cut and the sort of bright, bubbly smile usually reserved for mornings.

"One large coffee for one *very* large man," she says in a flirtatious voice.

"All the better to keep my hands warm for my date."

She slides her eyes to the booth where Maya is sitting, then back to me and shrugs with a conceding smile. "Enjoy!"

"Your coffee," the cashier says in a tone so droning and patronizing it seems practiced.

"Thanks," I say, paying in cash and letting them keep the change.

"Someone has an admirer," Maya says with a smirk as I arrive back at the table.

"Maybe she just likes hockey," I say as I sit down in the booth across from her. "At least now, my hands are warm."

"So just what do you think is going to happen with those warmed-up hands of yours?" she teases.

"Let's see where the night goes," I say, grinning over the rim of my coffee.

"Don't get any ideas," she says over the rim of her own mug.

"Wouldn't dream of it," I lie.

The way her eyes sparkle tells me she reads right through it.

Let's see where this night goes indeed...

"So, it was the wink that sold you?" I ask.

"I needed something to distinguish myself, and the wink was the only thing I could think of so you would know it was me."

"Right, as opposed to a blue butterfly," I say, thinking back to her profile photo.

"The blue butterfly was a...defense mechanism. I didn't want the whole world finding me on Instagram."

"Your account is private. I feel slightly cheated," I say with a suggestive smile.

"That account is definitely not first date material."

"Oh, now I'm really intrigued."

She laughs and shakes her head. "Not gonna happen."

"Fair enough. I'll leave it alone," I reply, sipping my coffee.

She twists her lips at me. "Your eyes tell a different story."

"Do they?" I ask with a grin.

"Mmm-hmm," she hums before taking another sip, not breaking eye contact with me.

There's a silence after that as we drink, but it isn't an uncomfortable one. This is the first time I'm seeing her without the distraction of hockey, giving me a chance to focus on her with something more than a passing gaze.

I have a feeling she's doing the same with me.

"So, are you a Blades fan?" I ask, moving on to the most obvious topic of conversation.

"It was my first hockey game."

"Ah," I say, setting my coffee down with a grin. "So that means I was your first—"

"Don't even go there," she says, her head falling slightly back to laugh.

"I should have known, considering how you were dressed," I say, moving on.

"Blame that one on Joey's mom who ambushed me at work, since she couldn't make it. Actually, blame his dad for not showing up in the first place."

I note something bitter in her voice and face as she stares down at her coffee to take a sip. I guess I'm not the only one here with father issues. No wonder I feel some kind of connection to her.

"Anyway," she says dismissively, her face clearing up as she brings her eyes back to me. "That explains the attire."

"The clothes certainly made you stand out."

"Is that what earned me the wink?" she teases.

"Not just that," I say, my gaze solidifying as I stare at her.

Hers begin to swim, as though the force of mine are turning her insides to lava. She blinks a few times, exhaling to release some of that internal steam.

"So, is this your usual modus operandi when it comes to picking up women at games? Hitting them up on Instagram?" she asks, raising one eyebrow.

I laugh and shake my head with amusement.

"What? Did you think I wouldn't ask?" she retorts.

"It's not that," I say, still grinning as I straighten my head to look at her. "It's that I'm usually the one setting my teammates up, helping them score, so to speak."

She chuckles, then her eyes fall to the table in thought. "The playmaker."

I raise my brow in surprise, wondering how a novice to hockey knows what a playmaker is, even if it is applied incorrectly. "You know the term?"

"Joey told me."

"I suppose it fits here too," I say, rethinking my earlier notion about the correct usage of the word.

"So what, you just play wingman? Or are you the designated team matchmaker?" She asks.

An idea comes to me and I darken my gaze just to draw her attention. "I have a very impressive move I've perfected that forces women to practically throw themselves at me. It's worked for my teammates in the past."

"Is that so?" she asks with a laugh.

"Mmm-hmm, would you like to see it?"

She shrugs and smiles. "Go for it."

I see the trio of girls, nervous and giggling, making their way to our table behind Maya and pause before I can even start. She follows my eyes, twisting her head around to see what I'm looking at, then bringing it back again with a knowing smirk.

"Excuse me," the one in front says, braces on full display. They can't be older than thirteen or fourteen. "Um...you're Erik Sørenson from the Blades, right?"

"You caught me."

The giggling intensifies.

Maya holds back a laugh, just barely rolling her eyes.

"My friend was wondering if we could get a photo with you?"

"Well, that depends. Only if my very pretty date here says it's okay."

Maya twists her lips, but I see the sparkle in her eyes. "I certainly wouldn't want to upset your fans. In fact, I'll take the photo for you all."

"Thanks!" Now, they're bouncing on their feet as I slide out of the booth.

The tops of their heads barely reach my shoulders, and they aren't shy about squeezing in, arms pressed into my back in some semblance of a hug. Mine are firmly in front of me, hands clasped together. I do manage a genuine smile, mostly at the teasing one Maya sends my way. She has to know how awkward this is for me.

"Say, 'go, Blades!'" she urges.

"Go, Blades!" The high-pitched squeal is almost enough to turn my smile into a wince, but I hold it long enough to get more than a few photos…with each of their phones…in various poses. Because, Instagram.

It almost feels like poetic justice.

"Okay, I'd better stop before my date's coffee gets cold," I hint, mostly as a reminder of the kind of woman that is in fact age-appropriate for me. And that I'm very much taken, at least for the evening.

Amid a series of thanks to Maya and checking and double-checking each picture, I ease myself back into the seat across from her.

"You're sooo lucky," one of them finally says to Maya, casting a quick, school-girl-crush glance my way.

"Kaitlyn!" another one squeals as she drags her away amid another round of giggles.

I wriggle my eyebrows at Maya. "Hear that? Lucky you."

She laughs. "They're what? Thirteen? Fourteen? What girl, or boy for that matter, has any sense about the opposite sex when they're that young? I had a crush on Chris Brown when I was their age. We all know how well that turned out."

"Some develop good taste early on."

She laughs again. "But I have yet to see this panty-dropping move of yours."

"Okay, can I have your coffee?" I say, directing my eyes to the mug in front of her.

She wrinkles her brow. "You aren't planning to secretly roofie me are you?"

"Roofie? You mean drug you?" A wicked grin comes to my face. "Only with my wit and charm, if this doesn't do the trick first."

She laughs and slides the mug toward me.

"Okay so, a bet. If I can turn this cup upside down without spilling a drop, you agree to another date with me. If I spill it then I owe you a new cup of coffee."

"I think you'll owe me more than a new cup of coffee," she says, pressing back into her seat as though I've already spilled the brown liquid all over the table and into her lap.

"Just watch and see. Do you agree to the bet?"

"Okay," she says, looking wary but intrigued.

My grin broadens as I slowly spin the mug on the table. "Turned."

Then, I lift it in the air. "Up."

I move it over while it's still in the air. "Side."

By now, Maya sees where this is going and starts laughing.

"Down," I say, setting the mug back on the table. "Turned upside down."

She slowly claps her hands and continues to laugh. "Bravo. So that's what gets you the ladies, huh?"

"Hopefully," I say, raising one eyebrow suggestively. "Usually, my teammates steal the move from me. One of them, Daniel Kelsey, met his wife with it."

"So, you're always the bridesmaid, never the bride? You sound like me."

"Oh?"

"Well, soon-to-be at any rate. With my friend, Gabrielle? She met her husband through me."

"Sounds like a story with a happy ending—for me anyway." Who was the man stupid enough to pass up the woman in front of me?

She bites her lip and smiles before continuing. "Marcus and I were working together on some group project thing while I was at Brooklyn College. Obviously, I considered dating him, mostly because he ticked all the right boxes. Smart, good looking, nice, funny. Checkmark, checkmark, checkmark, checkmark. But it was...you know, just one of those maybe, kinda, sorta things?

"*Anyway*," she says in an exaggerated tone, "in walks Gabby one day while we were finishing up and," she snaps her fingers, "just like that he went from Mr. I'm-Not-Quite-Sure-He's-the-One to Mr. I'm-Happy-For-My-Friend. They just...connected."

"Like lightning," I say softly, feeling it strike every one of my nerve endings. Fuck hockey. This is what that force of nature truly feels like.

"Like lightning," she repeats just as softly, her eyes trapped by mine.

CHAPTER TWELVE

ERIK

We're on to our second cups of coffee with no sign of slowing down.

"You haven't asked me anything about hockey."

Her eyes widen. "Um..."

"That wasn't a criticism. It's one of the things I like about being here with you."

She smiles with pleasure, those dimples killing me. "To be fair, I probably should be asking you about hockey, just so I know more about it. Especially since it seems you owe me another date."

I fully plan on holding her to that one.

"What would you like to know?"

"I guess how you first got into it?"

"That's a...long and complicated history."

"And you have plans for the rest of this Friday night?"

"It's more about weight than time. Heavy material."

"Ah, so in other words, not *first date* material."

I consider her for a moment. "Actually, I have no problem telling you. I just don't want to drag tonight into the deep end of my life."

Maya swirls her cup of coffee around as she eyes me. "So... let's start at the shallow end and work our way down."

God, this amazing woman!

I breathe out a light laugh. "I don't know that there is a shallow end."

"You seem pretty certain of that."

This time my laugh is sharper and less amused. "Let's start with the fact that my dad had sex with two women around the same time, both in different countries, both apparently unprotected. Hence the existence of me and my half-brother Liam. I'm four months older."

Maya coughs out a laugh, then brings her hand up to her mouth in shock. "I'm sorry. I Didn't mean to laugh. It's just..."

"I know. Deep."

"Like...*Jerry Springer* deep. Though I never thought I'd use that word to describe anything related to that show."

I grimace, being somewhat familiar with the reputation of the American show, even if I've never seen it.

"You know what? That was wrong. I shouldn't have said that. Let's swim back to the shallow end."

"Well, we're both already in over our heads so I might as well keep swimming deeper, yes?"

"You don't have to."

I swivel my cup in my hand, watching the dark brown liquid swish back and forth. "It feels nice to tell someone." I look up from the cup. "I don't know why, but I feel comfortable telling you. Do you feel it?"

She smiles softly and tilts her head to the side to consider me. "Yeah, I do. So let's go swimming."

I laugh silently, letting the feeling soak in a bit. Back in Sweden, my complicated family situation was public property as far as my peers at school were concerned. Liam had set the groundwork long before I even came into the picture. My arrival in Sweden coincided with that period in life when kids are at their meanest, and they spared nothing.

Once my success at hockey outgrew the target on my back, the tone changed. But it was always there, lingering behind every win, every eventual follower who latched onto me, every girl who batted their eyes my way. There was always an asterisk firmly attached to me that reminded everyone how easy it would be to drag me right down: Neither my mother nor I were my dad's first choice.

I can already begin to feel the bitterness set in, so I decide to lighten the mood. "Once upon a time, twenty-seven years ago..."

Maya smiles and shakes her head. "Erik..."

I shift gears, getting serious again. "I was born in Norway. It was just my mother and me. Well, a lot of my grandfather too."

"He's the one I saw in your Instagram photos?" she asks.

"So you've been snooping?" I say with a grin.

She laughs and coyly lifts one shoulder. "If you're going to make it so public... I especially liked the Christmas one with the cookie."

I wince. "That was a dare from my cousin, Bård. Each year we try to outdo each other on how—corny, I think you call it?—on how corny we can be. You obviously didn't scroll down far enough to see last year's with the reindeer hat. The *pepperkake* sent by my aunt Vilde was real, everything else was staged."

Maya laughs. "Wait, even the tree?"

I shrug. "I had one of those services put it up. I don't usually put one up myself."

There's a look of bewilderment on Maya's face, and I

continue before she starts asking questions. My Christmas memories don't exactly bring me joy.

"That photo for some reason has the most likes, second only to that *Ideal Gentleman* photo of me in the snow."

"That one is...*very* nice," she says, sounding impressed enough to make my ego do a little backflip. "But the one with your grandfather did seem the most authentic."

The smile on my face softens. "Yes, that's him. I probably spent half my time living in Norway staying with him. My mother had what you here call...wanderlust?"

Maya's eyes widen with interest.

"She was constantly going. My grandfather says it's in the blood. He was in the French Foreign Legion."

"Really?"

"True, he wanted to see the world. My mother? She was always going someplace. When I was nine, we spent the summer doing humanitarian work in Angola of all places."

"You're kidding!" Maya says with wider eyes.

"No," I say before taking a sip of my coffee. "Don't ask me anything in Portuguese though," I add with a grin.

Maya is still too in awe to reply.

"I have it too. I love to travel, though hockey season doesn't give me much opportunity to do it."

"I saw that in some of your Instagram photos."

"I still consider Oslo my home."

"Is that where you first started playing hockey?"

I laugh and shake my head. "You obviously don't know much about Norway."

"So tell me," she says with a tart smirk.

I grin and pull out my phone from my pocket. "It is played there somewhat, but not to the extent that it is in Sweden or Finland."

"What are you pulling up?" she asks, craning her neck to see the screen of my phone.

I lift my head. "It would be easier to show you if I sat over there."

She twists her lips. "Is that so?"

"Only if you want to really get to know Norway," I reply with a seductive grin.

She laughs but slides over to give me room. The booth is meant for four people total, so the benches would normally accommodate two people each. With her coat and purse and my larger than average build, the squeeze is…cozy.

Maya smells like a mix of coconut, vanilla, coffee, and something pleasant that I couldn't place if you forced me to. It's heady and distracting, like an aphrodisiac setting in at exactly the wrong time.

"This is Norway," I say, pointing out my home country on a map. "Next to it is Sweden. Notice anything different about the two?"

She peers hard at my phone. "The edges along the border? Norway has those sort of jagged—"

"Fjords. They are just one thing that makes our climate so varied. In Sweden, in Finland it gets cold. It snows. Lakes freeze. People play hockey."

"It doesn't snow in Norway?"

"It does, but we also have such an uneven landscape that what may be a popular snow sport in one town, is not as popular in another. Me? I wanted to speed skate when I was younger. Mostly to go to the Olympics."

"But then…hockey came along?"

I feel my mood drop a few degrees.

"Then, a piece of toast came along."

"What?"

I'm twisted slightly in my seat, so my body is facing Maya,

but my eyes fall to the table in thought. "You know those crazy stories about famous people who have lived amazing lives only to die in the most boring or ridiculous way possible?"

"I guess," she replies slowly, her tone matching the somber mood.

I bring my eyes up to her with a wry smile. "That was my mom. Did you know she almost qualified for the biathlon in the winter Olympics? That's cross-country skiing and shooting. She had visited almost forty different countries. She was a freelance journalist and lived for the next adventure taking her somewhere."

"She sounds amazing," Maya says, twisting around in her seat to face me, legs drawn up.

"She was," I agree, nodding my head. The wry smile reappears on my face. "She never slowed down...even when it came to making breakfast for us. I was upstairs in my room when it happened. One glass of juice in her hand and the toaster on the other side of the kitchen. She must have hurried to get the toast and spilled some of the juice, only to slip on it and hit her head."

"Erik," Maya says softly, reaching out a hand to touch my arm. I barely register it underneath the thick wool of my sweater, but even that light pressure is enough to calm the quiet storm brewing in me that comes every time I think about that day.

"The funny thing is, she seemed fine. Just another little bruise that comes from living an active life, this one on the back of her head. She wasn't the sort to go to the hospital just in case, and we both had a laugh over how ridiculous it was as we ate breakfast," I pause to collect myself. "Then I went off to school. By the time classes were over, I got the call she was in the hospital with a brain bleed. It was too late."

We're both silent for a moment afterward. I'm the first to break it.

"That's when I was sent to live with my father and his wife and son in Örnsköldsvik in Sweden. I was twelve at the time, which was lucky since I barely made the cut for getting involved with hockey. I had played a bit before in Norway and a history of speed skating and playing soccer in the summers helped, if only to make me more physically capable. Practicing as much as possible, mostly to avoid my new family pretty much guaranteed my success."

I can feel how tight the smile on my face is as I look at Maya. "So there you have the deep end of how I got involved in hockey."

She reads right through the fake smile. "I'm guessing life with your new family wasn't quite sunshine and roses?"

I laugh softly and shake my head. "That's a detour that's sure to ruin the mood...worse than it already is."

Maya leans in with a soft, encouraging smile on her face. "Try me."

CHAPTER THIRTEEN

MAYA

"My father wasn't horrible. He was just a man who did something stupid when he was young, like we all do."

"Is that so? Does that mean there are multiple little Eriks running around?" I say raising my brow at him.

It's enough to lighten the mood, and Erik laughs.

The bench in the booth is deep enough to accommodate me sitting sideways facing Erik, with both legs bent up between us. I lean against my heavy coat and purse as we talk.

Erik fills the space at the end with his large body. Many women might feel trapped or uneasy with the amount of room I'm left with. For some reason, I just feel secure and snug. I like having him sit here on the same side as me, closing me into this small space, like my own big, protective bodyguard.

"Okay, maybe his past transgressions were a bit more...*transgressive* than my own."

"So I don't have to worry about another woman in Canada or Mexico that you also take out for coffee?"

"If I did have a woman in each country, I know which

woman I'd choose first in a heartbeat," he says, fingering the rim of his coffee cup as he stares at me without any hint of teasing.

It's...bold. Confrontational. Unhesitant. Powerful.

Like lightning.

"Say something in Norwegian," I urge without thinking. His gaze deepens, and that wicked smile comes to his lips as he twists his body toward me even more. He drapes one long, muscular arm over the back of the seat and leans in so that the front of his sweater grazes across the shins of my jeans.

"*Kaffen din blir kald.*"

The way his voice sounds while he says it, he might as well be ordering me to take off my clothes right here and now. The way his face looks, eyes piercing me, jaw tense, the narrow nostrils of his nose flared...I'm not so sure I wouldn't.

"What does it mean?" I whisper, my body tingling with anticipation.

His grin broadens. "Your coffee is getting cold."

I blink once, twice, until I realize that's a literal interpretation of what he said.

"Erik!" I cry with a laugh, as I kick one of my booties out to tap his stomach. Even through the suede toe and thick wool of his sweater, I notice how unyielding the flesh underneath is.

I try to scoot my way back into my jacket balled against the window, just because. Erik grabs the ankle I kicked him with, then the other and straightens both out so they're stretched over his thick thighs.

"Do you mind?" he asks in a way that tells me he already knows the answer.

All I can do is shake my head no. Not. At. All.

"Good," he says, sliding in closer to me. The movement shifts my legs so my calves are hanging off the other side of him and my knees are bent slightly up, forcing them closer to the crotch of his jeans. The underside of my thighs, the part closest to my ass is pressed right up against the side of his.

Although my heart is racing like that of a jackrabbit running to escape danger, I feel even more secure like this. It's way beyond anything that could be termed "cozy," but that's the feeling it evokes in me.

I reach out to grab my coffee, mostly to give myself a moment to adjust without having to say anything.

"Bleh," I say, swallowing it, then laughing. "You were right. It's cold."

He grins. "Do you want me to get up and buy you another?"

"No." I meet his eyes, feeling bolder now. I want to stay like this forever.

"Tell me about your Dad, and what it was like in Sweden," I say softly.

He twists his head so that he's staring down at my legs across his lap in thought. One of his palms comes down to settle just below my right knee and his thumb circles the round curve of it.

I watch as a tiny smile touches his lips, and he turns his head to look my way.

"I don't even know why he wanted me to come live with them. Norway doesn't have as bad a stigma attached to unwed parents that America does, but most of the kids I knew in that situation could at least say their dad was involved in their lives. Mine was this man who I'd visited maybe a total of ten times in my life, a man who sent birthday and Christmas presents by way of communication. And now, there I was, living in his house. His wife, Freja was, at best slightly chilly at the idea. My half-brother Liam wasn't completely horrible at first, mostly just annoyed at having to share a room. Then came hockey."

He laughs and shakes his head, as though there's some joke in that, one that is more sad than funny.

"What?" I ask, jostling the leg surrounded by his huge palm.

"They lived in this town in Sweden called Örnsköldsvik, we call it O-vik for short. The thing about O-vik is, hockey is one of the most popular things to do there. I only started playing because all the other boys were. Then, it became an excuse not to go home."

"It was that bad living with them?" I say during the pause that follows.

"Not bad just...have you ever been at a party or meeting where everyone knew and liked each other and had this common interest and you had only been invited as sort of a sympathy offer or an afterthought? That's what it felt like. Like I was an afterthought. I had a tiny bed shoved into a corner of Liam's room before I insisted on moving to the basement. Dad was an accountant and was either lost in a book or working, ignoring the tension in the air instead of dealing with it. Freja seemed to go out of her way to make me feel left out, like cooking breakfast or packing a lunch for Liam, leaving me to make my own.

"I was constantly on the phone to my grandfather begging to go back and live with him, but for some reason, he kept insisting I stay there a little longer and see how it goes. That's how it was for at least a year; just a little longer, Erik, he'd say. Eventually, hockey replaced my need for comfort at home.

"I had played some in Norway, but nothing at this level. And surprisingly...I was good." He stops to look ahead, nodding his head as though to confirm it. "Damn good. *Naturally* good."

He exhales a laugh. "Which obviously did nothing to help things at home, but by then I didn't care. I had something to fill the void. Of course, it only got worse after that. Liam was supposed to be the superstar in the family. And then when—"

He stops suddenly.

"When what?"

This time he shakes his head with an easy smile. "That's pretty much it."

There's more. Definitely more. But he has a right to hold something back, so I don't press him on it.

Erik picks up his phone, and the map of Norway reappears. I feel the disappointment set in, thinking he's ready to call it a night. The coffee shop is a twenty-four-hour place, and I'd be happy to stay here just like this until the sun comes up. But he probably has hockey practice early in the morning or something.

"Would you look at that?" he says, closing out the map to show me the home screen. "I think we've officially crossed into second date territory."

I laugh, mostly with relief. Then I see the time, which is well past midnight. "My God, how long have we been talking?"

"Past your bedtime?" he asks, raising one eyebrow inquiringly.

"I'm a grown woman. I make my own bedtime."

"That's good to know," he replies, his eyes wandering down the length of me as I practically straddle him. "So now that it's past midnight do I finally get to see more of Barbackbutterfly?"

"Ohhh, no," I moan, throwing my head back. "I can't, it's too embarrassing."

"Come on," he says, squeezing my leg with one hand. "I told you all about myself. I'd like to know more about you."

It's a fair statement. I feel comfortable enough to tell Erik all about myself. I realize that it either comes down to opening up my private Instagram account or opening up the closet doors to my "complicated" family the way he did.

"Okay...barbackbutterfly it is," I say, twisting around to pull out my phone.

"Where did the name come from?" he asks.

"I started as a barback."

"Bar...back?" Erik repeats with a slight look of confusion.

"No, it doesn't mean what you think it means. Barback, not bareback," I say with a hard look, before laughing. "I helped out behind a bar before I became a bona fide bartender. As an aside, I always practice safe sex."

"That's good to know," he replies with a twinkle in his eye and a wicked tilt to his lips that indicates he's filing that one away for future reference.

I exhale slowly before opening the app. "Okay, I've accepted your request. Now you have full access."

Erik picks up his phone. "So the butterfly part?" he asks as he opens the app.

I relax and laugh. "That was from Ralph, the bartender I worked with. I guess I was a quick learner, but also good at staving off ornery drunks, basically quick on my feet, but tough as well. He'd always say that quote, 'float like a butterfly, sting like a bee'?"

"Ah, Mohamed Ali."

"It's so odd the American references you get and those you don't."

"Who doesn't know Ali?"

"True enough," I say with a tilt of the head in acknowledgment.

"Most Norwegians, and Swedes for that matter learn English from an early age in school. Then, we grow up with American influences through various media. My mother also exposed me to more English than the average Norwegian, being the world traveler that she was."

"So you speak Norwegian and Swedish?"

"They are similar enough for me to understand both, especially in the part of Norway I grew up in."

"Interesting," I say, wondering what it would be like to understand more than one language—let alone three. "So the language is different in different parts of Norway?"

"There are different dialects throughout the country," Erik says, nodding. "Some Norwegians might have had a harder time of it in Sweden than I did. Of course, they made fun of my accent when I first moved to Ö-vik. Apparently, to the Swedes, we Norwegians have an amusing way of talking. You know that Swedish Chef from Sesame Street?"

"Yeah?" I reply with a growing grin on my face.

"A lot of Swedes seem to think he sounds more Norwegian than Swedish, with his sing-song voice, especially those of us coming from Oslo as I did. That was a particularly favorite barb of my schoolmates."

I bite back a smile, remembering the muppet character from when I was a kid. "Don't feel too bad about it. I'm sure this American would completely botch both languages."

"I can laugh about it now," he says as he does laugh while turning his attention back to his phone. It stops abruptly when his eyes take in what's on the screen now that he has access to my photos.

"Oh," he says, now entirely focused on my Instagram feed.

I crane my neck to see that he's at the first and most recent photos posted of my friends and me on the beach in The Bahamas. Our bikinis and bathing suits are on full display as we pose with our drinks. He lifts his head and gives me a teasing grin, eyebrows wriggling suggestively.

"Don't turn it into something scandalous! We were on the beach!"

He laughs and continues to scroll through the photos. I scoot closer, leaning in so that my breast is pressed against his arm, my hand on his shoulder. I sense his breath get heavier, and my pulse quickens. The series of increasingly provocative photos doesn't help.

"Okay, so this is where it gets a little...crazy. Keep in mind the bar I worked at and the girls I worked with served as a sort of peer pressure in terms of how I behaved, and I was only twenty-one at the time."

"Hmm," is all I get from him as he continues scrolling. I can't help but wonder what he's thinking as picture after picture passes before his eyes:

Me and the rest of the girls from the bar, arms around shoulders, bare legs kicked up in the air like the Rockettes.

Another waitress from the bar bent over in those absurdly short shorts, as I playfully slap her ass with a tray.

Two of us, squeezed into one another, breasts pushed together so far more cleavage is on display.

Me with the back of my shirt lifted to show off the "cool tattoo" I'd just had made that was "sooo me."

Thankfully, the entire feed isn't all shots from that bar—one night of a big party specifically—but it's enough in a row to be a wee bit overload.

Erik continues to scroll until we're on to the safer territory of the average Instagram banality: a pretty day of snow; Gabrielle's surprise birthday party; me and my mom taking a selfie (he lingers on this one); a dressing room shot of me in a dress I'd finally decided on.

It ends pretty abruptly after that, and I'm quick to speak first.

"So the bar stuff, that was just—"

"You don't have to explain yourself to me...or anyone else for that matter." His gaze is perfectly frank as he speaks.

"Anyone who criticizes or judges you for what you did in your past, or what you do today doesn't deserve your time or energy. I'm not like that."

I feel the slow, silly smile creep to my face.

This guy.

"Thank you for letting me be one of your followers," he says with a grin, then leans in. "Just so you know, this doesn't count as the second date that I owe you."

"So when are we meeting again?"

"I have a game tomorrow—or I suppose at this point, it's tonight. Do you want to come?"

I almost instantly say yes before remembering my other plans. "I'm going to my mom's tomorrow—today."

He nods with understanding. "Well, after that I'm free until Tuesday."

"How do you feel about dating on weeknights? This Sunday is going to be…complicated."

I don't expound on that, and he doesn't press me on it.

"Monday it is then. I don't want to wait any longer than that."

"Me either."

"I suppose I should take you home now. Wouldn't want your mom accusing me of wearing you out," he says with a laugh.

I wrinkle my nose and slap him on the arm.

Erik slides out before me, and already I miss the feel of him underneath and beside me.

All this talk about my mom is a reminder that it's definitely going to be a topic of conversation when I visit her. I'll deal with that when it happens.

As for Sunday. I don't even want to ruin the moment with that business.

Erik's hired an Uber to take me to my apartment. To avoid the crazy cold weather, I've invited him in as far as the tiny "foyer" on the other side of the front door to my building. It's inconspicuously stuck between a nail salon and a very conveniently placed laundromat.

This should be the awkward part, where we wonder how to say goodbye. In reality, the lingering is just a matter of not *wanting* to say goodbye.

"I suppose it would be redundant of me to ask if I could come up for coffee," he says.

I laugh. "I have a roommate. The last thing I need is her seeing you."

"If you're worried about her stealing my interest, you don't have to be."

I let that one float around with the butterflies in my stomach before responding. "No, she's not like that, but she may try to sell you cheese or something."

I laugh at the confusion on his face. "She works at this cheese shop, and she gets a tiny commission if someone mentions her name, so she's always wearing these t-shirts from the shop with provocative sayings like....Brie Lovers Like it Soft and Creamy, or something like that."

"Oh, well I better not introduce her to *brunost*."

"*Brunost*? What's that?"

"*Brunost*," he repeats, correcting my horrible pronunciation with a teasing smile. "A type of Norwegian cheese...brown and usually slightly sweet. It's one of my favorites."

I laugh, pretty sure I'd be blushing if my coloring allowed for it. Norwegian cheese. Not *quite* the worst thing in the world to be compared to. Especially the way Erik says it. Brown and slightly sweet.

"Definitely don't tell her about that. The last thing we need is that phrase splattered across a shirt."

"So it'll just be our secret," he says, wrapping his arms around me and pulling me in closer.

My breath catches in my throat as he leans in.

I blink in surprise when he stops, only inches away from me as a slow smile creeps to his lips.

"You have this look of complete terror on your face."

"Wh-what?"

"Am I really that scary? I know my ancestors have a bad rap, but we ended all that raiding and pillaging a while ago, so—"

I get the hell over myself, and my lips are on his before he can even finish the sentence. I smile against the stunned paralysis that first meets them. There's something about catching this man unawares, frozen like a bunny caught in my trap, that has me excited.

That bunny quickly disappears, now replaced by a hungry wolf. Erik easily takes over from where I started, urging my lips to follow his lead, his tongue making a short, but memorable cameo before he pulls away.

I didn't bother zipping my coat up before leaving the coffee shop, and he moves his hands from around the outside of it, into the sides. I feel the rough fabric of my sweater bunch up under his palms, creating friction against the thin tank top underneath.

"Do you know what *vakker* means?"

"No," I whisper. Norwegian is hardly the most beautiful language but damn if it doesn't sound sexy coming from his lips.

"Beautiful."

I feel a helpless smile come to my lips.

Erik's coat is buttoned and I reach out to undo the brass

buttons of his peacoat. Underneath, the wool of his sweater seems prohibitively thick but I press my hands against it all the same. I feel the hard muscles of his abs and pecs thrilling my fingertips and palms.

"Say it again," I whisper.

He draws in closer, his arms now circling around my back underneath the coat. Mine are forced to do the same. He's so tall that, even with the small heel of my booties, our bodies press together into an incongruent fit, my breasts pressing into his diaphragm, his chin butting up against my forehead, his dick very noticeably creating an indentation in my stomach.

"*Vakker*," he whispers against my forehead before his hands quickly slide down to my ass and he picks me up.

I laugh as my back falls against the wall of mailboxes lining the tiny entry area. My legs wrap around his waist to help him along.

"That is better, no?" he says with a grin.

"Better," I say, staring hard at him.

His gaze darkens as he leans in again, his head now perfectly aligned with my neck. I throw my head back and give him full access, shivering at the first touch of his lips against my throat.

"Erik," I breathe, clawing my fingers through his thick hair to press him closer.

"Just as I thought," he says in ticklish mutterings against my throat. "So sweet."

I close my eyes and smile, ruining his hair as he ruins my body with soft kisses along the most sensitive parts of me—at least those that I can get away with exposing in such a semi-public area.

The idea that anyone could walk by and see us through that large glass window in the door, or that some neighbor could become curious at the soft noises we're making just down the stairs sends a thrill through me.

That thrill turns to electricity when Erik presses against me, trapping me between the metal mailboxes and his hard, unyielding body.

His tongue finds the hollow just below my throat, and I have to clench the insides of my pussy just to keep from crying out with pleasure. How did he find that so easily?

I feel him chuckle against me and I want to be mad, but instead, I laugh too.

"We're going to get into so much trouble," I say with a smile.

He pulls away and stares up at me.

"I'd love to get into trouble with you, Maya."

I stare at that handsome face—the same one that stared back at me from those pictures I took—and now sudden clarity hits me. Who knows who could be lurking in the dark beyond that front door. I've had enough of my fifteen minutes of fame —even if it was semi-anonymous. I don't need to add to it with photos of what we're doing here.

"I...I should—"

"Go," he finishes for me, sudden disappointment touching his eyes. He slowly lowers me back to the floor.

"I just—"

"I get it," he says with a reassuring smile. He reaches out to stroke my cheek with one rough thumb. It feels like heaven.

"Goodnight, Maya."

"Goodnight, Erik," I say, even though a part of me is begging for an encore of our performance.

I rush up the stairs and into my apartment before I can change my mind. Thankfully, Katie is out, probably at a party, so I don't have to answer any questions.

When I'm in my bedroom, I peek out the window that

faces the street. Erik exits the building, having seemingly waited until he heard me close my apartment door before he left. I watch him get into the Uber that he paid the driver to keep idling, shooting one last quick look up to my building.

Monday can't come fast enough.

CHAPTER FOURTEEN

MAYA

"Hey, Ma," I say hugging my mother as I enter her place, the very apartment I grew up in. A part of me loves the fact that it's still here, same as always. All my earliest memories, both good and bad, are stored here in this place.

Anyone looking at my mom and I would know we were related. I have a bit of my dad's nose and mouth, and the three inches I have on her 5'4" height are definitely from him, but otherwise, I'm all mom. She once showed me pictures of herself from college, and I swear it might as well have been me in those ridiculous bicycle shorts with ruffled mini skirts attached or drowning in colorful, oversized...everything.

"What's this?" I say as I enter the kitchen, looking in surprise at the new cabinets.

The dark wood with gingerbread trim that I grew up with has been replaced with something more modern and sleek. If I'm honest, it definitely needed an update, and this is what all the young urbanites are clamoring for these days. But it certainly doesn't make me think of "home."

"Oh, they're updating all the apartments now. Luis just

installed these for me. What do you think? They'll do the counters next."

"Updating? They're not trying to kick you out are they?"

"Oh no, at least not according to Luis. The neighborhood hasn't gone that far yet."

I can't help thinking that it soon will. Then what? After living here so long, my mom pays what many would consider an absurdly low rent. Combined with the money dad had to pay after the divorce, an inherently frugal lifestyle, and the salary she makes working in the Human Resources department of a large accounting firm, she could afford to move someplace decent, or even own something further out in Brooklyn.

But I like having her here. A lot of people would probably talk smack about how close I am to my mother, even living only a few blocks away from where I grew up, but I don't care. So what if I love my mom?

"What other changes are they making?"

"Well, they're redoing the floor. Ripping out the carpet for some kind of laminate that looks like wood, at least according to Luis."

That's the third time she's mentioned the new property manager's name. "What else have you and *Luis* been talking about?" I sass.

She gives me a slightly stunned look, then narrows her eyes. "I don't know what you're talking about."

"Well, I brought the wine, so talking is what we will most certainly be doing, especially about this Luis. I guess we should also toast to the old apartment before it becomes something new and improved."

"Speaking of what's new," she says, opening one of the shiny new cabinets to get two wine glasses. "At what point of the night were you planning on telling me about this hockey player of yours?"

"Who talked?" I say, spinning around as I open the bottle.

"Never mind who talked, tell me more about this Instagram thing...and what happened last night."

"Gabby," I confirm, then narrow my gaze. "Demi? I know it wasn't Zia."

My mom just sets one hand on her hip and waits.

"Did they show you the Instagram post?"

"You know I don't get involved with all that mess, Maya. Just tell me about him."

"Over dinner. What are we having? It smells good."

She just laughs and shakes her head as she opens the pot to show me the jambalaya.

"You are too good to me," I say, wrapping my arms around her from behind and squeezing tight. I won't have to worry about dinner for almost a week.

"Mmm-hmm," my mom hums, though I see the smile on her face.

I set the table, and she brings out the food, serving both of us. After pouring the wine, I feel the question repeated in her gaze, so I start talking first.

I tell her about Liza getting me to take Joey to the game and then get to the part about the photos, digging in my purse to bring out my phone. The table only seats four, and we're sharing a corner, so she's right next to me.

"So this is the player, huh?" She says, bringing the phone in closer and tilting her head back instead of putting on her reading glasses to see it. "I can't hardly see him through all those clothes and that helmet."

"Hockey is a pretty..." I think about that first fight between Erik and the other player, and then all the crashing into each other on purpose, "active sport. Like football."

She rolls her eyes up to me with disapproval in them, and I wince. Dad played high school football.

"But see how he stopped to pose with Joey?" I continue, trying to paint him in a better light. "And the last one of both of us is the post where he asked me out."

"Aww, look at the two of you," she gushes with a smile when she swipes to the one of Joey and me grinning at the camera. "Now where's this asking you out portion? Ah, I see here, underneath."

I watch her read it, not even realizing how much I'm holding my breath until she raises her eyes again. Her brow lifts with modest approval.

"Okay, I can see why you agreed to go out with him. Can't say I agree with the method, but the message is alright. I guess that's how they do it these days. In my day, a boy approached a girl in person and asked her out properly."

I laugh as I dig up a spoonful of rice and jambalaya. "Ma, you act like you grew up in the fifties or something. And no, most men don't ask women out over Instagram, it was just...the only way he knew how to get in touch with me. I think it's sweet."

Never mind what I thought about it just two days ago.

"Mmm-hmm," she hums before joining me to eat. "So what did you two get up to last night?"

I see my friends didn't leave much out.

"Don't you even want to see what he looks like without all that gear on?" I ask idly.

"You mean, do I want to confirm he's white?" she asks, reading right through me.

I smile around my mouthful of food and swallow. "Well?"

"It's ...different. But this is New York and that interracial stuff has been goin' on here since forever. Yes, even in my day. Frankly, I'm more concerned about this whole professional hockey thing, to be honest."

"What's wrong with hockey?" I ask, putting my spoon

down. "Do you even know anything about it?"

"No, but I know that it has the word 'professional' in it, which means fame and money. Successful men attract women. It's just a fact. And the more famous and rich and whatnot, the more women they'll attract. Women who don't care about cute little messages on Instagram, women who don't care about the one standing by his side, women who don't care about the wedding ring that may one day be on his finger. And just how long do you think the average man is able to resist all that?"

"We've been on one date, good grief," I say, laughing nervously into my spoonful of food.

I'm putting up a good front, but I won't lie to myself and say the same thought hadn't occurred to me from that first message on Instagram. Everything that came after that pretty much slapped me in the face with it. The messages from other women offering their numbers instead. Me basically becoming a public commodity in the form of a hashtag on Twitter, where any and everyone felt free to judge me based on one photo.

Then, I think about the tweens from last night.

You're so lucky!

I indulged their various poses and shot after shot, mostly because it was kind of amusing to watch. It's cute when they're fourteen. What about ten years from now when they're twenty-four?

"It's not even that serious yet," I say, shoveling another spoonful of food into my mouth.

"I'm not trying to burst your bubble, sweetheart; I just want you to prepare yourself when things do start getting serious."

"Got it," I say through a mouthful of food.

"Don't go being like that now," she says with a laugh as she nudges me with one elbow. "Go on ahead and show me this man, since you're so eager to show him off."

I smile through my mouth of food and pick up my phone.

"It's not like that, I just...we really had a good time last night."

I find Erik's feed and deliberately scroll through, skipping the shots of him playing on the ice until I find photos that paint him in the most mom-appropriate light.

"Here's him at Christmas. I know it's kinda corny, but that's the point. He and his cousin do this thing each year where they try to one-up each other."

She takes the phone, and a half-smile appears on her face. Just when I'm beginning to feel pretty sure about my selection, she frowns. "What's all this now? Ribbe? Lutefisk? I'm not even gonna try and pronounce this last one."

"So he really is Swedish, huh?" she asks, her eyes rolling to me, filled with uncertainty.

"Norwegian," I say meekly. "But...he's been living here for years now."

"And when this hockey thing is over for him. Is he going to stick around?"

"How would I know that? As I said, we went on one date—which you have yet to ask me about," I point out.

"Okay, how was your date with Erik, Maya," she asks in a teasing voice.

"If you're going to be like that, then forget it," I reply just as teasingly.

She purses her lips at me and continues to scroll through the photos.

"Well, now..." is all I hear, and it draws my attention away from the bowl of jambalaya I returned to. I crane my neck to see which one she's stopped on to find it's the photo from *Ideal Gentleman* of Erik in the snow.

"See? Tell me that wasn't worth at least one date."

She laughs and puts the phone down. "So are you going to tell me about it or not?"

I put my spoon down and wriggle in my seat, watching my

mom's eyes get soft at that. "I was with the girls, and they kept getting on my case, so I finally gave in and gave him my number. He called right back and...I said yes when he asked me out."

"Just like that? He asked you out the same night, and you agreed? I hope you don't plan on moving that fast for the whole relationship."

"Don't get all Victorian Era on me. I wanted to see what it would be like and...it was great. We just talked and drank coffee and kept on talking and talking until..." I stop before I point out what time I came home.

"That late, huh? Dare I ask if it was at least over before the sun came up?"

"He didn't spend the night—*not* that it matters and *not* that it's any of your business."

"You're right," she agrees. "But there's something to be said in the way a man treats a woman."

"And he treats me perfectly. I just felt...really at ease with him. Like I could be myself. He was nothing but respectful toward me, didn't even try to get in my pants."

"That's an important thing...in the beginning."

"And we're meeting again on Monday."

She laughs and shakes her head as she digs into her food. "You really got it bad for the boy, don't you?"

"I really like him."

"He's not bad on the eyes, I'll give you that. Even for a—"

"Don't even say it, Ma. This could be your future son-in-law," I tease.

"Oh, Lordy, here she goes."

I laugh and continue eating.

"So tell me more about this hockey."

"Umm," I say around my mouthful of food, before shrugging. I swallow. "I just learned about it while I was watching the game, so—" I stop, coming up with an idea. "In fact, he has a game tonight. We could watch it instead?"

Mom somehow got me hooked on that show *Claws* and saves every episode so we can watch together when I visit.

She mulls the idea over for a second before shrugging. "I guess I better start getting into it since my daughter seems to be so head over heels about this Norwegian."

"You'll love it," I say, suddenly feeling anxious as I think about the one and only game I saw. I was completely turned on by all the action—the fighting and crashing into each other, the speed on the ice.

I'm not so sure my mom will feel the same.

The table has been cleared and the dishes washed and dried. I have a huge Tupperware tub waiting in her fridge to take home with me when I leave—Katie will be ecstatic.

Now, I'm perched in my usual spot in the living room, on the floor between her legs as she sits on the couch. While I find the sports channel that's showing the game, she pulls the hair tie out to loosen my ponytail.

"It's about to begin it looks like," I say as I find the right channel. One thing my mom does splurge on is cable TV. At times it saddens me to think that it might be because she has no outside social life, but right now, it's convenient.

The two commentators are discussing tonight's teams and players in front of the ice rink that I remember from a few nights ago. I feel my heart begin to pitter-patter a bit as I anticipate seeing Erik on the ice again.

My mom parts my hair with a comb and I close my eyes, feeling that tingling sensation run through me as usual. She begins scratching my scalp with it before running a finger covered in hair product down the part. This is our thing, just another way of bonding. She's been doing this since I was a kid and it always calms and comforts me.

"You know, you could start your own YouTube channel like Zia. She makes some nice money doing that AMSR thing. People particularly love the videos with hair stuff, doing exactly what you're doing right now. I could even be your first model."

"Don't even get me started on that girl and her *videos*. Never mind what she got *you* to do. I'm not about to pimp my daughter out the way she did."

I laugh as usual when we get on this topic. Being a licensed masseuse and professional yoga teacher, Zia jumped on the AMSR—Autonomous Sensory Meridian Response, whatever that means—bandwagon early on. I didn't get it at first, just a bunch of YouTubers doing nothing but whispering into a microphone, or crinkling paper, or brushing hair. But I have to admit, it is soothing. I've watched several just to help me fall asleep.

With over five thousand subscribers to her channel now, Zia must be doing something right. And hell if I haven't happily taken advantage of getting a free back or head massage.

My mom views it differently.

"It's not porn, Ma."

"You say that, but I don't know anyone who sits around watching people gettin' their hair brushed or back scratched or *massaged* just to fall asleep or get some *tingles* or whatever."

I'm about to keep convincing her, mostly because I get a kick out of her reaction to it, but the music on the TV changes, indicating the game is about to start.

"Oh...here it goes!" I say, sitting up straighter.

I secretly cross my fingers, hoping Erik puts on an impressive show.

CHAPTER FIFTEEN

MAYA

Erik: Are you still awake?

The text message from Erik grabs my attention, and I snatch the phone from my nightstand to sit up in bed and read it.

After I sent a congratulatory message to him, my mom and I discussed the game for a bit. While we had been watching, she seemed to get into it as much as I did. Fortunately, there were no fights tonight, at least between Erik and someone else. But it was just as aggressive as the first game I saw.

As I headed out the door with my take-home jambalaya in my hands, I asked my mom point-blank what she thought about it. All I got was, "It was an interesting game."

Even pressing the issue landed me nothing more than a shooing out the door with the parting words to enjoy the jambalaya and a promise to tell my roommate she said hi. She finds Katie highly amusing for some reason, probably because she has yet to see her in any of her cheese-pimping t-shirts.

I push all that to the back of my mind and answer him:

Me: Yes

Erik immediately calls, and I laugh quietly to myself before answering.

"So, did you watch the game after all?" he asks with a smile in his voice.

"I did. That game was...intense."

"Yeah," he acknowledges with a seemingly apologetic sigh. "Did you enjoy it?"

"My mother certainly did."

"Your mom was watching too?" He seems both surprised and slightly upset about that. "What did she think?"

"It's hard to gauge," I confess. "She seemed to be into it while we were watching. What she thought after the fact...I'm not sure."

"In defense of my playing, I didn't get much sleep last night."

"You could have fooled me," I say with a laugh. "You seemed pretty fired up there on the ice."

"I had a lot of...frustration to blow off."

I immediately get where he's going, and my bottom lip gets trapped between my teeth with a smile.

"Well..." I say, unsure of how to finish that. I know what my body's telling me. My mind—not to mention my mother's words about moving too fast—have a different message to send me.

"Well," he echoes on the other end.

There's a brief silence before he's the one to break it.

"I made reservations for dinner Monday night. I hope you like seafood?"

"Seafood's nice," I say, as though either one of us gives a damn about dinner right now.

"And...tomorrow you have your complicated thing."

I feel my mood instantly shift. "Yeah...complicated."

"And you don't want to talk about it?"

"Actually, I don't know why I'm not telling you," I say with a small laugh. "It's my dad. I'm going up to Connecticut to see him. We do this about twice a month. Sometimes he comes here, sometimes I go up there. It's my turn to travel."

"Ah, I see. And he's..."

"Complicated."

There's another pause before he speaks again. "If you feel like talking afterward, call me."

My heart catches for a moment. I don't talk about my dad. I just don't. Not with my friends, definitely not with Mom.

But I have a feeling out of everyone, Erik gets it.

Still, it will take a bit more nudging to get me to open up just yet.

"I miss you already," he says with a laugh, to ease the moment. "I really enjoyed myself last night."

"Me too."

"Well, I should let you get some sleep. It seems like you'll need it."

"Yeah," I say, feeling the disappointment set in. I wish I could just skip over tomorrow and fast forward to Monday already.

"Goodnight, Maya. Until Monday."

"Goodnight," I say, then quickly add. "I hope you saved some of that pent up frustration for me."

I hang up before he can reply, then fall back onto the bed and laugh to the ceiling.

"What the hell did you say that for, Maya?" I ask myself.

My phone dings with another message. It's a volcano with steam rising out of it, followed by a text from him.

Just in case you were wondering what awaits. Until Monday...

I laugh and put the phone away, hoping this elation gets me through the day tomorrow.

The train ride up to where my dad lives in Connecticut is a little less than two hours. I didn't get much sleep last night, so I spend most of it dozing off.

By the time we reach the station, I'm wide awake and practically wired with anxiety. Daughters aren't supposed to feel this way when meeting their fathers, especially fathers who really haven't done anything to earn it. Dad was never mean or abusive or even neglectful, at least not purposefully so.

Mom was the one to ask for the divorce. By then, the tension in the apartment was so consuming it was a relief even to the girl who lived with them when he agreed.

The idea had always been for Dad to go to law school, but it was a dream deferred when I happened along earlier than expected. Once I was finally in middle school, he decided to pick right back up from where he left off. At first, we all seemed to make it work. Both my parents worked days, and he studied and went to school at night, while Mom took care of everything at home, including me.

But the cracks showed up early. Mentally, I know he tried, always promising that one day things would be less hectic for him, maybe after he graduated and took the bar.

That day only seemed to come when Mom had finally had enough. I hadn't even started high school by the time he moved out. After the divorce, I had specific pockets of time with him that were just ours. Those times were magical.

Then, he couldn't find a job in New York, so he moved to Connecticut to work, studying for and taking the bar there as well. That's when he started giving excuses not to come to New York but inviting me up there instead.

Then, he married Wanda. That's when the visits *really* fell by the wayside. It was once in a blue moon that he'd get in touch. It began to hurt emotionally and I realized whatever we had was dying.

Then, there was a new baby girl, Sidney. That's when he always had "so much going on with the new baby, maybe we could meet some other time." At the time, I was in college, and I myself had lost interest in the whole keeping in touch endeavor as well.

By the time Damien was born, all communication, period, had trickled to "special occasion" calls or texts. I did get a birth announcement in the mail, of course.

Dad had a new family.

He was starting all over from scratch.

Doing everything *perfectly* this time.

Then, a little less than a year ago, his interest in me was renewed. After the first few times I blew him off, I realized he wasn't giving up. So I bit...tentatively.

I'm still in that stage.

I'm the last one off the train. I slowly enter the station, my eyes wandering around to find the rare dark brown face in this part of New England. They eventually land on it, that nose and mouth that look a bit like mine, the six-foot-two height that my genes grabbed a few inches from.

I plaster a smile on my face to match his and walk over to let him hug me.

"Hello, sweetheart."

"Hi, Dad."

CHAPTER SIXTEEN

MAYA

"So, what's new with you?" Dad asks as he unfolds his napkin to set in his lap.

It's the usual start to every conversation. I'll either say "nothing" or "the same as usual," which is almost always true. He'll urge some tidbit out of me, even if it's something as banal as buying a new dress or some new cheese Katie has introduced me too.

Then, he'll fill me in on the details of his New and Improved life.

"I'm dating a hockey player," I blurt out for some reason.

Dad blinks in surprise.

"So I've heard," he says slowly. "Or at least the part about him asking you out. So you accepted then?"

"You know about that?" I ask in surprise.

He chuckles softly, "Well, you're not as active on social media as I am, which makes it hard to keep up with you, but I'd have to be completely cut off from the online world not to have seen that bit of buzz about my own daughter."

Of course he's on Instagram. I know he's on Instagram. The

photos he posts of his Oh So Happy family doing Oh So Happy family things are part of the reason I avoid it. *Here we are in our big, fancy house in the suburbs! Here we are at Disneyworld! Here we are making dinner together! Here we are decorating the Christmas tree!*

"So you were waiting for me to say something about it?" I press.

"Well, I figured it wasn't my place to bring it up, but since you did..."

"He's a nice guy. I really like him."

Why am I trying so hard to prove something to him?

Dad gives me an infuriatingly encouraging smile. That smile used to fill my stomach with a bubble of joy.

"That's good to hear, sweetheart. You should find a man that you feel that way about. But...this only happened, what? Wednesday? Thursday?"

"You're giving relationship advice now?" I say, with the usual heaping of sarcasm I can't seem to help when I'm around him. I always hate myself afterward for stooping this low, but in the moment it feels so righteously satisfying.

The only sign of displeasure from him is a slight tightening of his jaw as he takes a sip of water.

"I suppose that's a fair point," he says. "Heaven knows I probably didn't set the best example with your mom, and—"

"Dad," I say tightly. "You know the rule."

After years of subtle and not-so-subtle complaints, back-handed remarks, criticisms, and outright rants, I made it clear to *both* my parents that they weren't allowed to even mention the other in my presence.

"So...dating. Erik Sørenson, right?" He asks with renewed enthusiasm in his voice that only heightens the discomfort between us. "That must be exciting. I didn't realize you were a hockey fan."

"I'm not...not really," I say in a low voice. "It was my first game."

He chuckles. "First game and you managed to catch the man's eye. I guess I shouldn't be surprised. Even I know how special you are."

I feel an involuntary surge of pleasure fill me up. I know my dad well enough to realize this isn't the usual platitude from a smothering parent. Heaven knows he's not like that. He doesn't hand out compliments that aren't earned, which is interestingly enough one of the things I like about him.

The waiter comes by to take our orders, and when he leaves, Dad picks up where he left off.

"The boy you went to the game with, Joey? He's your coworker's son, right? I remember you talking about how you used to watch him for her after work. I guess that paid off," he says with a laugh.

I indulge him a smile. I'm surprised at how much he manages to retain from the mundane conversations over lunch or dinner.

"So, are you going to leave me in suspense, or tell me more about this hockey player of yours?"

"What do you want to know?" I say with a shrug.

The waiter comes back with our drinks, and I gratefully busy my mouth with a sip of wine.

"For starters, where did he take you?"

"We just went out for coffee...and talked," I add with a smile.

Dad catches it and matches with one of his own. "That must have been some talk."

My smile disappears. "It was nice," I say with a shrug.

Dad sighs and takes a sip of his wine. "Maya, I know how difficult these lunches are for you."

I become instantly defensive. "They're not—"

"No, no," he says gently, raising one hand to silence me. "I get it. You and I...at some point we just drifted apart. I realize that's completely my fault. We used to be so close. You remember testing me with those law school flashcards? Hell, you probably know all the hearsay exceptions in evidence better than I do even to this day."

"You aren't about to try and talk me into law school again, are you?" I say, feeling my irritation set in.

"No, I've said my piece on that."

"Yes, you have," I remind him. I like what I do, and law school just isn't for me. I see how stressed those attorneys are at my job.

"What I'm trying to say is, I want us to be close like that again. Why do you think I'm on Instagram in the first place? Why I tried to friend you on Facebook? You think I'd be anywhere near those sites if it wasn't for you? I wanted to stay in touch somehow. Let you know how I'm doing—how Damien and Sidney are doing. Without having to go through the obvious torture it seems to be for you to have a conversation with me."

"That's not fair," I say, feeling like a petulant teenager for some stupid reason. I hate this.

But I do have to admit, what he's just said is a surprise. I always felt the same way about it that my mother did—that he was showing off, somehow rubbing it in our faces, all the things we missed out on. Which is ridiculous in retrospect. My dad may have definitely dropped the ball a few times along the way, but being that petty and vindictive is not one of them.

"I know it's going to take work, Maya, but it's a two-way street, and right now I feel like I'm still the only one driving," he says. "This isn't me criticizing you, this is me...reaching out an olive branch."

I sip my wine, mostly to avoid having to say anything.

"So, maybe we can start with your dating life."

"What?" I say, almost spitting out my sip.

"You heard me," he replies with a laugh. "That's obviously what's front and center on your mind. Let's get it out."

I roll my eyes, but can't help smiling.

"Come on, maybe your old man can give you a few tips, let you know just how much of a player he might be."

"He's not a player," I say quickly.

"Ahh," he says as if that confirms something for him.

"What?" I retort.

"Nothing," he says, turning down the sides of his mouth to keep from grinning.

"What?" I repeat, laughing now.

"I just hope he's worth how bad you got it."

"Excuse me!" I ask, this time punching him lightly in the arm.

"Don't hate the messenger," he says, shrinking away from it as he laughs.

"I don't have it bad," I protest, but now I'm firmly caught up in the laughter.

"Well, at least you feel something for the man. That's always a good start. The question is, does he feel something for you?"

"Yes," I say without hesitation, smiling into my wine.

His eyes are on me, reading me like those infernal law textbooks he used to spend so many nights with. Then, he nods.

I feel slightly more at ease than I felt when I first sat down. This is almost how we used to be, the two of us. Back when I used to test him before his law school exams, eating Nilla Wafers with milk and teasing him every time he missed something. Back in the early days as a Child Of Divorce when my time with him was one-hundred percent all mine. Back before his time was divided and I was petty enough to decide he wasn't worth the effort.

"Enough about me," I say, if only to change the topic. "What's new with you?"

Dad's brow raises in surprise, which is understandable. I've never posed this question to him before. Usually, the conversation eventually wanes to the point he feels the need to fill the void with the latest news from his side.

"Sidney's birthday is in a few months and already the planning has begun."

"Six already?" I say after a painful swallow.

He nods with a grin. "And they're goin' all out for this thing. Already a little miss princess about it. Pink everything, and get this...a pony."

"Really?" I ask, feeling the fall come.

A pony.

It's so cliché I feel myself getting nauseous.

Of course, that's when our lunch arrives. I look down at the avocado BLT sandwich I've ordered, and the churn in my stomach gets more intense. Everything about this feels foreign or at least fake.

Avocado BLTs?

Ponies at birthday parties?

Hell, even the white wine at lunch.

This is the exact opposite of what life was like with him back in Brooklyn. What my life is *still* like.

I think back to Demetria's quip Friday about avocado toast food trucks and feel laughter begin to bubble up inside of me.

Hypocrite much, Maya?

"I need another glass of wine."

Dad wrinkles his brow, either in disapproval at the request or at the interruption of yet more tales of the birthday party... with a pony!

"Sure, Maya."

I signal the waiter and order another.

"Anyway, the neighbors have turned this into an *event*, closing off the entire cul-de-sac. Wanda has started conspiring with the other moms. I wouldn't be surprised if an actual petting zoo makes an appearance if the weather cooperates."

Cul-de-sac?

Petting zoo?

The waiter comes back with my wine, and I drown myself in it, tuning out the latest suspected upgrades to Sidney's Big Day. My sixth birthday had a homemade chocolate cake and ice cream with a few of my friends watching videotapes of cartoons in our small apartment. It seemed perfect at the time; I still think so.

So why am I so conflicted about my half-sister's special day?

"You should come. I know Sidney would love it. Wanda and Damien too. It'll be fun, even for us grown folk. I've been told there will be alcohol for the adults. You didn't come up during Christmas time this year. They missed you." He's twisting the knot pretty hard. They throw an annual holiday party, which would have been the perfect opportunity for another visit. I had an excuse not to come. "It would mean a lot to me as well, Maya."

"Sure," I say numbly. "I'd love to."

What? Shut up, Maya!

But my lips have already said it. The look on my Dad's face prohibits me from taking it back. I barely know Sidney from the few times Dad has encouraged me to "join the family" in something at their house. It was torture.

"Really?" Eyebrows raised in surprise. Smile so broad it threatens to break free from his face.

"Of course. She's my...my half-sister."

He nods, now almost teary-eyed.

Good grief...I need to go.

"I'm not feeling well. Do you think I could get this to go and leave early?"

Now, a look of concern touches his face. Not one ounce of judgment over the fact that I'm gulping down this wine.

"I'll definitely be there, Dad. Can't wait!"

That cheers him up.

Of course it does.

Maya finally playing along. Finally getting on board the happy, happy Jackson Family train.

Choo Choo!

I hiccup a laugh, then pretend to wince in pain, curling my arms around my stomach. "Really, I should get going."

"Got it," he says urgently, signaling the waiter.

On the ride back to the station, I stare straight ahead, the boxed sandwich on my lap as I wonder what the hell happened today. Usually, my body is slowly relaxing with relief on the ride back, reaching complete contentment only when I'm firmly on the train back to New York City.

Now, I just feel panicky. And it only gets worse the closer we get to the station.

When he parks, I stop him from turning off the engine so he can walk me inside as usual.

"Thanks for lunch, Dad. I...I'm looking forward to Sidney's birthday party. I can't wait!"

It's chipper enough to convince him. I think?

Either way, I need to go.

"Bye, Dad," I say, hugging him one last time. "I love you."

I feel him go tense underneath me.

That's one I haven't said in a long time, and definitely not before he's said it first.

He squeezes me tighter and I swear I can actually hear the tears in his voice as he says, "I love you too, Maya."

Once on the train, I feel like I want to scream if only to get the chaos in my head out. I stare out the window, and the landscape flying by does nothing to help things.

I need...something.

I pull my phone out of my purse and hit one button.

"Maya?" Erik's voice sounds surprised, happily so.

"Are you free? Can I...can I come over?"

CHAPTER SEVENTEEN

ERIK

"He can't just do this! Try to pick me up an insert me into his life like he didn't completely tune me out for over five years. And my sister's sixth birthday party of all things? He knows I can't say no."

Maya has been pacing the floor of my loft since she arrived, completely worked up from the "complicated" she just came back from with her father.

"I obviously don't hate them. How can I hate a couple of kids, my own *siblings*? Well, *half* anyway. Honestly, it's not even about them. It's about *him*."

She frowns before continuing. "I know I should be the better person here, at least try to meet him halfway, but it's still so...*raw*. I just—I hate that they get a version of him that I never got. I know that's petty, but I always have this feeling that I'm this black mark on his life, the daughter with so much *history* attached, the one who reminds him of that stressful period when everything went wrong. Do you get it?"

I do get it—more than she realizes.

When she called, I certainly had no objection to her

coming to my place, and not just for the obvious suggestion there. If anyone knows "complicated" with their father, it's me.

"Sometimes I wish he'd never tried to get back in touch. Not that today was too terrible. I mean, it started as usual," she rolls her eyes as she paces. "Then, it was actually good, like it used to be with us, before... Then, this birthday party thing came up and it just—I don't know, once again I felt like I was on the outside looking in."

I lean on the kitchen island and watch her walk back and forth. I had a car waiting to pick her up at Grand Central station, so she came directly from her meeting with her dad and hasn't even taken off her big, puffy winter coat yet. She did take off her boots as soon as she stepped past the threshold, probably as an effect of how clean and minimalist my loft is, by design. Her socks are black with pink smiley-faced hearts that are so incongruous to the weightiness of the moment, it's somehow amusing.

There's nothing laughable about those skinny jeans and where they send my mind, no matter how much I try to fight it.

"I'm sorry," she says, stopping suddenly as she turns to give me an apologetic look. "I shouldn't be laying all this on you. We've only been on one date, and here I am dumping my baggage and waving my red flags to you right here in your—" She again stops suddenly, looking around at my large, open loft. "This is a really cool place. It's so..."

"Scandinavian," I finish for her with a laugh.

I rented when I first moved to New York. When the Blades offered a five-year, $35-million contract, I figured it was okay to go ahead and buy. I wanted to stay in Brooklyn, as a matter of principle considering the team I played for represented that borough. DUMBO is cutting it close—I have a completely unobstructed view of Manhattan from my floor-to-ceiling windows—but it still counts.

Something about the stark, empty space I first encountered when I stepped foot in this place spoke to me. Nothing but exposed brick walls, cement floors and an entire wall of windows staring out at New York. It doesn't have the light, airy, and far more compact aesthetic of typical Scandinavia, but the way I've managed to transform it, you can see the influence. From the blonde wood bookcases to the stretches of blank space, it's all me.

"I like it," Maya mutters, turning around slowly to completely observe her surroundings.

"Then feel free to make yourself at home," I say with a grin as I push away from the kitchen island. "Starting with taking off that heavy coat."

She swivels to me with a guilty smile. "I didn't even think about that; I was just too busy—"

"Venting. I get it. And no, it's not a problem. Your red flags and baggage don't scare me off. But for now...relax."

She laughs as she shrugs out of her coat. Underneath is a sweater made of various shades of brown like ripples across her torso. It's shorter and more snug than the one from our date and I admire the way it outlines her body, at least what I can glimpse of it through the thick yarn.

If only it wasn't winter...

I take her coat and hang it up by the door, while she wanders around.

"Is this your mom?" she asks, and I turn to see her looking at one of two picture frames in one of the bookcases.

"Yes," I say, walking over next to her to look at the photo. It was taken one Christmas. Mom is hugging me from behind and looking into the camera with that mysterious, but genuine smile she always sported—the one that hinted at her own secret pleasure in the moment. I'm looking predictably reluctant, with a grudging hint of a smile on my face.

"She's …wow. She could be a model. She reminds me of that one from the nineties."

"Christy Turlington," I say.

"Right…except blonde and blue-eyed," Maya says, still seemingly mesmerized by the photo.

When I was a kid, I remember a lot of people mistaking my mother for the supermodel who was famous at the time. From the large, direct gaze, to the severely pointed end to her nose, not to mention her full lips, they could have been sisters.

My eyes have the same frank gaze but in the lighter shade of blue of my father's. My lips are slightly straighter and nose a little less blade-like, but there are definite mother-son similarities.

"And this is your grandfather? He always looks like fun," she says with a laugh as she stares at the photo of him holding up a mug of beer with a huge grin that is so typical of him plastered on his face.

"He is fun."

I smile as I look at the photo. *Morfar* never takes himself too seriously and was always fun to be around, especially when I was a kid. I specifically remember him encouraging an eleven-year-old me to take a long swig from that glass of beer after this photo was taken.

"What's this?" She asks, looking at a shelf of small glass vials filled with sand or rocks. She picks one up filled with black sand and reads the label on the bottom of it. "Diamond Beach, Iceland. 2017."

"These are my souvenirs from all the places I've visited. Rather than a t-shirt or magnet, I take a bit of those places back with me."

Her eyes roam the shelf, wandering over the small containers which number about thirty total. "You really have been a lot of places."

"I like to roam."

"Apparently," she says with a small, but surprisingly wary smile. "I've only ever been to Coney Island. I mean, except for that trip to The Bahamas."

"I think a beer sounds good. How about you?"

"Oh... I've already had two glasses of wine," she says, then twists around to face me and laughs. "But what the hell? If any day called for too much alcohol, I think this is one of them."

I pull out two bottles from a brand I like to drink when I visit home. "Nøgne Ø, straight from Norway."

She smiles and eyes the bottles speculatively. "Do you go out of your way to buy Norwegian beer?"

I consider her as I open one bottle and hand it to her. "Would you think less of me if I told you I bought it in anticipation of you coming here?"

Her grin belies any objection she might be inclined to voice. "You were that sure of your chances, huh?"

"I was sure that eventually, I'd be inviting you back to my place, yes," I say, giving her a meaningful look.

She swallows hard before even bringing the bottle to her mouth. "Is that so?"

I just raise my eyebrows in acknowledgment as I take a sip from my own bottle, still eyeing her as I do.

She grins and also takes a sip.

"What?" She finally asks with a giggle when I don't take my eyes off her. "You think I'm just another crazy woman with Daddy issues right?"

"No, I'm not thinking that at all. I was just thinking..." I set my beer down and come in closer as I talk. "Du er så jævlig vakker."

Her eyes are wide and her breath heavy. She swallows before responding.

"What does it mean?" Before I can respond, her gaze

narrows slightly. "And it better not be, 'my beer is getting warm,' or something like that."

I pull away and laugh, taking a long swallow before I answer. "No, nothing like that."

"So, what then?"

I feel my smile soften as I gaze at her. "That's how I would say ...you're so fucking beautiful."

She's back to staring at me with wide eyes a smile growing on her face. She squints slightly. "Really?

"Look at me, at the way I look at you, especially when you smile. Do you doubt that's exactly what I'm thinking?"

"No," she replies softly.

She brings her beer up to her lips, a smile playing at the edges before she takes a sip. After swallowing she pulls it away to inspect the label. "Not bad. So how do you say beer in Norwegian?"

I laugh at her attempt to change the subject. "Norwegian is a broad term. As I said, we have many dialects, so one way of pronouncing things is different from one part of the country to the other. That doesn't even count our writing style, which may also vary."

She smirks. "Okay, Mr. Linguistics, how would *you* pronounce it where you're from?"

"Well ...that's also complicated by the years I spent in Sweden, specifically in—"

"Oh, my God!" she laughs. "I can't tell whether you're just really opposed to me learning your language or a little too invested in me learning it in the proper way."

I grin, then shrug and answer the question. "Øl. That's how I would say beer."

She gives me a blank look than laughs. "Just...earl? Url? What was it again?"

I grin and say it again. "Øl, with an ø, like in my name, Sørenson."

Maya shakes her head in quick movements and wrinkles her brow. "I thought it was S*o*renson, that's how everyone has been pronouncing it."

"I don't mind. It's not easy to grasp in English. Better than being the ass who corrects people all the time."

"Okay, but seriously. I want to pronounce your name correctly."

I exhale an exaggerated sigh, then raise one eyebrow at her. "Fine then, Erik Sørenson," I say, pronouncing my first name in Norwegian with a slightly elongated and stressed "E," and my last name with a proper "ø."

"Wait a second. I've been pronouncing your *first* name wrong too?"

"Not really. That one can easily be attributed to a different accent."

"*E*-rik," she says, trying to mimic me. It sounds absurd, but fucking adorable coming from her lips.

I laugh. "Just stick to Erik S*o*renson, like everyone else. It's easier on the American tongue."

She smirks. "And what if I don't want to use my inferior American tongue?"

My mouth curls into a grin, and I set my beer down on the island. Her eyes widen as I come in closer, then she squeaks in surprise when I lift her up and set her down on the kitchen island. She's not a short woman even without shoes on, but I still have a good nine inches or so on her.

"What are you doing?"

"Helping you practice your Norwegian tongue, which I can't do if I have to keep staring down at you from up here."

"*My* Norwegian tongue, huh?" she says with a smirk.

"All yours, Maya."

"So then show me how it's done," she says, playing along.

"Well, first, you have to position your mouth just so," I say, leaning on one long arm against the bar so I'm right in front of her. "Like you're about to kiss."

She purses her lips and it looks so ridiculous that I want to laugh. "Less like an aunt about to peck me on the cheek and more like..." I lean in closer, showing her how to do it just right. "This."

Her mouth softens just enough for me to guide it with my lips. I taste her hot beer and wine tinged breath against mine.

"There," I whisper against her lips. "Now comes the proper position of the tongue."

"Show me," she whispers against my mouth.

I realize how much fun playing teacher can be, especially with a pupil like Maya. Which naturally conjures up all kinds of sordid thoughts. I shift my body so that it's between her legs, forcing them open slightly wider.

Not one to neglect my duties, I continue teaching her with my tongue, guiding it up toward the roof of her mouth then swirling around the tip, bringing the end down so that it rests against the edge of her bottom teeth.

"Just like that," I say, still just barely touching her lips. "Say it."

"Uhl," she pronounces.

"Getting warmer," I say, smiling against her mouth. "Øl,"

She mutters something incomprehensible, and at this point, I'm willing to chuck it all and say, close enough. I let my mouth and hands do the talking for me. With the lesson over, I'm ready for after-school playtime. My hands come down to her ass, pulling her closer to me, forcing her legs open even wider.

Maya's arms drape around my shoulders, her fingertips tickling the nape of my neck just below the edge of my hair.

"Did I do good?" she asks, smiling against my mouth.

"Good enough for some more lessons," I say, lifting her up.

"More Norwegian?" she asks, pulling away to give me a wicked grin.

"More than you can imagine. I hope you can handle it."

She laughs as I toss her onto the bed.

CHAPTER EIGHTEEN

MAYA

This.

This is exactly what I need.

Scratch that. This is what I crave. What I've been craving since Friday night (Saturday morning?).

Erik stands above me with his dizzying height. My filthy mind sinks to the most degrading fantasies about Vikings and plunder and everything the twenty-first century female part of me would normally rebel against.

Fuck all that.

Taken by Erik the Great!

I giggle at how ridiculous that sounds. The beer and wine in my veins—never having been buffered by the sandwich I have yet to eat, which still sits on the kitchen island—is turning me into some happily willing conquest.

"You're thinking naughty thoughts aren't you?" he asks, as though he's used to women happily playing damsels in distress, damsels who have no desire to be rescued by some pathetic knight in shining armor.

"I'm just thinking that I need more brushing up on my Norwegian, preferably with a hard...stern...teacher."

I kick one foot out—with those idiotic socks I threw on this morning, not realizing *this* of all things would be happening later on—to trace my big toe up along the inseam of his jeans.

Erik grabs it and pulls me closer to the edge of the bed by the ankle.

"Are you sure?" he demands, tearing the sock away from my foot, "because we Vikings aren't known for being gentle, or sweet and tender."

I feel my eyes glaze over at that. My breath comes in accelerated inhales and exhales.

"Yes," is all I can manage between those breaths.

His grin is wicked, showing no mercy at the lurid thoughts he so easily reads on my face. One hand reaches down to grab my other foot and rip away the sock, flicking it somewhere behind him to join the other.

He sinks down, leaning over so that I'm trapped between his two massive arms on either side of me. His knees are between my legs and he rises up to kneel above me.

"You know...we only chose the most attractive women to kidnap and take with us when we went raiding," he says, playing right into my fantasies.

"So you think I'm...*vakker*?" I ask with a coy grin.

"I think you're sexy as hell, Maya," he says, his eyes storming.

His hands come down to the button of my jeans and he practically rips it off trying to loosen it from the hole. His large hands pull the sides apart, not bothering with the zipper that comes easily undone as if by magic under the force of his urgency.

I lift my hips, a silent signal that he's free to do with me as he wishes. Erik doesn't even hesitate. Thick fingers are curled into my waistband, jerking the denim clinging to my hips and thighs away as easily as Saran Wrap off a piece of meat that he's been salivating over for days.

And haven't the both of us been craving this for a good minute?

I wriggle out of my sweater as he drags my jeans and underwear down my legs. When the frenzy of undressing me is done, all I have on is my bra.

"Wait," he orders as I arch my back to undo the hooks behind me.

I stare at him in confusion, only to be met with an icy glare that really does make me feel like some helpless damsel completely beholden to his mercy.

"That's my job," he says, his voice so demanding that I have no choice but to remove my hands and lie in wait.

"But first," he says, allowing a grin to appear on his lips.

I gasp in surprise as he drops off the edge of the bed to his knees and forces my legs open so wide I feel the strain of it in my inner thighs.

The heat is on in this large loft—I should hope so considering it's probably in the low thirties outside—but even that can't fight how cool the air feels against my wet pussy, now brazenly exposed to the open air.

"Don't even think about trying to escape," he warns just before his mouth takes complete control of me.

My eyes are the first to react, rolling back in their sockets as his beautiful lips surround the head of my clit. His tongue, so fluent in Norwegian, teaches another part of my body to appreciate foreign language classes as he guides the tiny bundle of nerves through a strenuous lesson in proper pronunciation.

"Fuck," I moan, in my filthy, basic American vernacular.

Erik punishes me with a rapid flick of his tongue, no doubt

spelling out some complicated bit of wickedly difficult Norwegian.

If my Spanish classes had been this...vigorous, I'd be fluent enough to star in the next telenovela. Then again Mr. Goode wasn't nearly the teacher Erik Sørenson is.

I gurgle something that probably *is* how one properly pronounces Ø, just before grabbing hold of his thick head of blond hair and screaming my head off as I orgasm.

Holy shit.

"Erik," I say, breathless after that very effective introduction to Scandinavian torture methods.

He stands up yet again, staring down at me like I'm some pathetic creature who deserves nothing more than the worst he has to offer.

Hell. Yeah.

He peels off his long-sleeved shirt and I finally get a glimpse of everything only my hands have experienced—very much filtered through the thick wool of his sweater back then.

Now, he's all mine for the taking.

His body practically glows from the muted winter light filtering in through the shades covering the floor-to-ceiling windows that look out on the East River and downtown Manhattan. From the rounded mounds of his shoulders to the sharp crease that lines the vee disappearing somewhere beneath the waistband of his low-hung jeans, it's rather awe-inspiring.

"How much do you want to play?" he asks.

My mind sinks further into the abyss.

I trust him.

Completely.

"All the way."

He stares at me, that glacial gaze penetrating me sharper than an icicle. I should be scared, but I feel the exact opposite.

I want it all. Everything.

I want him to take me so far down, the only language I remember when I come back up for air is Norwegian.

"Do it," I urge.

His eyes slide down to my bra, and he raises one eyebrow.

I raise one eyebrow in return.

He falls down beside me and traces one finger, up from between my legs to the hot-pink cotton of the cheap bra I have on. From Victoria's Secret of all places. The perfect sacrificial artifact to commemorate this moment.

Erik sits up and hooks two fingers of each hand into the thin scrap of fabric between the two wired cups and pulls. It takes a moment but eventually I hear the sound of fabric ripping apart.

I won't lie...I'm surprised. Even something as flimsy as what I have on, just barely supporting two slightly B-cup worthy breasts, should be able to withstand this.

It hadn't counted on someone like Erik Sørenson.

When the miraculous feat is accomplished, Erik flicks the two sides of the now useless bits of fabric and wire aside to reveal my tits.

As though I couldn't feel any more vulnerable.

And I love it!

"That's better," he says, his eyes impudently wandering over my naked body as though I was nothing more than his property, claimed from some unworthy territory that couldn't even defend my honor.

And the fantasy just sinks lower and lower.

His hand reaches out to take hold of my jaw, just firm enough to force my face toward him. "Say my name...properly."

I blink, trying to focus on my most recent lessons. "Erik...S*u*renson."

I know I've screwed it up—and isn't that the fun of it?

He clucks his tongue, shaking his head in disappointment. "You haven't been paying close enough attention, Maya."

His face comes closer to mine and a grin appears on his lips. "I think more lessons are in order."

"So teach me," I retort, like some recklessly rebellious student who has no idea just how bad detention can get.

Bring it, Erik.

And oh, how he does.

He slinks back to the edge of the bed, standing up again. I still have on the ruined bra, lying like rags on either side of my naked breasts.

Erik doesn't say a word as he slowly unbuttons his jeans, but his eyes are practically flashing neon signs, warning me about what's to come. I lick my lips with anticipation as he slowly lowers his zipper. He hooks his thumbs in the sides of his jeans and black underwear underneath and drags them slowly past his hips, gradually revealing each sharp crease and hard curve of muscle until...

Okay then!

He's half-mast, which is just enough to show that Scandinavian dick is indeed uncut, but certainly no less appealing. I mean really, who the hell cares when Erik is packing enough to end that debate just by revealing his.

"Oh...my," I whisper, feeling like some stupid girl who's never had sex before.

"Too much?" he asks with a grin and one eyebrow raised as the last of his clothes fall to his feet.

"Certainly more than expected."

"Is that a good or a bad thing?" he asks, reaching out to clamp both hands over my knees and pull me closer to the edge of the bed.

"I guess we'll see," I say, feeling my insides cream as his

eyes penetrate the area between my thighs just as hard as I hope his cock will.

"Oh yes we will," he says with a grin as he walks over to the nightstand next to the bed.

As I watch him pull out a condom, my eyes slide to the windows behind him. Even though the shades are down, obscuring almost everything, it still gives me a delicious thrill of pleasure knowing that we're about to do this so openly.

Erik comes back around, and I jump a little when he leans in over me again. My eyes widen as he guides the head of his cock along the slick folds between my thighs.

"Say my name, tell me you want it," he orders.

"I want it," I moan. "Erik...Sorenson."

"That's not how you pronounce it." He probes just enough to make my back arch in anticipation, then pulls out again. "Say it again."

"*Surenson.*"

"Wrong." He slaps the head against my clit, sending a jolt of pleasure through me. "Again."

His voice is so stern...so demanding. "*Suerenson!*"

I gasp in shock when he sinks into me. I gasp again when he pulls all the way out.

"You're so damn wet, so nice and firm...you don't deserve this dick, do you, Maya? You definitely need more lessons."

"Just fuck me," I groan, my hips bucking up to follow the huge cock that's been teasing me.

Erik gives me a wicked grin. "I like watching you beg for me, beg for this. That's how much I've wanted you since the day I first laid eyes on you."

I rise up on my elbows and glare, having no patience for flattery and sweet words. "So do something about it... Sørenson."

He laughs, but it dies quickly. It's replaced by a hard glare as both hands dig hard into my thighs, spreading them open as he forces his hips in between them. Even though I've already had the experience of him inside me, I moan with pain and pleasure as he shows me again, sinking as deep as possible, before drawing out only half-way this time.

One of his hands interlocks with mine, forcing my arm high over my head on the bed. He does the same with the other, so I'm stretched out beneath his hovering body as he bucks his hips in and out, screwing me slow and hard.

I've never done it like this before, so firmly held down in position as a man has his way with me. Erik's eyes are cast down, as though hypnotized by the vision of his huge dick sliding in and out of me.

My eyes are firmly on him, loving that hard, intense look on his face. His granite-like jaw. The deep crease created by his furrowed brow. The way his nostrils flare.

It does something...*very* nice with my insides. "That's it... keep going," I say, now unable to keep my eyes on him as they close with pleasure.

"Oh...God," he breathes. "You're so....God, Maya, you're fucking amazing!" he growls.

And that's when I feel it.

"Yes...yes...yes..."

There it is!

He doesn't even stop. In fact, his hips grind into me faster, spurring his own orgasm on, even as my body arches hard, then falls into the bed, a shivering mess.

"Maya," he finally utters, so strained that it's barely audible.

When he finishes and falls on top of me, I throw one arm around his back and smile up to the ceiling.

"That was...amazing."

"Agreed," he laughs, falling to his side next to me.

I twist my head. "How do you say it in Norwegian? Amazing."

"*Fantastisk.*"

I frown. "That's it?"

"What were you expecting?"

I shrug. "I don't know, maybe something...different, sexier."

"If you want sexy, you'll have to trade me in for an Italian or French man," he jokes, but I see his eyes smolder a little at the thought.

"Who wants French or Italian when I have a smokin' hot Norwegian?" I say, poking him in the chest. "I just expected something with more *urls* or those letters with the dots on top or something."

"We don't use those letters with the dots on top. We have ø, æ, and å."

I try to repeat the letters he's said, and he laughs at me. "We'll really have to work on your Norwegian alphabet. For now, we'll just have to settle on you," he turns so that I'm forced onto my back with him on top of me, "being fucking *fantastisk*, Maya."

I stare up at him with a smile. "You're pretty fucking *fantastisk* yourself, Erik."

CHAPTER NINETEEN

ERIK

"Are you serious?"

She stares at the box I'm holding in my hand.

"You said you were craving it—which I can understand after what we just did," I say with a wicked grin as I hold it out to her.

"I mean, I was mostly joking. You're letting me eat in your bed?" she asks with a smile.

"I'll let you do anything you want in my bed, especially if it keeps you from putting your clothes back on."

Her eyes flicker to the underwear I threw on to grab the box holding her leftover sandwich, and she smirks before taking it from my hand.

I walk back to the kitchen, which is part of the open area of the loft and grab both of us two new bottles of beer since the half-finished ones I first opened are no doubt flat and room-temperature by now.

"Thanks," she says through a mouthful of sandwich as she takes the one I hand her. She has a tiny bit of avocado on the side of her mouth, and I want to lick it right off, if only to taste her skin underneath.

The sex was the best I've had in a long time. The teasing. The playing. The language lessons.

The woman.

Suddenly, I'm craving more.

Almost as much as Maya seems to be craving that sandwich.

"You must be hungry," I observe with a laugh.

She rolls her eyes and smiles before swallowing. "I can never eat before those meetings with Dad. Maybe a coffee. That's it. I didn't get a chance to finish this before all the stuff about going to Sidney's birthday came up.

"So you're going?"

She shrugs and sets the sandwich down to take a sip of beer. "I said yes, so I guess I am."

"Will it be that bad?"

"Oh, I'm sure it will be fun. There will be a *pony* after all," she says sarcastically, then frowns. "Sorry, that was...petty. Let's just say, while everyone else is having fun, it will be extremely, uncomfortably, painfully awkward for me."

"Do you want me to go with you?"

She blinks in surprise.

Hell, even I'm surprised at the offer. It combines two things that pretty much scream "relationship" when it comes to women; and those two things I specifically try to avoid: family gatherings and parents.

But that comfort I felt with her that first night at the coffee shop is still there between us, now stronger than ever. So I get it. Whatever this thing is between her and her father, it's something I can relate to.

The awkwardness of being an outsider in your own family.

"I couldn't ask you to do that," she insists, taking another bite, but I do notice her eyes consider me hopefully as she eats.

"How about...if I have no game on the day in question, I'll go with you. Our coach gives us a one time get out of jail card when it comes to missing practice. I'll use it on you."

"You'd use yours on me?" she asks sweetly, overtly batting her eyelashes, but I note how relaxed her body is.

"Sure, I'll even drive you up."

She sets the sandwich down and gives me a deadpan look. "You have a car?"

"Yes?" I answer, wondering what's so surprising about that.

"In New York City?"

"Yes?" I repeat with a confused grin.

"Why?"

"I like to drive?"

"Where?" she asks in confusion. "The only people who have cars here are Uber and Lyft drivers and people who live in like...the suburbs or something."

"And people like me who like to drive?" I hint.

"People who like to drive still can't afford a car in this city."

"I can afford a car in this city."

She stops to stare at me, as though suddenly remembering who I am. "Oh."

"Oh," I say with a grin. "But I mostly use it to drive out of the city. So how about it? We'll be extremely, uncomfortably, painfully awkward together at the party."

She smiles, then laughs. I sip my beer as I watch her finish the rest of her sandwich.

"You know, I never asked you," she begins as she closes up the box now that she's done eating, "what made you send that message on Instagram. I mean, you must get hoards of women who are after you."

"True," I say, then grin when she glares at me.

She falls back onto the headboard, the covers still wrapped around her underneath her arms. "So, what was it? It couldn't have been that silly selfie of Joey and me."

I lean on one hand that rests on the bed and consider her. "It was that smile. The first time I passed you, and I think you were trying to get him to smile? It was just...really nice."

The same smile appears on her face right now. "That's so funny."

"Funny?"

"My mom, when I was first born, she'd play this song that was popular back then and said it always made her think of me, you know, when she was sad or having a bad day or something. She said I had these big, brown eyes just like the singer, and this smile that was almost too big for my face. Back then, my dimples were much deeper."

"What song?" I ask, suddenly extremely curious.

"Do you have your phone? Mine's still in my purse."

I walk over to the island where I left my phone and unlock it to bring it back to her. As she searches for the song to play for me, it occurs to me how easily I basically handed over my electronic life to her without a thought.

What is this? I'm sure the Americans have some interesting bit of slang to refer to it, probably with some underhanded jab at my masculinity. But I feel strangely even more secure in my masculinity somehow, like I'm strong enough to trust her with this.

"Here," she says, with a laugh as she hands the phone back to me. It's a YouTube video.

"Shanice. 'I Love Your Smile'," I read from the caption, then hit play.

It's a nice upbeat tune, and I can see how it might be uplifting for someone who's listening, especially if it makes them think about someone they care about. The singer is an attractive young black woman that does indeed have the same big brown eyes as Maya.

"I think she kind of looks like me, right?" she asks.

"Not nearly as *vakker*," I say.

She smiles and rolls her eyes, then sits up suddenly.

"Oh my God, it's snowing!"

I twist my head to look out the window and see the barest hint of tiny flakes floating in the dark gray light of the fading day even through the shades. I walk over to pull them up, and she turns to switch off the lamp to give us a better view...and help keep people from peering in, I assume.

"That's not snow."

"It's snow," she insists, tugging the sheets off the bed as she walks over to the window for a closer look.

I stare after her, watching her from behind. With her hair still mussed and the sheet draping down low in the back, she looks perfectly regal. The butterfly tattoo on her back is a nice touch, not at all as tacky as it should be. The flakes floating in the air beyond her get fatter and more noticeable, now falling faster to the street below us.

"See?" she urges, without turning around. "It's definitely snow."

If it isn't snow yet, it soon will be.

"Spend the night with me," I say suddenly.

She spins around in surprise.

"I have to go to work in the morning."

"You can go from here. I'll drive you in my car."

She grins. "And clothes. I can't very well show up in what I wore here, not to mention I need a new bra."

"I'll go and pick up clothes from your apartment and bring them back here."

It's a ridiculous proposition, and she laughs, shaking her

head. "Don't be silly. In fact...I should probably head home now."

I stare at her a moment longer, draped in my dark gray sheets like a ballgown around her, framed by the coming winter storm that's increasing even as she stands there.

"Smile," I urge.

She accommodates me, spreading her generous mouth wide, something in it hinting at her own secret pleasure in the moment.

That's it.

The one I'll cement to memory.

"I wasn't expecting something like this," Maya says, with a whistle of appreciation as we reach my sleek, black car in the garage of my building.

"Sixty-seven Mustang. This was my first gift to myself when I first moved here," I say, grinning with unabashed pride. I rarely drive it in the city, mostly because parking is a pain in the ass, but also it would be a shame to waste such an amazing ride only to get caught in the snarl of traffic that usually invades the streets of this city. Mostly, I enjoy taking it outside of New York City whenever I get a chance, just to explore nature.

"It's sweet."

We get in, and when I exit the garage, the snowflakes are definitely sticking. It's that moment during the first snow in this city where everything is white and quiet and perfect. Anyone stuck outside has quickly made their way back in. There are few other drivers on the street. Everything is coated in a blanket of white before the dirt and smog and heat get to it, turning it to brown sludge.

The two of us are quiet in the car watching the winter wonderland pass by. It feels like we're in a commercial, the kind that inspires aspiration. *Everyone should want this.*

I know I do.

"What's the word for smile in Norwegian?" Maya asks next to me.

"*Smil*," I say.

She turns to me and laughs. "I guess that's easy enough."

"Sure you don't need another lesson before I get you home?" I ask, giving her a wicked grin.

"I think my mouth can handle that one," she replies with a grin of her own.

After a pause, she speaks up again.

"Thanks for today."

I know what she's referring to, and it isn't just the sex. I reach out and take her hand, quickly squeezing it before returning my hand to the wheel.

"*Vær så god*," I reply, then turn to her with a smile. "That means, you're welcome."

She laughs. "That's one I'll probably have to work on."

"Tomorrow?" I say, with one eyebrow raised.

"Tomorrow."

CHAPTER TWENTY

MAYA

"You are officially Joey's favorite person, Maya. Ignore what all those idiots online have to say about you. We both think you're an absolute doll."

Once again, Liza is right there to meet me before I even reach my desk.

"That game he went to on Saturday was amazing, even if he did end up going with his dad," she says with a frown, but instantly brightens back up. "But he still knows it was all thanks to *mom* that he got those tickets and that jersey—well, via mom's friend, but you know what I mean."

"I get it," I say with a smile. "Glad he had fun. It was an exciting game. But what's this about idiots online talking about me?"

Are people still talking about #WhosMaya? Only a handful of people know that I not only replied to Erik, but also that we went out. Surely everyone else would have moved on by now?

"Well..." She pauses before continuing. "I for one didn't think the photos were that scandalous, but whoever went out of their way to take them—"

"What photos?" I interrupt, my heart dropping like a lead ball into my stomach. My mind races right back to last night. Those floor-to-ceiling windows. Could anyone see through those shades?

My God.

"They were on some hockey forum that Joey's into, posted just last night so—"

"Show me," I urge.

"Okay, okay," she says, looking at me like I've gone off the deep end.

As I wait impatiently for her to pull out her phone, I brace myself. She said they weren't that scandalous. I have no idea what her tolerance level for smut is, but even she'd have to claim everything Erik and I did at his loft worth taking a photo of would fall into the category of "scandalous."

"Here," she says. "A bit seedy the way they were taken through that door and all, but really not so bad."

I almost cry with relief.

The photos are just some surreptitiously snapped pics of Erik and me right inside my front door from our date on Friday. No nudity. No sex. No "language lessons."

Then again...

We are pressed pretty close to each other.

And our coats are open.

And my legs are around his waist.

And his face is buried in my neck.

And the look on mine is extremely...

How the hell did anyone even know about us being together that night? Other than the people who were in the coffee shop, the Uber driver, my friends, and Erik.

I read the message from the person who posted them:

Remember that sappy Insta message our favorite

Blades Casanova wrote last week to some chick? Looks like it paid off. My brother just forwarded these to me. Not saying how he got them but at least now we know why Sorenson was so fierce on the ice Saturday.

I wrinkle my nose with distaste and scroll down to read more. He didn't even spell Erik's last name correctly.

"Listen, I gotta go, Maya. All the attorneys are going nuts over this Gaultier Financial stuff. We can talk later." She reaches for the phone.

"What is this site? How do I find it?" I say, reluctantly ceding it back to her.

She scrolls through it. "Um...it's called...ah!" she says, showing me her phone once she finds it.

"*The Pucking News*," I read.

"Really, the photos aren't so bad," she says, reading my face. "Of course, I don't read the stuff posted there, and I keep telling Joey he isn't allowed to, but...well, you know kids."

When she leaves, I continue to my desk to dump my purse. After logging on to my computer and posting my arrival time, I quickly check my email to make sure there's nothing urgent, then grab my phone and head to the bathroom. No way do I want IT to have a record of me visiting this site, or to be caught looking at it from my desk.

Safely inside one of the stalls—Oh, I've never wanted my own office so badly!—I bring the site back up and seek out the thread with my photos on it.

It just gets worse and worse.

Looks like Easter came early for the Nordic Lightning. He found himself a chocolate bunny.

169

Not into black girls, but she could get it.

LOL...a nail salon and a laundromat. The only way it could get more ghetto is if there was a pawn shop and a Dollar Store.

This thread is full of incel losers who wish they could get laid period, let alone a chick who looks half as hot as her.

Frankly, I don't know how he could downgrade from Tessa Ogden to that. No matter how crazy the rumors say that chick was. [this one oh so helpfully includes a photo of my predecessor in all her pink lace bra and panty glory. I knew she was a Victoria's Secret model!]

Okay, no lie... I'm pretty sure I know this chick. I think my sister used to work with her at some sports bar. I'll hit her up and see if she has any pics.

"*Shit!*"

"You okay in there?"

I blink in surprise at the announcement. I've been too preoccupied even to notice someone has entered the bathroom. I look at the time at the top of my phone and this time, curse silently to myself. I really should be at my desk.

I flush the toilet just for appearances and...realize I have no pocket to put my phone to hide it. With a sigh and a roll of the eye, I exit the stall.

At least it's only Whitney Howard, the other young, black

female attorney that works in my department. If anyone couldn't care less about what I'm doing, it's her.

With her head full of long, thin locks, and her carefree attitude toward everything, including all things firm-related, I wonder how she's lasted here this long as one of the international law attorneys. Most likely it's because of all the pro bono work she does with refugees, which has earned the firm more than a few awards. Image is everything.

It's Monday, and she already has a cheerful look on her face as she stares at my reflection in the mirror. She has a slight overbite that lends to a wide but gorgeous smile and eyelids that seem to be permanently lowered in amusement.

"Sorry," I say, giving her an apologetic smile in the mirror as I set my phone down on the shelf in front of it to wash my hands. "Just some online crap I'm dealing with."

"Is it about that hockey thing?"

"What?" I say with wide eyes as I stare at her reflection.

She laughs lightly. "I mean, Liza won't shut up about it, bless her. I saw the photos." She raises her eyebrows in appreciation. "I also saw the photo of the player. I'd risk it for him. He's Norwegian, or Swedish, or something, right? I'm actually headed to Iceland next year with my friends. We do this international girls trip every year and don't even ask me how Charlene picked Iceland of all places."

"How many people know? I mean...how much has Liza, um, shown you?"

"First of all, Liza is—*yes*, she's a talker. The thing is, she knows *who* to talk to and who *not* to. You're fine, sis."

My reflection shows my mouth only slightly softening into a smile at that.

"Now, that's not to say some of these other attorneys won't find out about your business splashed all over the Internet. You can probably guess the ones who are into hockey. But if any of them give you shit, you just come to me, you hear? I'll handle it."

I bite back a laugh.

"At any rate, they're going to be too busy salivating over this Gaultier Financial business, and frankly, so will you, I'm afraid," she says briskly. "Dissolving a former Fortune 500 company is no joke, never mind the acquisition of the assets. The Christmas party this year is going to be bangin'. No rest for the wicked, as they say. At least it'll be something to take your mind off of this 'online crap' you're dealing with," she says with a grin.

CHAPTER TWENTY-ONE

ERIK

"Hey, you okay?" Peter Shaw asks next to me in the locker room of our training facility.

"Yes?" I ask, posed more as a question because, why the hell wouldn't I be? I'm sure the shit-eating grin on my face, leftover from yesterday with Maya, was evident to all my teammates as soon as they took one look at me this morning.

"I mean, it's just that—"

"Peter," LaPointe says, calling his attention away and not-so-subtly shaking his head.

That's when I look around the locker room and notice almost everyone's eyes on me. I sit up and feel that sense of unease start to set in.

"What?"

No one says anything at first, and I feel my irritation begin to grow.

"Is that site," Grigory finally says, making sure to give all of them a mild look of disappointment. *"The Pucking News?"*

Most of us have an unwritten rule about surfing the online hockey forums. It's a rule that's heavily broken by my teammates, mostly because they can't help themselves. Any *rare* bit of insight we might get when it comes to how to play the game is outweighed by snark and trash talk, which does nothing for morale.

Then there are the off-topic forums that tend to delve into the lowest of the low, punching well below the belt.

There's only one reason why I might be profiled on that site in such a way that would have my teammates tightlipped on the issue.

Maya.

If it was just a bunch of criticism about me or how I played or even my life outside of hockey, most of my teammates would probably ignore it unless it was something particularly noteworthy. Even then, it would be goodnatured ribbing that I probably deserve.

The looks of discomfort I see, especially from Shaw—who is too new to the team to know any better but suddenly realizes his mistake—mean that the photos and comments must be pretty bad.

I pull out my phone, mostly to the sound of protests telling me I should just let it go or ignore whatever I'm about to see.

Fuck that.

I search and find it right away. The first post on the thread is a photo taken of Maya and me right inside her building as I dropped her off. The way it's shot makes it look more illicit than it was.

The messages that come after it only make it ten times worse. What was just a bit of fun as we said our goodbyes now makes it seem like I'm having some secret tryst with a woman I shouldn't be involved with.

"Hey, I didn't mean to—" Peter begins.

"It's fine. There's a reason why we stay off those sites," I say, standing up and walking toward the exit to get to the rink.

"Let's get on the ice. I'm sure coach is wondering where we are."

I make sure I'm first out, so no one sees the murderous look on my face.

The venom is still in my veins during training.

I can't help but compare the things said about Maya to the taunts about my mother while I was growing up, especially once I moved to Sweden. Typically, no one would have cared about my dad abandoning my mother, leaving her to raise me on her own. But kids have a way of finding the chink in whatever armor you have on. Once it's pierced, they have no problem twisting the blade.

I feel the same sting spur me on through practice, forcing me to slam the puck harder, skate back and forth on the ice faster, spar with my teammates more fiercely.

Enough for the coach to finally pull me off the ice to cool off.

"I don't know what's going on in there," he says, tapping the top of my helmet, "but lose it before tomorrow's game."

When I get back to my locker after practice, I'm surprised to see there's a voice message waiting for me. From my father.

I stare down at the phone for a moment. My initial reaction is the same panic that hits anyone when they get an unexpected call from a relative. Has something happened?

I take a deep breath and hit the button to listen to the message.

"*Hello Erik, it's your father. I'm just calling to...to see how you are doing. I know we don't talk much and I understand why. Perhaps one day when you are free you can call?*"

There's a long pause as he seems to consider that absurd idea. "*On the other hand, perhaps I should call you back. I'd really like to talk to you. It's been a long time. Too long.*"

There's another shorter pause before he speaks again.

"*Congratulations on your hockey season so far.*"

I stare into space, feeling the tension in my face as I frown to consider what he's said. Christmas and my birthday, that's it as far as actual communication I get from him: a text message and a card.

Why does he want to talk all of a sudden? What's going on in his life to make him so interested in reconnecting with his estranged son?

Naturally, my mind can't help but try to read something into the last bit about hockey—still a sensitive topic within our dysfunctional little family.

My mind replays that fateful day in my head once again...

"*But what about hockey?*" *my father asks the doctor, bringing up the question that all three of us have been wondering.*

I actively avoid looking at Freja or my father as we wait for the answer.

Working in Örnsköldsvik, where hockey is as common as snow in winter, the doctor isn't surprised by the question. The look on his face tells us the answer before his mouth does.

"*There will be months of recovery before he can even think about going back on the ice. Even then, I'm afraid that any hopes of a professional career...*"

Freja is the first to break down into a sob, falling into my father's arms to hide her face.

I don't miss the look that briefly flashes across his face as he glimpses my way. A mask of calm collectedness quickly replaces it—but I'll never forget that first expression I caught a glimpse of. I know that look will leave a deeper scar than any cutting words ever could. It reflected all the accusation and resentment his wife is more than willing to hand out verbally.

But...my own father?

"It should have been you!" Freja screams, pointing a finger my way, her eyes filled with vindictiveness.

I stare back at her, completely numb to everything now.

My own father...

Her, I expected this from. I almost welcome it coming from her. It has the effect of eroding some of my internal guilt.

My own father...

"Freja, please," Dad says, holding onto her as he now looks away from me. "This isn't helping."

"I know he did it on purpose. He's always been jealous. He just had to—"

"Can we see him?" Dad asks the doctor, most likely to give her something to divert her focus away from me.

The doctor, who has been watching this with obvious growing discomfort, now shifts even more uncomfortably. "Actually, he...er...he asked to talk to his brother, Erik?"

His eyes land on me, correctly assuming that I'm the brother. His aren't the only ones on me.

"Him?" Freja practically stabs me with the daggers her eyes throw my way.

"Erik?" Dad asks, the confusion written all over his face.

I'm even more confused than he is. "Why?"

The doctor, who would have to be an idiot not to pick up on the tension between all of us, simply shrugs. "He asked to see you, and only you."

Freja breaks down yet again, and my father busies himself with calming her down.

"Come, let's go get some coffee," he hushes.

The bewildered looks on both their faces are probably no match for mine as I take a deep breath and head toward the room where my half-brother is. I feel like a prisoner walking the plank as I open the door.

Why in the world would Liam want to see me?

I fall back into the present, forcing that memory back into the recesses of my brain where it belongs.

Tonight is all about Maya. I don't need thoughts about my "family" interfering with that.

I wonder if Maya has seen it, the vile things said about her, the photos she certainly doesn't want to be public. If so, it will be just another thing to ruin the Monday night I was looking forward to.

I breathe deeply.

I won't treat Maya the way my father treated my mother. If she needs any reassurance that she's something more than a fling, a "chocolate bunny," then I'll give it to her.

I am not my father.

CHAPTER TWENTY-TWO

MAYA

Whitney was right. The firm was crazy all day with work. I didn't even get a break for lunch, instead, sitting in various meetings that were at least catered.

It's only on my way to the subway that I even get a chance to look at my phone and, sure enough, the poster has "hit up his sister" who used to work with me: Sarah Feeney.

We weren't especially close, but we did have some fun times together. As evidenced by the photos she apparently held onto...which are now being picked apart by the idiots on this particular forum.

The photos are in the same vein as my own private Instagram account, so the comments this time around are decidedly more despicable.

Before I close out, I note that one word in particular keeps making an appearance.

"What do you know about puck bunnies?"

Katie twists her head away from the TV she's lounging in front of. Thankfully she doesn't work Mondays and didn't have an audition today.

Because I have questions.

She swings her legs off the couch to sit up and give me a wicked grin.

"Well now, this sounds deliciously dramatic."

I just raise my eyebrows in exasperation.

"Come, come," she says, patting the seat next to her on the sofa. "Tell mama all about it."

I roll my eyes and bite back a smile. She always has this way of being just silly enough to pull me out of my funk.

"I was on this forum for hockey. *The Pucking News?*" I begin, dropping both my purse and coat on the couch next to me as I take a seat.

"Okay, I'm gonna stop you right there and tell you that was your first mistake. Don't ever go onto sports forums, at least outside of the areas dedicated strictly to the sport. They are cesspools of the lowest filth and brainless bacteria of society, each trying to outdo the others in terms of destroying all that is good and decent."

"Okay..." I say, not sure whether I should be relieved or horrified.

"It's like...accidentally walking in on your thirteen-year-old brother when he should have definitely put a do-not-disturb sign up."

"Gross," I say, not wanting to know where she plucked that analogy from.

"Exactly. No amount of mental bleach will wash that out."

"Katie..."

"Okay, okay, okay!" she says with a laugh, then straightens up, getting serious. "Puck bunny. Basically...a woman who's into hockey players. *Really* into hockey players. They can range from the flirty fan whose favorite player jersey is just tight enough to reflect that it's cold in the arena to...well, there are entire categories on PornHub dedicated to the other end of the spectrum."

"Ugh…" I say, cringing in horror. "How do you know all this?"

"Hello, did you miss the part about my two older brothers being into hockey? Second only to the game itself is discussion about who the players are fuc—going out with. This includes WAGs too, though I don't think that will make you feel better."

"WAGs?"

"Wives and girlfriends. The objectification never ends."

That doesn't make me feel better at all.

"Sooo," she begins. "How are things going with Erik?"

"Is that your way of prying?"

She exhales dramatically, throwing her hands up in the air for effect. "Well it's not like you're telling me anything! You come in at all hours of the night—or morning. And I try to be a good roomie and mind my own business without comment, but…a girl can only be kept in the dark for so long. Especially when it comes to a professional hockey player. Especially when it comes to one who looks like Erik. Especially since I thought we were—"

"Okay, okay!" I laugh.

"Well?"

"Well…he's…amazing," I say, falling back on the sofa. "We had a really great time Friday, just talking, opening up to one another. Then yesterday…" I let that one lie, not wanting to give her all the details.

"Ohh, girl!" she says, jabbing me in the side. "That good, huh?"

"Katie," I groan.

"Not to worry. Girl code! My lips are sealed. I can't believe it! My own roommate dating a Blades player! So when are you going out again?"

I sit up straight. "Shit! What time is it?"

Katie flinches in surprise. "Um..."

"He's coming to pick me up tonight and I haven't even showered or changed or—"

"What?" she exclaims. "He's coming here and you're just now telling me?"

I ignore her as I rush to my bedroom to find something to change into after squeezing in a quick shower. For some reason I hear Katie scrambling around as well.

Fifteen minutes later, I've done my best at a shower and changed into a soft, tan cashmere sweater, black leggings and over-the-knee boots, re-flat-ironed my hair and thrown on minimal make-up and, just in case, packed an overnight bag.

Katie is in a pair of shorts and another cheese t-shirt: Mozzarella Lovers like it Soft and Moist.

"What is that?" I ask, staring at her t-shirt and wrinkling my nose. Moist? Who the hell approved that slogan?

"What? You think I'm gong to pass up this opportunity not to pimp my cheese out? If I got Erik Sørenson of all people to come into the shop, they'd go—"

We both jump at the sound of the intercom to our apartment buzzing. Katie beats me to it.

"Come on up, lover boy!" she says with a laugh, not even waiting for him to announce himself.

"Katie!"

"What?" she says, laughing again. "I know he's Scandinavian but don't tell me he doesn't have a sense of humor."

I just roll my eyes and stare at the door, waiting for the knock, with two words still floating around in my head.

Puck and Bunny.

CHAPTER TWENTY-THREE

ERIK

"*Hello!*" I nearly jump at the exuberance with which the redhead answers the door. This must be Maya's infamous roommate. The white letters stretched across her chest on the black t-shirt confirm it.

"I'm Katie," she says, cocking her head to the side with a teasing smile. It isn't flirtatious, mostly the kind of smirk that comes from being in on a joke.

"I'm here for—"

"I know who you are," she laughs before reaching out to drag me in. "Maya is right here."

She most definitely is.

It seems like longer than just a day since I've seen her. She's dressed up a bit for tonight, but she would look stunning in an old t-shirt and shorts. Either way, it's all coming off later on tonight, and I for one, can't wait.

"Ready?" I ask.

She shoots me that brilliant smile, which has my dick

twitching already. It's interrupted by one quick dart of the eyes toward her roommate.

Something passes between them that I don't quite catch, but it doesn't bode well.

"What is it?" I press with a wary smile.

"Nothing," they both say in unison, though in different tones. Maya's is panicky while Katie's seems more exasperated.

"Okay..."

"Let's go," Maya says, perking up.

That's when it hits me. She's seen the online forum. It would explain the nonverbal communication between her and her roommate.

Faen!

I'm not stupid enough to bring it up first, so I continue as though nothing is wrong as I lead her back outside.

"You drove?" Maya asks when she sees my car double-parked on the street.

"Of course. I want everything about this to be a proper date," I say.

The snow from yesterday has mostly melted, turning into murky puddles. With my long legs, I had no trouble leaping over the large one between two cars, separating the sidewalk from the street where I parked.

"Here, I've got you," I say.

Before she realizes what I'm doing, I've got her in my arms.

"What are you doing?" she yelps with a laugh.

"Hold on tightly to your bag," I say, then leap over the puddle, landing safely on the wet street right in front of my car.

"People are looking," she says, suddenly panicky again as she tries to wriggle out of my arms.

"So let them," I reply, holding on tighter as I stare down at her with a grin. With any luck, she'll pick up on the fact that I have no problem being seen with her. "Why wouldn't I want to show off the fact that I'm with the prettiest girl in Brooklyn? Correction, *vakreste*, the most beautiful."

She stops struggling and stares at me. There's something in that look beyond the expected butterflies and rainbows, something I can't quite place. I stare back, trying to figure out what it is, before giving up and allowing her to slide down to the street.

After putting her bag in the trunk and opening the door for her, I make my way to the driver's side and get in. I put the key in the ignition but don't start the car.

"So, we can go to a nice restaurant, or I can cook for you at home. Which would you prefer?" The answer I'd like is obvious, mostly by the way I've posed the options.

The way Maya looks at me, you'd think I'd asked her to compute a complex math formula.

"It's not a trick question," I say with a helpful grin.

"Do you think of me as a puck bunny?"

And there it is.

I sigh and sit back to assess her. "Where is this coming from?"

"Nowhere, I'm just asking."

I stare at her a moment longer, not at all buying that. I feel my blood pressure rise, wishing I could reach right into the Internet and give a nice uppercut to the assholes on that forum for bringing about this kind of doubt in her.

"No. I don't think of you as a puck bunny, Maya."

She stares at me for a moment before exhaling. "Okay."

"I think we should go to my place. We obviously need to talk."

"I didn't mean to make a big deal about it, I just—"

"It is a big deal," I say, starting the car. "I don't want you asking questions like that, or thinking that way. We'll go back to my place and settle this."

"Okay," she says softly, settling into the seat beside me.

I turn on the radio, mostly to keep the conversation at bay. I need to collect my thoughts so they don't come out in a rush that completely overwhelms her.

Once inside my loft, I wait for her to take off her coat and drop her bag before I begin. I'm leaning against the kitchen island once again, this time with my arms crossed as I observe her.

"So do you want to tell me what happened between yesterday and tonight to bring this on?" I ask. For some reason, I don't want her knowing I've already read all that vile trash on *The Pucking News*.

I watch her inhale, ready to protest once again. She lets it seep out with a slow breath. "I was on this forum, *The Pucking News*, and...someone had taken a photo of us from Friday... while we were...you know, in my apartment building."

"Maya—"

"I'm over it," she says quickly, waving a hand in the air. "But someone else also got more photos from a girl I used to work with back at the bar, which just made it seem more...seedy."

Maya shivers with disgust, and I rush over to bring her into a hug.

"*Faen*," I curse in a whisper. "I should have warned you what it would be like. I'm used to this shit, but you don't deserve it."

She pulls back far enough to look up at me. "I'm fine, really. Frankly, I should have expected it. I just...I don't want you to think I'm just some—"

"I don't," I say firmly, making sure every part of my face confirms it for her. "To me, you aren't some puck bunny or hockey whore or—"

"Good grief, how many different ways do they have of slut-shaming a woman?"

A small, wry grin appears on my face. "Whatever you want to call it, you are more to me than that, Maya. This? Whatever it is at this point, I want to see where it goes. I like being with you, not just for the sex or...language lessons, which are great," she laughs at this, "but because I like you. Period."

She rewards me with that smile I love so much. "I like you too."

Struck by inspiration, I let go of her and lead her by the hand back to the kitchen where I've set my phone and keys down. I let go of her hand and pick up my phone.

"What are you doing?" she asks with a wary smile.

"Making it known," I say, pulling up the photo app.

"Making what known?"

"Us," I say, opening up the camera into self-mode.

"Oh my God, you aren't," she says with a laugh.

"Oh yes, I am," I say, pulling her into my side. With the boots that she still has on, her head just reaches my shoulder. "Smile," I say.

She laughs instead and I snap the picture. The resulting photo makes both of us laugh. Maya's laugh is just beginning to form and I'm grinning from ear to ear.

"I like it," I say. "It's...us."

"It's ridiculous," she says, though she doesn't seem entirely opposed to it.

"Okay, this time a normal one," she says.

"Got it," I say, wrapping my arms around her as we both smile normally.

"That one is so much better," she says once I pull the phone back to inspect the resulting photo.

"I like both."

"Both for what?"

"To post on Instagram," I say.

"No! You were serious about that?"

"Yes," I say, holding the phone out of reach.

"Erik...don't."

"Why not? Give me one good reason and I won't do it."

"Because..." She sighs. "I don't know. Because."

"Not a good reason." I bring the phone down again. "Maya, this is the start of us. This is me showing the world that you aren't some...insert whatever bit of slut-shaming you want. The point is, you aren't that."

She gives me a reluctant grin.

"This is me showing the world that you are special. So let me do it, stop all the trash talk and speculation and...making you feel like you have to question my motives, or that I'm questioning yours."

She softens just a bit more, staring at the phone with doubt.

"Instagram official. Yes?"

She laughs. "You're such a girl."

"I'll be happy to disprove that for you...preferably all night long."

She rolls her eyes and laughs again. "Okay, fine."

"Fine," I say with a grin as I pull up Instagram. I post both photos, making sure the Maya-approved one is first. I think about what to write, then grin as it comes to me and I type it out.

"Done," I say after posting.

"Wait...you posted without telling me what you wrote?" She asks.

I smile and shrug. "You'll just have to go online to read it."

She gives me a fake glare and scrambles for her bag to pull out her phone.

"I've got red and white wine for dinner, which do you prefer?" I ask idly as I head around to the kitchen.

I don't expect an answer right away, but when the silence lingers, I spin around to make sure she's okay.

Her eyes are still glued to her phone. I continue to observe her until she feels my eyes on her and rolls them up to meet mine.

"The only one I want to be with?" she reads.

"The *only* one," I assure her.

She twists her lips hard, either to keep from smiling or to keep from crying. "Erik...that's so..."

"Accurate," I say. "Now, red or white?"

She rests the phone down and laughs—though I swear there's a hint of a cry there too. "I don't care."

"Well, I'm making pasta with white sauce so, maybe white."

"Pasta?" she says, coming around to meet me near the refrigerator. "You mean you aren't making some Norwegian specialty to impress me, your only one?"

"God no, Norwegian food is not first, second, or third date material. Definitely not meant to be consumed by my only one. You have to develop a certain...taste for it."

"Oh yeah, I think I have a bit of a taste for it already," she says, putting her arms around my waist and smiling up at me.

I grin down at her. "Trust me, you might change your mind when it comes to our national cuisine," I say with a laugh as I put the bottle on the counter and wrap my arms around her. "In fact, it's best saved for when you've already decided you've fallen in love and you're willing to forgive all the faults of me and my home country."

Her lips press together in a repressed smile.

"So I have to fall in love before you introduce me to the food of your people?"

"It's the only way I'll ever let you anywhere near it."

"Even if I beg and plead."

"Be careful what you wish for. *Lutefisk* is not something to be jumped into lightly."

"*Lutefisk?* It sounds…"

"As terrible as it tastes."

"Well then, I guess I better fall in love."

"I guess you'd better," I say, suddenly wanting to do everything in my power to get her there.

CHAPTER TWENTY-FOUR

ERIK

The next morning we're woken up by a message alert from Maya's phone.

"Mmm," I groan in protest. "Leave it."

"I'll just take a peek," she says, laughing as she disentangles herself from me while I try to hold on tighter.

The phone is on the nightstand next to the bed, so all she has to do is roll over and reach for it.

"What time is it anyway?"

"Not even five yet," she says, sounding almost as annoyed as I feel.

"Oh no," she mutters after a while.

"What is it?" I say, instantly perking up at the tone of her voice.

She turns the phone to show me the message from Katie:

It's official, U have a bona fide stalker! Couldn't help myself and looked at the forum. There are

more photos…from yesterday! BTW it's on twitter too #ThisisMaya.

I sit up, coming in closer to her as she leans against the headboard. She clicks the link Katie provided.

"What the hell?" she mutters when she sees the pictures.

Even I'm surprised.

The first is of her in my arms as I leaped over the puddle yesterday. Another is of us in the car talking. Surprisingly, they also include some from us at the coffee shop, one of us across the table from one another and the other next to each other, her legs over mine.

The rest are all of Maya. Her leaving her apartment in the morning. Her heading down the subway stairs. Her seen through a crowd on the platform. Her standing in one of the subway cars, her hand hooked over one of the poles as she reads on her phone. She's wearing the same thing in each, so they must have all been snapped on the same day.

"These were taken just yesterday," she says, which confirms it.

She clicks over to Twitter and checks the hashtag Katie sent. Sure enough, the same photos are floating around there.

Neither of us bothers even reading any of the comments written, having learned our lesson last time. The creepy pictures are bad enough.

"Why on earth would someone be taking photos of me?" she asks, her voice starting to get panicky.

I wrap my arm around her and bring her in closer to me, trying to calm her, even though my own body begins to heat up with rage.

I have a pretty good idea of who might be this obsessed.

"Listen, I don't like this. I think you shouldn't go into work today. We'll both call in sick and stay here until I figure this out. I can skip one day of practice."

Maya shakes her head, still staring down at her phone.

"You're not getting in trouble with your team over this," she says. "Besides, I have to go to work. They're working on this big new case, and it'll look suspicious if I call in sick today when I was perfectly fine yesterday. It's the safest place I can be. I'd rather be there in an office full of lawyers with security at the front than here or in my apartment."

She has a point, which is the only thing that sets me at ease.

"I'm going to figure this out, Maya. Who's taking these photos and posting them online, even if I have to sue the damn website itself. You don't deserve this."

"No, but here it is," she says softly. "I guess this is what it's like dating someone like you."

"Hey," I say, reaching around to take her chin in my hand and lift it toward me. "No, this isn't what it's like dating me. Nothing like this has happened before, but it will stop now. Trust me."

There's a fleeting look of hope in her eyes before she gives me a weak smile and nods.

"I'm driving you to work today. I have an away game tonight, but I'm paying a service to pick you up afterward, okay. The last thing I want is for this to escalate."

The thought of how far this could go sends a wave of dread through me.

"I'm meeting my friends tonight to discuss Gabby's bridal shower. Don't worry, it'll be in a public restaurant."

"Okay. I'll give you the number to call when you're done. Don't go home on your own. Promise me that."

She smiles again. "I promise."

After dropping Maya off, I sit idle, ignoring the beeping horns of taxi cabs and truck drivers trying to get around me as I watch her walk through the front doors of her office building.

I pull up Doug's number and call him, putting him on speaker before I shift out of park and drive away.

"Erik, I know exactly what you're calling about and trust me, I'm on it."

"Tessa Ogden," I say through gritted teeth. "She's the only one I can think of who would be behind this."

There's a pause on the other end as he seems to consider that. "It's been a year Erik. Do you really think—?"

"Who else would it be?" I insist. "You have to be the one to talk to her or her people. Even if she hadn't blocked me in every way, I can't be held responsible for what I might do if I did manage to get in touch with her. This? This is completely unacceptable."

"I understand," he says in a placating tone that does nothing to douse the flames inside me. "I'll handle it."

"Do that. *Soon.*" I hang up before he can try talking me down.

My teammates are smart enough not to broach the subject when I meet them on the bus to our Pittsburg game. I stare out the window at the passing scenery, my insides feeling like a steam engine that's running too fast and hard, ready to explode at any moment.

Tonight's game threatens to be a fierce one.

My phone vibrates in my pocket, and I quickly pull it out, noting that it's my agent finally calling me back.

"Doug. So what did she have to say for herself?"

"Well, *she* didn't have much to say since *she* has been in Greece for the past week, on a getaway with some businessman she's currently dating. Her people assured me it couldn't have been her, Erik."

I'm officially dumbfounded. I'm tempted to accuse her of hiring someone, but that isn't her style. Every spiteful act she committed against me or the women I was dating after we broke up was her own dirty work.

"Maybe it's just some idiot who thinks he can get a few bucks with these photos," Doug suggests.

"No, this seems…personal. Who would be targeting her like that?"

"Personal," he repeats as though considering that thought. "Then it must be someone she knows already, someone with a grudge against her perhaps?"

"That's all I can think. Unless it's some random rabid fan."

"Listen, here's what I'll do, Erik. I'll pull a few strings, get the site to cough up who started all this and maybe even get a name."

"Do that," I say, feeling relieved that there might be an end to this.

The only question is, why did it start in the first place?

CHAPTER TWENTY-FIVE

MAYA

"Okay, so are we going to talk about these photos?" Zia asks.

"I don't think Maya wants to discuss it," Demetria says, giving her a frown.

We're at some expensive downtown restaurant Demetria chose (and promised to pay for) to get started on Gabrielle's bridal shower over dinner.

They both look at me expectantly, and all I can do is shrug. "It's ...scary, frankly. The worst part is not knowing who it is. One of Erik's exes? Was it some rabid fan?"

I think about some of the more lunatic signs I saw when I investigated the word "puck bunny," and I shiver. Hell hath no fury like a woman scorned.

What makes it worse is that these most recent photos were posted right on the heels of Erik posting the really sweet ones of us on Instagram. I can't help but wonder if the two are somehow related.

"Hell, it could even be someone I know."

They both blink in surprise at that.

"You really think that?" Zia asks, looking stunned.

"That's ridiculous, Maya," Demetria says.

"Is it? Why else would someone take photos of just me and not him? I'm not the famous one."

"It obviously has to do with you dating Erik," Zia says. "They didn't start getting posted until you started going out with him."

She does have a point.

"I mean, I'm a firm believer in true love, but your safety comes first," she continues. "I think maybe you should wait a while before you see him again."

He has an away game tonight, which means I won't see him until tomorrow anyway, but even that short a wait fills me with longing. I shake my head. "If this is all it takes for me to shy away, do I really deserve him?"

"It's only been a week, Maya, and you know I'm the first one who can tell you how reckless it is to fall for a guy so soon."

I diplomatically remain silent on that issue. Zia is the queen of falling fast and hard for all the wrong types of men.

But Erik is not wrong for me. I feel it, even now with all of this going on. Even after less than a full week.

"Listen, Maya," Demetria says, giving me an assessing look. "If you really feel strongly about him, then it's worth it. We both saw those Instagram photos. He's definitely into you, and you seem to be into him. A few creepy photos is hardly a reason to break up."

I feel a smile come to my lips. "That's a hard one-eighty from your stance just last week."

She shifts uncomfortably in her seat.

"You know what? Forget everything I said that night. I was…" She looks away then back to me, straightening up as she continues. "I was going through some personal things. It's obvious you like the guy, Maya. You and Erik can work through this and whatever else comes your way. You deserve that."

"Aww, Demi," Zia says, reaching out to squeeze her arm.

Demetria purses her lips with embarrassment, the way she always does whenever someone gets too emotional around her. Unlike Zia's hippy-dippy parents, hers were not the warm and fuzzy types.

I look at my two friends, grateful that I have such amazing women in my life with whom to talk this out. They're like sisters to me, especially considering we've known each other since at least middle school. I know, no matter what, they'll always be there to support me.

I have no idea who is doing this or why, but I trust Erik when he says he'll get it handled.

I'm at my mother's apartment, which I've been dreading all week.

"They figured out who it was. According to Erik's agent, it was just some random fan looking for attention on that idiotic forum. It's an anonymous site so they couldn't tell us his name, but they removed the posts with my photos and officially banned him, so that's probably why there are no more photos posted of me—or us."

In fact, it was the very next day that the issue seemed to be resolved. The morning after I met with Zia and Demetria I fully expected to find another round of shots posted of me getting into and out of the car Erik hired to drive me home, or even eating dinner with them. But there has been nothing since then. Even Twitter has given it a rest.

Thank God.

"I still don't like it," my mother says as she finishes putting relaxer in my hair to straighten it. Every five weeks or so, she'll do this instead of our usual routine when we meet up. I have yet to jump on the go-natural bandwagon, being as averse to change as I am. And why pay a hairdresser to do what my mom offers for free?

"I don't care if whoever it was stopped," she continues. "What if they get it in their head to start up again? Or what about the next crazy person who comes along and takes it further?"

"Then I guess I'll die for the sake of love," I say with a melodramatic sigh.

"That's not funny, Maya," she says, tugging my hair lightly.

"What?" I say, laughing mostly to lighten the mood. I thought telling her that the issue appears to have been resolved would make her a bit more accommodating. "What is it you have against the man?"

"Have you ever stopped to consider how different you two are?"

Now that she's done with my hair, I stand up to face her, but before I can even open my mouth, she continues.

"Before you get going, no, I don't mean because he's white."

"Then what do you mean?"

"Never mind this bit of fame and outright stalking, which he's probably used to. How much do you even know about hockey?"

"I'm learning."

"Okay. And where is it he's from again?" she asks in a leading way.

"So you have a thing against Norwegians?" I reply, laughing in disbelief.

"Norway, hmm. How much do you know about that country? I assume that's where his family still lives. When this hockey career of his is over is he going back there to live? Will he be taking you with him?"

"I don't know," I say, throwing my hands up in the air. "We've been dating for less than two weeks. That's not to say we don't see each other every day when he's in town," I point out.

"When he's in town."

"What's *that* supposed to mean?"

"How often is he gone? Because his leaving town for games is going to continue when you decide on a serious relationship. What's that going to be like when you have kids? Believe me Maya, I know something about what it's like to raise a child on my own even in a supposedly two-parent household."

Now my hands are on my hips. "Is this about me or you?"

"Don't," she says, pointing the comb at me. "Don't even go there."

"You just did."

She pauses, and I watch the anger inside her calm to more of a simmer.

"Okay fine, let's go there then. *You* also know what it was like. Do you want your kids to live through the same thing that happened with your dad and me, the same thing *you* lived through? One parent lost in the limelight of success while the other tries to maintain some semblance of a home life? One parent deciding that that's not good enough for him and he wants a new and improved life; a life with a wife who fits in better, a wife who's more like him now that he has his big house and fancy career and..."

She stops, realizing what she's saying, and I can see the hurt and shame all over her face.

"Ma," I say softly, going toward her and pulling her in for a hug, making sure the relaxer in my hair doesn't touch her. She's not a crier, but I know she needs this.

What's she's said isn't exactly how it happened, but I can see how she might feel that way. Just as with my dad, I don't talk about the other parent when I'm with her. Still, I know what happened between the two of them is always there, lingering beneath the surface waiting to come to a head like it has tonight.

I can also see why she'd be worried the same could happen to me.

It isn't as though the thought hasn't crossed my mind. Erik is a rich and famous professional hockey player from Scandinavia, a place I still know very little about.

What's to stop him from waking up one day and deciding that he was stupid to give up the Victoria's Secret model for this girl from Brooklyn?

What's to stop him from deciding that he belongs with some Norwegian or Swedish woman who at least understands his culture, where he comes from?

What's to stop him from deciding I'm not his "only one" after all?

I want to attribute it all to the typical second guessing that always comes from dating someone new. Mostly I've been able to temper it down, but it definitely still lingers at the back of my mind.

"I'm okay," my mom says, pulling away.

I squeeze tighter, making sure.

"Really," she says with a laugh that I finally believe.

I draw back, resting my hands on her shoulders. "Erik and I are just getting started, Ma. We like each other, and yes, I still have a lot to learn about him. It's a process, one that I want to invest myself in fully. I think—I *know* he wants that too."

She twists her lips into a smile, then rolls her eyes up to my hair. "Maya, you better wash that stuff out before you go bald."

"Yeah," I say, suddenly feeling that tingling sensation on my scalp. "It's starting to sting."

We both laugh as I rush to the bathroom to wash it out.

With my head under the water, I think about what I said to her and smile. I do want to learn as much as possible about Erik. So far, it's been fascinating. It doesn't hurt that he's a very effective teacher.

But what happens when the lessons start getting more advanced...and he decides he wants to move back home again?

CHAPTER TWENTY-SIX

ERIK

"Happy Valentine's Day...or at least the day after." There was a Blades game on the official date, so I'm here to pick Maya up the day after.

Maya laughs as she rushes in to hug me at her front door. She has on a red sweater dress, belted at the waist, with black textured stockings and over-the-knee black boots.

Nydelig. Gorgeous.

I'm wearing a black wool coat over my cashmere slate-gray turtleneck sweater and slacks in a darker gray with black dress boots.

"Wait, no Katie tonight?" I ask, looking past her into the small apartment.

"She said she landed a small role in some play. She was making a video with Zia, who does these AMSR things. Don't ask what it means. I couldn't even begin to tell you even though I've done a few videos with her myself. Anyway, she met Zia's brother, who's also an actor and they hit it off so—"

"Wait, what's this about you and Zia making videos?" I ask, picking up on the most crucial part of what she's said. With my crazy hockey schedule, I haven't met her friends yet, but I do recall the photo from Instagram of them in the Bahamas.

"Stop getting ideas," she says with a smirk. "What is this adventure we're going on tonight?" She asks, bouncing on the balls of her feet with a massive smile on her face.

"Well I had plans but now that I've learned you have the apartment to yourself," I say, my hands on her hips as I walk her back inside. "I think we should stay in and have a look at these videos of yours."

"Oh no you don't," she says, walking me right back out the door. "And get your mind out of the gutter. It's just a massage video."

"Massage?" I ask, raising one eyebrow as my mind goes right back to the gutter.

"Okay fine, we can stay in and watch videos of me getting a massage from my friend," she says, in a way that's somehow supposed to make me opposed to the idea. "But that means you'll miss out on the gift I have for you, which I guarantee is a million times hotter."

I twist my lips and wrinkle my brow as though considering that and she laughs and punches me lightly in the stomach. "Erik!"

I grin and pull her in, wrapping my arms around her in a hug. "You're right. My present is much better than that too. Are you ready?"

She stares up at me like a kitten, huge eyes gleaming with excitement. "Yes, I am."

Ten minutes later, we're in my Mustang driving along the parkway.

"So...not a fancy restaurant in town?"

"Stop digging," I say with a smirk as I shift gears to go faster now that most of the traffic has died down. "You'll ruin the surprise."

"Okay, okay, no more probing."

"Right. I'm the only one who gets to probe tonight."

"*Erik*," She groans, slapping my arm.

I sense her shift in her seat so that she's slightly turned to face me. "Do you know how sexy you were at last night's game?"

I turn to give her a grin. "Sexy, huh?"

"Mmm-hmm. I couldn't keep my eyes off you…at least when you weren't moving faster than lightning."

I chuckle. "Well, I'm glad I got you season tickets then, especially since it turns me on just as much to see you sitting there in the crowd looking sexy as hell too."

She laughs and twists back around in her seat to look around. "Are we leaving the city?"

"Yes, and that's all I'm saying."

She turns to look at me. "You really did plan something big, didn't you?"

"You'll just have to wait and see," I say with a grin, hoping she loves it.

CHAPTER TWENTY-SEVEN

MAYA

He looks so damn sexy! Just the way he handles that stick shift in this retro car is so...impressive. Being a New York native, I've never even learned to drive.

The city disappears behind us and apartments turn into houses spaced further and further apart, then...nothing. In my red dress, I feel like Little Red Riding Hood being whisked away by the Big Bad (Norwegian) Wolf.

As if I needed any more stimulation for tonight's romantic adventure.

Erik reaches out and turns on the radio, which is a modern update to whatever the original was. It's synched with his phone, and I'm surprised when the first song comes on.

"So you like Prince?" I say as "Take Me with U" begins to play.

"Yeah," he says with an almost embarrassed grin. "It reminds me of home."

"Prince? Reminds you of home? As in Scandinavia?"

"Norway," he says, his grin softening as he faces forward.

"My mom used to play this album all the time. She loved *Purple Rain*. I think she had a crush on the guy."

I laugh and shake my head in wonder. At least the woman had taste. I think about the picture in his apartment, which I've seen enough times now to have a mental image of. She was stunning enough that she probably had hordes of hot Norwegian men drooling over her. And Prince of all people was her crush. Then again, the man was pure sex.

I think about the conversation with my mom about how different Erik is from me.

"What was it like growing up in Norway?" I know better than to ask about Sweden, which always creates a distinct chill in the air around him.

He stares ahead long enough for me to think maybe I've said something I shouldn't have. "I was going to save it for later, but I think showing you will be better."

"What does that mean?" I ask, feeling giddy, yet wary at that ambiguous answer.

He smiles and turns to me. "You'll see. Just sit back and relax. Enjoy the scenery."

I sit back and look out the passenger side window, wondering what scenery he's talking about. It looks like we're heading to the middle of nowhere. Still, Prince's voice as "The Beautiful Ones" comes on after the previous song lulls me into a sensually lazy feeling as Erik speeds down the highway.

I've almost fallen asleep when I feel the car slow down. I perk up and twist my head to get a better look out the windows. We've pulled to a clearing on the side of the road. It's a semi-forested area, and the only light seems to be coming from the headlights of Erik's car.

"Okay, so either you want to make out like teenagers in a horror movie, or you need a place to dump my body after you kill me."

Erik breathes out a soft laugh. "You don't have much experience with pure nature, do you? No, I'm not going to kill you. The first option is still on the table."

"So, what is this?" I say, turning to face him.

"Here," he says. He turns off the engine, and the sudden silence is jarring.

"Here," I echo, looking around and wondering what "here" is.

"You always ask me about Norway, what it was like, what I did—well, this is it. At least one part of it."

"I thought you grew up in Oslo." I may still have a lot to learn about the place, but I at least know it's a city...with buildings.

"I did, but I also spent a lot of time with my grandfather who liked to be outdoors. It's very easy to escape the city, especially the area where he lives, and just wander the woods nearby. When I first came to America, to Florida, I had to drive to get away from the city, and there it's all pretty swampy, especially compared to Norway. Here, at least there are mountains and forests."

"So nothing about this scares you? All the emptiness?"

"But it isn't empty, especially when you look up," he says with a grin. He turns off the headlights and opens his door, causing me to blink in surprise. "Come with me."

He exits the car, closing the door behind him, and I follow his dark form with my eyes as he heads to the front bumper. He bends down to peer at me through the front windshield as though asking what I'm waiting for.

Gee, Erik, I don't know. How about the fact that it's the middle of the forest, pitch black, and pretty damn cold outside?

I inhale and open my door, grabbing my coat to throw on as I exit.

There's been a recent light snow, but this part of the road

has been cleared. A perfectly white, untouched blanket of powder still lingers on branches and the ground around us. It's a beautiful winter wonderland...in the middle of nowhere.

"I know this seems strange," he acknowledges as I lean on the front of the car next to him.

"I'm just a little freaked out is all."

"Don't be," he says, wrapping his arm around me and pulling me into his side. "Look up."

I do, and ...it's impressive.

The sky above is filled with so many stars it seems fake. "Wow, it's spectacular."

"Because you don't see this in Brooklyn. You don't even see it most places in Oslo. It was one of the first things my morfar— my grandfather, showed me when I was little and stayed with him. We'd camp for days and he'd tell me stories about when he was a soldier, some he probably shouldn't have," Erik says with a laugh.

I smile at that laugh, which helps me imagine what it must have been like.

"*Friluftsliv*," he says next to me.

"Pardon?"

"*Friluftsliv*," he repeats. "It's another Norwegian word but doesn't have a proper translation in English. It literally means 'free air life.' Norwegians spend a lot of time in the outdoors, fishing, camping, hiking, biking. Things like that. Those are some of the things I miss. I drive out here every so often just to get a feel for what those moments were like. Yes, Manhattan has Central Park, and Brooklyn has Prospect Park, but it's nice to be in a place where there isn't a skyscraper on the horizon."

I've never felt like such a New Yorker before. "I think I would go crazy if I had to spend more than an hour in a place this isolated."

Erik laughs and squeezes me tighter. "That's what I love about you. You're so...different."

"So you aren't disappointed or annoyed that I'm not into this? I mean, don't get me wrong, it's impressive. That sky alone..." I look up, only to have my mind blown again. "It's amazing, but I think I need the city."

He turns to look at me, and I see only the barest hint of the sharp lines and hard features of his face.

"Why would I be?" He asks in such an earnest voice that I'm surprised. "What fun is being with someone who's exactly like me? Who is only into the same things I am? I love that you introduce me to new things like AMSR, whatever that is. That's why I moved from Sweden, from Norway. It's why I love to travel, have new experiences, learn about different cultures. I love the fact that you and I are different in so many ways. In fact, I also love the fact that you're honest about this not being your thing. Some women would pretend to like it, thinking that's what I want to hear.

"No, Maya. I didn't bring you here to try and convince you to get into this. I brought you here because I want you to know a part of who I am, to see it first hand.

"In fact...I want you to experience it in my home country." In the darkness, I hear his clothes rustling as he pulls something from the pocket of his coat. "Hold out your hand."

I hold my hand out, and he places something small and cylindrical in it. It's a glass vial, just like the ones on his bookshelf.

"This one is for when we get there. We'll fill it with sand...together."

"Norway?" I ask, feeling my heart beat a little faster. "Is this you inviting me to your country?"

"This is me inviting you to my country," he repeats with a smile in his voice. "I'm going back in June. I go every year after hockey season is over, but this year, my younger cousin is in a band playing at some small festival and he wants me to come watch him. You can meet my aunt and uncle and other cousin and of course Morfar."

"Your grandfather."

"You're learning quickly," he says with a smile. "So...is that a yes?"

"Of course," I say quickly, my heart now beating a mile a minute.

Norway.

If someone had told me a month ago that I would be contemplating going there out of all the places in the world, I'd have thought they were crazy. The only foreign country I've visited was The Bahamas, and that wasn't even much of a culture shock, considering how many Caribbean immigrants live in neighborhoods around my area of Brooklyn.

But then came Erik.

"I can't wait for everyone to meet you," he says. Even in the dark, I can feel his gaze focused on me. "I can't wait for you to see what it's like there. I can't wait to be there with you."

I smile. "So you really want me to go with you?"

"Of course," he says, as though I'm silly for even asking. "Why wouldn't I want to be there with the most beautiful, funniest, sexiest woman I've ever known?"

"Well, now you're just trying to butter me up," I say with a grin.

"Except it's true," he says. "Going there without you this time just wouldn't feel right. Because...*jeg elsker deg.*"

I don't even need an interpreter, as the huge grin on my face makes clear to him.

"I love you too," I say, unable to hide the giddiness in my voice.

All of a sudden, I don't care if it's a visit to Antarctica or the middle of the Sahara Desert, I want to go to Norway more than ever. As long as it's with him.

"I can't wait!" I reach out to hug him and laugh. "So was this my Valentine's Day gift?" I ask, not even caring if it is.

"Come on," he says with a laugh. "I may have an ice-cold Scandinavian heart, but I'm not that unromantic."

"Oh?"

"Oh," he echoes. "In fact, we should get going before that pretty ass of yours freezes off. Your gift is another Norwegian take-away. This one I'm sure you'll like."

"Oh?" I say, getting excited again.

"*Koselig.*"

"*Koselig*," I echo. "What's that?"

Instead of answering, he leans in and kisses me. The chill of the air suddenly has a contender as his lips warm me from head to toe.

Erik pulls away. "*Koselig* is your Valentine's Day Gift. Let's get going, so I can show you."

CHAPTER TWENTY-EIGHT

ERIK

"Oh my God, it's gorgeous," Maya says, craning her neck to look out the windshield at the large lodge.

With a log wood exterior, it has the feel of a ski chalet catering to a wealthy clientele. It's popular year-round, mostly as a getaway for those who want to use the lake in back for summer, or enjoy winter in the snow-covered woods.

I smile as Maya's sense of wonder fills the air in the car. This is what I love about her. Being born and raised in New York has made her worldly in a way, but everything outside of that city is still exciting and new to her.

"So is this what *koselig* is then?" She says, falling back to face me with a smile.

"Just wait for it," I say, as I pull into the large circular driveway.

The valet comes around to open her door first. I exit and take her hand as I come around to lead her into the large foyer of the luxuriously rustic hotel. Massive antler chandeliers hang from the ceiling and over-stuffed, leather couches surround a huge fireplace that a person could stand up in. It has a roaring fire that instantly welcomes us in from the cold.

After checking in at the front desk, I'm handed the keys to the room I reserved for us tonight. It was a lucky break on my part. This place has the sort of intimate romantic vibe that draws a Valentine's Day crowd, at least those who can afford it. The massive suite that greets us when the man showing us to our room opens the door is a testament to that.

"Wow, Erik," Maya says, walking past us to explore the space.

Even though it's a large area, it still has a cozy atmosphere, especially when he starts up the gas fireplace—not quite as *koselig* as using real firewood but good enough. The lighting is warm and the furniture cozy. It's the perfect winter escape for two lovers.

"Your private dinner will be served at eight o'clock. In the meantime, enjoy champagne and strawberries. Will there be anything else?"

I shake my head and thank him, making sure to hand him a nice tip as he leaves.

"How long have you been planning this?" Maya asks as she sits on the sofa and takes a bite of one of the strawberries from the tray on the coffee table.

"Since I first laid eyes on you," I say with a grin as I walk over to sit next to her and pour champagne.

"Oh? You were so sure you were going to ask me out and I'd say yes?" she teases.

"Based on the look in your eyes when you saw me, I had a pretty good shot." I hand her a full glass.

She laughs and takes the champagne. "So, when are you going to tell me what *koselig* means then? I think I'm getting an idea, but I want to hear it from you."

"Lie back on the armrest and give me your legs."

Her brow wrinkles a bit, but she scoots back to rest against the arm of the couch and stretches her legs out over my thighs. Her long boots are still on, and I rest my hand on the suede rising above her knee.

"Remember this from our first night?"

"Yeah," she says with a soft smile.

"There's really no equivalent word for it in English, but that's part of what *koselig* is. It's a sort of cozy, comfortable feeling of being content or happy, usually with friends or family or other loved ones. I thought it was the perfect way to celebrate Valentine's Day."

"It is perfect," Maya says, leaning her elbow on the back of the sofa and resting her head against her hand. "I guess with all that snow in Norway, there's probably plenty of opportunity for it. Hot chocolate. Fireplaces. S'mores—wait, do you guys eat s'mores?"

"Yes, we do eat s'mores," I say in a dry voice. "But *koselig* is more than a winter thing. Fishing or camping with my *morfar* in summer was the same."

"So...Norway."

I look at her. "You do want to come, don't you?"

"Of course," she says quickly. "I just...I'm not sure what to expect. I don't travel nearly as much as you and, well, this is your home country. It's a lot to look forward to."

"Don't worry, I'll be there to hold your hand," I tease.

She kicks one of her legs and smirks at me. "I'm not going to faint as soon as I get off the plane. I'm actually excited."

"Good, it will be fun. Everyone will love you."

Part of the reason I want Maya to come is obviously to learn more about my home country. Prior to meeting her I always had this vague idea that I would return after my hockey career was over. However, I know she loves Brooklyn and can't imagine leaving. This trip will be a test for both of us; me, to determine if moving back is what I really want, and her, to determine if Norway is even a possibility for her.

Maya smiles, but before she can respond, there's a knock at the door.

"I guess it's time for dinner," I say as she swings her legs off my lap to let me stand up to answer the door.

Our waiter for the evening sets up the small table situated near the window, placing a white table cloth over it and adding plates, silverware, and glasses. He puts a small centerpiece in the middle made of roses and tea candles. With the view of the lake, it's almost over-the-top in how romantic it looks once he's done.

Maya and I take a seat and are given two menus with a selection of prix fixe dinners, giving us an option of three different four-course meals. Along with a bottle of red wine, we both order the steak.

Once he's gone, we stare at each other long enough in silence to eventually break out in laughter.

"I shouldn't laugh," Maya says. "This is amazing, Erik."

"Glad you approve."

"Of course I do, but you're giving me performance anxiety. How is my gift going to top this one?" She says, with a wicked smile.

"I have a feeling I'll enjoy it," I say with a wicked smile of my own.

The server comes back with our bottle of wine and throughout the evening, our salad, appetizer, main course, and dessert plates. During the hour-and-a-half it takes to finish, I tell her more about Norway, and she tells me stories about growing up in Brooklyn.

Now, we're finishing up the chocolate cake.

"...and when our parents found out, the four of us were grounded for over a month. Even Zia's parents, who are these free-spirited types, were pissed off. And Demetria, her parents are...*strict*. She was grounded longer than any of us. My mom," Maya pauses, "I think she was just more disappointed. She has this way of cutting you down with just a look."

That one has me thinking. "Have you told her about me?"

Her eyes widen briefly. "Of course I have!"

"And...?" I say as I sip the last of the wine in my glass.

"She...likes you. I mean she has yet to meet you, so it's hard to say but—I mean, she naturally has her concerns as any mother would, but she hasn't specifically objected to you or anything like that."

Her rambling tells me all I need to know.

"I think I should meet her."

Maya stares at me for a moment. "You want to meet her?"

"Don't most men eventually meet their girlfriend's parents?"

A smile grows on her face. "Am I your girlfriend?"

"After tonight you still have to ask?"

She laughs softly. "I haven't even given you your gift yet."

"This is true," I say with one eyebrow raised daringly.

"Well, *boyfriend*," she says, leaning in closer toward me. "Why don't you have them come and clear the table while I get it prepped for you, then meet me in the bedroom so I can wish you a proper happy Valentine's Day."

CHAPTER TWENTY-NINE

MAYA

Damn, I look good.
    If I do say so myself.

"Hello, *girlfriend*," I say to my reflection in the bathroom of the suite. It fits. Yes, it's been only almost a month but considering the amount of time Erik and I have spent together, even with all his away games, why the hell shouldn't we move on to being "official?"

I've heard the waiter come and go, which means we have the place to ourselves for the rest of the night. With the long coat firmly wrapped around me, I smile one last time to myself in the mirror, then open the door.

Erik is seated on the edge of the bed and grins when he sees me walk out with my coat on. Over my thigh-high stockings, I still have on my over-the-knee boots, which I wore just for this occasion.

"You know, you were right about one thing."

"What's that?" he asks, still with the grin of anticipation on his face.

"When I first saw you...I was like...woah." I pull my iPhone out of my purse and pull up my music app. "This is the song that was running through my head at the time."

Before I hit Play, I turn up the volume and rest it on the credenza. "I think it's only fitting that you be a party to it as well. After all, you are part of the fantasy."

I press the button to play the song, and Mýa's voice sets the mood with the opening spiel to "My Love is Like...Wo," assuring him that I know he's had his share of girls, but he no longer needs to search.

I got you...

As she begins singing in that seductive voice, I grin and sway my hips, playing with the belt to my coat. The way Erik's mouth widens into a broader grin spurs me on and I spin around so he can get a better look from behind as I snake my body, sticking my ass out. Just before the chorus comes on, I rock my body around to face him, untying my belt.

My love is like...

I open just as she gets to "wo" and almost ruin the sexy vibe by laughing at the look on Erik's face.

"Bet you weren't expecting this, were you...*boyfriend?*" I say with a teasing smirk.

He's speechless.

Considering the lacy, black bra, matching thong panties and garter belt holding up my stockings that I have on underneath he damn well better be.

The coat slips down my arms and drops to the floor. I kick it away with one heeled boot. Then, I come in closer, my hand coming up to Erik's face. I lean in and mouth the words as she repeats the chorus.

Before he gets used to it, I pull back and give him a better close-up view of this sexy get-up. I haven't really rehearsed anything, but I had a general idea of what to do. With this song, it's impossible for my body not to respond provocatively.

While she sings, I bring my arms up, taking my hair with it so it's piled on top of my head and I get lost in the rhythm. When I sense the chorus looming, I come back to him and grab his hands.

My love is like...

This time when "whoa" hits, I place both of his palms on my bare ass and jerk my hips to the side with each subsequent "wo."

We both laugh, but I don't feel self-conscious at all. This is way too much fun to take seriously. Besides, there's nothing funny about the considerable hard-on straining Erik's pants.

I push him back on to the bed and crawl above him. I kneel, knees on either side of him so that I'm resting right on top of his dick. I slide my hips up and down so the lacy strip between my thighs slides across the fly of his slacks. I feel his hardness press into me, and it gets me so hot I might just turn into flames. I wouldn't be surprised if I'm leaving an unfortunate wet spot right on the front of his pants.

I'm sure neither of us cares.

I have a pretty good idea how much is left to the song, so I lift up, crawling back to the edge of the bed and falling to my knees on the floor for the big finale.

The song continues, fading into a repeat of the chorus. By the time Mýa is ad-libbing the finish, I have his fly undone and his throbbing dick in my grip. I stroke lightly as the song ends, waiting for the next to begin before I bless him with my mouth.

"That was—"

"Not even close to being over," I warn with a devilish grin.

Erik rises up on his elbows to stare down at me as "Body Party" by Ciara begins to play. The song has to have been made specifically for moments like this.

I smile as I dart my tongue out, showing him just how much fun my body can be for him. With my eyes locked on his, I circle it around the head, which is fully exposed now. I sink down, following the slow beat of the music, coming back up just as leisurely.

As Ciara's voice leads into the chorus, I get into a rhythm. The soothing sounds create a perfect movement for my tongue to follow. My hands circle the shaft, slinking inside his pants to cup his balls and add to this body party.

I smile around the tip as I see Erik's reaction. Eye-contact is broken as his head falls back when I increase the movement sinking all the way down, faster and faster until he explodes in my mouth.

I pull back, resting on the heels of my boots. When Erik comes back up for air, I smile down the length of his body.

"Happy Valentine's Day, lover."

His gaze darkens.

"*Du er så jævlig fantastisk.* You are so fucking amazing."

I laugh, slapping his knee as I stand up. Erik sits back up, stuffing his cock back into his pants, apparently completely body partied out.

"Oh no you don't," I warn.

He chuckles and stands up. "In which case, let me finish where you started."

I stand there in my matching lingerie set, feeling like a dominatrix in this outfit, especially with these boots, while Erik undresses for me. It's like unwrapping a work of art. Every sculpted muscle, from his rippling abs to his broad shoulders, is like smooth, hard marble in the soft light of the bedroom.

He hooks his thumbs in the sides of his loosened pants, shoving them down his narrow hips, past his thighs, thick cords of muscles slowly revealed. Even though this is hardly the first time I've seen him naked, I'm still as in awe as ever.

This body is mine; my very own private party.

"Ready to keep playing?" I ask.

"Always," he says, his eyes hungrily devouring me in this special Valentine's Day wrapping I picked just for him.

"Then I guess you'd better unwrap me," I say, lifting one leg to rest the heeled boot on the bed. "Starting with these."

The grin that meets me is the same one that left me saying "whoa" the first time I ever saw him.

We have fun, slowly getting me into my birthday suit, then I fall onto the bed next to him. He's on his back, and I straddle his side, one leg draped over his, the hard swoops of his muscles pressing into the soft flesh of my thigh. I lift on one elbow to look down at him.

"This was amazing, Erik...*boyfriend.*" I say with a smile.

His eyes hold mine in a fierce embrace. "Say it again."

My smile softens. "Boyfriend."

"Again."

"Boyfriend."

"Again," he whispers.

My smile comes back. "How long do you want me to keep saying it?"

His face is just a serious as before when he answers. "Long enough for you to realize you're mine."

My smile fades again as my heart drags me back down to the heaviness of this moment.

"Boyfriend."

His hand comes up to stroke my cheek. "That's it...girlfriend."

I giggle under the feel of his thumb as it strokes my lip.

"I guess this means we're official."

"Should we take a picture for Instagram to commemorate it?" he suggests, now with a devilish grin.

I slap his chest and laugh. "I have enough scandalous pictures floating around the Internet, thank you very much."

"Well then, how about we continue this party. That image of you in that outfit is still fresh on my mind."

"Oh?" I ask raising one eyebrow.

"Oh," he confirms, his eyes leading mine down the length of his body to see his swelling cock.

"Well then," I say, getting up to straddle him.

He lifts his hips to help guide me along, and I sigh as he enters me. This time when we fuck, I feel the intensity and meaning behind it.

My boyfriend.

My man.

We come almost simultaneously, and I fall down next to him, completely worn out. Once again, I curl into his side, enjoying the way his strong arm comes around to press me closer.

That's what I call a Valentine's Day.

CHAPTER THIRTY

ERIK

Maya and I lounge in bed long enough to watch the sun come up. Tonight, I have a game.

Of course, I do.

"You'd better wipe that overly satisfied grin off your face before you get on the plane to Montreal. The guys are going to be merciless if you don't."

"Let them tease me," I say, giving her a quick squeeze. "So what if they know I spent the night with the most gorgeous woman on earth."

She laughs and traces her fingernail across my chest. "Say, I forgot to ask last night, how do you say—"

"Kjæreste," I say with a smirk. "It's the same word for both boyfriend or girlfriend."

"How very egalitarian. Not that I'm going to even bother trying to pronounce that one right now." She laughs again. "Does it bother you, me always asking how to translate things?"

I look down at her feeling something that adds a bit of density to this lighthearted moment. "No, I like that you want to learn about Norway."

"I guess it will make it easier when I go."

"Most people there do speak English."

"Yeah, but I don't want to be *that* American, the one who always assumes they will."

"Well considering how terrible your Norwegian is, they'd probably appreciate it."

"Hey!" She says, grabbing a pillow and slapping it in my face.

I wrestle her, grabbing her into a bearhug and...one thing leads to another, leaving me with an overly satisfied grin that would be impossible to erase.

Later we're driving back to New York in my car.

"So, you're still okay with my mom coming to the next home game?"

"This is the third time you've asked. I'm fine with it, of course I am. The question is, are you?"

"Why wouldn't I be? She has to go to one at some point and—"

She's interrupted by a message dinging from her phone.

"It's Katie," she says in a slight groan. "Three exclamation points, I guess I should call her."

"By all means," I say with a subtle smirk.

She chuckles before calling back. "Hi, Katie," she says in a droll voice. There's a short pause. "Yes, I'm still with Erik."

I turn to find her smiling and rolling her eyes at me.

"Um...okay?" she says, then whispers to me, "She wants me to put her on speakerphone."

I shrug, not caring either way.

"Okay, shoot," Maya says once she's tapped the button for the speaker.

"Hi Erik," Katie gushes.

"Hi Katie," I answer in the same droll voice Maya used.

"So, before you both hate me, just know I did this for your

own good, mostly Maya's but yours too. I didn't think anything would come of it since it's been a while, but this morning I saw it, from the alert that I set up. The thing is, Maya, stalkers are a real serious thing. They don't stop, and I knew that I needed to—"

"Wait, wait, Katie. What's this alert you've set up?" Maya asks, sitting up in her seat.

"For *The Pucking News*."

"And?" Maya urges, any hint of drollness gone from her voice.

"Well...there are more photos. I guess from last night when Erik picked you up?"

"What?" Maya gasps.

"Yeah," Katie says sympathetically. "Here, I'll send you the link."

"I've—I've got to go, Katie."

"You aren't mad, are you?"

"No, of course not. I've—just bye, Katie."

Maya hangs up and drops the phone like it's on fire. I turn to find her visibly breathing heavier, almost to the point of hyperventilating.

I quickly steer to the side of the road, finding a spot to park. The phone is lying on her lap and I grab it, clicking on the link Katie has just sent.

The photos are of Maya and me walking from the front door of her building last night, my arm placed around her shoulders. Then again of us in the car, Maya leaning in closer to me with a smile, looking like she wants to kiss me. My eyes quickly scan the comments, most of which are mocking words about Valentine's Day, my whipped status, vile commentary about what probably happened later on that night, and a few about my car.

"I thought your agent had taken care of this, Erik. You said—"

"He did," I say with quiet anger.

"So what's this?" she pleads.

All I can do is stare at the phone and think. It's been weeks since that last round of photos. Doug assured me that, not only was the guy posting them banned from the site, but also that this shit was over and done with.

"Why would someone still be doing this? We aren't even that interesting anymore. Who still cares?"

"It has to be personal, that's all I can think." It was my original thought and now, more than ever, that feeling hits me again.

"What, like a crazy fan of yours?"

I slowly shake my head in thought. "It's too…random. Or… maybe specific. How many people even knew I'd be with you that first night at the coffee bar? Or the day I came by to pick you up in my car? Or last night?"

Her brow lowers as she considers that.

"More importantly, why focus on you, like in all those photos without me? You're obviously the target here, Maya."

"Which means it has to be a fan. Someone who hates that I'm dating you," she says as though that's obvious.

"One who has this much free time to dedicate to it? One who's never pulled a stunt like this with any other woman I've dated?"

"All of whom were white," she points out.

That one gives me pause but doesn't discount one nagging thought.

"Okay but…how many people even knew I was meeting you that first night at the coffee shop? As far as the public was concerned, you hadn't even replied to me yet. I asked you out spur of the moment when you finally called, and only you knew where I was going to meet you. Well...you and your friends."

"Wait...are you suggesting that...?"

"No," I reply, but even I note the small pause.

"You are! Do you honestly think my friends would stoop this low? That they'd do something like this?"

"Of course not," I say, backing down now that I realize it was stupid to bring up.

"Never mind that *you're* the one with the crazy ex-girlfriend which you were certainly quick enough to dismiss as a possibility after the first time. But no, it must be one of *my* friends who is the culprit."

She's irate, but now I'm getting defensive as well. "Maya, I'm just asking you to consider all options, all *likely* options, based on the facts. Even if Tessa did have it out for you, how the hell would she know we'd be at that coffee shop that night? There are a handful of people, beyond those in the shop that night, who knew. Who knew then, *and* would know all this time where you'd be on a daily basis?"

"Okay, fine, let's entertain this idea of yours," she says in a scathing voice. "On my end, there's me, my friends, Zia, Gabrielle, and Demetria. That's it. And just who did *you* happen to tell? Perhaps your teammates or some of *your* close friends?"

"Just my agent who was with me at the time."

"Hmm," she hums sarcastically.

I cough out a sharp laugh. "Oh come on Maya. Yes, it was my agent trying to sabotage my life because...?"

"Maybe he's jealous, or secretly hates you, both of which you seem to be implying with my friends."

"I'm not implying anything. If you trust your friends, then I do too. I just...I just want to find out who's doing this dammit!"

"And I don't? Considering *I'm* the one being profiled?"

She's not calming down, and I know better than to suggest such a thing. Instead, I turn to start the engine, realizing that speaking will only dig myself a deeper hole.

We ride in silence, but the anger brewing between us is loud enough to fill the car. When I drop Maya off in front of her apartment, she doesn't even say goodbye but does manage to slam the door on me.

Which I probably deserve.

I scan the street around us, filled with Brooklynites, wondering who the stand out is, the one that might be secretly taking photos of her.

After making sure she gets into her building without hassle, I drive off, my anger still brewing. I pull over where I can, the car still in idle as I call up my agent.

"Erik, I know, I know," Doug says, sounding even more exasperated than Maya was.

"Fix this, Doug. Find out who it is and…fix it!"

"Trust me, I will," he says, sounding just as determined as I feel.

The anger is still there by the time I board the plane to Montreal for tonight's game.

I have no idea who this person is that has such a fixation on Maya. Even my teammates are suspect at this point. The thought fills me with a tinge of traitorous guilt since I know my teammates well enough. Besides, none of them have it out for me, as far as I know.

Now, I understand why Maya was so upset. She's known her friends for most of her life, much longer than I've known my teammates. But I know better than anyone that knowing someone that long doesn't mean they can't be bitter or jealous or resentful.

Still, I should have kept that thought to myself.

I'll give it time to cool off, get through tonight's game and deal with repairing the damage when I get back.

I just hope Maya is here waiting for me when I do.

CHAPTER THIRTY-ONE

MAYA

I'm at Erik's next home game. Alone.

I thought it best this way.

I watch the kids already lining up along the sides waiting for warm-up in hopes that they'll be lucky enough to get a puck. A smile comes to my face as I remember this is precisely how Erik and I first met.

When the lights dim, signaling that the players are about to take the ice in preparation for the game, I reflexively grip my cell phone tighter.

My eyes fall the text message still open there:

I'm sorry.

A soft smile comes to my lips. I haven't responded yet. I'm hoping my attendance tonight gives Erik my answer.

When the players begin skating out, unlike the first night I saw him, it takes me no time to zero in on #28. My smile broadens when, even through his clear shield, I see his eyes desperately scanning the area where my seat is. They rapidly pass over me before doubling back and widening in surprise.

I'm the next to be surprised when he cuts out of the loop

he's supposed to be skating in with the rest of the players and flies across the ice, slamming into the transparent partition right in front of me.

Just like that first night, his blue eyes practically leap across the distance between us to bore into me. They read me, trying to determine if all is well between us.

It's okay, I mouth, following it with a smile.

His lips widen into a grin and he follows it with a wink.

Jeg elsker deg, he mouths. *I love you*, he repeats, just for good measure.

I laugh, and he winks again before skating off, moving faster than ever.

"Did you see that?"

"Oh my God, that was so sweet."

"She's so lucky."

The whispers send a smug thrill through me...then a shiver of trepidation. It's only been two days, but there have been no more pictures posted of either Erik or me. I still have no idea who is posting them, but I *do* know it's none of my friends.

I still hate that Erik—even if only briefly—made me even consider them. But all the blame can't be laid on him. Hell, I considered everyone from Katie to my coworkers to the manager of the nail salon next door who always stands outside smoking a cigarette.

But none of that matters right now. We'll figure it out, Erik and me. All I know is that I've made the right choice by coming back to him.

Just because of the wink.

After the game, I meet him by the exit toward the locker rooms.

"I'm sorry, Maya."

"Like I said, it's okay," I reply with a reassuring smile.

I have to admit I'm not entirely opposed to this groveling

version of Erik, especially since he seems to have no shame doing it right in front of his fans standing nearby and his teammates that pass by on their skates back to the locker room. He completely ignores the smirks and eye rolls as he apologizes yet again.

"No really, I shouldn't have even hinted that it could be your friends, especially since I don't even know them."

"Well...I suppose we'll have to rectify that."

"I'm game," he says with a smirk.

"And of course my mother."

That one evokes an inhale before nodding his head. "Absolutely."

"Okay, so you have to be nice to him," I warn my friends as we sit at our usual booth at the bar, earlier in the week than usual. Even Demetria was able to make it, with the declaration she had to go straight back to her crazy job after this.

I certainly haven't told them about what Erik suggested. I don't need to taint their image of him before they even meet. Mostly because I kinda sorta like the guy.

Doug, Erik's agent, has once again urged *The Pucking News* to take down the photos and banned the newest account posting them. According to the site, the user—whom they still are unable to identify—is using a VPN to create new accounts without being recognized as the IP address that's been banned.

"Best behavior," Gabrielle says, sitting up straighter.

"Yes, yes," Demetria says with smile and roll of the eyes.

"I just want to see if he's as hot in person as he is in that *Ideal Gentleman* magazine," Zia says.

We're one drink in when I see him walk through the door. I'm not sure if it's my imagination, but the noise of the crowd seems to stop and time slows down as he walks toward us. Naturally, more than a few heads turn, some leaning over to say something to him. They're probably asking for a photo or autograph, but the man has only one thing on his mind, politely declining.

"Erik," I say, hearing how breathy my voice is.

"Maya," he says, looking down at me with a grin before taking the chair we've set up at the head of the booth. He turns his head to look around at my friends. "Hello—"

"Okay so who exactly is this crazy fan of yours that's been messing with our girl?" Gabrielle says, jumping right in, practically taking over the table as she leans across Demetria to ask.

"Are you sure it isn't this model ex-girlfriend of yours she told us about?" Demetria says, giving him a penetrating gaze.

"We just want to make sure our friend is safe is all," Zia says.

"Guys!" I say, giving them incredulous looks.

They all turn to me with expressions of innocence.

"It's okay," Erik says with a chuckle as he slowly swirls his beer and looks around the table. "It's good to know that I'm not the only knight in armor who wants to protect my girlfriend."

"Aww," Zia gushes, because of course, she would.

Gabrielle gives him a satisfied smile. Demetria's is more grudging.

An hour later, they're still just as smitten as I am. Especially when he pulls The Move on them.

"...down," Erik says, placing his half-empty beer on the table.

The reaction to a repeat of the trick he showed me that first night in the coffee shop receives a mix of laughs and groans.

"Okay, okay, I think we have to officially salute to our approval of Team Mayik," Gabrielle says, lifting her glass.

"Team what?" I ask.

"You know, Maya, Erik, Mayik. You can't be official unless you combine names and Eriya sounds too...girly. Marcus and I are *Marcelle*." She says this with a hard c in the middle, pronouncing it like she's announcing a new model of luxury car.

"Gabs, how many beers have you had?" Demetria says, wrinkling her face at her. She turns back to me, closing her eyes and sighing, before opening them and saying, "Maya, Erik, I really do wish you both good luck."

"Not good luck...congratulations," Zia says, raising her glass.

I laugh and lean into Erik, whispering in his ear. "I guess you've officially won them over."

"So, the two of you are headed to Norway this summer, Maya tells me?" Mom starts off.

It's the next weekend, and we're at a restaurant near Brooklyn Bridge Park, with a gorgeous view of the bridge spanning the East River to Manhattan beyond.

The waiter blessedly returns with the bottle of wine Erik ordered, and he waits for him to pour for the three of us before he answers.

"Yes," Erik says, giving my mother an easy smile. "I want Maya to see where I come from, where I was born and raised." He makes sure to reach under the table to grab my free hand and squeeze.

"But you lived in Sweden as well?"

"Mom," I say, giving her a hard look. I haven't told her the details about Erik's background, just that his mother died and he went to live in Sweden with his father before eventually being drafted into the NHL.

She just raises her brow my way as though she has every right to ask about it.

"It's okay, Maya," Erik says, squeezing my hand again. He turns his attention back to my mother, still with a gracious smile on his face. "Yes, I moved to Sweden when I was twelve, but Norway will always be what I consider my home. That's why I want to take Maya there."

"I see," Mom says, taking a sip of wine and leaving the air around us filled with tension. It gets worse with her next line of discussion. "It must be thrilling being a professional hockey player, all that fame and money and...attention."

"Mom," I say, a bit firmer this time.

"I get it," Erik says, interjecting. "You're Maya's mother, and naturally you have concerns about the type of man she's with. I'd be concerned too if my daughter was dating someone like me, someone who is in the public eye, someone who gets a lot of attention from other women, someone who is gone half the time to one city or another for a game."

"Someone who gets a lot of photos taken and posted online as well," she points out.

"Ma, I already explained that. It's been dealt with."

Hopefully for good this time.

"Until the next time," she says, raising her eyebrows at me.

Erik interjects to save the day. "I have little control over what the public does, but I promise I will do—*have* done—everything I can to protect her and make sure she's safe."

My mother sets the wine down to consider him, thawing only slightly.

Erik lets go of my hand and leans in on the table, his expression serious now. "As far as everything else, I know what Maya has told you about my background; I also know what she hasn't told you." He pauses, staring briefly at the table before bringing his gaze back to my mother, more intense than ever. "My father abandoned my mother and me before I was born. I know what it's like to grow up without a man in the house. I know what it's like to feel that sting of rejection from the person who should be there for you.

"Even though my mother seemed fine with it, it's something that has always affected me. I'd never do that to Maya, or any children we might have."

My heart lurches at that, then starts beating double-time. He turns to give me a meaningful stare. "She'll never have to worry about where my loyalties lie, because as long as she'll have me, they'll lie with her, and only her."

"As for taking her to Norway, it's not just for her sake, but mine as well. It's for both of us. I know about her, about her life in Brooklyn. Now, I want her to know as much as possible about me. I want her to meet the people and places that mean the most to me." He shoots me a grin. "I also want everyone there to meet her just as I'm meeting you."

He turns back to my mother. "I know these are just words, but I'm hoping over the next few months you'll see the truth in them. Ms. Jackson. I want to be with your daughter, and only her."

I exhale with a smile and turn my attention to my mother. Surely she can't object to that amazing confession. She gives me an indulgent smile, then lifts her glass to Erik in silent approval. I hope it's not just for show.

After dinner, Erik orders a car for my mother and me.

"That was amazing, Erik," I say, pulling him aside. "Thanks so much for going all out like that. You really impressed her."

He wraps his arms around me and stares into my eyes. "I meant every word of it, Maya. You're mine. I'm yours. I'd never make you feel any other way."

God, this man...

I lift up on my toes to kiss him, not giving a damn what

anyone around us might think. He's mine, and this is how I'm showing him.

I pull away with a smile. "Goodnight."

He smiles back. "Goodnight."

I run to the car and slide in next to my mother, feeling like I'm floating on cloud nine.

"So...what did you think?" I ask as soon as we're driving away.

I'm prepared for some drawn-out, begrudging acceptance filled with caveats about it being too early to tell, or about us still being too different, or about how they were just words, but she surprises me.

"I think," she says, reaching out to squeeze my hand, "You've made a good choice in that Norwegian hockey player of yours."

Well, that was better than expected.

CHAPTER THIRTY-TWO

ERIK

I'm on Maya's block, here to take her to her half-sister's birthday party. I know she's on edge about it, which is why I'm glad there's no game today, so I can take her myself.

When I turn the corner, I'm surprised to see Maya standing outside the front door to her building, even though I told her I'd come up to her apartment. She is nibbling on the edge of what looks like a pop tart.

It's been several weeks with no more photos, but I'm still concerned about her just hanging out in front of her place, especially on days when I come to pick her up. I do recall that being a particularly photo-worthy event for our former stalker.

Right at this moment that individual—who I'd happily drive a fist into—is replaced by another man, who appears to be hitting on her. Maya—my *girlfriend*—is gorgeous as hell, so she's bound to draw attention even of the non-photographic kind. All the more reason I'd have preferred meeting her up at her front door.

As I near the two of them, I'm finally able to pick up on the conversation. Maya is slightly turned away from me so she can't see me approaching. The young man with her has his attention squarely focused on her.

"So Maya, when you gonna let a brotha have a taste of your pop tart?"

"Really, Jarell?" she replies with a laugh. "Boy, *bye*."

"So it's like that, huh?"

"Yeah, it's like that," she says, still with a laugh in her voice.

I hang back a bit, just to see where this is going. Mostly, I find it amusing. It's obvious they know each other somehow. I'm just wondering how well.

"So it's been a minute since I seen you last. What you been up to?"

"Mostly avoiding men who ask for some of my pop tart."

Jarell chuckles, then does that thing with his tongue, sliding it across his lips in a way that indicates he's not even remotely done asking for some of her pop tart.

I'm just about ready to step in when I hear her next words.

"But right now, I'm waiting for my *boyfriend* to pick me up."

"So you got a man?"

"Yeah, I got a man. A man who will be here in any minute."

"But I see your man got you waitin' out here on the street though."

"I'm waiting out here on the street so my man doesn't have to walk up two flights of stairs to get me. That's what a *girlfriend* who appreciates her *boyfriend* does."

I smirk, feeling that rush that comes over me every time I realize this woman is mine. Forget birthday parties and words uttered in the heat of passion. To hear Maya so publicly proclaim that she's mine—I'm *her's*, that's what fuels that possessive nature in me.

"Which I for one do appreciate," I say, finally announcing myself.

The looks on both their faces give me even more satisfaction, for two different reasons.

"Hey, you," Maya says, with that fantastic smile that always makes me feel like I'm Thor himself.

Jarell looks at me like I'm some alien species who has just landed in front of him. It turns a bit hostile when I come in to place my arm around Maya's waist.

"Okay, I see how it is," Jarell says, trying to stare me down. "You found yourself a white boy. Now the brothas are no longer good enough for you."

"Only the ones that insist on asking for some of my pop tart," Maya says with a pert smile next to me.

"Yeah, well..." he lets his eyes finish talking for him, sizing me up and, most likely noting that I have a few inches of height and more than a few pounds of muscle on him.

I let my own eyes finish the conversation, staring hard enough to give him the hint that he should move on.

"So, hey," he says, rolling his eyes back to Maya. "Since we all down with the swirl, how about that roommate of yours. I hear—"

"No," she says in a flat tone.

He laughs and waves her off.

"Man, whatever," he says as he starts walking away. "I'll see you around then, Maya. Until homeboy here moves you up to *SoHo* or some shit."

I look over to see Maya watching him go with an amused smirk on her face. I squeeze her waist, and she turns to me with a laugh.

"Don't tell me you're jealous of Jarell of all people."

"I'm jealous of everyone," I say with a grin that makes her laugh. "Let's go before I have to start fending off every other boy in the neighborhood."

She wraps her arm around my waist to match mine around hers as we go.

"So...I said I'd pick you up at your door," I remind her.

"Is this about Jarell or the photographs? Because I told you, I'm done being worried about that. First of all, it's been weeks, just after Valentine's Day since it last happened. Second of all, I can't *not* live my life because of it. Even my dad said not to worry about coming out today because anyone who doesn't belong at this thing will stand out. It's the *suburbs*." She rolls her eyes as she says it.

"Yes, but we still have no idea who it was." I squeeze her waist again.

"Let's not talk about it, I'm nervous enough about today as it is."

"You still nervous about this?" I ask in surprise.

She shrugs against me. "It's a birthday party, so hopefully Sidney will be too preoccupied to spend too much time focusing on me and why I'm just now starting to show up in her life. I think it's fair to say that I'm at least partially to blame for that."

I stop walking and turn to her. "You need to stop that right now. Your dad was the one who decided he wanted nothing to do with you."

She stares at me, eyes concentrating hard. "Is this because of your father?"

I start in surprise, then sigh. "Sorry, I guess I'm projecting."

I start walking her toward my car again.

She laughs uncomfortably next to me. "Well, at least yours wanted you in his life. I think my situation is the exact opposite, at least until now."

I cough out a sarcastic laugh at that.

"What?" She says, looking up at me.

I see my car only a few feet away and urge her toward it.

"Let's get going. I don't want to ruin today with my baggage. You have enough—"

"Erik," now it's her turn to stop us. "Today doesn't have to be about me and my issues. If something is affecting you, I want to know about it. I want to know everything about you."

I stare over her head into the distance, thinking of all the things I haven't told her about my relationship with my father. If I'm going to be any use to her, she needs to know where I'm coming from. I'm not stupid enough to know that I can be impartial when it comes to dads.

My eyes fall to her, and I bring my arms around her to pull her in. "Okay, I'll tell you everything along the way," I laugh lightly. "It may even make you feel better about your situation."

She pulls back to look at me, scrutinizing that statement. A half-smile appears on her face. "Everything."

"Everything," I promise.

CHAPTER THIRTY-THREE

ERIK

"It started when I was about fourteen. I told you about the town I lived in while I was in Sweden, Örnsköldsvik—people call it Ö-vik for short. The thing about this town is that hockey is played practically by everyone there. A fair number of other players in the NHL come from that city."

We're in my car, heading north out of town. It's Saturday morning so traffic isn't too terrible, allowing me to concentrate even as I listen to the instructions of the GPS to get to the home of Maya's dad.

"Despite not having grown up playing hockey, at least not to the extent that most of the other boys in that town had, my brother included, I actually turned out to be pretty good at it." I feel a wry smile come to my face as I stare out ahead of me. "It helped that I spent so much time practicing. I was good enough to get into the junior leagues, which was good preparation for being in the professional Swedish Hockey League."

My smile disappears.

"My brother Liam was just as good, maybe even a bit better than I was. Then one day..."

I breathe slowly out my mouth, letting the pause linger.

"You don't have to tell me if you don't want to," Maya says softly.

"No," I say, without turning to her. If I look at her, I'll lose my nerve, filing away this part of my past, yet again, for a future date. "I'll tell you."

There's another pause before I continue.

"We were always fighting, especially around hockey. In Sweden, the sport isn't as aggressive as it is here. Not that it stopped us." I feel a soft chuckle in my chest as I remember some of our more memorable altercations. It evaporates when I come to the one that started it all; that day our lives changed forever.

"My brother and I had gotten into another fight." It occurs to me that I've said "brother" not "half-brother" as usual. It's always like that when I think about this day, especially with what happened afterward.

"We were on our way home and...words were said. I attacked him and...he fell. A compound fracture."

I hear Maya gasp next to me. "Jesus..."

I can still picture it, vivid as the day it happened. That jagged edge of something pale ripping through his pants. There wasn't as much blood as I expected. Frankly, I would have been less disgusted by that than the odd way his leg was bent.

"It took about five months to make a full recovery, or as much of one as he was going to make. We were in a city where hockey was as popular as football here is in a lot of states. He had a permanent limp; it was subtle after a while but still there. Certainly enough to prevent making it to any professional league."

I have yet to look at her since this revelation but decide now is as good a time as any to gauge her reaction so far. She has a thoughtful expression, adding a soft smile when my eyes meet hers.

"Go on," she urges. "I'm listening."

I nod and face forward again, feeling my determination come back.

"My life in that house wasn't exactly pleasant before that, but afterward...it was hell. Everyone looked at me with suspicion and resentment, which was odd because," I pause, taking an unconscious deep breath before continuing, "Liam never once pointed the finger at me, even though I was the one who pushed him."

"Really?"

"Really," I say nodding, still feeling my brow furrow in confusion this many years after the fact. "Liam told everyone he had simply tripped. I mean, everyone knew we had been in a fight during practice just prior to that, so it's no wonder most people were suspicious, especially his mother. But...it was my dad..."

This time I need the pause, mostly to stifle my anger.

"Just the way he looked at me. As though he assumed I had not only been the cause of Liam's injury but had done it deliberately. Just that split second of accusation and resentment in his eyes, the one that told me which son he favored, which son meant the most to him. As if I hadn't already known since the day I was born..."

"He must have seen the reaction in mine," I say, looking thoughtfully ahead. "The surprise and hurt and bitterness. Again, it lasted only a moment, but...we were never the same after that. I mean, it wasn't exactly perfect before, but we just stopped acknowledging each other after the fact. I think if I'd asked, he would have sent me back to Oslo to live with my grandfather as I'd wanted from the start, but I was invested in hockey by then. Mostly because..."

I hiccup a soft laugh. "Mostly because Liam was the one to insist on it."

"Really?" Maya asks again.

I turn to her with a half-cocked smile. "I didn't understand it either. When Liam was in his room after the surgery, it wasn't his mother or our father he wanted to speak to, it was me. I thought for sure it was just to lay on some verbal abuse, which I was perfectly willing to accept, but instead, he was almost...serene."

I turn back to the road and shake my head. "Maybe it was the pain killers they had him on. Before I could even apologize for what happened to him, he told me that I couldn't quit hockey. That I had no right to quit, certainly not because of him; that I was too good to let it go to waste. He said he knew how much I wanted to get out of there, out of that town, hell, even out of the country, and that hockey was my best shot.

"Neither of us ever revealed what he told me, and I'm sure our father and, especially his mother resented the fact that I put even more effort into hockey after that. As much as Liam must have hated me, all the more so after that, I'll never understand why he told me that."

I hear Maya exhale a soft laugh. "It makes so much sense now," she says, almost to herself.

I feel my brow crease as I turn to her. "What does?"

"Why you're so aggressive when you play. Why you get into so many fights. The guilt must be eating you up."

I don't respond.

"Don't deny it, Erik. You probably aren't even aware of how much you think about your brother and that day when you step out onto the rink."

"I don't *deny* it, I just...I don't think it has that much of an impact." As though that day doesn't flash through my head, only to be exiled by sheer force before each game.

"We're our own worst judge of character," she says with a small smile. "But at least I understand why your relationship with your father is so strained."

"Before I went off to join Djurgårdens in Stockholm, he and I fought over something. I don't even remember what it was, but If I'm honest with myself—judging my own character," I turn to her with a wry smile, "I most likely started it, giving him a reason not to help me move down there. Then later, by the time I was drafted by the League here in America, there wasn't even a phone call since I'd cut him off completely."

"So why do you think he's suddenly getting back in touch?"

Naturally, I've told Maya about the text messages I've been getting from him after each game.

I shrug as I stare ahead. "I don't know. I suppose he thinks enough time has passed."

"And...you don't want to call to find out why?"

"No," I say, almost to an aggressive degree. I relax and sigh. "There's too much there to unpack over a single phone call."

I sense her nodding in my periphery. "What about stopping in Sweden this summer, when you go back to Norway?"

I reach out one hand to take hers. "When *we* go," I remind her with a grin.

She laughs softly. "Okay, when *we* go to Norway. I'd love to see where you first started playing hockey."

My grin disappears and I stare ahead.

"We'll save that for another trip," I say noncommittally. This trip to Norway is meant to bring Maya and me closer together. The last thing I need is the sledgehammer of my father, and worse, Liam and Freja, coming in to shatter that.

I squeeze her hand before letting go. "Let's just get through today. I know it's been stressful for you. Forget about my issues for now."

"Right," she says, straightening up and exhaling slowly. "I guess I have my own demons to excise."

CHAPTER THIRTY-FOUR

MAYA

Erik parks along one of the residential streets away from Dad's house since the cul-de-sac has apparently been overtaken by the party.

I get out and stare back at the entrance to Hummingbird Lane—even the street name is like something out of a storybook—with a doubtful look. At least my dress is on point. I bought the light pink (definitely not my color) sleeveless shift specifically to match the theme of Sidney's party. With the white sandals I have on, I feel like something out of *Martha Stewart Living* magazine.

"It'll be fine," Erik says, as he gets out from the driver's side.

I give him a brief smile, which fades as I watch him head around to the trunk of his car instead of joining me on the sidewalk. When he opens the trunk, I realize what he's doing.

"You got her a gift?" I ask in surprise as I wander around to take a peek.

It's a large pink box, obviously professionally wrapped considering how intricate the fluffy bow on top is.

"I couldn't very well show up to a birthday party without a gift," he says with a grin.

"I only got her a gift card," I say, thinking about the pink envelope in my purse. The card is nice, one of those specially decorated ones with lots of rhinestones and butterflies. According to Dad, she's big into American Girl—she has two of the dolls—and considering the prices I saw online just for accessories I thought the $50 value was a decent enough gift from a big sister (half-sister).

"There's nothing wrong with a gift card," Erik says, trying to reassure me. "But just so that you don't feel like I'm trying to one-up you..." He flips open the small card on top of his gift.

From: Maya & Erik

I smile and tilt my head at him. "You didn't have to."

"Of course I did," he says, bringing one hand to the back of my neck and leaning down to kiss me.

"Do I at least get to know what it is?" I ask with a teasing smile after he pulls back.

"What fun would that be?" he says with a grin as he lifts the gift up and closes the trunk.

I laugh. "What if she hates it?"

"Then all is doomed," he teases, wrapping his free arm around my waist. "But she won't. I checked with Brian, my teammate. He has a six-year-old girl, so I have it on good authority that what's in this box is all the rage."

When we reach the street, the music blasting one of the latest pop tunes fills the air, but it's nothing compared to the noise of children enjoying themselves. I have to wonder if the entire neighborhood—Clear Creek *Estates*—wasn't invited to this thing.

Sadly, there appears to be no petting zoo. That doesn't

mean every other birthday staple under the sun is in attendance from women in princess costumes to clowns making animal balloons to a pink bouncy castle.

I see an area sectioned off for the really young toddlers and babies, my brother Damien included, all being supervised by a group of mothers.

I search the crowd of adults scattered in small groupings along the short street. I'm almost ashamed to admit I'm relieved to see that most of them have either beer bottles or glasses of wine in their hands. Apparently, this party has expanded into a bona fide neighborhood event for both adults and kids. Thank goodness. My nerves could use a little numbing.

Which is silly.

It's a kid's birthday party for Pete's sake.

"Ho, ho!" says a voice near us. Erik and I turn to find a man amid a small group of other men, pointing a beer bottle our way with a grin on his face. "You're that hockey player. The Blades?"

"That's me," Erik says with a gracious smile, still holding onto my waist.

"Oh man, who knew Rebecca dragging my ass to this thing would be worth it. First the beer now this," he says, walking toward us. The other three men in his group follow him. "Bruins fan myself, but hell if you aren't something on the ice. Sørenson, right?"

"Right," Erik says, and I bite back a smile as I recall learning the *proper* pronunciation of his name.

"You don't mind if I get a picture, do you? The guys at work are gonna love this."

"Actually, I should deliver this to the birthday girl first, but I'd be happy to later on."

"Oh yeah, sure thing," the guy says, as though just now noticing the huge pink box under Erik's arm.

The man seems to just now notice me as well. His eyes land on me, slide to Erik, back to me, then to his arm still around my waist. His brow wrinkles, almost as if these ingredients stirred together in his head create a very new and interesting batter for his brain to bake.

"Huh," he says, then seems to shake it off in the face of a bona fide sports celebrity.

We continue on, earning a few more stares as I lead Erik to the table where the mountain of presents is.

"Let's find the alcohol," I say quickly after we add ours to the pile. "I need a beer before I talk to anyone."

This isn't the first time I've met Sidney. She's a sweet girl, boisterous in that way that excitable kids her age are. The few times this past year that I've come to visit the whole family instead of just Dad, she's probably been the most enthusiastic about the experience. Too old to be indifferent like Damien, who's still only three, too young to realize how awkward the situation is like the adults around her.

As if on cue, I hear my name screeched from across the street.

"Maya! You came!"

I turn to find a brown-skinned girl in a pink cotton ball of a dress, pink bows in her pigtails bouncing as she races toward me. With all the power of a pint-sized linebacker, she crashes into me, arms wrapped around my hips as she laughs into my stomach.

I'm too stunned to react.

Two other girls, both white, have followed her over. The three of them have glitter butterflies in various shades of pink and lavender painted all over their faces, yet another birthday staple at this over-the-top affair.

"This is Maya, my big sister," Sidney proudly announces to her friends.

Like a hit of some drug shot right into my veins, elation flows through my body with surprising fierceness.

"Who're you?" one of the girls asks, giving Erik a curious look.

"I'm Maya's boyfriend," Erik says, once again wrapping his arm around my waist now that Sidney has let go.

"But you're white?" she says, looking even more confused.

Right then and there I decide I don't particularly like this one and maybe she isn't the best influence for my little sister to be hanging around.

"A white person can date a black person, Haley," the other one says.

This one I find perfectly acceptable.

"I know that," Haley says sheepishly, slightly softening my original opinion of her.

Look at me, judging six-year-olds. *Very mature, Maya.*

"Happy Birthday, Sidney," I say, finally managing to get a word in edgewise. I place my hand on Erik's shoulder. "And yes, this is my boyfriend." I can't help casting a pointed glance at Haley. "Erik Sørenson."

"Daddy says he's a hockey player. Is that true?" Sidney asks, looking up at him with the same frank curiosity that Haley had.

"He is. And he's a very good one," I say, shooting him a dazzling smile. I feel his body vibrate with laughter underneath my hand.

Hopefully, I'm the only one who sees the wicked tinge to the grin Erik gives me in return.

"Maya! You're here!"

It's my dad's voice, and my heart does a panicky little flutter before I turn to find him approaching.

"She came, Daddy! She came!" Sidney yells, bouncing up and down.

The smile I planted on my face, falters a bit. Was everyone so sure I *wouldn't* come?

"Yes, she did," Dad says to Sidney with a grin. I get a huge smile of grateful appreciation, thus answering the question for me. "Thanks for coming, sweetheart," he says, leaning in to kiss my cheek.

His eyes slide to Erik. "And this must be the infamous hockey player."

"Erik Sørenson," he says, reaching one hand out for my dad to shake.

"Nice to finally meet you," Dad says, pumping his arm with vigor. This reception is almost a complete one-eighty from that with my mom. Dad might as well be meeting the mayor of the city. "Why don't we set you two up with some beer or wine?"

"But I want Maya to come play in the bouncy castle," Sidney protests.

"I think Maya's too big for that, baby," Dad says. "Maybe after she's played with the grown-ups a bit, she can join you in...something? Maybe get her face painted like yours?"

I shoot him a panicked look. He grimaces with a shrug and a smile.

"Yes! But you have to get the pink and hot pink only, like me, Maya," Sidney says with all the authority of a mini dictator.

"Right," I say, hopefully sounding noncommittal before turning my attention back to Dad. "You mentioned beer?"

He guides us away, sending Sidney off back to the bouncy castle. "Sorry about that. There isn't much here for a twenty-five-year-old to do with a six-year-old."

"And face painting was your go-to?" I reply, though I can't help laughing at the idea.

"I for one would love to see your gorgeous face covered in glitter butterflies," Erik says with a grin.

Dad chuckles next to me as he leads us to a driveway where

I see several large metal tubs. Condensation drips down the sides, and several long necks from beer bottles stick out from piles of ice.

"Ha-ha," I say sarcastically. "I don't see either of you offering up your face as a canvas. What's good for the goose..."

"Here we are," Dad says. "Take your pick."

I grab something that is neither a Bud Light or the latest craft IPA. Erik does the same, then whips out his keys to remove the tops from both our bottles with a keychain opener.

I love a man who comes prepared.

We get precisely one second to take our first sips before Erik is once again accosted.

"I told you, Peter," the same man from before says, leading another man up the driveway toward us. "Erik Sørenson, in the flesh."

Erik plasters on a smile, and I subconsciously take a step away. I've caught the curious looks at this loud announcement, and pretty soon it'll probably be a mad rush.

"Dwight, you didn't tell me a bona fide hockey player would be at this thing. I woulda brought my buddy from work." The man turns back to Erik. "Say, how about that picture now?"

Dad turns to me and gives a guilty shrug.

I raise one cynical eyebrow as though I'm used to it.

"So this is what it's like then?" he asks me as Erik gets lost in a sea of suburban dads.

"Not always. Mostly it's the online stuff that bothers me. In person, people are more respectful. Online they can say and *post* anything."

I eye him over my bottle as I take a sip.

"Yeah, I saw the photos."

"What did you think?" I ask sheepishly.

He stares ahead in the distance and his jaw hardens

slightly. I'm prepared for a good talking down, but I'm surprised at what he says.

"I thought...that I was glad I didn't meet the person who posted those photos of my daughter because I don't know what I would have done to him."

Once again, that surge of elation hits me. So he's still my dad after all.

"Oh, here comes Wanda."

I feel my muscles tighten. Sidney may think I'm the shit, but with Wanda, the term uncomfortable doesn't even begin to describe what hangs in the air between us.

"Maya, thank you so much for coming. Sidney can't stop talking about it."

It seems so...genuine. Even the smile on her face doesn't have that tightness to it, making me think of a cracked rubber band threatening to snap.

"Glad I could make it. This looks like fun."

"I'm just about to bring out the cake, do you want to help me put the candle in?"

"Um...sure," I say, thinking maybe hell doesn't sound like a bad alternative.

"Sidney will love it if she knows you helped out," Dad says, urging me on.

"Not a problem," I say with a tight smile.

I turn to tell Erik where I'm going, but by now he's lost in a world of selfies. Don't ever let it be said that only teenaged girls are into that kind of shamelessness.

I follow Wanda into the Jackson residence. Like all the McMansions in Clear Creek Estates it's somehow customized just enough to make it both very different, yet somehow utterly the same as all the other houses sitting a comfortable distance from the street. Theirs comes in red brick with black decorative shutters.

The kitchen is sufficiently gigantic, dark wood and black countertops with stainless steel appliances. On the island sits a small three-tier cake with pink and lavender airbrushed around the sides, following a path of fondant butterflies.

"Wow," I say, looking at it. "It's impressive."

Wanda gives me a panicky look as she pulls out a fat pink candle in the shape of a 6. "It was made by a friend."

"I wasn't...commenting on it or anything, I just—I think it's gorgeous. Sidney will love it."

She seems to exhale some of her obvious discomfort. It's followed by an inhale, which has my senses on edge. I take a sip of the beer that I'm glad I brought with me.

"Listen, part of the reason I asked you to help me with the candle is...I'd like us to talk. One on one. I don't think we've ever had an opportunity to do that."

I take another sip of beer, longer this time.

"Okay," I horrifyingly almost burp out after swallowing.

A brief smile comes to her face before she's thoughtful again.

"First, I want to apologize."

That one has me blinking in surprise, wondering what the catch is. Wanda has never been outright mean or rude to me. She's no wicked step-mother. She's just the woman who brought a little too much to the table at which I was already sitting.

"I was already an attorney when I met your father. At the time, he was studying to take the bar in Connecticut, which is stressful. I knew from the beginning what I was getting into, that it was not just him starting a new career, but him with an ex-wife and a teenage daughter.

"What I didn't know was how that would actually play out in real life. I admit I wanted him, and *only* him. But I also knew that if I wanted him, I'd have to take everything else."

She stares down at the island, the candle still in her hand. Her head pops back up, this time with that tight smile I'm used to.

"We both know how that worked out."

I raise my eyebrows in acknowledgment and take another sip of beer.

"In your father's defense, studying and taking the bar is time-consuming. He'd come back from his days spent with you, almost devastated at the idea that you didn't seem to want to talk to him anymore or do things with him. I was the one to suggest waiting until he'd finished taking the exam before seeing you again. That one is on me. Well, on both of us, but blame me, I was the one to wear him down."

I recall that summer. It was the beginning of the end.

"When we were finally married, I won't lie, I wanted him to forget all about his life in New York." She gives me a wide-eyed look. "Not *you* of course, or even Tonya, your mother. I Just...I wanted him to focus on the life we were building. That's why I suggested he invite you up here instead.

"This is the part where you're going to hate me, and I wouldn't blame you if you did. We tried right away to start a family, and...it didn't go according to plan. I began to resent the fact that, for all intents and purposes, he already had a family in you. That, since you existed, it was proof that the entire blame lay with me. I was an emotional mess at the time, and I...I used your father for support. To the exclusion of everything else."

The things you learn in moments of truth...

"Wanda, I don't hate you. How could I after this? I was a stupid, angsty teenager. Part of the blame is mine."

"No," she says with a rueful smile. "No, this isn't on you. You were his daughter. You had every right to him, and I—I took that from you. By the time Sidney did come along, I was more than happy for him—for *us* to try and start over again with you. I completely understand why you were reluctant by then. Why you shut him out.

"Then Damien came a bit prematurely and Sidney has always been a handful, and...well, life went on in a very chaotic way. Now, Damien's a late bloomer and, as it turns out, Sidney is most likely dyslexic."

"What?" I ask in surprise. "Dad never told me."

She gives me a sad smile. "He doesn't burden you with things. That life you see on Instagram and Facebook, it only shows the best things, the things he desperately wants you to be a part of. That's why he posts so much."

"And you?"

She gives me a considering look. "I do too. For his sake, for Sidney and Damien's sake...for my sake. There's always been this hidden piece missing here, and I realize it's you. The way Sidney so quickly took to you, the way Dwight is when you're around, the way he talks about you... *You're* missing, Maya."

"I can't speak for you. To be fair, I can't speak for myself either, at least as far as how it will turn out. But I do know this," She gives me an earnest look. "I want to try. Really try. No more avoiding New York. No more half-hearted invites. You're family, Maya...our family. Let's try and make that a reality.

"I know I'm putting something on your shoulders that I have no damn right to ask, not after how I've been, but I'm hoping you'll agree to this."

"Of course," I say, feeling that weight all of a sudden.

She gives me a knowing smile. "You don't have to agree just like that. Think about it, maybe dinner some time here or in New York. Baby steps."

"Okay," I say, feeling a little lighter.

"Good," she says, now with that genuine smile again. "For now, you can start by doing the honors."

She hands me the candle.

I take it and stare at the cake, dumbfounded. "I hate to ruin it. It's like a work of art."

Wanda laughs. "It's about twenty minutes away from being destroyed. Just stick it on top."

I place it in a free spot on top, wincing as it punctures the frosting.

"Let's get this party started, shall we?" she says, reaching out to carefully lift the cake.

"To the birthday girl," I say, lifting my bottle.

The laughter that comes after that isn't quite forced, nor is it quite effortless.

Baby steps.

CHAPTER THIRTY-FIVE

ERIK

So this is what hell is like.

"Looks like you guys are well on the way to making the finals at least. Just a few weeks to go...you getting amped yet?"

"Hey, you're Swedish right? My brother did one of those DNA things, and it turns out my family's nineteen percent Scandinavian. We're practically cousins!"

"How the hell did you end up at a birthday party in the middle of suburbia?"

"Say, what are you? Like...six-four, six-five? I coulda sworn I was only two inches shorter than that. I must be shrinking."

"I heard your boss, whatshisname, that Magnus Reinhold? Reinhardt? Anyway, I heard he was looking to get Vasylyk in a trade. Please don't tell me he's getting rid of Grigory Mikhailov. Talk about a dumbass move."

"Could you sign this one too? It's for my nephew."

"Hey, you're looking pretty low there. You need another beer?"

Finally, a question worth answering.

"That would be great," I say, finishing off the last little bit of beer I've been milking to death to avoid having to talk too much. Where is Maya anyway?

"Actually," I feel a hand come from behind to gently touch my shoulder. "It looks like the birthday celebration is about to begin."

I turn to see a thin blonde who looks like she could be anything from twenty-five to forty-five, guiding me away from the crowd. She hands me a bottle of the same beer I've been drinking.

"Thanks," I say.

"No problem," she says with a laugh, hand moving down to my back. "The men aren't the only hockey fans here. The thing is, we women have a bit more tact and understanding about personal space."

"Right," I say, noting how her hand remains firmly on my back.

"So, a bona fide Blades player all the way up here in Connecticut. This must be an *exciting* change of pace for you."

I get that it's a joke, but I sip my beer instead of laughing with her. I do twist out from underneath her hand to face her, figuring small talk is relatively harmless. At least it's a distraction until the cake arrives.

"I'm sure you're bored to death talking about hockey."

"Actually, I enjoy it. It is my chosen career, after all." More importantly, it keeps specific topics of discussion from coming up.

"Is that so?" she says, her smile only deepening. "Then let's talk shop."

That's when I realize my mistake. The hand on my back. The missing ring from said hand. The half-empty glass of white wine in the other. The location she's taken me to, slightly further up in this cul-de-sac.

I should have known better than to think suburban moms were safe territory. Surely they have better things to do than try and hook up with a professional hockey player?

"This will be your first year making it to the playoffs right? At least as a Blades player."

"Right." I nod, deciding this is as good a segue as any to escape in as nice a way as possible. "I should—"

"You know, blond men have never really done it for me. There's something slightly incestuous about the whole thing." The gleam in her eye makes me think maybe she enjoys taking a dip into the same gene pool more than she lets on. "I'm a natural blonde myself, complete with Scandinavian roots."

What is it with Americans and ancestry, specifically of a particular type? Either way, it's not my concern.

"My girlfriend is probably waiting for me, so I should get back to the party."

"Girlfriend," she says, laughing lightly, as though I'm a lovesick teenager who's going steady with his first crush, instead of a *real* woman. She pats my chest and gives me a direct look that I don't need an interpreter to read.

"Yes, *girlfriend*," I stress, taking hold of her hand and placing it back down by her side. "As in the woman I came with. As in the woman I'm going home with. As in the only woman I'm interested in."

Her eyelashes flutter in surprise, and her head snaps back with an offended look, as though I've just slapped her.

The commotion further down, where the main party is, gets louder and I see Maya and Wanda walking toward a long table, the latter with a cake in her hands.

"Looks like it's time to cut the cake. Enjoy the rest of the party," I say, then walk past her without looking back.

I see Maya tilting her head at me with a cynical smile. She

detours my way, pointedly looking past my shoulder at where I left the woman and her wine.

"Don't tell me you're jealous of that woman, of all people?"

She brings her arms around my waist to look up at me. "I'm always jealous."

"Don't be." I wrap my arms around Maya and lean in for a kiss.

"Eww!" some of the girls nearby squeal.

I pull away with a grin. Maya bites back a smile. "I should probably go help wish my sister a happy birthday."

"Before we scandalize the entire neighborhood," I say with a laugh.

I watch her go over to stand next to Wanda as she lights the candle. Sidney is bouncing in place as she watches. I join in to sing happy birthday and clap along with everyone else when she leans in to blow out the candle.

The cake turns out to be an alarming shade of pink inside. I pass on a slice, which all the girls in attendance are more than happy to devour, including my girl.

"How is it?" I ask, frowning at the neon slab on her plate.

"Not bad," she says, tick-tocking her head side to side. "I think it's supposed to be strawberry. At least it's not as sweet as I feared it would be."

"Well, now I know what to get you for your birthday."

She laughs. "God, no. I think I aged out of this color fifteen years ago."

The presents come next. Sidney is ecstatic about Maya's gift, I suspect mostly because it's from her "big sister." She's also ecstatic about mine, hopefully because I chose right. It's some dollhouse for the latest "it" dolls. Considering it's nothing but pure pink fantasy, it seems to fit well within her color scheme.

"Maya, Maya!" she squeals, running up to us after the

presents have been secured away back to her home. "You promised to get your face painted like mine!"

"Did I?" she responds, with wide, wary eyes.

"Mmm-hmm," Sidney says, nodding her head vigorously.

"Well, I think your big sister is a little old for that."

"Please! Pretty please!" she pleads, hanging off Maya's arm.

She turns to me with a panicked look, and all I can do is laugh. That earns me a scowl.

"How about this? If Erik agrees to do it with me, then I'll do it. I don't want to be the only adult with my face painted." She twists her lips at me.

"You know what? Sure, why not?" I say, shooting a broad grin her way.

"Really?" she says, her brow creasing in panic.

"I'm secure enough in my masculinity to wear glittery pink butterflies on my face."

"Yay!" Sidney screeches, jumping up and down as she drags Maya toward the face-painting set-up. She returns to scowling at me.

Maya's first in the chair, and when she's done she comes out looking like some magical, mystical fairy. It gives me all sorts of sordid role-playing ideas.

When I take the chair next, the woman bites back a bemused smile. It doesn't prevent the brief bit of seductive morse code I get before she switches the dial back to professional birthday party hiree.

"Aww, you look so pretty," Maya gushes with a laugh. Sidney and her friends all giggle.

"Pretty enough for Instagram?" I tease.

"Instagram, now there's an idea," she says, digging into her purse for her phone.

"Oh, no you don't."

"What's the matter? I thought you were so secure in your

masculinity. Afraid the boys on the team might tease you?" she teases right back at me.

Now that she's said it, I can just picture it. The Valentine's Day cards flung my way on the bus at the beginning of this adventure will be nothing compared to what they come up with if they see me looking like this on Instagram.

I stare at Maya, who looks like something that just walked out of a fairytale with her pink dress and face covered in glittery butterflies. Suddenly, I want nothing more than to cement this moment for posterity.

"Okay, let's do it."

Her smile becomes lopsided as she gives me a skeptical look. "I was just joking."

"No, let's do it. It'll be a colorful addition to my feed."

The laugh she gives is hesitant, as though she's waiting for the punchline. When I reach into my back pocket to pull out my phone, she blinks in surprise.

"Come on," I urge, beckoning her closer to my side. I pull her in closer and lift the phone above us, tapping the phone app to take a selfie.

"Say...happy birthday Sidney," I urge.

She laughs, and I snap the photo, capturing it before she can even utter the words.

It's perfect.

"I wasn't ready!" she protests, craning her neck to look at the result.

"All the better," I say. "I'm posting this one."

She frowns but doesn't object, apparently finding her image somewhat acceptable. As though she could take a bad photo.

I post the image then type out the caption, showing it to Maya and Sidney when I'm done:

Celebrating the birthday of one special little girl, with my own special girl.

"You have over a million followers!" Sidney exclaims, noting what's obviously the most important factor here. "I want a photo too!"

Maya looks up at me with worry in her eyes, matching my sentiments about the idea. There's a reason I didn't even mention her half-sister's name. Even though there must be a thousand Sidneys in this part of the country alone, after what happened to Maya, I'm certainly not risking it.

"How about this? We can take one, all three of us and send it to your mom and dad to decide what they want to do with it."

She tilts her head to consider that, looking surprisingly mature as she does. "Okay."

"Great," I say as Maya shoots a relieved look my way.

Maya uses her phone and crouches down on one side of Sidney while I do the same on the other.

"Okay, one, two, three, happy birthday, Sidney!" she says. I smile as she snaps the shot.

"Looks good," she says, standing back up and staring down at it.

"I'd say it looks perfect."

Her eyes roll up to mine, catching me staring right at her and her face colors before she smiles.

"Better not speed. I can't even imagine what any police officer is going to think if he has to pull you over looking like that," Maya says, as she stares at me from the passenger side.

The sun is hanging low in the sky and she and I have both made our goodbyes after managing to disentangle ourselves from Sidney's insistence that we stay "just a little bit longer." It finally took her parents' intervention to allow us an escape.

"You could have washed it off before you left."

"But I look so *pretty*," I tease, shooting her a quick grin, which makes her laugh.

"Thanks for doing this with me, Erik," she says, falling back in her seat as I drive out of this labyrinth of a neighborhood.

"No problem. I had fun."

She laughs as though she doesn't quite believe that.

"No, really, it was worth it."

She laughs again. "So...how much shit are you going to get from your teammates for that photo?"

"They'll probably stuff my locker with fake butterflies and come up with stupid jokes or something, but it'll pass. Especially as we get closer to the playoffs."

"Are you nervous? About the playoffs, I mean."

I stare ahead. "I've made it to the finals in Florida, but we didn't win the cup. Still, being on the Blades from its inception feels different. It's like we're all part of an original family; even the ones who were drafted or traded in later on."

"Do you think you'll win?"

I laugh. "I never make that prediction ahead of time. If I don't, I still have two more years on my contract to make it happen."

"But you want to win."

"Of course. What kind of player would I be if I didn't? But sometimes getting there is half the fun. Besides, this year if we don't make it all the way, I get to go to Norway in time to see my cousin play at this event of his."

"Norway," Maya says almost in a sigh.

I turn to her. "Still want to go?"

She snaps her head around to face me. "Of course! I mean, it's only the second time I've left the country, so I'm a bit..."

"*Resfeber*," I finish for her.

She wrinkles her face. "Is that Norwegian?"

"Swedish," I confess. "Another one of those words with no real translation. It's that excited beat of your heart before a new journey begins."

"*Resfeber,*" she repeats, then laughs. "Yeah, I suppose that fits. My heart does kind of accelerate at the thought."

"Don't worry, I'll be there with you," I say with a grin.

She laughs. "But first, the playoffs."

I look thoughtfully ahead. "But first the playoffs."

CHAPTER THIRTY-SIX

ERIK

Maybe it's because the Blades didn't win it. We got as far as the second round before losing by one point to the Boston Bruins in the Stanley Cup playoffs.

I look down at my phone replay my dad's voice message again, feeling my irritation grow.

"Erik, I was sorry to see that you didn't make it all the way in the playoffs. Congratulations on getting as far as you did though. That is indeed an accomplishment.... I know you usually fly to Norway to stay for a few weeks after the season is over.... I would very much like to see you this time. Perhaps you can add a trip to Sweden as well? Please call. I would really like to talk to you. Goodbye, son. "

The last thing I need fouling my mood even more is a phone call with him. It's bad enough that my agent requested a meeting.

I actually don't mind meeting with Doug, he's amusing in his own way, and it usually means more money in my bank account, not that I need any more.

I declined meeting at his usual choice of an expensive

restaurant somewhere in Manhattan—which I'm sure he writes off anyway. The last thing I want is to make myself publicly available after that crushing loss. Instead, I'm here in his office.

"The good news is, you made it that far. Second round is damn good, Erik! Plus, you have two more years to try and win the cup."

"Thanks, Doug. Can we skip the pep talk? I'm supposed to meet my girlfriend in an hour or so."

"Right, right. After the year you two have had you're probably glad to be moving on to finding out what lucrative deals I've got set up for you. Better to be paid for getting photographed by choice than have some scumbag posting photos of you on some forum."

"A shame we still don't know who it is," I say in a mildly accusatory tone.

Doug doesn't miss it. "Listen, Erik, I tried, I really did. But you know these sites. People are anonymous. The best they could do was give me an IP address, and even that was useless since the guy was smart enough to use a VPN."

"I just don't understand what he thought he'd get out of it?"

"Some people are just weird that way. They do it for the attention, or hell, maybe he thought it would pay off somehow. I mean, you've got celebrity cachet and dating a black woman certainly is news even in this day and age. A few snaps of you and Maya on a coffee date. In your car. At your loft, even with the shades down—and Valentines Day? If only you were Kim Kardashian, the tabloids would have had a field day."

"Whatever, at least it's over now," I say, not wanting to think about that period in my life.

"Right, right," Doug says, visibly relaxing. "So, back to being photographed for profit. I have good news from our friend Sven Lindström. His hotel group is expanding into

Norway. Think of it, you and Maya getting a free stay in a five-star hotel while they butter you up with lots of money? I'd jump on the chance. Anyway, they've just purchased this unique property up in...well, I forget, but it's some sort of emersion in wilderness thing..."

The only reason I haven't stopped him is that something he said has lit a spark inside my head.

"How did you know?" I ask slowly, still deep in thought.

"Pardon?" Doug asks.

"You said something about photographs of Maya and me at my place with the shades down. There were no photos like that posted."

"Weren't there?" His brow is wrinkled in concentration. "I'm sure I saw some."

"No," I say in a steady voice. "I'm sure there weren't. And I'm sure if there were photos like that my agent would have told me about them."

Doug stares at me long enough for me to wonder if my suspicion is wrong. Then he swallows.

It's only by sheer force of will that I curb the instant surge of rage that overcomes me.

"What the hell have you done, Doug?" I demand in a voice so low that I even scare myself, mostly because I know that if I let go of the armrests my hands grip I'll do something regrettable.

"Erik." I can already hear him making excuses.

"Don't."

He stops and swallows again.

"Just tell me what you did and why."

Doug starts nodding his head, planting both palms on his desk and sliding them back and forth as though smoothing it down.

"It wasn't meant to go like that," he finally confesses.

My hands grip the armrests even harder.

"You know the Blades have been trying to...diversify their audience. I mean, why the hell else would they set up in Brooklyn? At this point in time, they probably should have just gone to the Bronx, but then they'd lose their entire base. No sane white person would ever go—"

I'm out of my seat and around the desk before he can even finish. I grab him by that stupid silk tie which probably cost more than season tickets for the Blades and lift him out of his seat. I shove him hard against the floor-to-ceiling glass window with a perfect view of lower Manhattan.

"Tell me why!"

"Erik!" He gasps.

"Tell me!"

"Okay, okay," he whispers through heavy breaths.

I loosen my grip since he's already turning red. But I don't dare let go.

"Like I said, it was...just an attempt to show that the Blades themselves were open to...diversification. Once I learned more about her, it seemed like a golden opportunity. A white player dating a black woman, and one originally from Brooklyn? It was a PR wet dream. I hadn't counted on the fact that the guy I usually have handle this stuff was going through a divorce at the time. I of all people can tell you how much it adds up. Bloodsuckers, all of them. Make damn sure you get a prenup before—"

"Focus, Doug," I warn him in a low growl.

"Right, right. He took more photos than he should have, the kind I had no interest in airing. That shot of you two kissing in Maya's doorway? The ones from your apartment, which you couldn't even see? Asshole wanted ten thousand! I told him to go to hell. I probably should have known what he'd do with them."

"After that, I paid him the money and thought that would be the end of it. But...he continued. Said he needed more. He figured Maya was a better target since no one would bat an eye at yet more photos of you. I hinted at bringing in the authorities for blackmail. He countered with the fact that he'd tell you I hired him if I didn't pay up. So I paid, twice as damn much this time. I told him if there was a third time, I'd go to the cops. I know how these people work; they just keep coming back for more and more. I kept waiting for the next time and...it never came."

I let go of Doug but keep both arms planted against the glass on either side of him. "So you know who it is, after all?"

He nods.

"And now you're going to do something about it."

He nods again.

"And then you're going to cancel our contract."

His eyes go wide in panic. "Erik! Let's not be hasty. Yes, I fucked up but—"

"It's over, Doug. I can't be with someone I don't trust."

I walk out before he can say another word. I'm sure the phone calls and emails will come, begging me to reconsider. The thought only adds to my foul mood.

Right now, I just want to escape back to Norway with my girlfriend.

PART II

SUMMER & FALL

CHAPTER THIRTY-SEVEN

ERIK

"What kind of cheese is this? Is good."

I turn to see Grigory inspect what's left of the cracker in his hand with some soft cheese spread on top that someone shoved at him as soon as we walked in.

We're at Wedge Appeal, the cheese shop where Maya's roommate works. According to Maya, this was initially supposed to be a small celebration in honor of Katie being made assistant manager. She somehow turned it into a going-away party for us just before we set off for Norway tomorrow.

Now, I'm not sure what to call it. Perhaps a violation of the fire safety code, considering how many people are here.

I see Maya making her way to me. Last night, she stayed in her own apartment to finish packing, instead of with me as usual, at least when I'm in town. One night is enough to stir longing in me, especially the way she looks in this gold slip dress that shows off her shimmery brown shoulders and just the barest hint of cleavage.

"Sorry about this, you guys," she says with an exasperated smile. "The play Katie is in with Zia's brother got some great review, so she invited the whole cast and crew to this thing as well."

That would explain the fashion choices of many attendees, which can only be described as "colorful." It also explains why most of the attention Grigory and I have been getting is in the form of "batting for the wrong team." I imagine there isn't much crossover between off-off-Broadway and professional hockey.

"Erik!" Katie squeals after squeezing through the crowd to approach us. Naturally, she's in one of her infamous cheese t-shirts, this one reading: Feta Lovers Like it Salty and Tangy. "Isn't this great! So many people came. I see you brought a teammate."

She flashes a smile at Grigory, who grunts something in the form of a greeting.

I brought him along because of the funk he's been in lately. If I didn't know any better, I'd assume it was due to not making it to the final round for the Stanley Cup But it's the same quiet brooding that's been eating him up for most of the season, long before the Blades even knew we were going to be in the playoffs.

Grigory is never one to give details, especially when it comes to his personal life, at least beyond stories about his younger brother who seems to be the only person about whom he cares. As far as relationships go, like a lot of hockey players, he was happy to ride the puck bunny merry-go-round for a while. Lately, even that seems to have come to a screeching halt. However, he has yet to mention anyone special that's brought it about. Either way, I can read him well enough to know that sitting in his large brownstone with nothing but a bottle of vodka to keep him company won't end well.

"We had some Norwegian cheese, but I think it got eaten by some of the cast members. Sorry!"

"Neither of us know half these people, Katie," Maya protests.

"That's the beauty of it. What better way to make new friends?"

"Katie," a man with light green pants practically painted on, a pink checked shirt, and electric blue bow tie calls out as he approaches. There's a pause before he continues and I'm the beneficiary of a dimpled smirk. Grigory gets a much longer lingering look, which is met with a hard stare. "We're completely out of white wine, and it's a perfect disaster. Christine is already throwing a hissy over the fact that there's no lactose-free, vegan option, so it's reaching Chernobyl status."

Katie heaves an exasperated sigh. "What part of cheese shop did she not understand?"

I watch the two of them head away to stop the nuclear explosion. A woman passes by with a tray covered with crackers and cheese. Grigory grabs a few with each hand.

"Maya!"

We all turn to see two of her friends winding through the crowd, Gabrielle and Demetria.

"Are you excited!" Gabrielle gushes, taking both of Maya's hands and squeezing them.

"Of course," she says with a laugh. "A bit nervous."

"You know what? I don't blame you. What was that weird-ass movie that just came out this year? Midsommer?" Gabrielle turns to me with a teasing smirk. "I don't want to hear about my girl getting involved in some freaky summer rituals or anything."

"Gabby, please," Demetria says, rolling her eyes before taking a sip of her wine.

"Good grief," Maya says with a sigh.

"If it makes you feel better, that took place in Sweden," I say with a grin. "We're staying safely in Norway."

"Maya, you just have fun. Don't fall too much in love with the place. We do want you back," Demetria says, giving me a quick but meaningful glance.

"And who is this?" Gabrielle says, turning her girlish attention to Grigory just as he stuffs his face with another cracker. "Wait...you're that Blades player aren't you? The size of you!"

They've all been to several of the Blades games and, despite all the gear we wear on the ice, it would be easy to pick Grigory out of a lineup.

"This is my teammate—"

"Maya!" We all turn at the interruption. It's Zia, most memorable to me as the one giving my girlfriend AMSR massages on YouTube. Right now, she's in one of her typical flowing dresses, this one a bright orange halter type.

"Sorry, I was congratulating my brother." She arrives somewhat breathless and wide-eyed staring around at all of us with her usual smile. "Oh my God, Norway! How amazing! I'm so excited for you!"

Something about her enthusiasm lightens the air around us. Even Demetria seems amused by her tone.

"I was just introducing my teammate," I say, clapping a hand on Grigory's shoulder. "This is Grigory Mikhailov, our fearsome defender."

When I turn to glance at him, his eyes are practically boring a hole into Zia, who seems completely oblivious. It isn't lost on Maya or her other friends, who all dart their eyes back and forth between the two of them.

"Hi, Grigory," Zia says brightly, resting one hand on his bare arm before turning her attention back to Maya. I can almost feel him turning into a statue next to me at that touch. "Seriously, ten whole days? I'm so jealous. I hear it's so green there. I read somewhere that the most popular car there is the Tesla? Is that true, Erik?"

"You and Grigory don't have wine," Maya interjects, giving me a secretive smile. "I think you could use it."

"I heard they're out of white and red now, so all that's left is the rosé," Zia warns us.

Grigory makes a noise next to me that fully expresses his thoughts on that option. I can sympathize. I almost regret taking him away from his vodka.

"This thing has turned into kind of a madhouse," Maya says. "I'm officially rescuing Erik from boyfriend duty."

"Really?" Zia says with a small pout of disappointment. She reaches in to hug Maya. I'm not surprised when I get one as well. I've learned that she's the touchy-feely type. "Bye, you two. Have lots of fun and take way too many pictures."

When she lets go of me, I can practically feel the radiating heat coming from Grigory next to me. Talk about Chernobyl. I'm pretty sure even that disaster wouldn't be as dangerous to me as the vibes I'm getting from him right now.

"Go on you two, get some rest before your trip," Demetria says, hugging Maya.

"*Definitely* get some rest in beforehand," Gabrielle says, a completely different insinuation behind her suggestion if that smile on her face as she hugs both of us is any indication.

"Again, have fun!" Zia says. "I've got to go back and talk to this actor I just met. He's introducing me to this guy Jason, who is supposedly some YouTube expert that promised to help me out with my channel."

She hugs both of us once again—of course she does—gives Grigory a brief but glowing smile, then disappears back into the crowd.

"I think I will leave as well," Grigory says in a gruff voice. "Thank you for the cheese, Maya. Have fun on your holiday."

"Thank you, Grigory," she says with an empathetic smile.

When he turns to leave, she gives me a meaningful look and tilts her head toward his retreating figure.

I shake my head with a smirk, but heed her unspoken suggestion, following him out.

"Grigory, wait up," I say, jogging onto the sidewalk.

He turns to me with a grim expression.

"What was that back there? Are you interested in Zia?"

His eyes darken, and he gives me a look that would make any other man turn to dust. "No."

"I don't think she's seeing anyone—"

"No. I have no interest in that woman...or any woman."

That pretty much confirms my earlier suspicion about a woman being the cause of his troubles.

"Listen, why don't you join Maya and me? We could go to dinner and just have a good time before she and I take off."

His expression softens and he smiles, shaking his head no. The hand that comes to rest on my shoulder feels like a fifty-pound weight. "Is good you have found a nice girl. I am happy for you. But I am going home now. Thank you, for...trying. You are good friend. Enjoy your trip."

"Are you sure?"

"I am sure."

I watch him walk off, now trying to picture him with Zia. I can see the attraction. She's extremely pretty in a bright-eyed, free-spirited sort of way. But the two of them together would be like fire and ice. Or more like brimstone and incense.

"So are we playing Cupid or not?" I hear Maya say as she comes up next to me, wrapping an arm around my waist.

"Could you imagine the two of them together?" I ask doubtfully.

Maya laughs, shaking her head. "Talk about the odd couple." She comes around to face me, both arms around my waist now. "Then again, I distinctly remember you saying that's what you love about me. That we're so different."

"Well, there's different and then there's...*different*."

She tilts her head to the side, conceding the point with a smile. "Speaking of which, just how much am I going to stick out like a sore thumb in Oslo? Do you think they'll like me, your family?"

"They," I say, kissing her forehead, "are going," I kiss her nose, "to love you," I finish, placing my lips against her mouth.

We stay like that for a moment, savoring each other as though we haven't spent most nights together.

When she pulls away, she smiles up at me. I see the hint of trepidation behind those eyes. "I guess I'll find out for sure tomorrow."

"Yes, you will," I say in as reassuring a voice as I can.

CHAPTER THIRTY-EIGHT

MAYA

The last time I was on an airplane was the three-plus hours it took to get to The Bahamas with my friends several years ago. Even then, it was nothing like this upgraded class.

One overly stuffed window seat that leans back almost far enough to sleep on is a far cry from being squeezed in next to someone who hogs the armrest (paging Gabrielle).

Not that I got much sleep on this flight.

The combination of a new adventure plus the man in the seat next to me has had my body pumping adrenaline since JFK. I'm sure at some point I'll crash, but for now, the excitement is still real.

Resfeber.

Now I understand what the term means.

I only get two weeks off a year for vacation and initially thought about using all of them for this. Spending that much time in a new country in close quarters with Erik—even though I spend almost every night at his place these days—seemed like

Norwegian overload. The happy medium was making it a ten-day trip, including both weekends.

I turn to look at Erik, who is not nearly as nervous as I am since he seems to be fast asleep.

"It'll be fine," he mutters, his mouth curling into a smile even as his eyes remain closed.

"I'm not nervous," I say with a laugh.

He opens his eyes and stares at me. "My family is great. They'll love you. It'll be a fun week."

"Right," I say, nodding if only to reassure myself.

He sits up and looks at me. "Maya, like I told your mother, I'm bringing you to Norway because I want you to see where I come from, my home."

His home.

There's something in the way he says it, as though it isn't him speaking about the past but the present. The future? He's always left what he plans to do after hockey open-ended and I'm tactful enough not to press him on the issue.

The assumption on his part has been that he'd stay in the United States playing hockey, even after his contract with the Blades is up, he'd sign with them again or go with a new team.

Even though I always thought I'd die in Brooklyn, the same place I was born, the possibility that he may end up on another NHL team has crossed my mind. That, I could definitely live with, moving with him to Chicago or San Jose or wherever.

The possibility that he may end up back in Norway long after his hockey playing days are over is something I've also considered, but pushed to the back of my thoughts until after this trip.

Could I leave the only place I've ever known to not just move to another state, but another country?

I suppose this trip will help me find out.

"Vilde," Erik announces with a grin on his face.

I follow his eyes to find a blonde woman with a broad smile staring at us. She has hints of his mother in her. The striking features of Erik's mom are slightly softened in this woman, making her pretty rather than stunning.

"Erik!" she exclaims, her smile growing wider as she comes over to hug him.

She quickly pulls away to focus on me. "And you must be Maya. So pretty!" She gives Erik a conspiratorial smile before pulling me in for a hug as well.

And here I was lead to believe Scandinavians were so stoic and cold.

"How was your flight? Are you excited to be here? We must get your luggage, yes?"

The questions keep coming even as she leads us away and I realize she's just one of those people who likes to talk, a trait that I suppose transcends national boundaries.

Once we have our bags and follow her to her car, there's a bit of a back and forth before both of them finally convince me to sit in front with her so I'll have the better view of Oslo as we drive in.

"We all love the Instagram photos," Vilde says as she drives. She looks up at Erik in the rearview mirror with a smile. "Your cousin Bård will tease you, of course."

"Of course," Erik says, shooting her a grin then winking at me as I turn back to look at him.

"Emma would not stop talking about that first one. She says it has become a common thing, boys asking girls out on Instagram or inviting them to join their bus for russ."

He laughs as though he knows exactly what she's talking about.

"Russ?" I ask, looking back and forth between the two of them.

Now, they are both laughing.

"Ah, you just missed it this year," Vilde says with regret, as though I've missed seeing Halley's Comet.

"Count your blessings," Erik says.

"It's fun!" Vilde says, giving him an admonishing look in the mirror. "Emma can't wait. Be prepared for her to talk your ear off about it. That's what you get for sponsoring her bus."

"What is russ?" I ask, feeling completely out of the loop.

"Oh yes, of course," Vilde says, shooting me an apologetic smile. "*Russefeiring*, it's a...celebration, you'd call it? For students who will be graduating. They buy buses and decorate them and have concerts and dress up in red and blue and—"

"And drink and party and go wild," Erik finishes with a laugh. "Bård invited me to join his a few years ago. The Blades didn't make it to the playoffs that year, so I was able to come back early. Let's just say, all of it stayed firmly off my Instagram account."

"Yes," Vilde says, breathing out a long slow sigh of resignation as she stares ahead.

Erik laughs.

"Okay, now you *have* to tell me about it," I say, twisting in my seat so I can face both of them. "Is it like a long weekend of fun or something?"

Erik laughs again. "More like several weeks."

"Weeks? They just party nonstop for weeks?"

"Well," Vilde says, "for the most part, yes. But the young are entitled to have their fun."

"So what did you do that's not fit for Instagram?" I ask, narrowing my eyes at Erik.

"Probably best left for when we're not around Bård's mother."

"I know what went on," she says, shooting him a look in the rearview mirror. "Unlike you, his friends had no problem posting their photos of all the dares."

She turns to me with a frank glance. "They went nude through the street. Streaking, is that what you call it?"

"You didn't!" I say, laughing as I turn to him.

He grins and shrugs his shoulders.

"Erik," I groan, wrinkling my nose. He laughs.

"It ends with our Constitution Day, and there's a big parade. Everyone dresses up in their *bunader*, our traditional dress," Vilde continues. "One day, we'll have to get you back here again for that."

"It all depends on the playoffs. Do you not want me to win the Stanley Cup?" he teases.

"Yes, yes," she admits. "Perhaps when you're done with hockey."

I twist back around in my seat to face forward.

"So your cousin, Emma, is doing it this coming year?"

"Oh no, not for another two years," Vilde says.

"And she's planning it *now*?" I ask, turning to face them in surprise.

They both laugh again.

"Planning is a big deal. In America, it would be like..." He seems to think about it before continuing. "Maybe like planning a wedding?"

"Is that so?" I say with a teasing smile.

Vilde laughs beside me, and Erik twists his lips, shifting uncomfortably in the back. I laugh with Vilde.

"So what dares did you do during *your* russ?" I ask, before realizing my mistake.

Erik's hint of a self-deprecating smile disappears, and he looks out the window. "It's slightly different in Sweden."

"Oh." I twist to face forward again, wanting to kick myself

for ruining the mood. He graduated in Sweden, so of course he wouldn't have participated in whatever graduates in Norway did. I'm curious about what it was like in that country, but I have no intention of sticking my foot further in my mouth to find out.

"Speaking of which..." Vilde says in a hesitant voice.

That gets both our attention, and Erik and I face her.

"Your father called me to find out what dates you would be here this year."

"Did he?" Erik says, sitting up straighter in the back seat. I turn to find him staring hard at the back of her head.

"I think he would like you to visit Sweden this time."

Erik doesn't respond, only turning to gaze intently out the window next to him.

"It's been years, Erik," Vilde says, trying to catch his attention in the rearview mirror. "Perhaps—"

"No." It's said quietly and in a deceptively mild tone, but the finality of that one word is unequivocal.

Vilde sighs next to me and stares ahead.

I turn to look back at Erik, but he doesn't look my way. Giving up, I turn to face forward again. He told me about the phone message from his dad after he lost in the finals, the one he never bothered to return.

The question is, now that we're here what does he plan on doing about it?

CHAPTER THIRTY-NINE

ERIK

Thankfully, Vilde knows how to keep the conversation going, even after a brief uncomfortable moment. By the time we've reached her house, she and Maya have been happily chatting about almost everything under the sun.

Even my mood is lighter when we exit the car.

"Alf, my husband is at work, but we will be having you two over for dinner one night so you can meet him. For now, Erik has insisted I treat you to a proper Norwegian lunch before we drop you off at Dad's house," Vilde says, shooting me a conspiratorial smile that Maya fortunately misses.

"Erik!"

We all turn to the front door where my cousin, Emma, is flying toward me. I open my arms just in time for her to jump into them like she's six years old instead of sixteen, legs and arms wrapped around me like a monkey.

"Emma," I say, giving her one good squeeze before she jumps down with the same agility. Before I can say anything more, she's speaking Norwegian to me.

"*Thank God you're finally here. The rest of the girls can't* wait to meet you. We have the most amazing plans for the bus. Sofie bought all these socks to sell and raise money even though I told her we had enough, but she says we have to because it's what all the other groups are doing. So when they come you have to buy some socks."

Emma has the same propensity for talking that her mother has, which I find odd. It's so unlike my mother and me even though we're all related.

"Emma, this is Maya Jackson, Erik's girlfriend," Vilde says in English, giving her daughter a slightly reproachful look.

"Oh, my God!" Emma exclaims. I'm not sure if it's from embarrassment at having missed her or excitement at finally meeting her. The way she races around the car to greet her makes me think it's the latter. "You're here!"

"Nice to meet you, Emma," Maya says, reaching her hand out.

Instead, Emma takes it and ropes it around her arm to walk her inside, now talking her ear off instead.

"You're so much prettier in person. Not that you are ugly on Instagram! Everyone thought it was so sweet how Erik asked you out. I loved the photo with the butterflies on your faces. Bård laughed at Erik, but I thought it was cute. Who doesn't like butterflies? Fortunately, my brother is practicing with his stupid band today for his thing Friday. So I have you all to myself."

Vilde gives me an apologetic look as we watch them walk away. I grin back at her and follow them into the house.

"So this is what you usually eat?" Maya asks, looking skeptically at the food laid out before her. I can't blame her. The various selections covering the table, from the *brunost* cheese, which she's promised to save for this trip, to the infamous *lutefisk*, which at this point probably has a mythical status when it comes to Norwegian food, is probably overwhelming.

"Yes, we eat this all the time," Emma says in such a giggling way that even Maya has to know this is a joke at her expense.

"It is traditional Norwegian food, but some of this is either for special occasions or...an acquired taste," I say.

"Don't start with the lutefisk," Emma says, gagging for effect.

"I actually like it," Vilde says with a shrug. "But yes, as Erik says, it's an acquired taste."

"And smell," Maya says, as she leans down to inspect it. She looks up, apologetically, even though we're already laughing. "No offense."

"Why not start with the brunost? Gjetost made with goats milk," I say with a grin.

Her smile mimics mine. "Brown and slightly sweet?"

"Delicious," I say with a wink.

"What's going on there?" Emma says, looking back and forth between us suggestively.

"You should have it on bread or something," Vilde says, utterly oblivious to what Emma has caught on to.

"It's fine. I'll take a slice," Maya says, using the cutter to peel some off.

I watch her as she takes a bite, eyes rolled up to the side in thought. "You're right. It is kind of sweet...not bad though! I like it."

From there we all join in, taking samples of our favorites as Maya works her way through the *lefse*, a type of flatbread with butter and sugar (she loves it) to the whale meat (she finds it tolerable). Vilde thankfully left some of the more obscure items off the menu like *smalahove*, salted and smoked sheep's head, which even I've never had.

"Okay, now the *lutefisk*," I say, staring down at the one plate that's been left untouched.

Maya looks at it uncertainly then eyes each of us. With one deep breath, she grabs the fork and stabs a small piece to pull away.

I'm sure Vilde and Emma are both holding their breath as I am while we watch her reaction to it. The way her face crumples is amusing.

"Oh...that's ...just foul," she says, her tongue hanging out as if to air out the taste of it. "How in the world—just, no."

We all laugh as she pushes the plate away.

"Congratulations," I say. "You've passed your first Norwegian test."

"I'll take Brooklyn any day," she says, gulping down the glass of water near her.

"If you want to be really Norwegian, you should have just microwaved a frozen pizza," Emma says as she forks a *kjøttboller*, our version of a meatball.

"Sounds like my typical Wednesday night," Maya says with a smile.

"So what are you going to do while you're here?" Emma asks idly.

"Show Maya around. Play tourist."

"Frogner Park?" Emma asks, rolling her eyes. "Americans are always so surprised by it. Such prudes."

"Frogner Park?" Maya asks.

"He didn't tell you about it?" Emma asks, perking up a bit.

Maya twists her lips at me. "Erik wouldn't let me google anything. He wants to show me firsthand."

Emma laughs. "That's so sweet! But just be forewarned—"

"And surprised," I say, shooting my cousin a hard look, which only makes her laugh, and completely ignore me.

"Then, of course, there's Ekeberg Park which is even more—"

"I think maybe we should head to Morfar's house," I say, coming around to place my hand over her mouth. Emma squeals with laughter underneath it, trying to squirm her way out.

Maya laughs as she watches. "No, I want to know about this park."

"Everyone goes there, and I don't understand why. It's a lovely park but...there's so much more to Oslo and Norway than that," Vilde says, shaking her head in disappointment. "Anyway, yes, we should go see if Papa is back from his morning hike."

"Thank you for the food. It was....interesting," Maya says, grabbing another lefse for the road.

"Enjoy the naked bodies," Emma says with a laugh once I let go of her.

"What?"

CHAPTER FORTY

MAYA

Erik refuses to expound on Emma's parting statement. "You'll see when I show you around tomorrow," he says from the backseat. "But Vilde's right, the park is usually crowded with tourists."

"You should take Maya to the palace. Did you know Norway is a constitutional monarchy? We have our very own king. You can walk the grounds around it. That would be nice."

Erik's opinion of that idea could be read from Brooklyn.

We've been driving for a bit, and the nicer apartments and largish homes of Vilde's neighborhood have transitioned to smaller houses with nature creeping in from backyards that seem to be nothing but forest.

"Ah, it's a good thing I called first. He's just now getting back from his hike," Vilde says, as she turns into the driveway of a house. It's a light blue, two-story home of a size that might be called "quaint."

I peer out the windshield to see the same older man from many of Erik's Instagram photos heading down a trail toward the front driveway with a walking stick. His white beard partially obscures that cheerful smile of his as he comes closer to greet us. He's dressed in shorts, hiking boots...and an I 🤍 NY t-shirt, which I find hilarious. Erik is the first one out of the car.

"Morfar!" he says, jogging over to embrace him in a bear hug.

"Erik!" his grandfather responds. The sinewy muscles of his forearm go taut as he hugs his grandson just as hard.

"Those two are practically best friends," Vilde observes with a fond smile as she watches them through the windshield.

"I can see."

I open the door just as they are pulling apart and Erik's grandfather greets me with an even broader smile.

"And this must be the famous Instagram model!"

I laugh as I lean in to hug him. It's lost in the strength of his embrace. His lean figure must be made up of pure muscle. For Erik's sake, I hope that means a long and healthy life.

"Maya, this is my morfar, Arvid Sørenson. Morfar, Maya Jackson."

"Yes, yes!" Arvid says, waving the introductions away as though the two of us are old friends. "Let's get you two settled. I hope you don't mind staying with an old man while you are here in Norway."

"Nonsense, I insisted," I say as he hands his walking stick to Erik and wanders to the car's trunk that Vilde has just opened. He leans in and pulls out both suitcases.

"Oh, we can do that!" I insist.

"*Nei, nei, nei!*" He pooh-poohs wheeling both suitcases up the driveway.

I turn to Erik, who is just standing there holding the walking stick. He slides his eyes to me and smirks, subtly shaking his head as though he's used to this treatment.

"Well then, I'm off." Vilde walks over to hug both Erik and me. "Remember, dinner at some point this week. Probably Wednesday?"

"It's a date," I say, squeezing her one last time. "And thank you again for the introduction to Norwegian cuisine."

We follow Arvid through the front door, him wheeling the suitcases behind him. The inside of the house is just as homey as it appears outside. It's the cozy kind of decor one would imagine an older active man to have. It's comfortable, and I can see why Erik usually stays here instead of a hotel when he comes to visit, especially considering the greeting I witnessed.

"I've set you up in your usual room, Erik," Arvid says, heroically carrying both suitcases up the stairs to the room. "This is the same room he stayed in when he'd visit during the summer as a boy."

It still looks like a boy's room, painted blue with dark plaid bedding. There's a king-sized bed, thank goodness. Otherwise, I'd probably be dwarfed by Erik's larger body. The walls are covered with posters for movies or bands, some with Norwegian names I can't pronounce, but mostly American.

"*Spaceballs?*" I say with a laugh as I walk over to look at the particular poster.

"He watched it about a hundred times that one summer. One of your friends introduced you to it, no?" Arvid says.

"Who says I don't have a sense of humor?" Erik says with a grin.

"Come, come, I've got some beer for us downstairs. I want to learn all about you, Maya."

"Beer?" I say, absolutely loving that idea. The taste of lutefisk is still in my mouth. "Øl, right?"

"Very good!" Arvid says.

"You can thank my teacher," I say, giving Erik a grin.

The grin he returns isn't lost on Arvid. "Now, now, you

two. Beer first, then you can snuggle. Not to worry, my bedroom is downstairs, far away."

I cough out a laugh as I follow both of them downstairs. Erik grabs me by the waist, hanging back a bit.

"See? What did I tell you?"

I got a sense that Arvid was fun based purely on the photos I saw of him. But he's so much more likable than I would have ever thought. Now, I'm glad we chose to stay here instead of a hotel, which Erik did offer and I patently refused. I want to experience Norway the way he does.

While Arvid gets beers for us, I note the various photos he has sitting on shelves or hung on walls in the living room. Unlike Erik, he doesn't have a spartan approach to collecting memories, and I learn even more about the family just by looking at them.

"Aww, is this you as a little boy?" I ask, leaning in toward one of a small towheaded boy who couldn't be older than three or four as he squats down to inspect something on the ground.

"That's me," Erik says, coming in beside me. I turn to see him staring at it with a soft look in his eyes, as though he remembers the exact moment that was taken.

"Did you see the one of me in New York?" Arvid says as he approaches me with an uncapped beer.

"No," I say with a laugh. "Which one is that?"

He leads me to a shelf where there is a small six-by-four framed photo of him and Erik, arms wrapped around each other.

"This was when Erik first moved there for his hockey team."

Arvid is wearing the same I ♥ NY t-shirt he has on today, but paired with one of those foam Statue of Liberty crowns tourists wear around the city.

"How in the world did you survive on the streets of New York looking like this?" I question with a laugh.

"They loved it," Erik says with a smile.

"So did you like New York?" I ask, taking a sip of the beer.

"Of course!" Arvid says, with a grin. "I did all the things. That Brooklyn Bridge, the Empire State Building, the Central Park. I do like our hot dogs better, *pølse*. You must try one while you are here."

"Don't let New Yorkers hear you say that," I warn. "So have you been back since?"

"Oh *nei, nei*. I only go to a place once, and that's it!"

"Really?"

"Too much in the world to explore. I have the...how do you say it, wanderlove?"

"Wanderlust," Erik corrects.

"Yes, yes, wanderlust. Ingrid had it. Erik has it." He raises his bottle, waving it around the room. "But we always come home eventually."

I take a sip of my beer, eyeing Erik next to me. There's a nostalgic smile on his face.

I file it away as I sip my beer, focusing on his grandfather instead.

"Come, come!" Arvid says, leading us to the couch. "Tell me all about this romance of yours."

I get caught up in his grandfather's evident enthusiasm. I'm glad we chose to stay here.

CHAPTER FORTY-ONE

ERIK

"So this is the same bed you slept in every summer when you were a kid?"

Maya and I have both showered and changed into bedclothes. I'm in nothing but a pair of boxers, and she's wearing a nightgown that's so prim and old-fashioned I want to laugh. It's a far cry from what she usually wears to bed with me.

"Yes," I reply, pulling her in closer. I can't wait to take off this ridiculous thing she has on. "If only fourteen-year-old me could see the grown-up me with this beautiful, sexy woman in my bed."

She laughs and tries to resist my hands slowly creeping along her thighs, sliding that white cotton fabric up. "That's so perverted."

"You have no idea what goes through the mind of a fourteen-year-old boy, do you, Maya? But rest assured, Salma Hayek has nothing on you."

She twists to face the poster nearest my bed, a personal homage to the movie that pretty much threw me right into the deep end of puberty. "Oh my God, is that why you have the *Dusk Till Dawn* poster on your wall?"

"Come on, that scene in the bar—"

"I know the scene," she interrupts, her voice icy.

Naturally, my mind snatches that well-used file from the archives of my brain. Salma Hayek in a bar wearing nothing but a bikini costume, a headdress, and a boa constrictor, dancing along tabletops ending with one bare foot in Quentin Tarantino's mouth as she drizzles liquor down her leg.

"Which has nothing on your Valentine's gift to me."

"Oh?" she says, sounding slightly thawed.

"Oh," I echo, sliding my fingertips underneath the hem of the gown which she's allowed me to drag up thigh-high.

"We're not having sex in your grandfather's house, Erik," she says, placing a hand on top of mine.

"He doesn't mind. He'd be disappointed if we didn't."

"Erik!" she protests but not without a giggle.

"Mmm," I say, twisting around so that I can nibble on her plump bottom lip. "I like it when you say my name that way."

"Erik," she protests again, her hand sliding up my arm that's still perched on her thigh. If she thinks I'm avoiding tasting, touching, exploring this smooth expanse of skin for the entire week just because of some prudish sensibilities, then she's sorely mistaken.

"We could recreate that scene," I offer.

She laughs against my mouth. "In this thing? It's the exact opposite of sexy."

"So take it off." I press my lips against hers before she can dismiss that idea too quickly.

She moans against me, her body going lax enough for me to slide the nightgown up to her waist. Even her underwear seems to be modest, white cotton covering most of her hips and ass. It only makes me that much more eager to rip them away like some barbaric...Viking.

I smile at the played-out stereotype of my ancestry. The Norway of today is nothing like the raiding and pillaging, ruthless take-no-prisoners image that's recently become popular on TV. That doesn't mean I can't let my mind play pretend.

I hook my fingers into the elastic of the waistband, slinking my other arm up so that hand can join in. The sound of the fabric ripping causes Maya's hips to jerk involuntarily. Her hand grips my bicep as I continue to tear her panties off.

"Open your legs," I urge.

The sound of her thighs sliding across the sheets as she obeys is the only thing drowning out the sound of our heavy breathing.

My palm traverses the soft skin of her stomach as I push the nightgown further up. One hand rests on her breast, enjoying the way it fits into the concave of my palm.

"Erik," she moans as her nipple hardens against the thick skin. I leave my hand there, not wanting to ruin the intimate feel of it even to help her take the nightgown completely off.

Maya's fingers scrabble across my body, seeking out my underwear. The delicate fingers aren't strong enough to rip the fabric the way mine did, but they are no less urgent as they tear the one piece of clothing down my hips, scratching the skin as they go.

I'm surprised my dick doesn't detach from my body considering how eagerly it springs free. I remove the hand from her breast to find more savory fare between Maya's legs.

By now we're past the point of worrying about either STDs or pregnancy—Maya is safely on birth control—but something about the idea of fucking her raw and unprotected, leading to who knows what, specifically here in Norway has me especially hard.

The wet sound my fingers make as they explore Maya's pussy tells me that she's just as eager to get a bit primitive as I am. I kick my legs, losing my boxers somewhere in the sea of sheets until I'm completely naked.

Without bothering to remove her nightgown, I twist over so that I'm between her legs. She brings them up around my waist. We're like magnets, our bodies connecting with a force of nature.

I begin fucking her fast and furiously, spurred on by the silent gasps and moans she tries to hold back for the sake of propriety. Something about that only has me bucking my hips harder, wanting to bring out the noise if only to prove that I can.

"*Erik*," she mewls, a pathetic attempt at appeasing me.

"Louder," I order in a harsh whisper, holding back until she accommodates my request.

It's only when I shift my body, arching it up so that I hit the spot I've learned pushes just the right button inside her, that she gives in.

"Erik!" It's good, but I know I can do better.

I sink into her, snaking my hips rhythmically. I love this, the way she responds to my movement, the way her fingers dig into my back, the way her breath feels against my neck.

I love everything about her.

I love her.

That does it.

"Say it," I growl, feeling the heat from my manically beating heart spread to combine with the heat radiating from the urgency building up in my groin.

She inhales, which I know by now means she's on the cusp. I work my hips just the right way to build that wave.

"Maya," I whisper.

"*Erik!*" Maya cries out, loud enough for everyone in Oslo to hear.

I pull up to watch her face, releasing the tension that held me back until this moment. When I come, it's hard, lasting so long I'd be surprised if there's anything left of me when I'm done.

My body is nothing more than a limp piece of meat, falling to her side. I feel her wriggling her nightgown back down to its modest length before she curls into me.

"We shouldn't have done that," she says, laughing softly into my arm.

I bring it around to pull her in closer. "I had to introduce you to Norway properly."

That causes her to laugh louder. "You're so bad."

"So are you. That's why I love you."

"I love you too, Erik."

We have a whole week here in Oslo. Plenty of time for her to learn about where I come from, maybe even grow to love this place as much as I do, as much as I love her.

I'm up early for a reason.

Maya was still sound asleep as I snuck out from under the covers and put on nothing more than a pair of pants.

"*God morgen*," I say, greeting morfar with a mug of black coffee as he ambles down the trail behind his house.

"*Takk, takk*," he says with a cheerful smile as he takes it, his face still ruddy from the exertion of his morning hike.

I follow him inside, sipping from my mug.

"*So, out with it. What is so important that you stupidly left the side of that beautiful girl upstairs?*" His eyes roll up from the mug he's drawn closer to his mouth before sipping. "*Or do I even need to ask?*"

"*Has he called you?*"

This is another question he doesn't need to ask about. He knows exactly which "he" I'm talking about. I watch him take a long sip of coffee, savoring the taste of it before he leans back in his chair to assess me.

"*He did.*"

"*And you didn't tell me?*" I ask, slightly surprised.

"*The two of you need to learn to communicate. Nils has never really been direct about things,* most *things anyway,*" Morfar says, frowning to the side at some thought. His eyes come back to me with a hard look. "*But he's your father, Erik. He may not be around for long. You of all people should know this.*"

I feel my jaw harden at the idea of him comparing that man to the memory of my mother.

"*Yes, your* father," he stresses. "*I think you should go to Sweden. See what he wants. It's obviously important.*"

The sound of creaking on the stairs silences us both. Maya makes an appearance from around the corner to the kitchen, an apologetic smile on her face. She's still in the nightgown from last night and, despite the seriousness of the conversation she just interrupted, I can't help but wonder if she's bothered replacing the panties I tore off last night.

"Sorry, the smell of coffee and your voices woke me."

"*God morgen,*" my grandfather says in his usual cheerful tone. "Come join us for coffee."

"Thanks," she says.

Morfar pours her a mug, and she gratefully accepts it.

"So, Erik will be showing you around Oslo today?"

She takes a sip, surreptitiously eyeing me over the rim

before she answers. "Mmm, that's good. Yes, that's the plan. I'm supposed to play tourist."

"Good, good. When you come back, we can go for a nice hike before the moose come out."

"Moose?" she asks, her eyes wide.

"He's joking," I say with a mild smile, feeling the tension in me start to fade.

"Oh no, moose are a very serious thing here in Oslo. They especially like tourists. We'll have to be careful," he says with a wink that makes Maya laugh.

That's the thing about Morfar, he has this ability to shift the wind completely, so whatever river of negativity on which the room has been floating instantly changes direction. Even I've officially put all thoughts about my father—along with the disturbingly nagging curiosity about why he's been so communicative the past several months—to the back of my mind.

CHAPTER FORTY-TWO

MAYA

"This is the park Emma was talking about?" I ask, looking past the ornate black gates that serve as the entrance to Frogner Park. There's a long stretch of grass beyond that leads up to some sort of rounded obelisk-shaped statue in the distance.

We drove Arvid's car into Oslo, since, according to Erik, taking public transportation from that far out would have taken too long.

I don't know what Arvid and Erik were saying this morning when I came downstairs, but I don't need to be fluent in Norwegian to know it probably had to do with Erik's father. He must have called Arvid just as he did Vilde. Erik never once meddled in my issues with my father, and I plan on affording him the same respect, even though I can see how much it's affecting him. Just as he did for me, I'll be there for him when he finally decides to do something about it.

"Yes, this is the park. As you can see, Vilde was right about the tourists."

It's only mid-morning, and indeed there are crowds of people milling about, wandering in through the front gates.

"Still, it's worth seeing," Erik says, as he takes my hand.

It's a spectacularly gorgeous day, a far cry from the sweltering humidity we left behind in New York, but I'm still surprised at the number of sunbathers I see on the patches of grass along the path toward the largest statue. Every inch of green—other than the main stretch of lawn—seems to be covered by slowly baking, mostly blonde bodies wearing nothing but bikinis or shorts.

"I guess they really like sunning."

"When half the year is spent in the darkness you soak up what you can. Six months from now, the sun will still be low in the sky this time of day."

I wrinkle my brow at the thought. I definitely notice the later evenings during summer in New York, but nothing this drastic. Erik's room at his grandfather's house had blackout curtains, so I didn't get a clear idea of exactly when nighttime fell.

All thoughts of the oddities of Norwegian daylight hours disappear as my eyes land on one of the first statues. It's a naked man carrying two naked kids under each of his arms.

"That's not...so bad," I say. Most statues in the world are naked, after all, including every childlike cherub shooting water from their mouths—or other parts of their anatomy.

"It gets more interesting," he says with a smile.

He's right, of course. By the time we've passed the bridge, and several more instances of naked adults seemingly getting more and more frustrated with naked children, I'm practically immune to it all.

Then we get to the *pièce de résistance*, the gigantic statue made of intertwined bodies, all of them naked.

"It's like one big orgy!" I say with a laugh.

"A perfect representation of our culture," Erik says with such a straight face, I can't tell if he's joking or not. I punch him lightly in the arm, and he coughs out a laugh.

"So what does it mean?"

He shrugs as he stares up at it. "Does it matter?"

I think about it for a moment, then laugh again. "I guess not."

"So, is the city growing on you yet?" Erik asks.

We're walking up one of the slopes of the blindingly white Oslo Opera House. As with all the popular attractions in this city, it's crowded with tourists.

It's been a few days here in Oslo, and I've seen a pretty good bit of what the city is about, at least as far as tourist attractions go.

One of the first things he showed me was the apartment where he and his mother lived. Today it's been the various schools he attended, places he used to play, the center where he first started speed skating.

Over the past few days, I've played tourist with Erik. He took me to Ekeberg Park, dragging me all the way to the statue of a woman squatting...and pissing. The "water" that escaped the statue even smelled slightly odd.

I've tried the *pølse* (yes, better than the New York hot dog) while sunbathing on a tiny spot we managed to snag by the Sørenga Seawater Pool (which gave new meaning to the term sun-worshiping).

Naturally, we've toured all the museums, including one with a recovered Viking ship.

We had dinner with Vilde, and I finally got to meet Alf—

whose name I was amused to discover the spelling of. He is definitely more sedate than his wife.

Emma managed to lure Erik back to Vilde's house so he could meet all the girls on her bus for russ. It was like running into a casting call for *Teen Vogue*—good grief these Norwegian genes! All of them melted like ice cream in root beer floats upon introduction, turning into one big gooey mess over him. It was very reminiscent of those tweens from our first date at the coffee shop. Was I ever that gaga over a guy when I was sixteen?

He did end up buying ten unnecessary packs of socks.

I look out at the city, most of which is visible from one of the higher slopes of the Opera House, which is certainly the crowning jewel of Oslo.

"I like it here," I confess as Erik takes my hand, pulling me out of the way of two children running full speed down the slope we're on.

"Me too," he says thoughtfully, looking out at the water.

"Why don't we do something non-touristy today? I want to see more of the parts of this city that you experienced growing up."

Something passes over his eyes. I can't tell if it's a good or bad thing. "That's a good idea."

"This isn't one of your *freelovsliv* activities is it?" I say with a slightly apprehensive laugh.

"*Friluftsliv*," Erik corrects as he continues leading me through the brush and trees. "Trust me, this will be worth it. Either my mother or Morfar used to take me here to go swimming all the time."

I smile as I watch his back, muscles flexing underneath the

t-shirt he has on. All he told me in preparation for today's adventure was "wear a swimsuit."

"Of course, we could always head back that way," he says, nodding his head toward the direction from which we came. "Huk beach is popular with locals. There's even a nude beach connected to it."

I roll my eyes at the grin he flashes my way. "Not happening."

He laughs and continues on, my hand still in his. Eventually, we reach a clearing with a tiny beach of sand and calm dark water beyond it. It's like a small oasis, surrounded by green as far as the eye can see behind us instead of sand. Ahead, the water stretches on forever, with just a hint of more green land in the distance.

It's so serene and quiet and beautiful, we might as well be the only two people left on Earth.

"This is gorgeous."

"And private," Erik says, setting the bag he's carried in down on the sand.

I drop my things, picking up the towel to unfurl onto the sand. I stare out into the glistening water, the sunlight creating starbursts against the gently rippling surface. I imagine Erik as a kid with his beloved mother or way too much fun grandfather, splashing around in it. It presents a nice picture, and I can see why he's brought me here.

This is the part of Norway that I really wanted to see, the part that shows me more of who Erik was. Something beyond just the few photos he has or memories he's revealed to me.

"Let's go in," he says, and I turn to find him already stripped down to his swimming trunks. His eyes, glance across my shorts and tank top with mild impatience.

"Why do I get the feeling you just want to see me in my bikini?" I say with a smirk.

"I won't deny it," he replies with a broad grin.

I laugh and oh so slowly peel off my clothes, just to make him suffer. He pays me back by grabbing me once I'm down to nothing but the black bikini I had on underneath and carrying me into the water.

"Erik!" I squeal, laughing despite myself.

He doesn't let go, even once we've reached chest level, holding onto me as we bob in the refreshing water. I didn't learn to swim until I was in college, and beyond that, I rarely have an opportunity to go into the water, so this is something new for me. Although it's mildly chilly, I find it enjoyable.

Mostly because of the man holding on to me.

"I really am glad you agreed to come," he says, staring at me, his face dripping from the splashing water that accompanied us to this point.

"Me too."

"Do you need me to hold onto you?"

"Need or want?" I reply with a smile.

He laughs and pulls me in closer. "I could stay like this all day."

"Me too, but," I splash him with water. "I'd rather swim."

Before he can return a splash, I wriggle free with a laugh, wading away on my back, which, along with the dog paddle, is one of only two ways I remember how to operate in the water. It's no surprise that he's a much stronger and more practiced swimmer and he readily catches up to me. I dip below the surface, but he finds me anyway, dragging me back up above the water in his embrace, both of us laughing.

We play around for what seems like hours, but I'm sure is only half of one. Having not spent most of my life vigorously practicing for an athletic career, I get worn out far earlier than Erik does. I paddle to the point where I can stand up and head back to my towel, falling on it to watch as he swims a few laps in the water. I nibble on some of the *lefse* we've packed as I watch him, enjoying the way the sun, which hasn't even reached the halfway point in the sky, feels on my wet skin.

My stomach is practically bloated with *lefse* and *brunost*—the brown cheese, which is another thing that's growing on me—by the time Erik stomps out of the water, looking like some mythological god of the seas.

"I have a surprise for you," he says with a grin.

My brow shoots up with curiosity as he falls onto the towel beside me to rifle through his bag. It rises at least another inch when I see what he pulls out.

"I figured you forgot yours, so I brought one just in case."

In his hand is a tiny glass vial, empty just like the one he gave to me on Valentine's Day.

"I did pack mine," I say with a smirk. "If I'd known what we were up to today I would have brought it."

"Save it," he says, his eyes intense. "For our next adventure."

That's when I fully understand the importance of this moment. My eyes fall to the glass container in his hand.

"I want this to be the first of a thousand adventures with you, Maya," he says as he grabs a handful of sand from the beach we're lying on and pours some into the glass.

My eyes slide back up to his once he's done. "I'd love that, Erik."

"Good," he says, nodding, his gaze more intense than ever. He reaches out the hand he used to pour sand and cups my face. Even though the sand-covered surface feels rough against my cheek, I can't imagine a more wonderful sensation. "Because I mean it. Every trip, every journey, every adventure, every waking moment, I want you there. *Jeg elsker deg.*"

"I love you too," I laugh, leaning in to kiss him before he can even react. He chuckles against my mouth, dropping the tiny vial to pull me down on top of him.

"Still glad you came?" He says once we've had our fill of each other's tongues and lips.

"Absolutely," I reply.

The momentous day isn't lost on Arvid once we get back to his house.

"So, another good day in Oslo?" he inquires cheerfully, his eyes darting back and forth between us with conspiratorial glee.

"Very," Erik says with a grin.

For some idiotic reason, maybe because I'm still caught up in a wave of happiness, I start giggling. It's contagious, and soon all of us are laughing.

"I think perhaps something stronger than beer, or *øl*," Arvid says, winking at me, "for tonight."

"Sounds good to me," I say.

Before Erik can add his agreement, his phone rings. Something about it breaks the mood, as though foreshadowing who lies on the other end of that call.

"Take it," I say softly.

Erik's jaw hardens as he stares at me. I note the briefest nod before he pulls his phone out, staring at it for a second before another ring shakes him out of his trance.

I don't need to ask who it is.

"*Hallå.*" The way Erik answers is enough to figure out that his father has finally decided to get in touch with his son directly.

I watch him as he listens in silence, not uttering a word, his face expressionless. He says something in Norwegian, or perhaps Swedish, and my eyes slide to his grandfather, who is just as stoic as he is, giving nothing away.

"*Ha det bra*," he eventually says in a curt tone—I've learned enough Norwegian to know it means *goodbye*—sounding weirdly formal before he hangs up.

I wait, not even noticing that I'm holding my breath. Erik gives me a wan smile, which brightens hyperbolically as he shifts it toward his grandfather.

"How about that drink?"

CHAPTER FORTY-THREE

MAYA

Once again, I'm holding back. Erik didn't tell me anything about what was said during the short, one-sided phone call, nixing any questions about it with the easy distraction of sex when we finally went to bed.

It was enough to remind me even this morning that his father is not up for discussion.

My thoughts have firmly moved on to tonight's festival, where Erik's cousin Bård is performing. I didn't get to meet him during dinner at Vilde's since, according to her, he was busy practicing with his band all week.

I was told this event, which I didn't even bother trying to pronounce the name of, was a student-run thing with mostly amateur bands performing.

"What is this place?" I ask, looking around at what seems to be a small college campus, or at least the residential portion of one. There are large yellow buildings arranged around a quad area.

"Blindern Studenterhjem? It's housing for university

students." A grin comes to Erik's face as he continues. "Though I suspect more partying goes on here than studying, at least according to what little I've learned from my cousin."

Having lived at home during my years at Brooklyn College, I never got the full "college experience," so I'm suddenly more excited about tonight.

We end up at a slightly sloped hill of grass leading down to a raised platform with microphones, speakers, and other gear set up in preparation for the performing bands. There's a colorful banner across the top that reads: **Bukkehaugfestivalen!**

A nice-sized crowd of young people is already milling about; most seem to be in their early twenties or late teens. That's about all they seem to have in common. I see everything from blonde bombshells in bikini tops and shorts to pure goth, complete with dyed hair and Doc Martens. One young man has a Norwegian flag tied around his neck like a cape. A few others seem to be wearing some sort of formal traditional attire, the girls in long embroidered dresses and the boys in red vests or overalls and short pants that end just below the knees. Most are casually dressed like Erik and me, him in a t-shirt and jeans and me in a black sundress.

"I don't see him yet," Erik says, his brow creasing as he searches the crowd. "I think his band goes second so let's get a beer and find a seat on the grass."

I follow him to the keg that's set up near the event. Having made an alcohol run with Erik one day after an enjoyable late-night drinking and chatting session with his grandfather, I know that the heavier stuff in Norway is sold in state-run stores called *Vinmonopolets*, and is not cheap.

Even beer, which can be bought in grocery stores has a hefty price tag. Thus, it's no surprise that the people here in attendance are happily overindulging in plastic cups filled with the stuff for the low, low price of 45kr, or about $5.

"So you and your cousin are close?" I say before taking a sip now that we've found a spot from which to watch the bands perform.

Erik sips his with a thoughtful look on his face. "We became closer once I moved to Sweden. My summers were mostly spent here in Oslo, and by that time he was old enough to be...interesting. He's six years younger so prior to that he was too young to do much with."

"So seeing him perform makes up for not winning the Stanley Cup?" I ask with a smile.

"Well..." Erik says, tilting his head to the side.

I laugh and nudge his arm.

"Yes, I'm glad I could make it," he confesses with a smile. "There will be other opportunities for the Stanley Cup, but this is a once in a lifetime thing. It's a reminder of why I keep coming back home, so I don't miss things like this."

There's that word again. Home.

Before I can reply, a young man takes the stage to get things started. After welcoming everyone to the festival, he introduces the first band, and I forget about what Erik's said to enjoy the beer and the show.

It starts with a bang—literally. The first act is a proper head-banging, heavy metal band screeching out tunes in Norwegian. Enough beer has been flowing prior to the start of the event for the crowd to get caught up in the intense current, jumping around and snapping their heads up and down, long hair whipping in the air. Although it's a sight to behold, I'm mostly just feeling my adult-ness, happy that Erik and I are sitting near the sidelines.

By the end of their set, I'm starting to enjoy the music, nodding my head to the heavy beat. It's probably because of the second beer that Erik bought for me. Bård's group takes the stage and I perk up. Their sound is more palatable to my tastes, reminiscent of grunge bands from the 90s—less screaming and more crooning, all in Norwegian, which makes it more interesting.

"He's the one on the guitar to the right," Erik says, pointing to the tall blond near the edge of the stage. Bård is lanky in a way that shows off a few muscles, the kind of physique that's fitting for a future rock star. Like the rest of the Sørenson clan, he looks like something that's just stepped off the pages of a magazine. Even in nothing more than a black t-shirt and jeans and Converse tennis shoes, he could turn heads.

When they finish their set of songs, Erik and I stand up to applaud along with the crowd. One small clique of girls near the front are especially boisterous.

"They're outstanding," I say, still clapping as they exit the stage.

"Yeah, I've only heard songs from their YouTube channel, but they sound much better live."

The band disappears somewhere, and we sit back down for the next group, which does a hilarious compilation of songs filled with sexual innuendoes. Even though the songs are a mix of English and Norwegian, I get enough of the double entendres to understand and laugh along with the crowd.

By the time they're done I see Bård and his bandmates coming back to join the audience, now without their instruments. Instead of joining us, he smiles and nods his head our way then makes a detour to the small group of girls who were cheering him on. One girl in particular, pretty with a decidedly dark aesthetic, hair dyed pitch black and a dark, ripped t-shirt and black skinny jeans, seems to grab most of his attention.

"It looks like we've been delegated to a lower priority," I say, nodding toward them.

"She's probably more appealing than the beer I'll buy for him," Erik says with a shrug.

I laugh and sip my beer as I watch Bård lean down while the girl whispers something in his ear. The smirk that comes to his face suggests Erik might very well be right.

The band that's on by the time he makes his way to us has a lead singer so melodramatic he almost seems to be crying on stage. It's definitely canceled out the upbeat mood that the last band left the crowd with.

I tune them out while Erik makes his introductions. First, the two of them hug like long lost friends, saying a few words in Norwegian before they finally turn to me.

"Bård, this is Maya," Erik says in such a proud way that I feel my cheeks get warm with pleasure.

"Ah...Instagram!" his cousin says with a grin, pointing two finger guns my way before laughing and reaching out to shake my hand. "Welcome to Bukkehaugfestivalen! Are you enjoying it?"

"Very much," I say, while Erik escapes to buy another round of beers. "Your band is really good."

"Thanks," he says with a self-deprecating smile and nod. "Erik has been great about sponsoring us."

"*En øl*," Erik announces as he returns to hand a beer to his cousin.

"*Takk*," Bård says, thanking him before downing half the cup in one swallow. Oh, to be that young again.

Having finished my second beer, I'm feeling pretty spry myself.

"There's an after-thing in one of the buildings. You should come," Bård says, frowning at the performance on stage for some reason.

"Sounds like fun!" I say, sounding ridiculously chipper even to my ears. I must be tipsier than I thought.

Erik gives me a strange smile then shrugs and nods in agreement. "Sure, why not?"

Bård only seems to be half-listening as his eyes remain glued to the stage. When I turn my attention to the singer at the microphone, I notice him practically boring a hole right back at Bård.

What's that about?

I drown the rest of my beer just in time for the next band to make an appearance. It's another rowdy bunch, this one more punk rock than metal and decidedly more fun. I laugh, dancing around like the rest of the crowd. I feel like some free spirit at a pagan ritual as I completely let loose. It's surprising how many inhibitions a few rounds of beer can shake free.

By the time they've finished up the last song, half the people around us are already making their way to one of the yellow dorm buildings nearby. I drag Erik along, following them like part of a drunken conga line.

This is so much fun!

Although Erik holds his alcohol better than me, even I notice how much more laid back he is, easily amused by the antics of those around him.

Bård catches up with us. The pretty girl who stole his attention earlier is clinging to his arm. Up close, she's perfectly stunning, despite trying to drown it out with all that black.

"Hi, I'm Hanna!" she says, clinging tighter to Bård as she eyes me.

"Maya," I say, planting an arm around Erik's waist, assuring her that she has nothing to worry about from me. I feel the vibration of his chuckle under my hand, and I look up to give him a mocking glare.

"I owe you a beer!" Bård—seemingly blind to what's transpired—shouts at Erik over the noise of the crowd. "Let's go to the bar."

"There's a bar in here?" I ask in surprise. I really did miss out in college if that's the case.

Bård leads us to an open area where there is indeed a bar. Billa Bar, according to the name painted across the wall behind it. He somehow manages four beers, and we each take one.

It's probably one too many for me, but...when at Bukkehaugfestivalen!

From there, it's a wild blur, and I'm pretty sure whatever I missed out on in college, I make up for in the hour, or so that passes by with more beer.

A friend of either Bård or Hanna inserts himself into our little quartet to give me the grand tour.

I laugh when we pass by the blindfolded head of a goat mounted on the wall, for some reason finding it absurdly amusing.

"You know the Nazis occupied this dorm during World War II," our tour guide announces in a conspiratorial voice. "They kicked everyone out during the occupation."

I nod as though this is fascinating information. Somewhere in the back of my mind, it actually is.

"This is the party room!" he announces as we reach a door with "Valhalla" painted in red.

It's much louder and more crowded down here, which is fine by me.

A girl practically crashes into our tour guide, whose name I realize we never even got. She immediately zeroes in on me. "American?" she asks with eager eyes. Before I can even answer, she is tugging up the hem of her shirt to show me a massive tattoo of a koi fish on her waist, so fresh it's still slathered with ointment. "What do you think?"

I love it!" I gush, actually jealous for some reason. Why didn't I think to get a pretty koi fish on my waist instead of stupid butterfly tramp stamp all those years ago?

"There used to be a bullseye you could throw your empty beer bottles at!" Bård shouts with a grin as he points to a red wall. "They painted over it."

I pout, feeling childishly disappointed that I can't throw my empty beer bottle at the wall.

At some point I desperately need to use the bathroom and the Girl with the Koi Tattoo—as I've officially labeled her in my head, making the obvious connections to the popular Scandinavian book, the *Girl with the Dragon Tattoo*—laughs as she takes my hand to show me the way.

"There's a piano!" I announce, staring dumbfoundedly at the upright piano sitting right next to the urinals. The girl playing a stilted version of "Moonlight Sonata" right next to them is enough to almost shock me into sobriety.

I wrinkle my brow as I belatedly notice the row of drunken boys shamelessly relieving themselves right next to her.

"Are you sure—?"

The girl who dragged me here laughs.

"It's coed," she says, her voice filled with amusement.

I'm too close to bursting to care about propriety and quickly make my way to one of the stalls, thankfully with a door, to relieve myself.

What a crazy place!

Back in Valhalla, I find our little group again and laughingly tell Erik about it. His smile is indulgent, more amused at me than at what I've revealed.

"I think I need to visit it myself," he leans in to whisper in my ear before escaping the room.

"You're American."

I turn at the announcement, and find the lead singer of the band that Bård was staring at during the show. He has a slightly sullen look on his face that quickly disappears when I give him my attention.

"Yeah?" I reply warily.

Bård says something to him in Norwegian, placing a hand on his chest as though telling him to back off.

He replies in a slurred voice. It shifts to something bitter as he spits harsh words to Hanna standing next to him.

Her voice sounds exasperated as she responds.

Despite my drunken state, it oh so plainly falls into place for me. This newcomer has the hots for Hanna, who is decidedly Team Bård.

The drunken interloper waves an angry hand at both of them and turns his attention to me with a lazy grin. "I'm talking to the American girl."

I busy myself with my beer, mostly to avoid getting involved in this messy triangle.

"You like Kanye West?" he says, laughing, and twisting his fingers in some interpretation of gang signs. "Jay-Z? Snoop Dogg?"

Oh, good grief.

I roll my eyes, my mouth thankfully still filled with beer so I can't respond the way I'd like to.

"Wha's up ma nigga!" he says before laughing again.

"What did you say?" Erik's voice calls out behind me as he returns from the bathroom, sounding pissed the hell off. I'm still swallowing my sip of beer, so I can't calm him before he tears into the boy.

He growls something angry in Norwegian. The boy, obviously too drunk to realize the fighter he's up against just smirks, saying something back in a pompous tone. His eyes slide to me, and he adds another little verbal tidbit, his voice and gaze so lecherous that it defies the need for a translator.

Hanna gasps in shock.

Bård shouts something in scathing Norwegian.

Erik responds in the way that has become his modus operandi.

The first punch has the boy flailing. The second has him flat on his ass, his nose a bloody mess.

There's a brief silence surrounding us on the cusp of that. It's quickly filled by a mix of stunned chatter in Norwegian and a few titters.

"Erik!" I say, grabbing his arm with my free hand. "It's fine."

He's like a statue, planted in place staring down at the boy as though he'd like to add a few good kicks as well. His target has quickly found his anger, his face snarled in preparation for revenge.

"Let's go," I plead, tugging hard. I feel his muscles tense in resistance, happy to go a few more rounds.

"Erik!"

He twists his head to face me, his expression filled with angry surprise that I don't want him to completely destroy the guy to save my honor.

"Let's go," I say in a surprisingly sober and level voice.

He sighs and allows me to lead him out as he studiously ignores the other partiers staring at us as we leave.

I shoot an apologetic smile at Bård and Hanna, both of whom give me looks of understanding. Like Erik, I ignore everyone else as I quickly try to retrace our steps out of the dorm.

It's still light outside, which completely throws me for a moment. It has to be almost midnight by now.

How the heck do people here live like this?

"What the hell was that, Erik?" I say as soon as we're outside.

"You have no idea what he said," he retorts, his face and voice still filled with rage.

"So what? In case you've forgotten, I used to work at a sports bar. You think he's the first drunken boy spouting offensive shit that I've had to deal with?"

"He shouldn't have said what he did." He's like a bull still seeing red, exhaling through his nostrils in anger as he paces back and forth.

"Listen, I get it. You want to defend me, but this isn't hockey. You can't just go swinging punches."

I have enough clarity to see it now, and just enough lingering *under the influence* to blurt it out.

"You need to go to Sweden."

That stops him in his tracks, erasing the look of anger and replacing it with one of surprise. "What?"

"It's obvious that whatever is going on with your dad is something you need to stop avoiding. *Now.*"

"You don't understand."

"I understand enough to know this has been eating away at you since we got here, maybe even long before now. What's the harm in just going?"

He glares at me, jaw hardening with renewed anger.

"Listen," I say softly. "I know probably better than most what this must be like for you. How about being the better man and flying out there? If nothing changes, at least you can tell yourself you tried."

Erik's only response is to stare even harder at me, his blue eyes turning to icicles. I can't tell if I've managed to make an impact at all.

CHAPTER FORTY-FOUR

ERIK

"I'm coming to Sweden. Tomorrow."

There's a moment of silence on the other end of the line, long enough for me to rethink the whole thing.

"I'm glad, Erik," my father says, sounding relieved for some reason. "*There is...a lot to discuss.*"

I feel my eyelids flicker at that. It isn't lost on me that there must be something of dire importance going on, enough to end this wall of non-communication he and I have had between us the past several years.

"*I'm bringing someone with me, a friend. Someone close to me that I'm seeing. Her name is Maya Jackson.*"

"That's good," he says, sounding surprisingly pleased. "I look forward to meeting her."

"What's this about? Why are you so anxious to see me?"

There's another pause, longer this time. "*I think it would be best to discuss all of this when you come. Let me know what time your flight arrives, and I'll meet you at the airport.*"

I can tell by his tone I won't be getting any more from him.

Dad has this way of stating things with a certain quiet finality that's far more effective than any angry rant.

"*I'll see you tomorrow then.*" I hang up before he can reply, feeling frustrated once again.

How the hell did I let Maya convince me to do this?

We're on a small plane, having transferred in Stockholm to a flight bound for Örnsköldsvik.

"This is a good thing," Maya reassures me yet again.

As annoying as the repetition of it is, I find her words reassuring. I don't know why I'm so tense about this.

Maybe because it's the first time I've seen this side of my family in almost seven years.

Maybe because I still harbor some of the resentment that kept me away all this time.

Maybe because I know there's bad news waiting for me when we land.

It's the only plausible explanation as to why Dad would get in touch after all this time.

He is waiting for us when we arrive, as promised, and my eyes search him carefully looking for any indication that something is physically or mentally wrong with him. Other than a seemingly lingering sadness, I see nothing.

I have his eyes, though mine reflect a bit more intensity when I look at myself in the mirror. Otherwise, there are vague similarities that hint at our relation to one another, the same full head of blond hair, square jawline, above-average height. It's his posture and resting facial expression that give away his more tempered resolve, the one that always chose complacency over challenge.

"Erik," he says with a smile on his face that would probably mimic the one he'd have if I'd risen back from the dead. I suppose in a way, for him at least, I have.

"Dad," I say, feeling the discomfort set in.

Before we can do that awkward dance where we aren't sure whether to hug or shake hands, he pulls me in for an embrace, holding me with surprising strength and longer than expected.

When he pulls away, he searches my face either studying it to memory or searching for something. I'm not sure which.

"This is my girlfriend, Maya Jackson," I say, mostly to escape that look. I direct my gaze toward her. She seems to be assessing my father with the same scrutiny, no doubt just as curious about this visit as I am.

Dad flashes her the same pleased smile he gave me, again surprising me by bringing her in for a hug. He had a tender side to him, but even for him, this sort of hugs and smiles sentimentality defies what I remember.

"Hello, Maya. I'm Nils, Erik's father." He leaves off the last name, Norquist, which I never bother to adopt.

"Nice to meet you," she replies with her trademark smile that could melt even the coldest heart.

"Well, let's go, shall we? I know everyone is excited to see you."

I feel my brow wrinkle, watching him even more studiously to see what brought about that lie. I know for a fact Freja would have no interest in seeing me after all these years. Liam? At best, he'd be indifferent.

What the hell is going on?

This time it's Maya insisting I ride in front with my father as we drive. I seem to be the only one feeling the tension since she and my father amicably chat on the drive into town. They might as well be old friends.

"...and then I tried the lutefisk, which, I'm sorry, but it was disgusting," Maya says from the back seat.

Dad laughs lightly, looking up at her in the rearview mirror. "Yes, we do love our preserved fish. While you are here, you can sample some traditional Swedish food. Our meatballs are popular. We also have smörgåstårta, which is like a sandwich cake."

I twist to face both of them, eyeing him as though he's someone completely different from the father I knew, and frowning her way.

"I'd love to," Maya says, giving me a pointed smile.

I turn to face the front, focusing my attention on the scenery. It's quite a drive back to the city I left and never looked back on when I joined the professional Swedish Hockey League. Thankfully, Maya keeps my father occupied for most of it, allowing me to tune out as I watch the Swedish landscape fly by. There are long stretches of nothing but open land eventually dotted with the occasional house. As civilization begins to creep in, I feel my muscles get more and more tense. Ö-vik isn't a large city, especially compared to either Stockholm or New York. Yet, as I watch familiar landmarks pass by, I realize it has the ability to affect me far more than either of those two cities. It's all so familiar, I might as well have never left.

"Where are we headed?" I ask, remembering enough to realize we aren't headed back to the home I spent the latter portion of my adolescence in.

"I thought we would stop at Liam's home first," Dad says in a deceptively idle voice. "Everyone is already there, Freja, his wife, Linnea. He has two children now!"

I snap my head around to look at him. It isn't the news that my half-brother is married with kids that has my senses tingling, it's the way my father has mentioned them. It's too...cheerful.

"That'll be nice. Seeing everyone again," Maya says, matching his cheerful tone, completely immune to the undercurrent of deception in it.

Now, my body is tenser than ever. Part of it is seeing the half-brother whose life I ruined once upon a time. I suppose it's only fitting that the prodigal son come face-to-face with his sins upon his return home.

The house we arrive at is smaller than my father's, tucked into one of the many quiet areas of the city. There are already a few cars in the driveway, and we park on the street in front.

"Here we are!" Dad says, still in that chipper tone that is beginning to grate on me.

I step out of the car and stare at the house where my brother supposedly lives. Having been out of touch for the past seven years, I have no idea when he married or had kids. How old are they? How did he meet his wife? What does he even do for a living?

It occurs to me that he might as well be a stranger I'm meeting for the first time.

Dad and Maya both come around, the latter taking my hand and squeezing encouragingly as the former leads the way to the front door.

It's no surprise that it's unlocked. Örnsköldsvik isn't exactly a hotbed of crime.

Freja is in the front hallway on her way to another room, and I feel my stomach instinctively clench when I see her. The mild wave of resentment flows through me as she comes to a stop.

"Nils," she says with breathless surprise, as though we've arrived earlier than expected. She flashes him a brief smile, deliberately avoiding eye contact with me.

She looks surprisingly older than I remember. Freja isn't an unattractive woman, though compared to my mother, she might as well have been beige wallpaper. She has brown hair and a face that's a bit too long, with a jutting jaw and widely spaced cheekbones. Her blue eyes are perfect for cutting right through a person, which I know all too well. A generous mouth and pert nose are the only things softening her features, giving her a more proportioned look that some might find appealing.

Eventually, she has no choice but to acknowledge me, those blue eyes settling on me with a surprising amount of trepidation. The only expressions I'm used to receiving from her were resentment and annoyance at my very existence.

"Erik," she says. Again, I'm surprised to find something in her voice that isn't quite tenderness, but close enough.

"Freja," I reply, sounding as neutral as possible.

"We're so glad you've decided to come back," she says, with a seemingly genuine, if a bit hesitant, smile. She's speaking English, having noticed the woman standing next to me who is obviously not Swedish.

I narrow my eyes with suspicion, causing hers to drop with embarrassment.

"He's brought his girlfriend, Maya Jackson," Dad says, apparently trying to lighten the mood.

Freja's eyes flit back up, landing on Maya. She smiles. "It's nice to meet you, Maya. Thank you for coming."

"Thank you for having me. It's so nice to finally meet all of you."

I watch both my father and Freja visibly relax under that cheerful tone in Maya's voice, diminishing all the tension in the air.

"Where's Liam?"

My father and Freja immediately catch each other eyes, a brief spark of fear flashing in them. Freja plants a smile that's too large to be real as she turns back to me.

"He's outside with the rest of the family. I was just on my way to get the food. Nils, why don't you show them out?"

Before he can respond, she quickly turns, heading on toward the kitchen. I watch her go, then turn my attention to my father.

He inhales before planting the same overly bright smile on his face. "Come, they're all dying to meet you."

It's obvious now why I've been summoned back. Liam. Whatever it is that has caused such an upset among the Norquists has to do with him.

I brace myself as I follow my father to the backyard, still holding firm to Maya's hand.

The first person I see is a young woman, her light brown hair braided and wrapped up around her head Heidi-style. She's pretty in a soft, pleasant way with a round, open face and an easy smile. She has on a pair of loose jeans and a sleeveless blouse, paired with sandals.

She doesn't notice me, too preoccupied with the children running around blowing bubbles. It's a boy and a girl, the boy about four or five years old and the girl teetering after him on the unsteady legs of a toddler.

"Linnea, this is Erik and his girlfriend, Maya."

She blinks over at us, her eyes going wide as though I'm an apparition. "Oh...oh, yes! *Hallo!*"

I give her a distracted smile, my curious mind having found the man sitting in a deck chair, his back still to me. The only thing visible is the back of his head. The brown hair is shorter than I remember, perhaps a bit curlier as well.

"*Torn, Matilda, come meet your uncle!*" Linnea says, walking toward us. She speaks to them in Swedish, being that they're probably too young to be quite fluent in English yet. The two children stop chasing the bubbles the older one is blowing and stand in place, eyeing me with curiosity.

As fascinated as I am by Liam's young family, I can't take my eyes away from him sitting in that chair, still facing away. While his kids are still stuck in place, wondering if I'm worth the interruption of their playtime, he finally stands up and turns my way.

That's when I understand why I had to return home.

CHAPTER FORTY-FIVE

ERIK

I hear Maya's soft inhale next to me. Even though she's never met my half-brother, anyone who saw him would know there was something wrong.

I always figured Liam would become a brawnier version of himself as a teenager. Instead, he looks like he's just stepped out of a brutal prison camp. Although he isn't entirely emaciated, his skin and what little flesh he has hangs off him like someone who has suffered rapid and extreme weight loss.

"I know, a bit of a surprise," he says with a wry smile as he sees my expression. "Hodgkin's lymphoma, specifically. Don't worry, it's in remission now."

"*Come, Torn and Matilda, you'll have a chance to meet your uncle later. Let's give Papa a chance to talk to him,*" Linnea says.

I'm still too stunned by my brother to even pay attention to anyone else. It's only when Maya lets go of my hand that I fall out of my stupor.

"I think I'll go help inside," she says, rubbing my back once before she follows everyone in.

"*Let's sit and catch up,*" Liam says, switching to Swedish. He still has a soft smile on his face. I watch him slowly walk back to the chair, still with that hint of a limp in his leg. On the way, he grabs two bottles of beer from the large bucket filled with ice that I see has been set up on the patio.

I settle into the chair next to him, still watching him with wary regard. He opens one bottle and hands it to me, then the other, taking a small sip for himself.

"Should you be drinking that?"

He laughs. "*I think a visit from my long lost brother warrants it, no?*"

I don't laugh with him.

"*It will be fine,*" he assures me.

I sip my beer, not taking my eyes off him. "*When were you diagnosed?*"

"*December.*"

I nearly choke on my beer.

"*Yes, it was surprising,*" he says over the sound of my coughing. "*But fortunately, it went into remission thanks to chemotherapy.*"

"*Why—*" I cut myself off before I can finish the question, why didn't anyone tell me. I know I have myself to blame.

Liam answers anyway.

"*You had your life in America,*" he says, staring ahead. "*It went into remission fairly quickly after chemotherapy. Your team was doing well enough to make it into the playoffs.*"

"*We didn't make it past the second round.*"

"*I know,*" he says, still lifting his beer in salute.

It's an uncomfortable topic, one that has been the primary source of conflict between us since I first moved to Örnsköldsvik.

Still, I've come this far...

"*That day in the hospital, after the—after I pushed you. Why didn't you tell anyone? Why did you tell me to keep playing hockey?"

He stares out at the lawn. I follow his gaze, my eyes resting on some pink plastic thing that must belong to Matilda.

"I think by then, I'd had time to process what happened — not just the fight, but everything that had led up to it. I'd been jealous of you since you first came. I thought Dad liked you better; he had to if he'd gone to all the trouble to bring you to Sweden."

Once again, I'm surprised. I turn to Liam, my eyes wide.

He feels my gaze on him and laughs. *"Don't look so surprised. Everyone liked you. Girls fell all over themselves. Guys always seemed to want to be with you even though you only ever wanted to be alone it seemed. And Dad...well, I couldn't figure that one out. I know my mom hated you coming here. So did I."*

"So did I," I say, and we both chuckle. His confession is startling, mostly because everything he's said no doubt comes from having viewed my life here through some blurry lens. I don't remember our classmates liking me as much as he claims —at least until I started excelling at hockey.

"In the hospital, I was so angry at first, especially when the doctor mentioned how long the healing would take. But the first day gave me nothing but time to put everything in perspective.

"You'd lost your mother. You'd been uprooted from everything you knew, even the language with which you were most familiar. I still remember our classmates making fun of your accent, me joining in with them. Without hockey, you would have had nothing."

He pauses, not even taking a sip of his beer before he continues.

"I knew you were going to quit after that. I won't lie, a part of me hated the fact that you'd then just become a martyr, with

everyone blaming me. You had a talent, a natural talent that was too good to waste."

I sip my beer and ponder that. After swallowing, I turn to him. "I never apologized for what happened. I'm sorry, Liam."

"There's no need," he says with a smile. "I have a pretty good life, after all. An amazing wife, two great kids. I beat cancer!"

He pauses, staring at me with a curious look before continuing. "I sometimes think about how life unfurls. If this minor or major thing had happened differently, what would my life be like? I think my life has gone exactly the way it should have... thanks in part to you."

"You never think about what it would have been like to be in the NHL like me?"

He laughs softly. "You're the adventurous one, Erik. You always have been. Yes, I wanted to be in the Swedish League, but that's about as far as my goals would have taken me. You are exactly where you belong."

I consider his words, thinking about how they apply to my own life. If I'd quit hockey, I'd probably still live here in Örnsköldsvik, or perhaps back in Oslo. I'd never have made the Swedish League, then the NHL. I wouldn't have been on the Blades team, living in Brooklyn, skating past a woman with the most beautiful smile I've ever seen.

Maybe he's right. Maybe I'm exactly where I belong, there in Brooklyn.

I sip my beer, turning my attention back to him. "So you said you're in remission? Is that why you didn't want Dad to tell me about it?"

His expression becomes serious. "I wouldn't let him tell you during the season, especially after I went into remission. That seemed...unfair. He told me he would ask you himself to come visit, said something about owing it to you to ask *himself, that it was his duty. I wanted to wait until you were here before I asked you about this, not through Dad or my mother or any of your family in Oslo. I felt that was only right."*

So Dad was playing the long game. He must have started texting the moment Liam became sick, hoping to wear me down little by little in the hopes that I'd eventually say yes to coming to Sweden this year. And that part about owing it to me? My mind snaps back to that moment over a decade ago in the hospital. My own father...

"What is it you wanted to ask me?" It's only after I've said it that the answer is obvious.

"This remission may only be a temporary thing. This disease has a pretty good survival rate, especially at the stage I had it. But all the same..."

"You want me to get tested. Bone marrow transplant, is that it?"

"Stem cells, specifically. The only reason I waited is...well, Dad wasn't a match. Thus, the chances that you are—"

"I'll do it," I say before he can finish. "Of course, I will."

He nods, a grim smile on his face as though he's already jumped to the conclusion that I won't be a match, but he appreciates the offer.

As I sip my beer, a chill goes through me at the idea that I almost didn't bother coming out. I'm sure Dad would have defied Liam and told me about his condition eventually, remission or no remission.

"I'm glad I came, Liam," I say, staring ahead.

"I am too, brother."

Later on, we're inside eating the late lunch that Freja and

Linnea have prepared. Part of it consists of smörgåstårta, which is something I've personally missed since I've been gone.

Maya eyes the slice of layers of bread stacked between prawn salad with skepticism, but eagerly helps herself to a second after finishing the first.

Now that Liam and I have made our peace, I have a better chance to learn more about the rest of the family.

"*Are the buildings really, super big in New York?*" Torn asks in Swedish.

"*Really super big!*" I say, lifting my long arm in the air as high as I can to show him.

He laughs and his sister, who I've learned mimics everything he does, joins in.

Torn is big for his age, the same way Liam and I both were. He has Freja and Liam's brown hair and his mother's kind brown eyes.

Matilda has the wide, thoughtful blue eyes of her grandfather, my father. Her hair is so blonde it's almost white, the way most Scandinavian children's hair is at this age. By the time she's her brother's age, it may be as brown as his or as blonde as mine.

Maya is chatting with Linnea and Liam. Freja and my father watch us all from opposite ends of the table. Though I have yet to come to the same understanding with them that I have with my half-brother, I can at least sympathize with what they've been through this past year. I'm sure thinking about the one son who made it all the way to the United States, with his multi-million-dollar contracts, supermodel girlfriends, and international respect and admiration—just thinking about that "Northern Lights" spread in *Ideal Gentleman* wracks me with guilt—couldn't have helped things as they watched Liam dance with death.

Still, this feels more like home than it ever did when I lived here as a teenager. Freja is much more relaxed, basking in the adoration of her grandchildren. Dad is content, for once noting that his sons aren't fighting. Linnea is every bit as amazing as Liam claims she is. His kids are just as great.

It makes me realize what I'm missing out on.

That night, I'm lying in bed with Maya. We're in a hotel to avoid imposing on my family and for privacy.

"Today was nice," she says, resting her chin on my chest as she smiles up at me.

I smile back down at her. "It was. I'm glad you encouraged me to come."

She laughs and pokes a finger into my chest. "You would have come eventually."

I'm not so sure about that, but I don't say so.

I stare thoughtfully over her head. "I know you have to go back to work by Monday, but I need to get tested."

"Of course," she says. "I can manage my way back from here."

I nod, still staring at the wall.

"I think you *should* stay longer," she says, as though answering a question I have yet to ask. "You have a lot of catching up to do."

I bring my attention back to her with a smile. "You don't mind?"

"Erik," she says, rising to give me a mildly scolding look. "What kind of girlfriend would I be if I came between you and your family?"

My smile turns into a grin. "I knew there was a reason I loved you."

"Oh yeah," she says, easing into a grin of her own. "How you gonna show me?"

"I can think of a few ways," I say, rising to twist my body so that I'm on top of her.

The way she laughs underneath me, wrapping her arms and legs around me feels so damn perfect.

That's when it hits me. I have everything I want, right here, right now. Maya. My family. My home.

Even here in this generic hotel room, I know I'm right where I belong.

CHAPTER FORTY-SIX

ERIK

"Negative."

"Oh, Erik, I'm so sorry," Maya says, her face sympathetic as she stares back from the computer screen.

We've agreed to FaceTime every day while I'm here in Sweden.

Liam, out of all of us, was the most realistic about my chances of being a stem cell donor for him and took it better than anyone.

"So what does that mean for Liam?"

"It isn't a death sentence. As Liam said, the fact that he responded so well to the chemotherapy bodes well for him. The stem cells would have just given him a greater fighting chance."

She nods, her face somber as she looks off to the side in her bedroom back in Brooklyn.

"But..."

Her eyes snap back to the screen.

"I think it's a good idea for me to stay, at least until training camp."

"I think that's a great idea," she says, with surprising enthusiasm. "You should spend as much time as possible with him and the rest of your family. Family is everything."

I smile, feeling a certain sense of relief relax me. Now that she's said it, I realize it's true. Family *is* everything.

"*Okay so, you have to hold the stick, right at these two points,*" I say, showing Torn the best way to hold a hockey stick, even though we're on the grass of his parents' backyard.

I've learned that my nephew is pretty adept on skates and has already started learning the bare minimum of the ins and outs of hockey.

Now that his professional playing uncle is in the picture, his once lukewarm interest has turned into a full-fledged obsession. Every time I come over, he practically assaults me with questions about America or demands for "training" in hockey.

It reminds me of my time at Big Brother back in America. I enjoy spending time with kids. The fact that Torn and Matilda are my blood relatives—no matter how tenuously—makes it all the more enjoyable.

Naturally, what Torn does, Matilda must do as well. Despite his protests (which I have to keep from laughing at) I happily indulge her, planting her tiny hands on the stick that they don't even fit around as I show her how to swing it.

Kids have always been an abstract thought in my mind, mostly something to think seriously about once my professional hockey career was off the ground. Being here with my niece and nephew has made me realize that I've never moved on from that point.

It's yet another thing that being back here in Sweden has opened my eyes to.

And there's only one woman I can imagine moving on with.

"Zia's trying to get me to do the big chop and go natural."

"Big chop?" I question, looking at Maya on my laptop screen. I'm still living out of a hotel having spent the day with Liam and his family.

"Cutting all my hair off and starting from scratch, no relaxers to straighten it," she explains with a tight smile as though worried about what I'll think of it.

"You know I'll always think you're beautiful."

She rolls her eyes and laughs. "That's what boyfriends are supposed to say."

"Especially when it's true. All the better, since it helps keep you from hiding that gorgeous face of yours."

She can't help but smile at that. It fades as she tilts her head to consider me through the screen.

"I always feel like I'm talking about stupidly inane things while you've got so much going on back there."

"These stupidly inane things are what I live for; it's what I need right now," I say. "Talking with you is the best part of my day, Maya."

She smiles in that pretty way of hers.

"Now, tell me more about what's going on out there in Brooklyn."

After considering me for a moment, letting my prior statement sink in, she perks up and rolls her eyes again. "Zia is in love, *yet again*. This YouTuber she met through some guy at Katie's party. I'm not going to be the one to say *anything*. I know Demetria is itching to give it to her. He plays video games all day. That's it—aside from making constant sarcastic remarks. Plus, he has one of those annoying floppy haircuts where it's always falling in his eyes and he always makes this big show of swiping it back."

I laugh, enjoying the casual feel of this. I could listen to Maya talk forever, especially if I get to see her beautiful face while I do.

She thinks this is trivial, considering the gravity of what's going on here in Sweden. She has no idea how much of a life preserver she is, keeping me afloat as I navigate this new experience.

"*Okay, okay, I think Uncle Erik needs a break,*" Linnea says, calling her children back in the house.

She's right, Uncle Erik does need a break. I'm loving them to death, but who knew kids were this exhausting!

I watch Torn and Matilda reluctantly head into the house as Linnea shoots me an appreciative smile. Liam is still easily tired out, and I've slid into the role of de facto babysitter as she helps him and takes care of the ordinary obligations of running a home.

Today Freja and my father have come to visit for dinner.

Dad steps out into the backyard as I pick up the toys we have been playing with for the past hour. I notice he has two beers in his hand.

"*They really have taken a liking to you,*" he says with a smile.

"*They're great. I'm glad I'm able to spend so much time with them.*"

When I'm done with the toys, I wander toward him, taking the beer he reaches out to me.

"We haven't had a chance to really talk since you've been back."

I sip my beer, waiting to see where this is going. He's right. I've spent most of my time here in Sweden at Liam's house. I only see Dad and Freja, who has warmed considerably toward me, when they come over for dinner.

"So, let's talk," he says, nodding toward the same deck chairs that Liam and I sat in that first day I came back.

I feel my muscles go taut but follow him.

For a while, we sit and drink beer, the trademark introduction to any man-to-man or, more to the point, father-to-son talk known round the world.

It's summer, which means the sun has yet to even reach the horizon even at this late hour, especially further north here in Örnsköldsvik. Dad stares ahead at the grass where I just spent the last several hours playing with Liam's kids.

"*Did you know that I asked your mother to marry me once I found out she was pregnant?*"

Of all the ways he could have opened this conversation, that's the last thing that would have ever crossed my mind. I'm speechless.

He laughs softly as though I've visually or verbally reacted in some way. Even though my insides are going haywire, I have yet to show it.

"*I don't know how much your mom or grandfather or aunt told you about our relationship.*"

"Nothing," I say, hearing the tinge of bitterness in my voice.

He must hear it as well since he gently nods his head.

"*I was in Norway for the summer. This was after I had graduated from university. It was supposed to be a tour of the country with some friends from school, one of whom lived in Bergen. Your mother was working on one of those boats that tours the fjords?*"

I vaguely remember my mother mentioning that as one of the many brief working stints she had throughout her life.

"She was the most beautiful woman I'd ever seen in my life."

That one has me stunned again. Not because of the words—I know my mother was an attractive woman, bewitching many a man long after my dad left the picture—but because he's confessing such a thing.

As though reading my mind, he turns to me with a smile. "Don't get me wrong, I love Freja very much, but your mother had this...otherworldly beauty to her. So much so that it was almost terrifying."

He turns to face the fence again. "Back then, I was less... cautious about life?" He says it in such a way as though he's not sure that's the correct word. "I had said something funny—I wish to hell I could remember what it was—but she laughed, and I was...gone. From that point on, I stayed in Oslo. I have no idea what she saw in me, but she was more than happy to spend the rest of the summer indulging my affection."

He takes a long swallow of his beer.

I haven't even touched mine.

My whole life, I've wondered what happened between my mother and father. Part of me also wondered what the hell she saw in such a meek and defeated man. Now, I slowly realize part of who he is today is because of my mother, who consumed life so fully that she couldn't help but steal a bit of it from those around her, my father included.

"I would have happily stayed there in Oslo with her before we even knew about you. But summer passed, and she made it clear that that was all there was to us. I knew it as well. It would have ended that way, nice and neat. Except...two months later, she called."

Now, I do take a sip. There's no need to fill the silence with what that call was about.

"*I was surprisingly ecstatic. She was...pragmatic. Strictly for my information, she said.*" He smiles into the distance. "*As though that would have stopped me. I was going to be a father.*"

I feel my heart beat a little faster.

"*To me, it all seemed so obvious. I'd move to Norway, marry her, and we'd live happily ever after. But when I got there...she had gone. It was your grandfather who told me. He was sympathetic about it, but he knew his daughter. She wasn't one to be tied down that way. You were hers and hers alone.*"

I feel my face harden. No wonder neither of them told me about this. My father wanted me. He wanted to be a family. It was my mother who denied me.

"*That's when I came back to Sweden. Freja and I had known each other from before, and we reconnected. She was exactly the kind of woman I should have been with from the start. That, I knew. Liam came about not too soon after. If I had to guess I'd say it was a combination of me being careless, trying to erase the memory of Ingrid. Or perhaps it was the mistake of telling Freja about your mother, which made her equally careless in some jealous way. One drunken night was all it took.*"

He takes a sip and stares ahead. "*But it worked for us. I have no regrets about Liam or Freja at all. Other than the few times I flew to Oslo to see you, I didn't hear from your mother again.*"

I'm still feeling the bitterness of what I could have had.

"*Don't blame her. She can't help who she was,*" Dad says, as though reading my mind. "*Just as you can't help who you are. I should have never brought you here. I just...I thought that when that terrible thing happened to her, I felt it was my chance to make it up to you—to be the dad I wanted to be in the first place.*"

I was blinded by what I thought was my duty...and, to be fair, what I thought I was denied."

I sip my beer.

"Now, I'm not so sure it was a good thing. I was guided by pride, not by what was best for you."

I think about what Liam said, about how life unfurls. About where I'd be if things hadn't happened exactly the way they should have.

Mostly, I think about Maya.

"No," I say after swallowing. "It *wasn't easy, I'll agree. But...I'm exactly where I need to be, Dad. Partially because of you moving me here."*

I feel him looking at me, so I turn to smile at him. I lift my beer to him, and he smiles back, tapping his to mine.

"Skål," we both say in a Swedish salute.

"Thanks for telling me all of this." I know he's told me more than he probably should have, but it served to create a clearer picture of my past, and for that I'm grateful.

"You deserved to know the truth, son."

I sip my beer and look out onto the lawn again, now more than ever feeling like I'm finally home again.

CHAPTER FORTY-SEVEN

MAYA

"Erik's moving back."

It's Friday and my girls and I are at our usual bar after work. Erik has been in Sweden for a few weeks now, and we've been FaceTiming almost every night.

"What?" Zia says, looking at me in surprise.

I shrug, circling the rim of my glass of beer with my fingertip. "He pretty much made it clear last night. All this talk of how if he were to move back, Stockholm would be the best fit since it's easy enough to get to both Oslo and Ö...Ö-vik—I can't pronounce the full name yet—where his brother lives."

"What about hockey?" Gabrielle asks.

"Obviously it will be when his contract with the Blades is up."

"But he hasn't said anything definite," Demetria confirms, peering closely at me.

"Why else would he bring up living in Stockholm?" I say, giving her an exasperated look.

There's a silence that follows that as we all drink our beer to absorb this information.

"So...would you consider moving to Sweden?" Zia asks.

I laugh. "Me? In Sweden? I was there for less than two days. I didn't even get to see Stockholm beyond the airport. Oslo was nice, but again, I was there for about a week."

"The question is, do you love him?" This is coming from Demetria of all people.

"What? Of course I do."

"Well then stop making excuses."

"I'm not making excuses," I say, looking across the table at her in surprise. It's mostly at the idea that she's the one saying this rather than what it is she's said. Even Gabrielle next to her and Zia diagonal to her are staring at her in mild shock.

"Yes, you are. I can already see you finding a way to justify breaking up with him in your head over this. Which is crazy."

"I never thought you'd be in the love conquers all camp," I say with a hint of a smile.

"I'm not saying love conquers all. I'm saying that..." She sighs and looks at her beer before bringing her attention back to me. "I'm saying that if you love him and he loves you, then ...it's worth trying."

'Where is this coming from?" Zia asks with a skeptical smile.

"Nowhere," Demetria snaps, and I swear if she had the sort of peaches and cream coloring of my roommate, she'd be beet-red right now.

"No," Zia presses, circling one finger at her. "There's something going on here."

"You know what? Fine, break up with him," Demetria says, her attention on Zia instead of me.

"I'm not breaking up with him!" I say. Even though the intensity of my voice was mostly out of frustration, as I make the statement, I feel it.

There are still a few more years on his Blades contract.

That's plenty of time to visit Norway and Sweden enough to become at least familiar with both places. Plenty of time to learn the language and figure out the immigration requirements. Plenty of time to figure out a new career since I'm sure my legal skills would be pointless there.

I sip my beer, suddenly feeling overwhelmed.

"Let's leave Maya alone," Gabrielle says, flashing a sympathetic smile my way, then turning to Zia with a sparkle in her eyes. "Tell me more about this YouTube guy."

I sense Zia perk up next to me, as usual floating on that bubble of happiness she always lets carry her away with each new relationship.

"Jason? He's amazing."

I try to keep from rolling my eyes. Every new guy she's with is "amazing." I think back to Grigory, Erik's teammate, mostly, the way he looked at Zia that day. It's the same way plenty of men—and boys while we were growing up—have looked at her. I feel a stab of sympathy for him. But with his handsome, albeit gruff good looks and career as a professional hockey player, I have no doubt that he'll find someone to help him get over her quickly enough.

"So he does what again? Just posts videos of him playing video games?"

"It's the most popular subject area on YouTube," Zia says in a slightly defensive tone. "As his two million subscribers attest to."

Gabrielle sighs and rolls her eyes as she sips her beer.

"But he's expanded to other things too. That's where he's really been helping me. Diversity is key. Stay in the same universe, but expand that universe." She says this as though it's some sage advice from the Buddha himself. "I'm moving on to minimalism and healthy eating, all within the same AMSR theme."

I listen to her go on and on about Jason-this and Jason-that, happy that the focus is no longer on me. As I sip my beer to ponder my own relationship, I see Demetria's eyes on me. She's practically repeating her earlier words with that gaze.

It's worth trying.

"Okay, I'm going to be the one to say it," Gabrielle begins, and I feel a lecture about insta-love coming on.

"Oh my God," I interrupt, having just caught sight of who walked through the door. I shake my head, thinking I must be mistaken. A bar in this part of Brooklyn is bound to attract casually-dressed, white males in their mid to late twenties.

But how many with hair that particularly blonde?

And how many that tall and with that build?

And how many with those blue eyes that could easily cut across a room?

The same blue eyes that have just found me.

"Is that Erik?" Zia says, sitting next to me with a view of the front entrance.

All I can do is nod slowly as he grins and makes his way toward our booth near the back of the bar.

"Maya," he says, his eyes still glued to me once he arrives.

My friends are just as dumbfounded as I am at his appearance.

I finally find my voice.

"I thought you were in…?" I can't even finish the sentence. Where was he last?

"I came back."

Why? I'm too scared to ask aloud.

"Can we talk?" he asks, his face getting serious.

I feel the lump in my throat go down hard. This is it — the part where he confirms my suspicions.

"Sure," I say, sliding out of the booth. "I don't think anyone is outside in the back. It's still too hot."

He nods, and I lead the way, feeling completely numb.

Outside, twilight is turning into night. I'm sure back in Sweden and Norway the sun would still be clinging to the sky. Yet, another thing I'd have to get used to.

I suddenly find my voice. "Listen, Erik, I know you want to move back to Sweden or Oslo or wherever once you're done with hockey here in New York. I get it. It's your home. You should be with your family. Who knows how much longer your brother will be in remission? And you've got your grandfather and dad and…everyone. I don't want to be the one to take that from you. I think this could work. I do. No, I've never left Brooklyn, but that doesn't mean I can't get out of my comfort zone and do this. The thing is, I love you, I really do. And you said you loved me—Oh!"

I stop, for some reason spellbound by the firefly that's just landed on his shoulder. That's when I look around and note that the air is filled with them. It's the beginning of July, still the perfect season for them to appear.

Erik looks down at one that's dancing around his hand. "This city…it never ceases to amaze me," he mutters. His eyes slide up to me, filled with the sizzling electricity of a hundred lightning bolts. "Everything about it."

Now, I'm speechless again.

"Maya, you're right. Norway is my home. So is Sweden. But so is Brooklyn. You're also right…I do love you. It took going home, specifically being there without you to understand."

"Understand what?"

"That I don't want to be there without you. I don't want to be anywhere without you. Listening to you talk, watching your face through the screen of my laptop really was the highlight of each day while I was there. That was no lie."

Now the lump in my throat is back.

"Our last conversation, it only occurred to me afterward how it may have come across—like I wanted to move back. Has the thought crossed my mind? Of course. But...I don't want to be anywhere without you, Maya. If that means staying here in Brooklyn then—"

I silence the rest of that with a kiss, reaching up on my toes and throwing my arms around him to bring him in closer. My eyes close to the sight of fireflies glowing around us. It's perfectly magical.

When I pull away, I find Erik grinning down at me.

"We have a few years to figure it out," I say.

His grin broadens, those eyes dancing with devilish amusement. "Starting with tonight."

CHAPTER FORTY-EIGHT

ERIK

Jul (Christmas Eve)

"Can you see us?" I say into the laptop.

Through the screen, I see my morfar, Vilde, Alf, Emma, Bård, and his girlfriend Hanna at the dinner table. All of them are dressed in holiday sweaters that would make the average person cringe.

"We can see you all just fine," Vilde assures me.

Here at Liam's home in Örnsköldsvik, all of us, from Dad and Freja to his wife and children, are similarly dressed in ridiculous Christmas attire.

Maya is wearing a pink sweater with snowflakes made out of tacky silver sequins. I have on a black sweater with multicolored ornaments splashed over the front and back.

Ugly Sweaters.

Just one of the few American traditions we've decided to bring back with us for the brief holiday visit.

The NHL only gives its players December 24-26 off. I had a game on the 23rd (of course I did), but Maya and I managed an early morning flight to Stockholm, then to Örnsköldsvik in time to celebrate on Christmas Eve when most Swedes celebrate.

"Okay," I say in English, which even Matilda and Torn are picking up quite well these days. "I just wanted to wish everyone God Jul or...Merry Christmas," I finish, turning to Maya.

She smiles at me, mostly filled with the happiness of the holiday spirit around us.

"And while I have everyone around who means something to me, I think it's the perfect time to...ask this beautiful woman sitting next to me if she would be my wife."

Before she can even answer, both the laptop and the room around us is filled with cheers and laughter and clapping. Everyone but the woman sitting next to me knew this was coming.

Maya is stunned into silence...even more so when she sees the five-carat ring I present to her.

It's only when the noise dies down and everyone is looking at us that she realizes she hasn't yet answered.

"Oh...I mean, *yes!*"

CHAPTER FORTY-NINE

MAYA

The Wedding

Norway this time of year is perfect.

I've visited often enough to know.

We've picked July for the date, long enough after the playoffs to be a safe bet, just in case.

Hopefully, the man waiting at the end of the aisle considers me a prize worth winning as well. Or at least he'd better have the tact to say so if ever pressed on the matter.

I laugh to myself as Zia places the flower wreath on the hair she finally managed to convince me to go natural with.

I'm in a simple white, knee-length lace dress and white sandals, holding a bouquet of purple heather, Norway's unofficial national flower.

My four friends and I are in a secluded spot away from the main "venue" which is the beach Erik took me to the first time I visited Oslo.

"How in the world do you look so Scandinavian and decidedly not Scandinavian at the same time?" Gabrielle asks, scrutinizing me so that everything is perfect.

"Well, I've certainly had enough Scandinavian in me, so maybe that explains it," I say with a perfectly straight face.

Demetria is the first to laugh. That sets the rest of them off, and pretty soon we're all laughing uncontrollably.

"Okay, okay, okay," I say, waving my hands to quiet them. I look around at each of them feeling so blessed, trying to keep myself from crying. "You guys..."

I can't even finish since the tears start flowing.

"Girl, we know," Gabrielle says as she's the first to come in and hug me. Another round of laughter breaks out as the others follow suit.

When we're done, they are the ones to escort me to the spot closer in where both my mom and dad are waiting. I wasn't about to choose one over the other to walk me down the aisle and, fortunately, they both agreed to be as civil as possible to do this for me—their daughter.

"Oh, Maya," my mom says, almost ready to break out in tears and cause me to do the same all over again.

"You look beautiful, sweetheart," my dad says.

They were surprisingly less civil about the "casual" mandate of the affair but gave in at my insistence. Just as Erik and I instructed all the guests, they are simply dressed in a summer dress for her, and khaki pants and a shirtsleeve white button-down shirt.

"Let's do this!" I say, feeling suddenly giddy.

The wedding is small by most standards, but big enough to not only fill the beach but fill the needs of the bride and groom. We invited people who meant the most to us.

Mom and Dad stand on either side of me, walking me down the "aisle," which is just a part in the group of people leading up to the man that means everything to me. I make sure to meet all their happy gazes, acknowledging each in turn as we pass.

Arvid, who insists I officially call him "Morfar" after today, Vilde, Alf, Emma, Bård and his girlfriend Hanna. Nils and Freja. Liam, Linnea, Torn, and Matilda. Wanda and my sister and brother (just like Erik with Liam, I've officially dropped the "half). And even Luis, Mom's "someone special" that I had an inkling might eventually turn into something.

There will be another ceremony back in Brooklyn to accommodate a larger group of loved ones, including extended family. And of course Liza and Joey, as well as my former roommate Katie—still in the process of taking complete ownership of the cheese shop she once worked at, otherwise she'd be here too—all of whom helped make this happen.

But right now there's Erik Sørenson.

The man I'm going to marry.

Those same eyes that struck me like lightning the first time I met him, now strike again. Who says it can't hit the same spot twice?

Woah.

CHAPTER FIFTY

ERIK

The puck drops.
I don't even think. I just go. That's what I do best: go. On the rink at any rate.

The Blades are tied with the St. Louis Blues. Considering these are the final minutes of the third period of the game, every heartbeat in the arena is probably pumping hard. Not nearly as hard as mine as I pass to Peter Shaw.

The crowd in the seats is in a frenzy, half black and light blue and half royal blue. With the Blades having won three out of the last four games, they know that if we win this one, the Stanley Cup is ours.

I hover around the neutral zone just in case we lose control of the puck and I need to step into action to recover it. My muscles react when Shaw gets overtaken by a Blues player, but before I can even push off with my skates, LaPointe gets it back again. After trying for the goal and missing, a Blues player hits it back into the neutral zone.

My teammates scramble out of the attacking zone to prevent offsides, but I'm focused on the Blues player who has the puck. I crash into him and quickly recover it in the aftermath, guiding it back into the attacking zone.

I can almost hear the minutes ticking down in my head as the end of the game approaches. With nothing but the goal on my mind, I speed past two defenders, almost losing control of the puck with one. After a brief struggle, I swivel, taking the puck with me and, operating solely on instinct, slap it toward the goal.

It feels like slow motion from there, watching the puck fly in the air, the goalie arching his body to stop it. Even my reaction is delayed when I see the back of the net quiver in response to the impact of the puck.

It's only when one of my teammates crashes into me from behind that I wake from my stupor. The roar of the crowd fills my ears.

"Yes!" Screams Shaw as he lets go of me.

The Blues are scrambling into action but I still take a moment to look up at the time left. Only a little more than a minute. No wonder the black and light blue in the arena is already in party mode.

Further down the ice, I watch Mikhailov body check a Blues player and gain control of the puck. There's a brief battle for it as the Blues players desperately try for a goal in the final moments.

I hear the crowd begin to count down from ten seconds, and I know it's over. My eyes seek out one area of the arena in particular.

And there she is.

Maya's already standing, slapping her hands against the glass as she cheers with the rest of the crowd. There are other familiar faces around her, the friends of hers who could make it, Shaw's girlfriend who I remember helping introduce him to at a bar in Philadelphia years ago, and of course Morfar, who flew out to witness this moment.

I know back in Norway and Sweden, my family is also celebrating a few seconds prematurely as well. After so long in remission, the doctors are hopeful about Liam's condition, and I look forward to seeing him and the rest of my family as well. In a couple of weeks, Maya and I will be flying back, as usual, to spend the summer between both countries, with a brief trip thrown in to some new and interesting locale to collect another bottle of sand.

Maya's new volunteer job working as a paralegal for a nonprofit organization that one of the attorneys she used to work for started allows her the entire summer off to accompany me to visit my family. It's a happy compromise for the both of us, one that will continue on this way indefinitely.

After tonight, I have no doubt that my new—and far better—agent will land me an even better multi-year contract with the Blades. Which means I'm staying in Brooklyn, something with which I'm perfectly fine.

So long as it's with my wife.

When the buzzer sounds, I'm lost in a sea of teammates who surround me in celebration. I focus my attention back on them. After all these years together that led to this moment, they deserve that much.

It seems to go on forever, helmets and sticks scattered around us like oversized confetti on the ice. When it dies down, I separate myself and skate over to Maya and my grandfather. They are both still standing and jumping up and down in congratulations.

I focus on Maya, coming to a complete stop in front of her. I wink, and she laughs and blows me a kiss.

"*Jeg elsker deg!*" she shouts through the clear partition.

"I love you too," I shout back.

That's our thing, started when she began learning Norwegian. She's still terrible at it, but I do so love correcting her pronunciation.

My eyes fall to her oversized black and blue Blades jersey, which just barely obscures the soon-to-be newest addition to the Sørenson family. The love I feel for her is almost doubled when I consider this one. There's so much to discover there, so many adventures that await. Which makes life so much fun.

I wanted to be surprised. Maya wanted to know.

It's a boy.

I can't wait.

EPILOGUE

ERIK

"*En gang til!*"

I lift my four-year-old son just as the water reaches us from the wave that just crashed. He laughs as I swing him in the air then back down as the water recedes.

We're in Hawaii, knocking off a checkmark on the bucket list of bottles of sand to fill. The elusive Papakōlea beach took a while to get to, but the green sand—supposedly one of only four places in the world this color—is worth it.

My son is already a much darker shade of the naturally barely brown coloring he usually is. His head of light brown curls has yet to get wet, considering his apparent aversion to the water. Or maybe he just enjoys making his papa work.

"*Again, again,*" he repeats in Norwegian.

Maya was the one to insist he learn it. She read somewhere that children retain languages best if they learn before a certain age, so "Mama" speaks English with him and "Papa" speaks Norwegian.

It makes for an interesting life.

But I have to admit he's picked up on both tongues quite

well. My wife is an amazing Mom. But then I knew that would be the case when I married her.

I pick Martin up one more time and swing him in the air. Before he can request another round, I speak up.

"Okay, okay. Papa needs a break. Let's go sit with Mama and eat lunch."

I can see his little face crumple in disappointment, but before he can express his full outrage, I calm him.

"*I think she made some lefse and we have brunost.*"

His surprisingly blue eyes brighten, and he wriggles out of my arms to run back to the beach where Maya is sitting back on the blanket, with our daughter Astrid.

I take a moment to admire them. Astrid is not even a year old yet, but already growing into her looks, a full head of wavy light brown hair and the huge eyes of her mother, a few shades closer to hazel than brown. She laughs as her older brother comes running toward them, the same dimples denting those cheeks that her mother now sports.

"Mama, Mama!" Martin screams. "Papa saved me from the water!"

"Did he?" she gasps in surprise. "Well, I guess that makes him a superhero."

I grin as I slowly walk toward them. It softens as a specific memory of my mother comes to mind, as vivid as the day it happened.

Ingrid Sørenson had an inclination toward frequent, but brief moments of tenderness with me in between the chaos that was the rest of her life of wanderlust.

"*Some of the most exciting adventures of my life have had nothing to do with leaving home,*" she told me as she curled up in the corner of that couch we used to laze on. She'd be reading or doing some research, and I'd be on the other side, most likely playing video games. It must have been in between games when I had stopped to get something to eat or take a bathroom break that she told me about it.

"The time it hit me the hardest was the moment I first felt you kick while I was pregnant with you."

I remember rolling my eyes and being someone grossed out by the idea at the time, which just made her laugh and ruffle my hair, another thing I hated—or at least pretended to. Obviously, now I'd give anything to have those days back.

But now I get it. Being with these three has been the greatest adventure of my life. Nothing, not any of my travels or even hockey itself compares.

And I can't wait for the adventure to continue...

The End.

Psst! Be sure to sign up for my newsletter to get some eventual Bonus Chapters for this series.

Newsletter sign-up: http://eepurl.com/cbc3BD

Interested in being on my ARC Team? Follow me on Booksprout: https://booksprout.co/author/1984/camilla-stevens

CONTINUE ON FOR A PREVIEW OF THE NEXT
BOOK IN THE
INTERNATIONAL ROMANCE SERIES...

THE MONTE CARLO SHARK PREIVEW

COMING OCTOBER 2019

TWENTY YEARS AGO

"I know for a fact that my husband was murdered!"

My mother's words are etched into my brain. They were spoken three days before she, like my father months before her, was murdered.

Both of them at the hands of people here in attendance at her funeral.

As the widow of a publicly disgraced husband, the crowd of mourners should be sparse. As the daughter of one of Monte Carlo's most notorious gamblers, who died penniless, the number of those wishing to pay their respects should be near nonexistent.

But even the loss of status and wealth has its draw. Especially when tied to such a sordid past as that of the Reinhardts.

Only a handful of attendees are here to mourn. At least half the others have come out of morbid curiosity. The remainder have a score to settle—or at least a score they hope to see laid to rest with my mother.

I'm sitting in the front pew next to my younger sister, her

THE MONTE CARLO SHARK PREIVEW

tiny hand gripping mine for dear life. I make sure to keep my eyes firmly on my mother's casket, which will soon be buried in a plot next to my father's. I don't allow my gaze to stray beyond the five-year-old girl sitting next to me.

Wandering eyes would imply curiosity.

Curiosity can be deadly. I don't need some overused adage about a cat to remind me of that.

At thirteen, I'm old enough to know how dangerous information can be, or rather, how dangerous it can be to let others think you either seek, or worse, have it.

Just like grandpa taught me during the rounds we played when I was younger, keep your cards well hidden. From there, it's all a matter of bluffing and carefully watching your opponent.

A boy focused on his mother's remains during her funeral gives away no tells.

There is no quirk indicating that he's well aware his father was killed to cover up a ring of money laundering and embezzlement reaching even the most pristine banks of Luxembourg.

No twitch to signal that he knows his mother was killed because she got too close to the truth.

No tic to alert them that the only thing on his mind is pure vengeance.

My sister and I are going to live in Monaco with our aunt. We'll no longer be wealthy, even in that playground of the rich and famous, but that's fine. I've learned there are more important things than wealth.

Things like intelligence...cunning...ruthlessness.

Power.

Just like the sharks from the book my father gave me when I was a boy, I'll move with stealth and determination, progressing with a single-minded focus on my prey.

Then I'll strike.

And just like the shark in his territory, when I'm done I'll be more formidable and merciless than anyone in this sea of ours.

Especially with those who dare to get in my way.

CONTINUE TO READ MORE ABOUT THE NEXT BOOKS IN THE INTERNATIONAL LEGACIES ROMANCE...

NEXT UP IN THE INTERNATIONAL LEGACIES ROMANCE

If you hadn't guessed from reading this...not to worry! Yes, the other women in this book will have their own HEA (after long and winding roads...it won't be as straightforward as you think!)

Just so I'm not a total jerk about keeping you in anticipation:

Sloane's Story ~ **The Monte Carlo Shark** (Coming October)

Whitney's Story ~**Her Icelandic Protector** (Coming November)

Zia's Story ~ **Her Russian Defender** (Coming 2020)

Demetria's Story ~ **The Luxembourg Betrayal** (Coming 2020)

And much more...